About the Author

As a first-generation Bengali-Canadian who grew up and currently resides in Toronto's Regent Park, my upbringing as an immigrant from a low-income family drives my passion for social, economic, and environmental justice. As a new writer based in Canada, my intention was to produce a literary fictional piece of work which upholds and shares such values with the wider world.

Voyagers 1

Saquib Ahsan

Voyagers 1

Vanguard Press

VANGUARD PAPERBACK

© Copyright 2025
Saquib Ahsan

A CIP catalogue record for this title is
available from the British Library.

ISBN 978-1-83794-221-3

This is a work of fiction. Names, characters, businesses, places,
events and incidents are either the product of the author's imagination or
used in a fictitious manner. Any resemblance to actual persons, living or
dead, or actual events is purely coincidental.

Vanguard Press is an imprint of
Pegasus Elliot Mackenzie Publishers Ltd.
www.pegasuspublishers.com

First Published in 2025

Vanguard Press
Sheraton House Castle Park
Cambridge England

Printed & Bound in Great Britain

Forgive yourself for the decisions you've made without agency,
I judge nature as nature judges me

Voyagers - August 20th

143 Years After New Acadia

"We can't leave them behind" said Maaria, clutching her school bag with both arms and her life.

"That's not up to us," replied Hiran, wiping the rain from his face with the back of his palm.

It was noisy and difficult to breathe inside the dampened freight car. The tail end of a windy rainstorm continued its charge through a wide-open door, while birds once thought to have gone extinct, now cried from inside cages which were welded shut.

"And I left my girl behind so I could leave with these guys" he continued, ignoring the birds as he made his way towards the side door.

"If they cared about any of it they'd be here with us now"

"And not back in Queens"

"Or wherever the hell they went"

Gripping the cold handle with both hands, he straightened his shoulders and widened his feet before tugging back with all he could.

"T-They d-don't care a-about us"

It quickly occurred to the two of them the door wasn't going anywhere, but he continued on, persistent nonetheless.

"Hold on" said Maaria, placing her school bag down and walking to meet him.

"Let me help"

He watched as she wedged a foot against the wall of crates behind her, using the space to support a push against the metal door. The freight car creaked, like fingernails to a chalkboard, as the door loosened and slid along its well-corroded frame. Together they escaped the storm, but still left some space to slip out if they needed to. The birds seemed to settle.

"Thank you Mars" said Hiran, walking towards her with the school bag she seemed to have forgotten about.

"We got lucky finding this train, the next stations' a whole day away",
"We needed this"

Damn, I really needed this.

He had spent the last few miserable months aimlessly trampling the Highlands of Middle Acadia, working for and against the armies carving out Queens for all her worth, as well as the gangs preying on the leftovers. Now here he was, *cold*, *wet*, and without any idea of what was awaiting ahead.

But it's just the cold, he thought

If it takes me I'll be gone and with God.

With that in mind, sitting in the damp next to *some overgrown chickens* didn't seem so bad.

"Thanks" said Maaria, finding her place next to a short stack of nearby boxes.

"Just leave it on the floor"

At nineteen, she was about a year older than him with chestnut brown skin a shade or two darker than his own and tangled black hair which fell just below her chest. For clothes she wore a green shirt which covered her arms and neck, while a grey pinafore hung from her shoulders to just above the knee. She appeared ordinary, even a little fashionable with the tears around her black leggings, but other than the wet mud and bird feathers coating her bare feet, nothing about her suggested she was fleeing war.

It was an otherwise standard school uniform and she was an otherwise normal school girl.

"The train ain't gone yet" he said, noticing the narrow stream of tears sneaking down her rain-soaked cheeks.

"And even if it does, they'll meet us there"

He meant to reassure her, but his efforts sounded half-hearted, even to him.

"Yeah" she said, squeezing the water out of the unwanted knots she once kept in a bun, visibly upset.

He didn't need to wait for her to finish her sentence to understand her feelings. It was hard to leave her brother Tavaar and their friend Zoh behind, especially after losing what they've already lost.

They had set out earlier in the day, the three of them with rations and clothes packed in their school bags, and him with whatever he had left in his courier bag. Their plan was to catch the train travelling through She-Loves-Me-Not Valley to Windlehem, but after learning the last train leaving Queens left days ago, they decided the safest plan was to follow the tracks to the next town ahead before deciding what to do next.

For a while it even appeared as if things were going to be okay. None of them were gravely injured and there was even enough food and water to last them several days. They might have lost their homes and missed the train, but they were *lucky* to still have one another.

This was it,

This was our best chance.

The four followed the tracks for nearly half the day until a violent rainstorm arrived without a cloud or warning and forced them to settle into a nearby forest in search of shelter. To their surprise, it was there they discovered an empty train yard tucked away behind the hill of an Old Acadian mining site. A train yard which he had assumed was no longer in use, until a freight car as long as the trees were tall, emerged from somewhere deep within the forest and came to a screeching halt before them.

Mother was watching us today, and we really made it out,

All four of us, and we were really going to be okay.

It was on their way to board the train, however, when Zoh and Tavaar decided to head back towards Queens without an explanation of where exactly they were going or why they were heading there.

They just left us, and I can only blame myself for it.

"Mars" said Hiran, breaking the silence between them before they both grew too fond of it.

"Hm?" said Maaria, returning from her thoughts.

"You should know this is all my fault"

She was a little startled by the abruptness of the comment, but seemed curious as to what he meant.

"What are you talking about Hiran? How?"

"It's a long story" he said trailing off, "Trust me"

Hiran I – May 1st

Almost Home

It was late in the morning when he arrived at Guildmen's General Store, unsure of why exactly he was there.

"What took so long?" asked a large old man with a gruff voice and a faint smile.

It was Arther Guildmen himself, and he stood behind the desk of a long wooden counter, watching, with arms crossed, as he closed the door behind him and set aside his bicycle.

"My mom kept me," replied Hiran, "I told her it wouldn't be long."

"Well, good thing you made it," said the old man, mildly raising his voice. "Your uncle would've lost his lid. Said he couldn't trust anyone with it."

"What is it?" asked Hiran, curiously stepping into the store in his mossy green leather sandals, a brown shirt torn at the shoulder like a soldier, and black shorts cut above the knee.

Something seems different about the place.

An entire winter year had passed since his last visit, and his eyes couldn't help but wander. The rusty iron beams once barring the windows were exchanged for glossy new steel ones, black rockwood replaced the ageing hardwood floors, and a new counter was still being built as an extension to the current one.

What's he been up to?

Tucked somewhere inside Queens' usually bustling Newtown District was Guildmen's General Store, a place regarded both for the uncommon goods it housed as well as the history it represented. It stood as one of the few businesses known to have survived both battles fought for Queens in the past few decades. Battles which nearly ruined the Ancient City.

"You really cleaned up the place," said Hiran.

"Yeah, it's gon' be a big pilgrim year," replied Arther Guildmen, beginning his count of the early morning earnings.

"Finally some real peace round here."

"Yeah? Why's that?" he asked half-heartedly.

Faith wasn't always his favourite subject, but still he was a *believer*.

"Ain't you hear?" replied the old man. "The Police sent out new treaties."

"New treaties?" said Hiran, fading away into the store, lost in the vastness of it all.

"Yeah, to the Liberation Army and even the Frontier," answered Arther Guildmen.

After a few steps forward, his nose had quickly picked up what his eyes had mostly missed.

The air was filled with the aroma of unfamiliar goods, goods long overdue, and even of goods thought to have perished from the Biosphere some time ago. There were boxes filled with bags of black rice, crates containing rare tea leaves and endangered cured meats, as well as shelves stocked with various dried roots and *things* pickled inside tightly sealed jars.

"*Starmilk?*" he said to himself, reaching into one of the crates and retrieving a glass bottle.

It contained a sticker of a smiling green cow with two gold horns, and the words *'Forget-me-not Ranch'* written beneath in bold red letters. The milk itself appeared no different than any other cow's milk, except when he put his nose to the lid, he could smell the *forest* imbued within.

"And Highland honey!" he said aloud, setting the milk aside and picking up a jar of what appeared to be dark raw brown honey.

"But I thought the Highland bees were all gone?"

"Y-Yeah," said Arther Guildmen, clearing his throat.

"That's some real Highland honey."

"It, uh... came in from the south not too long ago."

Damn, things are really pickin' up.

He continued his search through the nearly overstocked store, like a stray cat scouring every corner of its new home. In cartons pushed to the side came rosewine from Rosetown, in the corner were barrels full of potions and elixirs from Lindblum, and in sealed boxes marked with

Military Police stamps were eggs the size of his head. There was even a box filled with his favourite blue cheese from Cratertown 23.

"All that came in last night," yawned the old man. "Had to put up some new idols too"

"It's gon' be a long summer."

"New idols?" asked Hiran, curious as to what exactly he meant by *new*.

"Yeah," replied Arther Guildmen, pointing to the wall behind him.

"Next to the Sun."

He turned his head back to the front door where he found ornaments, figurines, and idols hanging along the walls. Some to welcome foreign travellers and traders, others to bridge the gap between Acadians and Queenspeople. Next to the clay sculpture of the Smiling Sun dangling by the window for the Westerians, were rag-dolls nailed to the rockwood.

Yeah,

Never saw those before.

He swept his eyes through the room, glancing at the many supposed gods and their faces, but only recognizing them by their uncommon names at most and the materials they were made of at best. Understanding them as anything more was to recognize another force in the world, and there was no room in Mother's Home for believers of other deities, unless they were among her Ancient children *of course*.

Some gods laid idle and forgotten, like the Stone Serpent coiled around its nesting tree, while it was unsure if others, like the Winged Ship and the Nightbird, were gods at all. There was also something for those who worshipped the flags of their country over the gods of their people, and Guildmen's General Store was one of the few places throughout Queens where one could find the flags of both Old and New Acadia hanging under the same roof.

"So why am I here?" asked Hiran, turning back to the old man.

"Your uncle didn't tell you?" he replied, setting aside several stacked pillars of coins and paper notes.

As old as he was, he was *still* a large man, with arms as wide as most men's legs, and freckled skin which all Westerians were proud to wear. Decades ago, he had worked as a merchant-trader, travelling between the many old and new cities of Rodina, before settling into Queens. He now owned and operated the General Store with his sons Morten and Garet, and his nephew Eon.

"He told me to just wait," said Hiran, searching the room for his own deities and finding them in the same well-kept corner.

Resting as they always were.

He approached the decorated shrine with eyes to the floor, unsure if he deserved to stand before the figurines of the First Mother who birthed the universe, and her daughters Romina, Rodina, and Wilona, who populated it with the moons, stars, and planets. It took a moment to gather the courage to face his sovereigns, and when he did, he found a woman dressed in a long crimson robe cradling a newborn boy, and three little girls dancing under a leafless iifa-tree. There was some guilt and shame in the prayer-song he mumbled under their presence, but he hoped they didn't mind.

I haven't been to the Temple in months,

I hope they can forgive me this time.

"Yeah, well it's for a package," said Guildmen, brushing his grey beard with a handful of brown freckles. "One of the richest merchants in *all* of Rodina made the order,"

"Okay," said Hiran, with a sceptical, but curious voice, nonetheless.

Rodina was a large continent and there were many rich merchants occupying its Lowlands and Highlands. To be ranked as one of the wealthiest was a nobility in its own right.

"Where's it going?"

"Roilmont," answered Arther Guildmen.

"Roilmont!?" he said, "You can't really expect me to go into Roilmont?"

There was something odd about the dead Acadian city of Roilmont, lying just north of where they stood. It had been deemed off limits by both the Liberation Army and the Military Police, and there were countless horror stories about its streets, *and its rain, and its folks.*

"Don't worry, it's just at the city-limits"

"Eon is downstairs, he'll tell you more."

"And take this down to Emmi while you're at it" said Guildmen, handing him the bottle of starmilk over the counter which he took by the neck.

Behind Guildmen was an open door nearly kept out of view by his body and it led into a narrow hall where dozens of crates were stacked to one side in neatly organised rows and columns.

He strolled down the hallway with a finger gliding along the wall, until it snagged against a small hole in the wood. It was there he waited for a moment, listening intently and looking both ways before sliding the wall to the side and revealing a set of stairs leading to the basement below, where the real business was kept.

Daaria I – May 5th

Almost Alone

She sat atop her bed with her legs crossed, watching the others as they awoke reluctantly to the sound of erupting bells and yawning girls.

I dreamt that dream again,
The one about the lowland-
Wait-
You don't have time for that Daaria,
Don't fall behind.

Lifting the covers over her head, she checked her sheets and underclothes for blood where it could and shouldn't be. The bed was *dry*. She also checked her dark olive brown skin for any red sores resembling bug bites, but she was *spotless*.

C'mon, let's go.

Back in the dim lit dormitory, she found the other girls following the same routine. With their blankets over their heads, and their hands searching frantically over their bodies.

Hurry-

She rolled off her bed before any of the others were finished, folded her things in a mess, and walked them to a nearby hamper before slipping into the washrooms.

It's been five gruelling years since she learned this would be her life for as long as she remained a property of the Citadel. Rushing out of bed every morning just to beat the other thirty soldiers occupying a dorm with only five showers and three toilets. Conditions hardly suitable for a supposed unit of top-ranking officials.

Though, at least it's not back home,
Or the Generalist Force
No, I shouldn't say that-

It's unkind.

After a quick trip to the toilet and a shower with a cap on, she dried herself, brushed her teeth, and happily saluted the others with her right hand crossed over her heart while they lined impatiently for the stalls.

She did this all without once bothering to glance at the mirror, knowing well enough she had bags of blue and purple below her olivine eyes.

Laying on the night desk beside her bed was her standard dark blue Peace Officer's uniform, a pair of black leather boots which never suited her, and half a glass of water which she downed in two swigs.

As she tidied her bed, she wondered about all the girls who might've laid their hair on her pillows before it was hers. She also thought of their crushes, whose names were still etched inside love-hearts on the wooden underframes.

Those must've been different times,

I wonder if any of them ever kissed or if they ever wed,

Probably not.

When she finished tidying her bed, she quietly dressed herself in her uniform, wondering about all the girls who might've called it their own before it was hers. One of them had even made adjustments in the stitching and cut. Adjustments only the next wearer could ever know of, but the way it fit her petite frame made her feel as if it was made just for her. Though, she couldn't say the same for the Army-issued bras which always left rashes under her armpits.

She brushed the excess thoughts aside, detaching herself from her things and upbringings before placing her wavy black hair in an uninspired ponytail and carrying on down the hall. She never *once* had a chance to look her best and all she ever needed was some sleep, *but life was no handout,* and every day had its need.

Eyes to the front, not to the side.

Luckily for her, the measurement most interesting to the Citadel was how useful she was, beauty was not typically assessed.

At one end of the dormitory, Wilona and Gwendolyn stood complaining about some recent assignment to Roilmont, and on her way out she found Jaana, Orina, and Gadolin discussing the recent news around Mineraltown. She wanted to ask if they had heard anything coming in from the excavation site there, but there were too many rumours going around, and she was already worried enough.

Don't stress yourself out,

Just wait for the official report.

Everything's fine,

I hope so.

As she neared the door to the dormitory, she met a girl with dark honey brown skin, sharp red eyes, and unbrushed curls of short flowery golden hair. She was over a head taller than most of the other girls, and wore a metal prosthetic in each arm from the elbow down.

"Daaria," she said, with a yawn and a handful of bedsheets.

"Omaara," replied Daaria, with some concern.

It was difficult to ignore the slight purple and sickly appearance of her skin and face.

"You look terrible."

"I know," sighed Omaara, placing the sheets in a nearby hamper.

"I'm *still* bleeding heavy." she whispered.

"What? Really? No way," said Daaria, trying her best impression of an unsurprised person.

"Yeah," said Omaara, "It's been two weeks."

"And it hurts all the time"

"Two weeks?" asked Daaria.

The charade was getting harder to keep up.

She didn't talk about it for a few days,

I thought she was done-

She smiled her best smile and placed a hand on Omaara's heart. "You'll be fine," she said, calming herself down if anything. "I wouldn't worry about it."

I had a period for eight days once,

Two weeks isn't that far off, right?

"Do you think it's hemovar-?"

"No" she hissed, "Don't say that".

"That would've killed you by now" she said, knowing it sounded a little crude, but continuing on nonetheless.

"What about you?" said Omaara. "You look like shit."

"Hey!" said Daaria. "That's not nice."

"Sorry," she giggled, for the first time in weeks, "But it's true."

Even if it came at her expense, she was happy Omaara was amused.

She looks like a sunflower when she smiles.

"I just barely slept the last few nights," said Daaria.

"Did the Citadel say anything about it yet?" asked Omaara.

"No," sighed Daaria, "I just hope Will is safe."

"You hope who is safe?" asked another girl from a few beds away.

She turned to find a black-haired girl with piercing bright-red eyes and a shade of skin similar to Omaara's.

Her name was Olisa August, but she preferred just her orphan-name, *August.*

"My brother, Wiluss," said Daaria. "He was working at the Research Facility in Mineraltown—"

"Oh, that," interrupted August, dropping interest in the conversation and moving on.

"I'm sure he'll show up somewhere," said another, with a practically monotone voice.

She didn't have to turn around to know it was Briaana Cryheart, a girl who wove pink ribbons into her boxer braids as if she was meant to.

Along with August, she was one of several elite recruits from the Firstlands. A place not so distant on the map, but worlds apart in space and time.

"T-Thanks," said Daaria, unsure if her response was too little or too much.

Him showing up somewhere, that's what I'm most worried about.

An image of her brother's lifeless corpse flashed through her thoughts, but she was careful not to wince or shudder in front of the other soldiers.

"What about you, Briaana?" asked Omaara. "Are they really sending you back to the field already?"

Oh wait- That's right-

Though one could never tell from the unrelenting look of indifference on her face, Briaana had recently returned from a failed explosives mission which left four soldiers dead and two others missing.

We used to share the dorm with Roxanne and Glenanna, they even sat at their table and still, nothing.

Didn't even lose sleep over it-

"I'll be fine," said Briaana, placing a hand on her shoulder before leaving with August.

They waited until after they had left before speaking again.

"So we're finally getting an assignment huh?" whispered Omaara.

"Yeah," replied Daaria, "I wonder what it is."

"It sounds like a real one," she said, peeking both ways out the door before stepping out onto the hallway. "From what Jaxas heard, at least."

"Well I hope he's right," whispered Daaria, "And he also better not be late."

She followed Omaara out the dormitory, though not without first leaving her upbringing at the door.

"I don't want to get in trouble again."

Talius I – May 3rd

The Young Commander

A cool misty ocean breeze sailed into his apartment as he stepped out onto the weather-beaten balcony, pleased with the sunny clear skies and the early summer wind.

Thank you daughters, for such a beautiful day.

The salty cold mist coated his skin and put pins to his eyes, and in the time it took to wipe the ocean from his face, an orchestra of summer birds had quietly perched atop the concrete guard. They watched along, with their curious little heads as he took his own seat atop a three-legged chair, and put his eyes into an Ancient gizmo they called a telescope.

If there's anything out there, I'll find it on a day like this.

He adjusted his line of sight to match the source of the mist, before dialling the scope forward past the slums and factories which made up the bulk of the Citadel, as well as the Highland plains which housed the rest of his small empire. It was there he found the dark purple waters of the ocean Primordia, and it was here he began his weekly search for the fabled clear, still-waters of the Ruined Sea.

According to the records of their Old Acadian ancestors, their predecessors among the Gran Acadians had landed on a similar and not too distant rocky shore after fleeing their homes with just the food in their bellies and the wind in their sails. For several centuries, the extent to which the past was understood had simply ended there as well.

Other than the likelihood this occurred somewhere between two and twelve thousand years ago, it was not known precisely when this great migration took place, or just how many years had passed since then.

If it was, then it was lost.

For many centuries, the details regarding the journey was much of a debate among Old Acadian history keepers who, along with their doubts about the claims made within the Gran Acadian scriptures, also questioned their motives and sources.

It was written their forebears had crossed an ocean home to prehistoric storms and sea serpents which swallowed entire fleets whole, as well as a great civilization buried under a clear and calm sea, all before discovering a Highland thought to have existed only in legend.

This great odyssey was referred to as the 'Great Voyage', and such a tale was thought by many to be the work of fiction, written by scholars who were out of touch and not of the times, and then later retold by grandmothers and playwrights. This changed, however, when the Old Acadian Military attempted to return to Gran Acadia centuries later.

What little remained of their countless failed efforts were washing ashore still to this day.

"Talius!" shouted out a man from outside his apartment door.

"Open the door! It's Hellin!"

Hellin?

He sucked his teeth and reluctantly set the telescope aside, re-entering the dampened living room and navigating the scattered mess of old and used gizmo parts in his Army-issued trousers and black leather boots.

Shouldn't he be assembling the regiments?

War is at our door.

As he approached, he heard voices whispering from the other side of a heavy metal door, but it receded the moment his footsteps neared.

What does he want?

He turned his attention to a nearby electrical panel which not only contained the controls to the magnets responsible for sealing his apartment shut, but also an Old Acadian Military periscope refitted to observe beyond the walls. There he found three men in three different uniforms, all Army-issued and littered with ribbons and medals.

Each awaited with their hands to their hearts, knowing well enough they were being watched.

"Colonel?" he asked through the mouthpiece.

"Commander!" answered a tall young man with silvery white hair like a lynx and a skin tone as dark as his black uniform. He was also quite handsome with a slightly square face and strong shoulders to match.

He removed himself from the periscope and flipped on a switch labelled *'release'*.

A buzz spread throughout the apartment like a bee's nest as the door swung open.

"What's going on?" asked Commander Talius, watching the men as they entered the apartment to stand before him.

"Commander!" they said aloud together, with their hands to their hearts.

"Officers," he replied, with a hand to his heart as well.

"Where's your hand radio?" asked the colonel, stepping forward.

He was quite tall, even compared to other tall men, and his hair under the right lighting appeared to be missing all texture and depth. It was almost as if the First Mother herself had painted a white cloud with little detail atop his head.

Almost like a painting itself.

"Oh," he said, turning back and pointing to the mess on the kitchen counter.

"It's probably over there, why?"

"We've been calling," said the colonel, as sternly as was acceptable.

"It's bad news," added Peace-Sergeant Briggs, a man well into his forties.

He wore a black beret over a blue Peacegaurd uniform which he insisted be tailored to include as many secret pockets as possible.

What he was concealing wasn't a mystery, however.

It was peanuts.

"What is it?" asked the commander.

"Windlehem's lost," said Colonel Hellin, in a tone he often reserved for funerals.

"Lost?" said the commander, withholding a reaction. "What do you mean?"

"A transmission call came in," answered the peace-sergeant.

"The Holyfields are retreating and the Rocklanders have abandoned the march."

"What!? Why?!" asked the commander.

"Commander Thornheart couldn't retake the nearby villages-"

"The campaign was a failure," interjected Colonel Hellin, "Over eight hundred soldiers dead."

Hmm.

No, that doesn't make much sense-

Eight hundred soldiers?

He turned back to the analogue clock hanging over the entrance to the balcony and scratched his head.

The 3rd of May, a Wednesday, and the military hands read 2.30.

"That sounds like some countryside shit to me," said the commander.

"I'll believe eight hundred soldiers are dead when they're piled outside by apartment"

"I know," replied Major Waltz, "But it's coming directly from Colonel Vanfall."

"And when did this transmission come in? How come I never learned of it?"

"You told us not to disturb-"

"We have to abandon Windlehem," said Colonel Hellin.

"No," said the commander, "There must be some mistake."

He stood tapping the five medals pinned to his black commander's coat, wondering if this marked the beginning of the end for the Liberation Army.

"We have all of Peaceland," he said, pleading more than making a case. "And Rockland hardly sent a third of their forces." he said, pacing around the apartment like a fox digging for its cache of leftovers, before settling on the Old Flag of Acadia.

She was draped over the windows like a curtain, and he stood there for some time, watching her catch the wind like a spider's web.

"Here," continued the colonel, retrieving a device from his pocket and pressing down on a button.

It was a recording of a tired, but well-spoken man, speaking against the wind.

"Hello Commander Talius, this is Colonel Vanfall of Rockland's Outer Forces. I don't know what the time is, but the day is May 1st and it's been one hundred and forty-three years since New Acadia."

"Commander Thornheart is currently fighting a lost battle near Windlehem along with several of our supporting forces. Our main regiments were caught by a surprise attack on our way to the City, and now we are on a full retreat back to Liberated territory. We managed to cross the bridges leading over the Nine Rivers, before the Frontier tore it down, but the Holyfield Forces are stuck on the path to Windlehem, and the only way around requires them to survive a journey through the Bloomwoods"

The Bloomwoods?

"This campaign has been a disaster, we must abandon this fight Commander—"

The recording stopped there.

"The Bloomwoods" said Major Waltz, with both arms crossed and a head down. "It's going to take a couple weeks to make it back at least"

"Maybe months" suggested the peace-sergeant,

"Spring is over"

They might never make it back entirely, he thought to himself quietly.

The Bloomwoods was a beautiful name for a dreadful place, and as was suggested, it was home to polliniferous trees which bloomed toxic flowers during the end of every wet season.

"The ice has melted and now the woods are to be flowering soon"

"We have no choice but to abandon Windlehem," continued the colonel, "But we still can't leave them behind."

No-

Not Windlehem-

The Ancient City of Windlehem, one of the three sacred Highland Cities of Rodina, once belonged to the Liberation Army before falling to the Military Police a year ago. It didn't last under their control for too long, however, as the city was recently seized by the Frontier Army after a series of clashes in the countryside.

It was an odd sequence of events for the times, but an important one to remember. History was a narrative as much as it was an experience, and those controlling the understanding of past events could justify any present social order, or affect the outcome of a future one.

We had a coalition with the Frontier Army,

We even sent them the supplies to take Windlehem back, and they betrayed us.

They had initially celebrated the Frontier Army's conquest as a victory for the Liberation Army's cause of reunifying Acadia, and he had even sent a handwritten letter congratulating their top generals for their triumph over the Military Police.

Though he was not without fault in this, as Colonel Hellin and the others had argued. Along with his congratulatory message, the letter contained detailed instructions on how to ease the rapid transition of Windlehem back to Liberated control. A demand which had been returned with a fiery redeclaration of war between the United Liberation Army of Acadia and the Free Acadian Frontier Army.

Probably should've waited on that part, but it did show us where their hearts were,

War was unavoidable.

His fingers continued to tap on the medals long after the thought had ended. Each one represented a Stronghold and its communities, united under his command through contracts and conquests, and altogether they formed the Liberation Army of Peaceland.

"Commander?" asked Major Waltz.

"We can't lose Windlehem..." he said trailing off, gradually wandering back to the balcony. "We won't ever be able to reunite the country if we do."

From twenty stories above, he could see enough of the Citadel and its grace to understand its importance to the very idea of civilization, as well as why his enemies hoped to pry it from his cold dead hands. Though before he could entertain the fantasy of heroically responding to and defeating an invading force, the faint sound of parading unionizers in the foreground interrupted him, and it reminded him of *the problems at home.*

He had Landlords to arrest for treason, a small government in the nearby city of Mineraltown to investigate for treason, and a worker's union to disband for civil disobedience. Which, though not treasonous, was still illegal.

"Do you have a plan then?" asked the colonel. "A good one?"

"Are Thornheart's officers still trying to unite the Holyfields?" asked the commander, returning to the balcony.

"From what we know, yes," answered Major Waltz.

"Then assemble a retreat force to Windlehem, and ask the Holyfields what they need from us to set their differences aside," he said, pausing for a moment to gather the right words. "Tell them we need them, too."

Hiran II

Like many places throughout Queens, Arther Guildmen's General Store was less of what it claimed to be and more of what it claimed it wasn't. After a terribly long walk down a creaky wooden stairwell, he reached a door leading into a bustling space twice the size of the store above. It was one of the many saloons littering Newtown District's underground scene, and where Arther Guildmen made a small fortune.

A dozen road workers slept the day away in a darkened corner while a group of uniformed Police-soldiers sat singing with a crowd of foreign travellers and traders. Some were Westerians, others were Astormi, but wherever they came from, they came for the same reason. To spend some time and money on the best liquor, laced milk, and corner fights in Newtown.

His eyes darted around the well-lit room, searching for a *pretty girl* his age with curly black hair and a brown apron. He found her working behind the bar at the other end of the saloon.

Emmi,

Where've you been?

He walked towards her, ignoring the men who were resting in-between their exploits in the surface markets, as well as the drunks bloating their bellies with drinks and laughs. The closer he approached her, however, the more his legs began to tremble, and by the time he reached the bar, his knees were practically rattling in their sockets.

D-Does she miss me?

"H-Hiran!" she said, staggering and spilling the drink she had been preparing.

The glass shattered with a loud crackling thud as it hit the floor, but the patrons were unconcerned.

"You good?" asked Hiran, smiling at the mess she made, and *was*.

"W-Why are you standin' there like a creeper?" shouted Emmi.

"Sorry," he laughed, exchanging the bottle of starmilk for a light blue tablecloth which he found on the counter. He then used it to help collect the shards of glass scattered across the wet floor.

"Ugh..." she groaned, walking over to help him clean the spill.

"You better clean it right, I can't get in trouble again."

After the bar was wiped and the floors were swept and dried, they shared a long hug by the till.

"I grew more than you," she smiled, after removing herself from his embrace.

She was a brown-eyed, brown-skinned girl, with a nose matching her pretty face and a right eye which fell slightly. She worked as the saloon's dishwasher, and when it was required, helped out by the bar. There was also *always something about her*.

Something which reminded him of the summerbirds known to pass through Queens, but never settle for the Ancient City.

"Yeah, that's true," said Hiran, scratching his head. Unable to deny the small gap between them had narrowed further since they last met.

She returned to the counter and placed a handful of fresh leaves from a nearby basket into a bowl made of a shiny black stone.

"What' you doing?" he asked, peering over her little shoulders.

"*Well,*" she said, dragging on the word longer than she needed to, all to express some attitude. "I *was* making something for you before you messed it up," she said, reaching over for an empty cup.

"Huh? For me? How'd you know I was coming?" said Hiran.

He placed a hand on a nearby grinding ball, another blackstone object which she had been searching for, and rolled it towards her.

"Oh... I, uh... heard Guildmen on the phone," said Emmi, catching the ball and setting it aside.

"And, uh... Eon is looking for you, by the way," she said, pointing into the room. "You should stop bothering me and go talk to him."

"But I like bothering you-"

She blushed.

"You should go," she said, under her breath and with some sadness in her voice.

"He's over there"

He followed her finger into the saloon, and it led to a freckle-faced boy who was already approaching with a dirty apron.

"Hiran!" said Eon, navigating through the crowd and offering him a hug which was well received.

"I ain't seen you since... I don't even know."

"How 'you been?" asked Hiran.

"I'm good," said Eon, patting the back of his shoulder. "You' here for the delivery, right?"

"Yeah," said Hiran, a little distracted by the sound of Emmi applying the grinding ball to its bowl.

Wait... How'd he know?

"How'd you know?" he asked.

"Huh? What you mea—"

A ringing interrupted them, it was the telephone by the bar.

Emmi was within arm's reach of it, but she was made to ignore it as only members of the Guildmen family were permitted to answer.

"Hello?" said Eon, after rushing over and picking it up.

Emmi stopped her striking.

"Yeah, he's here," said Eon, glancing toward him with darting eyes. "Mhm... Yeah, okay, bye."

He set the device down and walked to a door kept locked behind the bar.

"C'mon, let's go," said Eon, unlocking it with a key tied to his wrist and stepping forward.

"Who was that?" asked Hiran, following him into the saloon's concrete back halls.

"Morten," answered Eon.

Morten? Was he asking about me? Why would he be asking about me?

"Oh... where's he at?" asked Hiran.

"He's out right now," replied Eon, "Don't really know where."

After a few locked doors and several turns in the dark, they entered a well-lit hall with a vault-like door at the end. Here he was made to keep a watch out while Eon operated a switchboard in a darkened side hall out of view. How the door was unlocked was also something only for the Guildmen family to see, but he knew from Emmi it had something to do with a hidden panel behind some electrical board.

Eon emerged a few moments later and together they walked towards the vault.

"Let's go," he said, waving him closer.

This better only take a couple hours,

I can't be running around town like last summer.

He followed him into a cold concrete room, well-lit and well-stocked with goods most would be jailed for just seeking out, but not Arther Guildmen. He had friends in important spaces and an unfair share of the underground black market as a result. This was just another one of his well-known secrets, the '*blackstore*'.

Talius II – May 5th

He was on his way to search the dark purple waters of Primordia when a voice on his hand radio called out to him from the kitchen.

"Commander!" said the soldier, "Colonel Hellin is on his way up to greet you."

"Thank you," said the commander, taking the device and setting it on his hip.

Hell, what now?

He walked over to check the periscope and found Colonel Hellin approaching straight faced with Major Waltz.

"Don't forget this," said the major, handing the colonel a newspaper which he had rolled under his arm.

"Huh?" said the colonel. "Where are you going?"

"Back to my post," answered the major. "We have a lead on the Landlords, I can't say much about it now."

"Just tell Commander Talius it's not looking good for Lord Hariya Baltiar," he said.

"I hear you, Major," said the commander, buzzing the door to the apartment open.

"It won't be long, Commander," replied Major Waltz, "And it's exactly what you suspected."

The major turned to the top right corner and offered a salute over the periscope before parting ways.

"Read this," said Colonel Hellin, wasting no time with formalities as soon as he entered.

It was a copy of the *Westerian-Prefecture Times*, and the headline read '*Westerian Victories in Ladria*' and included a photo of a dozen Westerian Hellraisers linking arms, smiles, and flamethrowers next to what likely was a pile of scorched bodies.

"Ladria?," said the commander, a little desensitised with the image.

Another whole country, taken off the map completely.

Ladria was another one of the many nations at war with Westeria, but they were thousands of kilometres away, on the other side of Rodina. It was likely the last Acadian to have ever set foot on those lands had died hundreds of years ago, back when Acadians lived united under their own sovereigns and were free to roam what remained of the world.

"Also, check under it," said the colonel.

He grunted and drew his eyes to a smaller article below. It read '*The Road to Rebuilding Acadia!*' and contained a photo of some fifty workers repairing the roads next to a concrete wasteland.

"That looks like Downtown Queens," said Commander Talius.

"That *is* Downtown Queens," answered Colonel Hellin, "And most of those workers are from Liberated communities."

"What? What do you mean?" asked the commander.

The colonel reached into a pocket concealed within his uniform, carefully removed a slip of paper, and handed it to him.

"This just came in," he said, "From Thornheart's top officers."

He unravelled the note and found a transmission coded in Military Braille, a language developed by Old Acadian Military leaders during their final years. Few knew of its existence and even fewer knew how to read its seemingly thoughtless and disorganised rows of raised dots.

"*Our assembly is on hold,*" he read to himself while running his fingers through the text. "*Two of ours defected to the Dogs.*"

Dogs-?

The Military Police-

He took his fingers through the braille several times over to ensure he wasn't overreacting or misreading the text.

"*They cut us off from the rest of Easton, we can't unite if we tried.*"

"That violates our treaty!" he said aloud upon finishing the text.

"Does it?" replied the colonel, taking a seat on the worn-out couch positioned beneath the Old Flag.

"A Police-soldier never set foot in Easton."

"But if any more of their communities open their gates—" said the commander, under his breath.

"They might find a way into Lowtown," said the colonel, finishing his sentence.

No, this can't be happening-

There has to be a mistake-

Though the Military Police were out of contention for Windlehem, their presence in Queens was hard to ignore. In their first attack some forty years ago, they razed the entirety of the Downtown core, as well as the Liberated communities occupying it. Though the surrounding Liberation Forces did manage to unite and eventually stave off the invasion, the damage to the land was enough to lose the war. Thousands were displaced and left homeless as a result of the destruction to the Ancient world. A world which no Acadian ever had a hand in constructing, but still relied upon immensely for shelter and life.

This crisis was made worse during their Second Invasion in the year 128 After New Acadia (A.N.A). It was a brief war, lasting only a few weeks, but it marked an important turning point in history. It was the first time the Military Police had managed to successfully carve out and retain a space for themselves in the Highlands of Rodina.

We can't let them get to Lowtown,

We could lose the entire country if they find it.

"What do we do now?" he said, pacing around the living room in complete circles.

"We can't abandon Thornheart or her people," said the colonel, "Especially not while she is gone."

Yeah,

We wouldn't hear the end of it.

Several months ago, the Military Police Chief tasked to Queens had claimed she did not want to see another war in another Ancient City, and at the time it appeared she supported mutual cooperation between the remaining Liberated communities. In a letter directed to him, she had declared the Military Police too were fractured in their organisation and that the struggle for Windlehem was not their fight. Many within the ranks and coalition held strong opinions about signing a treaty with the Police, but he and his uncle, Commander Braxas Baltiar of Rockland, believed it was in the interest of the Liberation Army to agree to the terms set forth.

It only made sense,

I made the best decision I could.

Though signing a treaty meant a legitimation of Military Police authority on the land, their presence proved useful on several occasions.

From quelling the city-rebels who terrorised the streets of Easton District, to establishing a welcoming space for Westerian pilgrims and foreign traders seeking to worship and supply Queens with trade. The treaty had also made no mention of Windlehem or supporting other battles, which he had reasoned would only allow them to pursue its capture without having to worry about fighting a separate battle within Queens or elsewhere.

"We should've listened to her when she said to reject their treaty," said Commander Talius. "She warned us her people were starting to forget."

This illness must run deeper than we thought.

"We have to wait for them to figure out their next step," said Colonel Hellin, "And maybe do what she says next time."

"If there is a next time"

It's been about a decade since he last faced Commander Valta Thornheart of the once united, but long since scattered, Liberated communities of Downtown Queens. Yet he could still feel the butterflies in his belly when he first learned she would be marching her forces through Peaceland on the way to Windlehem. He had spent an unreasonable amount of time getting dressed and working up the audacity to face her, only to later discover from her officers that not only did she refuse to meet him, but she also refused almost every opportunity to make a stop during the three-day trip through his territory.

She's still mad at me, even after all these years.

"I know you want Windlehem," said Colonel Hellin, walking towards the door and waiting for him to buzz it open.

"But it'll have to wait, we have assignments to hand out today," he said, with a foot out the door and a hand to his heart. "Don't forget."

"I haven't," saluted the commander. "I'll see you there."

Damn, I forgot about that.

He returned to his apartment, unsure of what to make of the news or of his time. In the kitchen he found a *broken typewriter* resting over the counter and a glass of water sitting next to it. He was quite thirsty, but instead of drinking it, he swirled it in his hand, watching the twister inside fade almost as quickly as it formed, wondering if there was ever a worse moment in his life.

Many competing memories came to mind.

Why didn't I see this coming? I thought I was being strategic, but they were a few steps ahead. What's wrong with me? No. It's not me. It's that disease,

They're all forgetting their history and there's nothing we can do about it.

History was important to remember, especially considering if all it took were a few headlines and a couple rumours to mislead a people. In a country where more than a quarter couldn't read and another quarter were practically losing their minds, it wasn't too difficult to rewrite the past for an unearned legacy. It was even a competition.

I-I have to figure something out, I can't end up like the men I look up to.

'C-Commander?" stuttered a soldier's voice from the handheld radio, a woman's.

What now?

"What is it?" asked Commander Talius, reaching for the radio and placing it under his chin.

"It's a message," replied the soldier. "From Colonel Wilona Flowers."

Wilona I – May 4th

A Tree Without Roots

She stood atop South Station's tallest observation tower, watching as tens of thousands crowded the Citadel's busy streets. Many with somewhere to go, others with nowhere to be.

Attached to her hip was an auto-pistol belonging to some Baltiar war hero now forgotten in time, on her feet were a pair of Army-issued boots which still hadn't broken in after all these years, and all around her was an unobstructed view of what many regarded as the new capital of the Liberation Army.

Peaceland.

She watched as they went about their afternoon, Citizens and noncitizens alike. Some searching for a place to sell their labour to, others already at their stations grateful for the luxury of work it provided. There was a great deal of uncertainty resulting from the rising tensions throughout the country as well, especially after the recent events in Windlehem. In addition to the worries of refugees swarming their territories, and of markets collapsing due to the damage to the land, it was widely understood each defeat meant a step closer to the end of their empire and collective cause.

We don't have too many wars left to lose before they're at our gates, and it's not like there's much left of the Highlands either,

All these people and nowhere to place them.

There were many others wandering and working within the Citadel. Those who were just as concerned about the world and its affairs, but were too busy trying to manage the unpredictability of day-to-day life to give it much more than a passing thought.

In Peaceland, rent and taxes were not scaled to match the wants or to meet the needs of its people. Every migrant, resident and even Citizen were expected to pay not what they should or could, but what they always *must*.

As it's always been.

Though not nearly as populated or well-constructed, Peaceland was about twice the size of the Ancient City of Queens and thrice as large as her Old Acadian neighbour, the City of Roilmont to the west. Split between five Strongholds representing three major regions, some thought of it as its own small country within a greater Liberated Acadia, while others understood it as a city state with countrysides in-between its Strongholds.

Whatever it was, she considered it their *best hope* to reunify the country.

To the north beyond the walls of the Citadel, the Highland gradually receded into Peaceland's Midland Plateau. It was there the Honoured families and their Landlords enjoyed the wealth and privilege of a special protected class status. Their contributions to the Cause were found in Midland Stronghold, where the descendants of those who conquered and consolidated Peaceland continued the unrelenting legacy of its founders.

To the south-west stood the Iron Mountains and an Ancient Highland peninsula now home to the Firstlanders, a community of Acadians who enjoyed their well-earned sovereignty. They were the first to resettle on the land after Old Acadia fell, and possessed something close to a small army of their own in their new capital Southern Stronghold. Though they remained largely independent from the rest of Peaceland, they served as loyal allies and servants to the Liberation Army and its cause.

Maybe I should retire, it's not like I got much time left anyways,

I should try to enjoy these years,

Or maybe months.

She clutched the medals which were pinned to the left side of her breasts. They were awarded to her for her most distinguished achievements, and for someone losing their memories to illness, she was as proud as one could be.

Three gold ribbons symbolising her rank in the Army, a raw piece of silver stamped with a set of numbers in honour of her ascension from a war orphan to a full class Citizen, and an eagle made of maglith in memory of the Third Battle for Queens, of which she apparently led to victory. There were many other medals as well, each only valuable for the soldiers who fell in line at their sight.

But I couldn't leave now, not when Talius needs me—

The sound of something collapsing burst from the markets below, and its noise echoed throughout the corridor of makeshift apartments and complexes.

"Huh?" she said to herself, creeping to the edge of the rooftop in search of what might have caused it or where it could have come from.

"What was that?"

Spread across the Citadel's urban grid she found the institutions responsible for making use of every child born a Citizen to the land. The University, the Guild Academies, and the Army Colleges, as well as the surrounding communities which were tasked to populate its classrooms and training sites.

At the easternmost edge she noticed an array of stalagmite-like structures and it reminded her of a kingdom made of sandcastles, but with cement and stone instead. It was the *Fortress*, the largest Stronghold within Peaceland, and where Commander Talius Baltiar resided, ruling over all those who had pledged their lives to the Liberation.

Looks like there's nothing over there,

They would've raised the alarms.

She turned her sights to the centre of the Citadel, where the day markets were still bustling with trade and commerce. Right next door to the west of it, across a massive rift on the land they called the small river, were the slums. As desolate and dejected as they always were.

It's probably just some slum cleaning, or maybe they finally arrested those unionisers,

Or maybe it was an attack-

No, who could even attack us? Our defences are airtight, it's our offence which always seems frail.

As much as she tried to fight it, her thoughts wandered back to Windlehem, and with it came an unnerving feeling. One which seized the hairs on her skin and ordered them to stand upright like an officer. It was a national tragedy, one she was certain would change the political discourse of Acadia, *if it hadn't already.*

But it wasn't her duty to think about it, not when there were other problems.

Problems closer to home.

Cradled somewhere in the lands between the Citadel and the Firstland Peninsula, was another Ancient settlement. A dense cluster of highrises surrounding an old mining village known as Mineraltown. It was a place left mostly true to their original built and purpose, and considered by worshippers of the Ancients to be as sacred as any other Ancient Highland City.

The town was governed by the local Temple of Zaaj, led by Mother Maaria. a priest-woman who administered the small municipality outside of the Liberation Army's normal affairs. She was a warm-hearted woman, as kind as a newborn's smile, but a little over a week ago she had closed the town's walled gates and held all those inside captive. Including the pilgrims and foreigners who ventured to their land and were protected under international law.

They had made several attempts to contact her over the course of the week, but every effort was ignored.

What is she planning? What is she thinking?

Her hands began trembling uncontrollably, as they always seem to whenever the world didn't match her expectations.

This isn't like her-

Her hand radio buzzed.

"Yes?" she asked, answering the call.

"Colonel Flowers!" said a soldier.

It was *Major San*, and there was some urgency in his voice.

"Where are you?" he asked

"At the observation tower," answered the colonel. "Why?"

"An explosion by the market," said the major, "We need you downstairs."

Daaria II

"You know, these aren't so bad after a couple thousand," said Omaara, chewing on a ration-bar made for soldiers to eat in-between meals and in trenchfields.

"Yeah," agreed Daaria, reluctantly taking a bite out of hers.

"They really couldn't come up with a better recipe though?"

"And where's Jaxas? We're goin' to be late again."

After retrieving their Army-issued pistols from the armoury, the pair marched toward the courtyard with their best strides. It was raining, though rather unconvincingly, and the wind was absent, a rare occurrence on the Highlands where it often stormed even on the sunniest of days.

She watched as the other soldiers assembled into their lines, ready to set out for the day under the direction of their respective captains.

"Nevermind," said Daaria, pointing to a boy through the crowd of soldiers.

"There he is."

From the distance, approached a handsome boy with a dark brown complexion, he was more or less the same height as Omaara and had long curls of shaggy black hair which covered his face and eyes as much as it did his head.

"Good morning," said Jaxas, with a yawn and a hand over his heart.

"Good morning," replied Daaria and Omaara, both returning the salute.

The three Peaceguards began their walk through the Fortress, greeting every soldier and officer with the same gesture.

Their path was paved with coloured earthstone, blue and green, brown and yellow too. It was a common material in Rodina, but its use in construction and architecture was still something only mastered by the Ancients.

It's been several years since she first laid eyes on the Fortress, and she still couldn't help but reflect on how *strange* her structures appeared, both from a distance and especially up close. The buildings themselves were built entirely of Acadian-concrete, a respectable attempt to recreate an Ancient secret, and they resembled the apartments, towers and other complexes found throughout Queens, but all a little misshapen, and at times, *distorted*. Misplaced windows and balconies, whole watchtowers placed where it no longer made sense to be, all next to lingering walls and barricades which were more of a nuisance to the surrounding space than they were useful. It was quite clear that not the best minds or hands went into the construction of the Fortress, almost as if they were built without a care or plan, and from what she understood, this was partially true.

Unlike the Ancients, who led their constructs with the precision only achievable through an advanced understanding of engineering, or at least architecture, the Acadians had constructed their spaces out of emergency. In Rockland it was to survive, in Peaceland it was to occupy.

"Hey, you going to finish that?" asked Jaxas, pointing to the half-eaten ration-bar she had forgotten about.

"No, have it," said Daaria, handing it over without any resistance.

"Yes!" said Jaxas, excited.

"I love this shit."

As they neared the Commander's Tower, they passed the barracks which housed new recruits from across Peaceland's three regions, the Highlands, Midlands, and Lowlands. Many were on their way to the training fields and circuits which the soldiers called the Playgrounds, while others were preparing for Army College. A place where soldiers with some promise were admitted into to make themselves useful to the Liberated Cause.

"So, y'all hear about Windlehem?" said Jaxas, with a mouthful of rations.

"Yeah," said Omaara, frowning.

"All those soldiers and their families."

"Yeah no kiddin'," replied Jaxas, "How many' you think never made it?"

"A thousand at least," answered Omaara.

The Liberation Army of Peaceland, under the direction of Colonel Hellin, planned to send several hundred Generalists, backed by a few Specialist regiments to support the recapture of Windlehem. Some of her friends from South Station were within the pool of Generalists to be sent, and she worried for them. They had all grown up together in the Eastern Lowland town of Notwell and it's been months since they last spoke. Now there was a strong possibility she would miss them on their way to the frontlines and never see them again.

I hope they didn't get selected yet,

I didn't even get a chance to say goodbye.

"Well at least we're safe in the Peaceguard," sighed Jaxas.

"Yeah, well we ain't," said Daaria. "Look what happened to Roxanne and Glenanna."

"Elara and Wilow" added Omaara, under her breath.

There was a recent assignment handed to several Peaceguard teams to charge dynamite atop the Great Gorge separating Peaceland from Queens. A sudden explosion, however, caused a mudslide, sending more than half of them down into the Forest Gorge and River below. Some bodies were recovered by the land survey and rescue team, while open parachutes were all that remained of the rest.

"We're not safe either," continued Daaria. "No one is."

"Unless you're a high-officer."

Unlike most soldiers stationed within the Citadel, they belonged neither to the Commander's Generalist or Specialist force, but rather to an entirely different branch. The Peaceguard.

While the Generalists supported the hard labour efforts of the Army during peacetime and fought in the frontlines during wartime, the Specialists found their place serving the Army's technical needs and mechanical operations. Fighting only after the frontlines perished or as their services were required.

The Peaceguard, however, were an elite branch of soldiers, selected from the Specialist branch and placed in more distinguished positions. There were only a few hundred spread throughout Peaceland, and the main concern of their officers were not managing a war or its battles, but rather administering and policing its Citizens, noncitizens, and other soldiers.

As a result, they enjoyed special privileges, such as being the only force permitted to open and concealed carry, as well as make arrests. Like all soldiers, however, they were still expected to sacrifice their body and life to the Cause when the time arrived.

"Well, if we die, I hope we die together," said Jaxas.

"Yeah," agreed Daaria

"What?" burst out Omaara. "Don't say that!"

"I'm just saying," laughed Jaxas.

"Well I can't die yet," she said, taking her metal claws to her head and hair.

"What would my mom say?"

"And my dad!"

As Omaara began, a man wearing a black Old Military coat decorated with five distinct war medals appeared from around the corner of another thoughtlessly built building. He had a face as hard as rockwood, and smelt a little like *wine?*

She and Jaxas placed their hands on their hearts the moment his presence was made, but Omaara hadn't noticed with her back turned.

"My parents would kill me if I died without a promotion. You know, I think I should ask the Commander for a promotion, I think I deserve it and he knows my dad and—"

"Uh, Omaara?" said Jaxas.

"Hm?" she replied.

"Behind you..."

"Yeah right, I'm not falling for that again."

"No, seriously," said Daaria, saluting her best salute.

"Huh?" she said, turning around and bumping into him.

He was of similar height to her and Jaxas, with irises as bright and red as the red stripes found in the Old Flag. His windswept hair, while shimmering even without the sun, was cold and black like a Lowland night. He was quite handsome too, but could use a shave.

"C-Commander!" said Omaara, quickly stiffening her posture and saluting.

"Soldiers," the commander saluted. "Good morning."

Hiran III

A calming blue light glowed from above their heads as the vault-like door shut behind them.

"This way," said Eon, leading the path to and through the maze of well stocked shelves.

It was impossible to say for sure what lurked inside the jars and crates scattered throughout the room, though he had a few good ideas from the deliveries he had made for Arther Guildmen and his uncle Commander Braxas over the years. Some goods came from faraway trades, others were from just down the street, some were only passing by, others were made to stay in Queens.

There was some money to be made in this holy city and Arther Guildmen sold whatever he could without stepping too hard in the interests of others.

From perishable goods like poisonous treesaps, coloured truffles, and dried toad skins, to precious and heavily contested metals like maglith, and rare commodities like the horns, feathers, and furs of creatures considered extinct, such were the sorts of things found in Guildmen's basement. Some served as useful components for medicines and machinery, others were taken for a high, but they all had at least one thing in common. Such commodities were purchasable only with an Old Acadian coin they had long ago split into two, the pushed-out centre of silver now simply referred to as the *good-coin*.

The air cooled and thickened the further they travelled through the damped concrete room. There was an odd putrid smell as well, something like roadkill drying under the sun as it rotted. It was hardly noticeable at first, but it gradually proclaimed itself before suddenly seizing the space around them.

"What' you doing later?" asked Eon, opening a wooden door at the end of one of the halls.

It led into a long closet where lost and stolen Ancient artefacts were kept.

"Nothing," replied Hiran.

He watched as Eon set aside boxes containing Ancient batteries, cables, disks, and other pieces of hardware and gizmo parts. Things purchased from the blackmarket and only to be sold to the highest bidder, who were at times, their original owners.

"Let's get high," said Eon, handing him a metal capsule the size of Arther Guildmen's fist.

"This it?" asked Hiran, staring down at the thing.

It was a cylindrical object, a type of protective container he was familiar with.

"Yeah," replied Eon.

"Cool," said Hiran, "And yeah I'm down."

"What we smoking?"

"Hex."

"What?" laughed Hiran.

"I'm kiddin'," said Eon. "Jinx, what else?"

The two made their way out of the blackstore, taking a different path through the maze from which they came. Cold winds trickled in from a nearby freezer-room, where Ancient bones and fossilised remains continued to ferment until they were ready to be consumed.

According to Emmi, there was another door somewhere, one sealed shut and hidden within the walls. He searched for it whenever he had the chance to, and to his surprise did find something once. A rusty red door which could only be seen from the tiny gap between the floor and the shelves concealing it. He wasn't sure, however, if it was what she was talking about or if it had been hidden on purpose as she claimed.

I should ask her about it,

How did she know anyways?

"Wait," said Hiran. "Where exactly am I taking this?"

"Uh... you gotta ask Guildmen," said Eon. "He's the one who made the trade."

"Oh... okay," said Hiran, taking one last look at the container before carefully placing it inside his courier bag.

It protruded a little, but it was safe and snug.

"What's inside anyways?" asked Hiran

The warm lights glimmered quietly above and though it was brief, they revealed a tense expression sweeping across Eon's face.

It was quick, but he was sure *it was there*.

"I-I can't tell you," said Eon, as the vault-door slammed shut behind them.

Raamina I – May 1

The Queendom of Acadia

She stood behind the safety of her royal purple linen curtains, watching the world as it passed with eyes peeking out the balcony of an Ancient spire. The star they called the sun continued to creep over the early summer afternoon, while an orb as teal as a robin's egg settled quietly behind a nest of clear blue skies.

It was thought long before the Great Highlands of Rodina had ever formed, waves of emerald and sapphire crashed endlessly against the sea moon Maaria's storm-ridden shores. Shores once worshipped by the ancient Gran Acadians, and storms still thought to have been the cause of all rain on the Biosphere.

From twelve stories above she could see enough of the world to tell a thousand stories of it. A few blocks west, Ancient factories once responsible for manufacturing steel and coloured concrete, now served as cowsheds and chicken coups. In the Honoured Sanctuary located a few apartments east lay some of Acadia's youngest soldiers, forgotten by seasons past, and several kilometres to the south, an Ancient bluestone pillar glistened under the sun like glitter. It was called the Salt Pillar and it rose far above every building belonging to Rodina, dwarfing even some clouds.

Where are they? They should've arrived by now.

Concealed from the public eye, she watched as soldiers formed a ceremonial line-up by the northwest gates to Outer Rockland. She tried many times to ignore it, but her eyes kept returning to the hordes of Rocklanders gathering anxiously around the outpost. The crowd of a few dozen at dawn had grown to several hundred by the early afternoon, and the news was still getting around.

What did this treachery buy me?

Just more anxiety?

Troubled by the sight, she brushed the view from her mind, turning her attention instead to the workers tending to the Baltiar family's fields. She watched on, in her black and silver trimmed priestess gown, as the workers pushed ploughs into the semi-frozen soil and the servants continued to slave away in the kitchens.

Watching the men, women, and children who were responsible for attending to her property was something she often did whenever she felt the years were unkind to her. It reminded her of those who fought to enjoy the warmth of summer, and of those who toiled to survive the winters.

Not too many summers ago she was also still a woman who longed for her lover's letters. This was when he used to write to her occasionally, before the years passed and there was less to say. Before she had wasted her life preoccupied with a Lordship she never cared for, while he wasted his rotting away on the battlefield. She still wanted to see him, *but it wouldn't be the same.*

They had learned not too long ago he had been taken as a prisoner of war by the Military Police along with a significant share of his forces. Accepting she would never see him again would have been harder than birthing the children he left her alone to raise, and it was for that very reason she had simply refused to accept.

When watching the workers didn't work, she escaped through the stories told to her by the women and men of her childhood. Particularly the ones which made her feel grateful to be alive today, and not some other time ago. The tales told to her by her great aunt Wila Baltiar often came to mind.

"*The Lost Years,*" she once used to say, with an astute and dignified voice. A trait expected out of every Baltiar, Landlord or not.

"*The time in-between Old and New Acadia, when the Westerians tore through the Old Country, razing every village, raping every woman, and forcing our people out of their cities and into the graveyard they discovered upon arriving.*"

"*For countless summers the Westerian Siege continued, and for countless summers they failed. To survive waves of attacks, the Old Acadians melted down whatever they could to craft makeshift walls, some of which still stood tall. To withstand the decades of occupation, the Old Acadians tore into the Highland to smuggle in whatever they could, and to survive the cold winters, the cold dreaded winters, they kept everybody in a huddle, even the dead."*

"Existence meant suffering, birth was a tragedy, and it was unsure when or if the years would be counted again." she spoke aloud, recalling her words.

"A time when naming a newborn was the worst thing a woman could do for herself,"

"Knowing one day there'd be nothing left to eat but the children."

These days women also hardly gave birth, and even when they did, they often bore little monsters.

Reminding herself of these tales and truths left her grateful to be alive today, especially with the class status she inherited.

The sounds of marching drums erupted from the roads of Outer Rockland and the deafening cheers from crumbling balconies and crowded alleys followed shortly.

I-Is that them?

The noise echoed through the Interior of Rockland. Passing through the dense clusters of apartments and industrial space, before finding their way to the Baltiar Palace where she awaited.

After the drummers passed through the gates, the flag carriers followed with the Flag of Old Acadia, an iron vessel stranded between a field of red and purple ribbons.

It is-

Like a child being tucked to bed for the last time, silence quickly blanketed the land when, instead of marching soldiers, corpses were carried in on the back of Army trucks. Soldiers once paraded out of Rockland in the uniforms of their forefathers, now returned in blood stained bags stacked together like firewood. Many broke down at the sight of it, while many others rushed to the trucks, likely in search of their own.

She knew there would be sacrifices made, so as not to raise suspicion, but she was surprised with how many trucks arrived with bodies.

A-And it's still early in the retreat, they're going to be trickling in for months-

Her heart leapt when she quickly lost count of the bodies, and again after a knock on the door broke out.

What was that?!

She stood still for some time, too timid to answer, too afraid of what awaited her if she did.

Not now-

Please, just go away-

She eventually worked up the courage to call out to it, figuring it would provide her with enough time to jump if she needed to.

"W-Who is it?" she asked, softly so as not to give away her intention.

"Mother Raamina," whimpered a woman from the other side of the Ancient chamber. "Lady Isaarith is here—"

"I told you she was in there" screeched a *creature* on the other side, "You stupid servant bitch!"

Talius III

The lights radiated inside Colonel Hellin's office, a room located inside a bunker built several floors beneath the Fortress.

"The rebels burned down another outpost three days ago," said the colonel, taking a cup of water by the projector and having a drink.

"It was guarding a guild site and we were forced to abandon it."

"Along with the nearby villages."

"We sent a team of Peaceguards there a month ago to investigate," said the commander, turning to the three soldiers standing before them. "You'll be carrying on their work. Any questions?"

"Where's their base?" asked a red-eyed soldier with flowery golden hair rivalling the sun.

She was about as tall as him, which wasn't much of an accomplishment for a man, but she was over a head taller than most women he'd ever met.

"We don't know," answered Colonel Hellin, scratching the back of his head.

Their eyes followed him as he walked over to the scaled map of the Eastern Lowlands projected onto the wall. It contained a bird's eye view of its regional stronghold, the villages surrounding its Army towers, as well as an outline of every Lowland hill, building, cave, road and river.

"But we know the first few uprisings started in Goodwater, Notwell and Cratertown 8"

"We think they're spread out somewhere around those four towns," he added, pointing to the wall.

"So we're helping them?" asked another soldier, a red-eyed boy who looked a little bit like a woodcow with the way his shaggy black hair fell over his face. "The Peaceguards there, I mean."

"No," replied the commander.

"They went missing some time ago"

"What?! Missing?!" spoke the three Peaceguards in near unison.

"Go to Eastern Stronghold first. Brigadier Stormwater will tell you more. Understood?"

"Yes, Commander!" they each answered, again in near unison.

It was expected of those recruited into the Generalist Force to sacrifice their bodies for their country and cause. While for soldiers with more useful technical skills, insightful observations, and other traits deemed essential to the Army's operations, a well-deserved position in the Specialist Force awaited them upon graduating Army College.

Here, however, were well-distinguished soldiers who he had personally pulled out of the Specialist line and reclassified into the Peaceguards. Soldiers who achieved top of their class in Army College and were deemed necessary to the supremacy and progress of the Citadel, and therefore, the Liberation Cause itself.

"Also," said Colonel Hellin, "We're sending a supply truck to the Lowlands tomorrow. There won't be another one heading there for a while, so don't miss it" he continued, sealing an envelope and handing it to the soldier named Omaara Strong.

She was the daughter of Antolin Strong, an Honoured Family as old as the Liberation Army itself and some of her truest allies.

Her father would turn his own grandmother's bones into cannon fodder before he would turn a back on the Army.

"Yes, Colonel!" she answered, with a warm-hearted salute.

Though he was in command of the Liberation Army of Peaceland and its vassal states, he always wished for a smaller unit. A unit which could be managed personally and sent off to pursue his direct interests without worrying about a chain of command to shout orders down to. This is what led to the formation of the Peaceguard.

It was a fairly new branch, created as a small network resembling the underguilds of Rockland, though instead of street gangs and the gutter-born children of Queens, he was commanding highly specialised soldiers who presided over his Army, and people during peacetime as its law enforcers.

They had also proved their usefulness during the times in between war and peace, investigating threats to land, as well as doing the dirty work only specialists could do without sparking the war.

"Um, Commander?" asked a girl who stood at the shoulders of the other two. "I have a question, but it's not about this."

"What is it, soldier?"

Her name was *Daaria Earthwind*, a young soldier who had been transferred to the Citadel after achieving one of the highest overall test scores in the official Peaceland Classification Exam. A standardised exam designed to stream students into their correct stations as soldiers and civilians. Instead of the civilian path, however, she decided on soldiership.

She made a brave choice and I'll reward her for it.

"I also never had the chance to tell you," he continued, "Good work on your last assignment."

It was a simple but important delivery assignment from Newtown, though one which nearly failed if it hadn't also been for her quick thinking and determination.

I would've been in so much trouble if it hadn't been for her.

"T-Thank you, Commander Baltiar! It's an honour to serve you!"

"What's your question?" he asked, turning the projector off.

Though she had spent the last few years training in the Citadel, he could hear it in her voice.

She's still a Lowlander at heart.

"Mineraltown," she said, pausing to collect the right words.

"Is it true there are defectors?"

Colonel Hellin immediately glanced his way with a straight face.

"We'll find out soon," said the commander, raising a hand and casting a dismissal. "You're to return to your stations until then."

"Yes, Commander!" they said together.

Emmi I - April 21st

God save us

She walked her bicycle down a crowded stone tiled road, sneaking glimpses of the pilgrims and market goers as they wandered about the ancient city in awe. Rose stained skies were cast above the Highland and there were watchtowers overlooking every entrance into the market district the Military Police had renamed *Newtown*.

"Alright, this looks like the place," she said to herself, turning into a back road and stashing her bicycle away inside a nearby bush.

Where are those two?

I don't have all day,

We're lucky Guildmen even gave me a break.

She relaxed her shoulders, let out a deep sigh and placed herself down atop a concrete bench, gazing at the Ancient world and its towers made of marble, white granite, and concrete found in all sorts of colours like gemstones.

Things were slowly returning to where they were before the start of the war. The overworld merchants were returning to Queens, hopeful for new and meaningful opportunities, the Lowlanders began their ascent of the plateaus, expecting to sell off their early spring harvest, and the working folk continued to scramble as they always have. Spreading throughout the city streets to put a price on their time like the very goods they bought and sold.

It was believed by many throughout the land that the Ancients were once a magical people dwelling within magical cities they had constructed out of hard labour and *sorcery*. Their towers even dazzled as such, nearly unweathered by the countless storms which had undoubtedly passed, and under the right sunlight, she was *convinced* they were made of precious emeralds, rubies, sapphires, and of course, *magic*. Though they had vanished from the annals of time, the Ancient world still persisted atop the

Highlands, void of an owner or ruler for countless millennia. Their buildings, however, continued to glitter as if they had just been constructed, and their homes were still complete with running water, gas lines and something the people called *electricity*. All things that were beyond the understanding of the Acadians who first set foot upon the continent they named Rodina.

The thought was captivating and it led her to begin searching for meaning behind the colossal walls and ornate pillars overwatching the town, wondering if they were meant to serve a purpose beyond what had become of them, or if they were destined to house those who took them for holy sanctuaries.

Were they always worshipped?

Or was it some sort of farce?

Did they always have idols dwelling inside?

Or was that just a recent fabrication?

A screeching roar soon split her train of thought, and with it arrived the sounds of halting engines, and the parade of marching boots. It was likely a *Military Police* truck passing along the main road, and quickly reminded her of all this world and the pursuit of its grand marvels had stolen from her.

It made her spit on the street out of spite.

I get so angry whenever they're near,

I need to relax-

I can't let myself do anything stupid.

The Military Police were a force mainly made up of Acadians, loyally serving a foreign sovereign and surviving largely within remnant Westerian territories, carrying on their brutal legacy of oppression of Acadian people.

Blood-traitors, she spat,

Dogs, she cursed once more.

It's been half a century or so since they first arrived at the gates of Queens with their Westerian gifted technology, taking a fragment of the City with coercion while displacing hundreds of thousands in the process. It was said when the Liberation Army originally resisted this expansion into the Highland, the Police had responded by decimating their defences with rockets and flamethrowers. Razing much of Queens and her core to the ground and before claiming it on behalf of Westeria as a part of her reconquest. There were many other conflicts in more recent times as well, with the Military Police claiming victories over several failed Liberated campaigns, and at some point Newtown eventually came to split the City into two. Easton District to the east and Westown to the west.

I've lost so many friends over the years and I really miss home,
If it wasn't for the Pilgrimage I'd still be in my room,
And if it wasn't for the Military Police I'd still be in school.

During the present day, the Military Police had ended their practice of destroying Ancient buildings and instead competed with the Liberation Army to carve out Queens' lucrative pilgrim market. This was a part of the City that was lost to war and as a result, what remained of it was regarded as something special by those who took the Highland for worship in the dark years of Acadia. Her own neighbourhood of Jacktown had been included among the several communities seized by the Military Police for its Ancient sites. Now only pilgrims and tourists were permitted to enter its locked gates, now a Zaaj Temple stood where her beloved tree temple used to be, a brothel where her school used to be.

We're slowly getting pushed out of the Highland,
Just so they can turn our homes into temples that disgrace the Mother,

Temples that prayed to some Ancient king they took for a sovereign and saviour.

A saviour who was dead before any Acadian ever knew him.

For worshippers of the Old Faith like her, the Zaaj reformists had betrayed Acadians with their worship of the Ancients, and they had disgraced the Old depiction of the Mother by tearing apart the tree she had tamed and rested under.

So many reasons for the Blacksheeps to take back the City,
Queens doesn't belong to the occupiers, it belongs to its settlers.

She was so preoccupied with her thoughts that she hadn't noticed an arm reaching around her neck until after it had grabbed her by the shoulder and reached for her breast.

What-

"Hey baby" said a creeper from behind her.

"What the hell-"

Struggling free from his hold on her, she reached into her pocket for her knife and blade in hand she turned to the assaulter, assured she was going to stab someone on her lunch break today.

What she found instead only agitated her more.

It was just a girl dressed in boy jeans like a woman.

It was *Nia!?*

"Nia?! What the fuck! You scared me!" said Emmi, as upset as she could be.

"Don't do that!"

"Relax" laughed Nia, revealing a gorgeous smile and some braces, "I just wanted to catch feel"

"Stop!" replied Emmi, hitting her arm.

Her name was Hania but they called her Nia for short, and she braided hair to get by and always kept lipgloss by her side. She was a *beautiful* girl with brownish-red cat-like eyes, steel braces and light black skin, and an uneven smile which also revealed a pair of misshapen dimples.

She was seventeen and in her senior year at Eastern Commerce, a nearby high school in Easton District.

"Where's Ashley-Ann?"

"Ashley-Ann, here I am!" sung another from their rear with a melodic voice.

"Ashley!" said Emmi, immediately embracing her in a tight hug.

She had silky black hair which she wore down to her lower back and fuzzy peach skin with a face shaped like a *chipmunk's*.

"You look so cute today" said Emmi,

"I like your top"

For clothes she wore a pink crop top over a pair of black denim shorts, and on her feet were a pair of black leather boots which though Military Police school issued, were ironically trending in the underground world of teens.

"Thank you babygirl" she said, ever so politely as she always did.

She was also known to be a bit of a ditz, but charming nonetheless, and *absolutely gorgeous* like Nia who was *just stunning*.

"Did you two bring the stuff?" asked Emmi,

"In here" said Nia, pointing back to her backpack.

"And here" said Ashley-Ann showing off hers.

"I only have an hour off work so we have to be quick"

"We have class too" said Nia, "But can we go shopping first?" she asked, taking the lead, "I have to get some school supplies"

She didn't reply, but only gave her a stern look.

"Please?" pleaded Nia

"It's on the way, and it's only 12:04" she added, flashing her old analog wristwatch.

"Okay fine" surrendered Emmi, "But we have to go now"

"Then let's go," said Nia, happily leading the way.

"Can we go get some food too?" asked Ashley-Ann trailing behind her. "I'm so hungry"

"We should have time" said Nia, "Our practice run only took us twenty minutes"

I hope this ends well.

The trio carefully began their stroll through the marketplace, passing by alley cats and sewer rats as they crossed historic plazas surrounded by farmer's markets and spice traders. In a nearby animal bazaar they watched over a small group of temple keepers leading another group of merchants and patrons behind a cart full of wild hens and their chicks. At some point the party of market-goers turned into a side alley which reeked of blood, and rot, and it was there they overheard some sort of foreign chanting before one of the hens were taken by the neck. One had even plucked a smaller bird from its mother and continued to chant as he carefully slid a sharp blade under its neck. The three watched on in horror as the man then allowed its blood to spill onto those gathered before releasing it to circle the road. It was a small ritual sacrifice to their god as a way of commencing the opening of the market for the rest of the summer.

"*Gross*," said Emmi, plugging her nose, "I think I'm going to throw up"

"I don't think I can eat any meat after that," said Ashley-Ann.

"I know where we can get some rarefruit for free," said Nia.

"Is it on the way?" asked Emmi.

"Yeah it's just down the street,"

"There's a few stalls I steal from all the time"

The path was paved with concrete as they pressed forward into the district, and when the animal bazaar ended, boutiques welcomed their march deeper into the market. Above the storefronts were apartments built to house an occupying population of Westerian citizens, who along with the Pilgrims, received protected class status in Newtown. Inside such communities were bustling merchant-stalls specialising in exotic grains and spices, ancient vegetables grown from distant lands, salt and sugar, and special fruits believed to quell any illness. Though the markets were heavily crowded, there were a great deal of blind spots in the busyness of the plaza. As a result it triggered something within them.

"Hey this place is great" said Ashley-Ann, pocketing a piece of jungle-fruit with an impressive sleight of hand.

"Isn't it?" agreed Nia, casually taking a slice of terramelon and placing it into her mouth as if she had purchased it.

"You guys are like monkeys," said Emmi, quietly giggling to herself.

She tried resisting the urge to steal, but couldn't help but to treat herself to a thornberry here and a piece of highfruit there, snatching whatever she could from the stands like they had when they were younger. It was a bad habit which had only developed over the years as the three rose within the ranks of the Blacksheeps, a guild of street performers and part-time thieves.

They were made up mostly of Tautau boys and girls from now conquered or abandoned communities, but they took in others as well. If they weren't already working and assuming a second identity in the market somewhere like her, they were performing plays and committing petty crimes by day. In the night, however, they dedicated themselves to smuggling and robbery, and when the times called for it, they responded to the expansion of other Acadian forces with their own armed resistance.

At some point during their pilferage through the open market, a unit of five police-soldiers had crossed into their plaza on foot. They wore red and black uniforms like the Westerian Army with barking rottweilers stitched to their coats.

"Guys" she hissed back to Nia and Ashley-Ann.

"What?" said Nia, toneless and finishing the last of her terramelon and wiping the sugary juices from her lips.

"*The Police*" she whispered.

They just know when to show up.

"It's nothing," said Nia, dismissively.

"I wouldn't panic"

From the corner of their eyes they watched as the police-soldiers quickly made their rounds through the plaza, quietly pocketing bribes instead of counting for sheep. They took every royal note handed to them before saluting off toward the next stall, and it didn't take long for them to approach their tent, leaving them within earshot of the conversations taking place nearby.

"How can I help you officers?" said one of the market vendors, already reaching under the desk for some cash.

"We're looking for permits" answered a police-soldier, a woman with black hair and darker sunglasses.

"Right away" said the man handing them several hundred in Old Acadian royal notes, the most common currency used in Acadia.

Unlike their metallic coin counterpart, the paper currency known as the royal note was worth about the same number printed on its face, while the coin was split in two and typically used to separate the poor from the market.

"We should stop stealing" said Emmi, "We could get caught"

"But I wanted to get some makeup said Nia, "I even made space in my bag"

"Wait-

"So *that's* why you wanted to go *shopping?*"

"I thought you said you were getting school supplies-"

"Yeah, the makeup is for school"

"Hania-" she said, staring at her, unable to complete her sentences.

I thought she meant-

I should've known-

She nearly made her tear out her own hair with the way she had an answer for everything, and that almost made her laugh out of sheer frustration.

I can't handle her anymore,

And on such a pretty day too.

"What!? You didn't tell me you wanted to get makeup" blurted Ashley-Ann, "Hold on, I'm going to go make some room too"

"We're not getting makeup," said Emmi.

"What? Why not?!" asked Ashley, stomping her feet like a terrorbird.

"Because both of you are supposed to be carrying plaster bombs inside your backpacks"

"Please tell me you brought it Hania" she said turning back toward her.

"Don't worry, I have it" she replied, "It's my homework I didn't pack"

"And I also wouldn't forget" she continued, "I just wanted to go before we shut the market down"

The three of them were on a mission to detonate an Ancient temple, a particularly important site situated within a crucial juncture in Queens. It stood along one of the most contentious points in Newtown, to the east was a community stubbornly loyal to the Liberation Force, to the north housed a Military Police outpost, and to the west was the start of the Red Light District, a sex haven for foreigners at the expense of the local people. The temple itself was under control of a Westerian sex cult and was being used as a gathering site for elite members of the Acadian sex trade.

"Now be quiet" she hissed, "I'm trying to listen to the Police"

They watched on as the soldiers continued to make progress in the plaza, sizing up the locals with unimpressed gazes until a particular vendor had interrupted their easy streak of bribe collecting. They side-eyed the tent and their interaction with the man.

"This permit doesn't match any of our policies," said a *handsome* police-soldier of average height and golden hair, holding the paper to the sunlight.

"That's because it's Liberation Army issued," replied a much taller soldier with brown hair, his uniform adorned with a fair amount of medals.

He must be the squad leader-

"What are you talking about? My stalls 'been here for years" shouted the vendor, loud enough to catch ears and turn several heads in the market.

"This plaza has been under our control for the past four months now" answered the tall soldier, "It's no longer protected by The Liberation Force"

"Having this could get you arrested"

"Arrested? That's ridiculous! Arrested for what!?"

"Lower your voice!" ordered *sunglasses*.

I don't like her.

"For selling on Military Police property without a proper permit" replied their squad leader, "Which can and will be cited as the possession of illegal paraphernalia"

"Although, completely forgettable for 20 good-coins" he said, scanning their immediate surroundings to make sure the others were minding their own business.

For a moment she even made direct eye contact with him, and he squinted as a warning.

"We'll even write you a new pass"

The vendor chuckled as if it was the most absurd thing he had ever heard.

"20 good-coins, you're out of your minds"

"We'll take 25,000 in Old notes" said another police-soldier, a *tough* looking young man with muscle protruding out of his uniform.

"I'm not paying you a single bad-coin!" protested the vendor.

It seemed as if everyone was now secretly eyeing the altercation.

"Then you're getting arrested and the price of that permit just went up tenfold" said the tall police-soldier,

"And lower your voice, that's the last time we tell you" added sunglasses, once again.

"There's no way in hell you're arresting me!"

Their squad leader didn't respond, only extending his compact night baton and ordering his officers to arrest the man.

"Merrill, Heizer", "Take him into custody"

"Yes Captain!" said sunglasses and the overtrained soldier.

"Reus, you watch and take notes" He continued, gesturing back to the blonde one.

"I haven't done anything wrong! I know my rights in this market"

"Stop resisting arrest!" said the female soldier.

Merrill huh?

I'll have to remember that.

"Keep it moving folks" said the squad leader, "Nothing to see here"

"Come on" gestured Emmi, "It looks like none of our business"

"Let's get out of here before someone catches on to us-"

"Get away from me!" yelled the merchant, reaching underneath his shirt. It was there he removed an auto-pistol and it was then three loud pops rang out into the plaza. First there was bewilderment, then came disbelief, followed by yelling, screaming, and pushing.

"Emmi!", "Emmi!" called out Nia and Ashley-Ann amidst the chaos, sneaking underneath a nearby tent just outside the line-up of panicking market-goers.

"Over here-!" Nia yelled, just before more deafening shots were fired in quick succession.

She turned to find the members of the Military Police caught in a firefight in the marketplace and there were two vendors who appeared to have been caught in the crossfire. There was writhing and yelling, and more shots fired until there suddenly wasn't.

She was surprised by how much blood had fallen and permeated over the concrete floor. It appeared as if someone had let loose the headless chicken into the market.

"Shut the plaza down" ordered the squad leader, "And arrest anyone who refuses to identify themselves"

"Come on let's go" hissed Nia, catching a wave within the crowd.

"Before they bring the dogs"

Wilona II

The sun had set many hours ago and the injured were rushed to the Citadel's Hospital where many were still receiving emergency care. What was initially thought to be an explosion, was in actuality, dozens of civilians digging tunnels through the foundation of two houses, collapsing them both. Out of the forty pulled from the rubble thus far, only thirteen survived.

She watched her husband through the window into the emergency room, as he spent the last few hours in the day sowing strangers back together.

He works so hard every day and never complains.

They had spent countless nights apart, closer to their work than they were to one another, as well as the bed they were meant to share.

I miss him.

There never seemed to be enough hours in the day to appreciate the joy they were told was marriage, but still they understood their responsibilities to the Cause was more important than the time they could've spent together. Love was hard to find and make space for in a society perpetually at the edge of not working hard enough, and fearing the outbreak of disease and war. It was the sacrifice several generations of Peacelanders, and Acadians in general, were made to make for survival.

She stepped away from the window, wanting to wait for him but knowing he wouldn't be finished anytime soon. In the hallways she found more nurses, medics, and doctors tending to the other survivors. There were women, men, and even children, all broken, half-starved, and worked to the bone, while those with lesser injuries were taken away to be questioned by the Peaceguard.

It was an odd event to say the least, but she wasn't going to spend any energy thinking about it. Her high-officers were handling the investigation, and she wasn't going to interfere unless it was required of her.

Resting further down the hall, on floor blankets and mattresses, were a dozen soldiers from Rockland. Soldiers who were sent to recapture Windlehem for the Liberation, soldiers who were paraded through and out of Peaceland as champions of their united cause. They left with long-rifles strapped over their shoulders like school bags, and now spent whatever lingered of their youth, resting broken wills over bloody stumps. Unaware of the passing time like laundry left out to dry.

These are just the stragglers who made it back, and the ones too injured to make it home.

The soldiers were stratified according to the severity of their condition as well as the urgency in their required treatment, and nearly all of them were given a very high dose of witchleaf, a drug derived from a rare thorn-bush native to the Forest Gorge. It was used to place patients in medically induced comas, not necessarily for just the pain, but also to remove any idea of worldly attachments, including a sense of ownership over joints and limbs.

They just marched to their ends,
What were Vanfall and Thornheart thinking?

"Colonel Flowers" saluted a woman in a dark blue and crimson patterned robe, a priestess from the Citadel's own Temple of Zaaj.

She along with several others were enlisted to ease the hearts of patients at the hospital and together they hymned prayersongs from the New Book of Zaaj, but at times like these it seemed as if they had just overcrowded the place.

"Sister Jully" she replied, with a hand to her heart as well.

"A moment of your time, please, I wish to speak to you. It's an urgent-"

"You have me"

"There's some hope," said the emerald eyed priestess.

"For?" she said quietly and rather unconvincingly.

Hope for what?

The war?

In her decades within the Army, she had never heard of such a devastating and embarrassing defeat, especially before the battle ever began. She was relieved, to say the least, when she learned Colonel Hellin of the Specialist Force had called his reinforcement campaign off after requesting four hundred of her Generalists.

They would've just followed them to their graves, I could never let that happen to my soldiers.

It's been many years since she was surrounded by this many sick and injured. The stench of blood in the air raised memories of a war she could not remember, but was certain she lived through.

The dilemma was giving her *a headache.*

"Colonel?"

"-Oh, my apologies"

"I meant to say, hope for exactly what?"

"The dead lay all around us"

Sister Jully was silent for a moment, but was resilient in her voice. "They're at the hands of the gods now, Mother and her children, and Zaaj"

"But you're still here-"

"And looking rather well to be fair" she added.

"I'm not quite following"

She's saying there's hope for *you*, Colonel" said another priestess, approaching with the same garments and deep emerald jewelled eyes.

"Hope for *me*?"

"Please, follow us" saluted Sister Jully, before trailing off along the hall.

I should go home, she thought to herself following behind.

Yeah, maybe take a long bath too.

She followed the women as they led her through a maze of turns which appeared endless to the passing eye, and past rows of crowded rooms evenly spaced between one another, and walls which widened with each step. Her feet were sore but she followed the pair nonetheless and rather reluctantly, first because she was curious as to what they meant by '*hope for her*', and secondly because her mind began to gradually slip away to illness, as it so often did.

Wait- I think I'm lost,

And where are they taking me?

At some point she noticed the sound of her footsteps taking a loud sharp turn, the ceramic tiles had been replaced with a glittering concrete floor, brown, green, and blue.

Have I been here before?

She refused to ask out of embarrassment and the fear of appearing weak and too unfit to lead, and instead followed the signs on the walls. At first they were a haze and a mess, but she continued to glare with determination until the text and symbols slowly regained meaning.

"E-East Wing",

I think-

At some point the walking stopped and one of them motioned the other to continue ahead. She then led her to a room where inside was a woman who stood out to her from within the sea of patients. A woman with pale skin and beautiful short hair, smiling from her wheelchair. The way she sat with her hands gently placed over one another reminded her of the portraits women from Landlord and wealthy Honoured families posed for in their palaces.

Yet here she was, her only comforter, the calm Ancient lights.

She's beautiful-

No, elegant!

"She was suffering from the same condition as yours" said one of the women, who she once again recognized as Sister Jully.

"*Was?*" she asked, perplexed.

"We performed some white magic on her, a sort of fire ritual"

"*Magic?*" she almost chuckled, but didn't out of respect.

"I've never been a believer of magic"

"The doctors tried everything and no new research from the University regarding your illness led us to back to magic, Colonel"

My illness?

There was no cure for the illness which was quickly catching up to her. Many believed it was the result of the last war, as that's when it first appeared in a mass. Almost everyone afflicted went hairless and blind as they aged, others went toothless and frail, and all gradually came to forget their place in the world as the seasons passed.

But magic?

"Well, is she healed?" she said unconvinced, but going along with it nonetheless.

"No, but we-"

"W-We managed to cure parts of her" interjected the other priestess.

"Can she talk?" she asked, resentfully.

"Can she walk?"

"Can she *work*?"

"No..." she said, regretfully, "But she can eat without a tube, and her pain seems to be fading"

"Oh-" she said, livid but quickly understanding the gravity of her situation.

"That's comforting-"

"Colonel!" hissed a man from the other end of the hall.

She turned to find Major San awkwardly running towards her.

He was a brown-eyed man with short brown hair and a handsome face which kept him younger than his true age.

"Major," said the colonel, exchanging salutes. "Are you finished with the investigation?"

"N-No, well, still taking reports," answered the major, catching his breath.

"Okay, leave it on my desk when you're finished," she said, trying her best to regain focus.

"I'll read it first thing tomorrow morning. I'm going to bed-"

"No!" shouted Major San, undoing the effort he made to stay as quiet as possible.

On second glance, it was clear he was visibly upset. There was sweat trickling from his forehead and collecting over his moustache and beard.

His hands were a *little shaky* as well.

"You need to hear what they're saying," said the major. "They're all from Mineraltown"

"I-It's serious"

Valtus I – May 3rd

Lost Cause

He was already awake and moving before the morning bells could erupt inside the dormitories of South Station. Gathering as much of himself as he could before the others were aware of the new day, and the race to be ready and line up on time. Something had bitten him in his sleep, and he felt it swelling with an itch as he hurried over to the bathhouse with his toothbrush, a fresh set of underclothes and towel. Though as much as it bothered him, there wasn't anything he could do about it without quickly falling behind the early morning rush. A sacrifice required of anyone searching for privacy in an Army Station with twenty-five dorms, each containing twenty-five beds stacked three beds high.

I'll be fine,

It probably won't kill me.

In the bathhouse he found a mirror and a face worth ignoring, though it was poor discipline to glass gaze anyways, so he didn't mind the appearance.

He wondered, while brushing his slightly misaligned teeth, if it would ever feel right to wake up in South Station and call it a home. The only place he had ever regarded as anything close to such was found somewhere inside the mostly quiet rows of makeshift apartments in a small Lowland town called Notwell. A town where they thanked the First Mother, and only the First Mother, for every meal they ate. No matter how small.

At least the water here's warm, even if it's still a little grainy.

Life was harsh in the sun beaten town, and he always missed waking up under the same roof as his family. Though, he did sleep better at night knowing he was doing something for his village, even if it was just caring for his own. So sometimes he awoke happy.

After a quick shower, he dried his scruffy black beard and eventually the rest of his body, before returning to his dormitory where he dressed in the dark. It would be several more minutes before the lights would be turned on, but it didn't take too long to see the plain brown uniform he was expected to die in.

In school they were taught many if not most of the assigned uniforms were a continuation of a legacy. A legacy responsible for the lives they were living today, as those before them fought and died bravely for a unified and Liberated Acadia.

A Newer Acadia.

It was never quite clear who those people were and what exactly was achieved with their sacrifice, however, and this uncertainty bothered him. Not because he particularly cared for his country or was in fear of dying a similar death to those who wore his suit before him, but because it frightened him to think another would be in his place one day, long after he was gone.

Before he set out, he checked under his bed to see if the metal box which contained all his precious belongings was still in its place. It was where he kept photos of his family and the portraits he drew of his friends. There was also a letter from a girl he should've written back to, but he had nothing new or smart to say, so he didn't bother replying.

In the dark he could only make out a shadowy outline which resembled something like what a box would, and that was enough for his peace.

I almost forgot, the reclassification test results are in today,

I hope I passed.

Like most enlisted into the Generalist Force, soldiership was his only trade. Though, he still hadn't given up competing to achieve some rank above the frontlines, a useful distinction to have if one still possessed the will to live. This was his third time taking the test, however, and the last opportunity afforded to him by the Army to distinguish himself.

No, I studied and trained so hard.

I know I passed.

For many years it felt as if no matter how hard he tried, there was always a gap between how useful he was and what the world was looking for.

But today felt different.

Today was going to be a good day.

Raamina II

She opened the door to the chamber and found a small fair-skinned woman with enough freckles on her face to pass as a Westerian, and enough rags covering her plump body to be mistaken for a sack of potatoes. It was her head servant-woman *Maggy*, and she stood there with a baby on her hip.

"S-Sorry to bother you, Mother Raamina," said Maggy, cradling the child.

"I hope "

"It's fine!" shouted another, barging from behind with a limp and two young boys by her side.

It was the head priestess of her Zaaj Temple, a creature named Lady Isaarith.

"Get out of the way and leave us alone!"

"S-Sorry," said the servant-woman, turning her head to the floor and leaving before she was scorned any further.

"What is it, Isaarith?" asked Mother Raamina, approaching the cloaked woman whose misshapen body she could not hide.

"Mother," replied the lady, with the same crackling voice they had discovered her crying as a babe.

"We have to talk," she said, following the smaller of the two boys by the hand as he guided her through the room.

He was more or less her walking stick, no older than eleven and just as freckled-faced as Maggy. Though unlike Maggy, who was somewhat still regarded as a free-woman by Acadian standards, he was born to serve and bound to work.

"About what?" answered the Mother.

"Oh… that's right," she said, nudging him back to the door when his work was finished. "Stay outside. I'll fetch you when I need to."

Maimed by birth, she was a hideous and disfigured thing. Blotches of brown sores spotted her greenish skin, less like the freckles Westerians were proud to wear and something more reminiscent of mosquito nests lying across a still pond. She could hear quite well, but owned no ears. Possessed two hands, but with fingers missing found elsewhere, and placed inside the hollow sockets where her eyes would've been, were painted stones. Never blinking or seeing, but always judging and *prying*.

She owned many pairs of eyes, today she decided on red.

"You should leave too, Callum," said Mother Raamina, turning to the other boy who stood by the door.

He was one of her personal slaves and was a few years older than her son Hiran who would be turning eighteen this summer.

Speaking of that boy, where in Hell is he?

"Hm?" said Lady Isaarith, "You're still here? I thought I told you to stop following me, out of my sight—"

"Wait!" said Callum.

The boy was clearly trying to be careful not to shout, knowing it could cause the lady's ears to bleed, but still, she wasn't having it.

"What is it, Callum?" interjected Mother Raamina, before Isaarith could act out again like an *undeveloped child.*

And just like a child, she strikes and claws at her servants and slaves whenever they irritate her.

"M-Mother," said Callum, the slave-boy, "They need help at the Zaaj Temple."

"There's too many bodies coming in"

He was a dishevelled boy, also with faint freckles on his face, but with the characteristic golden eyes expected from a Solarite.

"Go tell the daughters to start the blessing ceremony without me," said Mother Raamina.

"They already started, Mother," answered Callum.

"Then tell them to finish it!" shouted Isaarith.

Her ears seem to be fine whenever she raises her crackling voice.

"Tell them I'll be there in a few," said Mother Raamina, as softly as she could.

Callum bowed and took the younger one by the hand with him. She locked eyes with him before they left the room, but couldn't remember if he had ever been given a proper name before he was sold. The Westerian traders who imported Solarites like him into the Highland had removed his tongue and his boyhood on the day of his birth before selling him off to wealthy Acadians like them to use as eunuchs.

73

"Isaarith," said Mother Raamina, walking over to ensure the boys were not lingering in the halls. "Why are you like this?"

"For no reason other than I must," answered the head priestess.

"Hm," replied the Mother. A fair answer, considering what she was.

"Also, shouldn't you be at the Temple with the other priestesses?"

"There's something more important, Mother"

She concealed her most horrid deformities under curtains of dark blue silk which she wore like a shell, almost as if she had crawled out of a swamp herself.

The only normal thing about her was that she was as much a woman as she was a man in-between her legs. Such a thing was uncommon, but not unheard of.

"But do you need to yell all the time?"

She watched as she considered the answer for some time.

"No, I guess not," she eventually replied.

"Here," said Isaarith, handing her a slip of parchment.

"What's this?"

"I don't know, read it for me,"

It was a transmission written in Old Military Braille, one of the many trade secrets kept by those specialised in rulership and war within the Baltiar family. She placed her eyes and fingers on the text and began reading.

"The Honourable Commander Braxas…"

She stopped to roll her eyes.

The Honourable Commander.

The same honourable commander who never once fought a war, the same honourable commander who sat in Rockland's Outer Fortress day drinking and sleeping with saloon girls when he should be making important decisions about the lives of all Rocklanders.

She continued reading. "…Requests your presence at the Outer Fortress to discuss matters relating to the nature of the outcome in Windlehe—"

Her heart skipped a beat.

"Nature of the outcome? What is that supposed to mean?" she said aloud.

"W-What does he want?" she asked, expecting a reasonable answer.

"Sounds like he's trying not to scare you, maybe they know-"

"No" she proclaimed, believing it herself, "There's no way they could know about our pact with the P-," she said, running back to the purple linen curtains.

"Unless…"

Unless-

She checked the balconies both above and below, and even behind the curtains before sliding closed the retrofitted metal cage which served as its gate.

"Unless Vanfall turned his back on us," finished Isaarith.

"I doubt he would" she reasserted, again as if it were the truth, "He's had a hand in this as well-"

"I-I don't feel good about this," stuttered Isaarith, pacing around the Ancient chamber like a frog.

"Calm down," said Mother Ramina, "And you're twisting what hair you have left"

She took some time to carefully select her words.

"I'll worry about it when the time comes," she said softly.

"They might have their small empire, but we have ours, remember?"

For kingdoms were at times, women.

Daaria III

"Eastern Stronghold? Where did that come from?" asked Omaara, scratching the back of her head.

"What' you think is going on, Daaria?" asked Jaxas. "You hear anything?"

She shook her head. "No, it's all news to me. I thought they dissolved the rebels years ago."

She had heard stories about how unstable the region was from others in the Army, but her parents never had anything to say about it in the mail they sent her. There were no mention of rebels taking over villages and burning guildsites, just sketches of her baby sister who was also *just the cutest*.

"And what are we really doing?" asked Jaxas. "They're sending us to take over for some missing Peaceguards, but what's that even mean?"

"Yeah I caught that too." said Omaara, wilting a little whenever she frowned. "They didn't really tell us, did they?"

"It could mean tonight's our last good night's sleep," said Daaria.

Outside of policing duties, Peaceguards were instructed to further the direct interests of the Citadel. Whether it be demolishing bridges and other buildings, disabling pipelines and electrical lines in enemy territories, or even spying and arresting political dissenters, unionizers, and soldiers within their ranks. As a result, they had earned their reputation as an elite force, obstructing and undermining in the name of the Liberation.

It seemed unjust at times, but the Army taught it was necessary to ensure the peace and liberty Peacelanders enjoyed. So she did what she was told without question, like any decent soldier would.

"Who was the Commander talking about anyway?" asked Jaxas, "And why were they there?"

She shook her head. "No idea."

"I was thinking about it the whole time, but nothing," replied Omaara, shrugging.

"Could've been some secret assignment."

"They're always hiding things from us," said Jaxas.

"I guess we're gonna have to find out," sighed Daaria, wincing at the thought of having to take another order from Brigadier Stormwater.

Though she was happy to be nearer to home, she wasn't exactly excited to return to the Lowlands.

Especially Eastern Stronghold,

I don't get it-

He praised me for my recent work, but this assignment feels like a punishment in disguise.

She was being sent back to a place she had worked so hard to escape, and right when her brother needed her the most.

"I'll go see what this truck is about," said Jaxas. "Let's meet at the cafeteria before our shift starts?"

"Can you tell them to make some space for us?" asked Omaara, "I really don't want to sleep next to some goats like last time."

He didn't answer her question, but instead leaned over to whisper something into her ear, she giggled.

When he was sure no one other than the three of them were in sight, he wrapped an arm around her shoulders and kissed her on the lips. They held one another for some time before he walked away.

It reminded her she liked *boys* too.

Unsure of what to make of the rest of their morning, the pair wandered the empty courtyard before agreeing to rest under the shade of a wispy leafed Highland-tree. The rain had come and gone, but there were no rainbows over the Fortress, only low hanging clouds and grey skies indistinguishable from the concrete complexes.

"What was your last assignment?"

"Hm?" said Daaria, returning from her thoughts.

"Your last assignment," said Omaara, taking a seat on the steps leading into the Medical College Tower and looking up to her.

She's even prettier from up here.

Is that what the boys see?

"Commander said you completed some assignment by yourself? You never told me about it."

"Oh," said Daaria, laughing but only to hide her panic. "I-It was nothing."

"Well." Omaara smiled. "He said good work, and if anyone's up for a promotion, it's you."

"Yeah, well," replied Daaria, clearing her throat and spitting off to the grass. "I doubt it."

"If anyone of us were getting promoted they wouldn't assign us to *fucking* Eastern Stronghold."

She was seventeen when she was transferred to the Citadel with enough honours to enrol in Army College. That was six years ago and she never once looked back.

"Remember when we first met?" asked Omaara, reaching out towards her.

There were a few loose strands of hair falling over her face, one of which Omaara curled a finger around before pulling it.

"Ow!" said Daaria. "Why'd you do that for?"

"Sorry," she replied, "I don't know."

It was in those first few days at Army College when she discovered a golden-haired girl crying to herself, under a similar tree they now sat beneath. She had approached her to make sure she was okay, and found a pair of metal claws holding onto a small gold necklace with a secret compartment. Inside was a picture of what was *still* the most handsome man she'd ever seen.

"How many times did I say sorry that day?" asked Daaria.

"I don't know," giggled Omaara, "I only remember I couldn't stop giggling."

Without asking, she took a seat next to her, and without thinking, told her, *"He's not even that cute,"* and *"You could do way better anyway."*

Only to later learn it was actually an older brother who was serving as a Specialist in the Salt Wars. He was expected to return after the victory in Riverland, but the Battle for Cratertown 26, another one of history's tragedies, broke out on his way to Peaceland. His tank-unit was among the many forced to turn back, and that was the last time he was ever seen.

I'm so lucky she took it well, I can't imagine not having her with me,
I'd have no one.

They sat and spoke for hours that day. Just two girls trying to understand the world and one another. They spoke about all the people they missed and all the people who missed them, all the boys they kissed and all the boys who tried to kiss them, and after learning they were both studying Acadian machinery, they became inseparable.

She's grown so much since then ,

Truly like a sunflower.

Her smile quickly gave way, remembering what she had told her this morning about her bleeding.

Another thing to worry over and nothing to do about it.

The disease hemovaria, or more commonly known as '*blood-cramps*' afflicted women who were mainly at the prime of their lives. One began to bleed and continued for a month, until a quick and sudden fever took them away. It was not known what caused it or if a cure would ever be discovered, but it was a disease which seemed to spread with each passing generation. Redefining what it meant to be a woman wherever it went. Twenty years ago, a girl was not a woman until she reached twenty-five, now she was considered lucky to have survived her very first week of bleeding.

There was a worry it was something men carried and passed onto the opposite sex, and the Army worked hard to ensure such breakouts never happened.

The afternoon bell rang out, signalling the end of morning classes and the start of lunch, and within minutes the empty courtyard was crowded with student-soldiers rushing out of the Medical College Tower and the next door Artillery Institute Building.

Similar to University, Army College was a space open only to those who performed well on the standardised exams distributed across most regions in Peaceland. It was here student-soldiers specialised in a discipline or trade, while advancing their training as a soldier. A mandatory requirement for anyone hoping to join the Specialist Force.

From somewhere within the crowd, Gadolin and Jotan, two soldiers from adjacent Peaceguard units, approached them with hands by their hearts.

"Hey!" said Jotan, a tall red-eyed, brown-haired boy with a mechanical prosthetic for his left leg.

"Long time!" said Omaara, "Where've you been?"

"Literally right next door," replied Jotan, "That's about the only place we ever are."

He was a childhood friend of Omaara, and like the majority of Specialists and Peaceguards, they both grew up in the Citadel as children of wealthy Honoured families.

"We've been stuck doing paperwork for weeks," said Jotan. "What about you?"

"We just got moved," said Omaara.

"Oh... Where are you guys stationed now?" asked Gadolin, feigning cheerfulness.

"To Eastern Stronghold," answered Omaara.

"Oh..." replied Gadolin, with a hint of condescension.

"They're sending Daaria back?" She laughed to herself for a moment. "Speaking of which, where is she?"

"Just kidding Daaria, you're so *small* and *cute*"

Don't react, don't give her that.

Ugh, Jaxas hates her too, he's lucky he missed her.

"No," said Daaria, "It's a team mission. That's what 'we' means."

"That's too bad," said Gadolin, "I'm sure your family could've used the help."

"They're fine," said Daaria, "Mind your business."

Gadolin was a *strange* young woman, and the relationship they had with one another was just as *strange*. She didn't know much about her, other than she hated her post as an office clerk, and belonged to an Honoured family.

Though unlike Omaara and Jotan, who belong to Honoured families residing within the Citadel, she came from the Midlands where they still retained their special class status. They were also often mistaken for sisters, something which always seemed to offend her more than it should have.

It was a completely reasonable response considering how undeniably similar they looked, especially when standing next to one another.

Same hair. Same skin. Same eyes.

About as pretty too.

But for whatever reason, she never smiled at the girl whose reflection might as well have been hers.

Is it 'cause I'm from nowhere and she isn't? What year is she living in? I'd rather be friends with Olisa August and Briaana Cryheart-

"You' hear about Windlehem?" asked Jotan, attempting to redirect the conversation.

"Yeah all those Rocklanders," replied Omaara with some sadness.

"They just pulled back the Generalists heading over 'cause it was so bad," continued Jotan.

"What? Really?" asked Daaria.

"Yeah," answered Jotan, "They're only sending a couple trucks over to support the retreat."

"Not like they would've made a difference," added Gadolin, "They would've just been target practice."

She knows I have friends in the Generalists.

"Well," laughed Jotan awkwardly. "I don't know about that, but uh..."

"Have you guys heard about Mineraltown? Crazy," he said, nervously attempting to change the subject once more.

"W-What about Mineraltown?" asked Daaria as calmly as she could.

"Is it true the guards defected?"

Jotan shrugged. "Don't know yet, but they're saying a couple hundred dug their way out of there."

"What?" said Omaara

"Yeah, they crashed a couple houses too," said Jotan, "They're still counting the bodies, from what I hear."

Her heart sank.

"W-Where are they keeping them?" she asked, shaking but keeping her composure.

"The Hospital," answered Jotan.

"Did you hear anything about the Excavation Site?"

"Jotan!" interrupted Gadolin. "We have to go."

She had already distanced herself from the conversation and began walking away without him.

"I don't know, sorry!" said Jotan, running to join her. "And good luck! Don't forget to write to me!"

"Well she isn't a bitch at all," sneered Omaara, after Gadolin had left their sight. "And it's funny, she's only a Peaceguard 'cause we got paperwork."

"I have to go to the Hospital," said Daaria.

"You okay?" asked Omaara.

"No, I have to find my brother. What if he's one of the people who—"

"Nah," said Omaara. "I wouldn't worry about him."

"Omaara!" said Daaria, wondering how she could even suggest such a thing. "That's my brother!"

"Yeah," said Omaara, "And isn't that him right there?"

"Huh? What? Where?" said Daaria.

Her eyes scanned the courtyard, searching frantically for what she meant.

"Are you messing with me?"

"No! Look," said Omaara, taking her face by the cheeks and turning her head slightly to the left. "Right there! With Briaana and that girl Olisa or August or *whatever* she wants people to call her"

Not too far away stood a short boy with short wavy hair and glasses nearly the size of his head.

"You're right, it is him!"

"Wait—"

"Why is he with Briaana and August?"

Hiran IV

"Here," said Emmi, sliding forward a wooden cup.

"Um…" said Hiran, absolutely disgusted with what he found inside. "What the hell is that?"

"It's tea," replied Emmi.

"Are you sure?" asked Hiran, "It looks like alley water."

It was a greenish-brown substance and smelled as slimy as it looked.

Is she trying to kill me?

He took the cup to his nose, and immediately regretted it.

What the fuck! She is trying to kill me.

Why?

"Why are you trying to kill me?"

He looked up to find her standing unimpressed with both hands on her hips.

Okay. Well, no choice I guess.

Here it goes.

"I like it," said Hiran, setting the cup down the instant it touched his lips.

It smelled worse in his mouth and was even slimier.

"It's good," he said, sliding the cup back to her.

"Good," replied Emmi, sliding it back with a smile.

"Finish it all."

"What?!   I   can't   do   it,   he   groaned. "It's too much!"

"It took me so long to make and now my hands hurt," replied Emmi.

"Please don't make me drink this," he begged.

She didn't respond, but instead put on *the face* she knew he couldn't say no to, a glare.

He finished the rest of it in a single swig, though not without first mumbling his resentment incoherently, which she heard but ignored.

It was *disgusting*, but there was a pleasant bitterness to it at least.

"Good, now I can go on break," said Emmi.

"You were really waiting for me?" replied Hiran.

"Maybe," she said, smiling and tossing her apron to him before heading towards the door leading up to the General Store.

He was trailing her out the saloon, until a boy calling his name caught his attention.

"Yo! Hiran!"

Huh? Who's that?

Waving to him from a small round table was a boy with a black bandana tied around his head.

Taryn?

"Hey!" Hiran waved, walking over with his courier bag.

"Brother," said Taryn, extending a hand.

The two exchanged a Rockland handshake, two high fives, a pinky swear, and a small prayer.

"What's good?" said another boy sitting next to Taryn.

It was his cousin, *Quail*.

"I'm good, bro'," said Hiran, reaching over and performing the same handshake.

Other than their hazel eyes and the size of their noses, the two didn't look all too related. Taryn was much darker with short curly blonde hair while Quail was a full head taller than both of them with black curls left uncut for many years. Both were members of The Grandma's Boyz, one of the larger street gangs in Easton working under the umbrella of Rockland's underguilds. The two others at the table kept quiet and to themselves, likely in understanding there would be no introductions, nor expecting it.

Sitting next to Quail was a fair skinned boy with a baby face. He looked a few years younger than the others and *just sat there*, watching the corner aimlessly with bleeding eyes.

That boy's gone.

A girl next to him sat quietly with her hood up and head down. Though he couldn't see her face, he knew she was a girl from the way her black leggings tightened around her curves and legs.

They were both wearing Military Police issued boots cut, standard pieces for any Westerian sponsored school uniform, which he figured they were likely hiding under their hoodies.

"What' you doing this summer?" asked Taryn, patting his back.

"Nothin'." Hiran shrugged. "Just helping Mom."

"Mother," he said, under his breath and mumbling a short prayer.

As many did whenever she came up in conversation.

Quail leaned in and tugged on his shirt. "We got a blackhouse going," he whispered, "Down by Westown."

Westown?

"Westown?" asked Hiran, a little concerned.

"Yeah," answered Taryn, "If you need some shit to do."

"What y'all need?" he asked, almost impulsively.

"Everything," said Taryn, "Cooks, dealers, *shooters*."

"Runners," added Quail. "We just laid some boys off, stupid ass kids couldn't beat a runny nose."

He considered the offer.

There wasn't much of a difference between his work as a blackstore courier and what was expected of a typical blackhouse runner. The work was similar, and more often than not, was assigned from the same source, his uncle commander in Rockland. Both were usually neighbouring stalls in the same marketplace as well, and much like agreements made between the City-states of Acadia, the only rules they recognized were the ones established amongst themselves.

He learned all this over years of dipping his toes into the many operations of the Liberation Army, including the ones that were far beneath him. It was there he had the most fun and made the most friends.

No, I can't do that any more,

These guys are crazy.

The Grandma's Boyz had built a reputation on the streets of Queens as an invasive gang. One willing to cross territories without a concern for agreed upon boundaries, or the result it would have for the well-established rules of the Highland streets. They had their agreements with other gangs, but were unafraid to *smoke* those they regarded as competition, even if it meant breaking treaties. Currently, they were engaged in a *nasty* war with The Summer Boyz and The Westown Mob, the two largest gangs in Westown.

Mom would beat me if she found out,

Even send me to the frontlines,

And I did promise her I'd pick up the family land.

Wait... I can put Tavaar, Zoh, and Roxas on though, they've been looking for work.

"I'm good," said Hiran, "But I know some boys who might be down."

"Who?" asked Taryn.

"You know 'em," said Hiran. "Zoh, Tavaar, and Roxas"

"Oh those boys?" asked Quail. "'They *shoot*?"

"Yeah them," answered Hiran, "And nah, they hustle hard though."

"'They gon' chirp?" asked Quail.

"No," said Hiran, "They're like us—"

"Can we leave?" said the girl, interrupting him.

Her voice was sweet, but she made it clear she wasn't asking.

"Yeah we cuttin' right now," replied Taryn.

"A'ight," said Quail, "'They always chillin' at the Hallways, right?"

"Yeah," replied Hiran. "You'll find them there."

"Cool," said Taryn.

"Aight, we good," said the girl, standing up and walking over to the lost boy sitting next to her.

His eyes were wide open, but he was somewhere else.

"Hey, baby'," she said, shaking him by the shoulders a few times. "Wake up."

He was still.

"C'mon, babe', we cuttin'."

She propped him upright and he began walking to the door without a change in his expression.

"Don't take it personal," she said, turning back to him.

It was just enough to catch a glimpse of the pink gloss on her naturally pouty lips.

"We got a lot of shit to do today and don't have time to meet new folk"

"I gotta get some sleep, I like to look cool for school."

Talius IV

"Defectors?" asked the colonel, powering on the projector once more.

It was an Acadian replication of an Ancient device, so it took some time.

"So that's the rumour going around?"

"I'm wondering how she even knew about Mineraltown," replied the commander. "I only learned after you left. I should've asked where she got it from."

"Word gets around fast," said Colonel Hellin.

"Yeah, we have to do something about that. We can't have soldiers knowing as much as they do. That's a problem."

"Leave it to Flowers," continued the colonel, softening his voice and face slightly, so as to reassure him.

"We'll just get in her way, and besides, we have our own problems to think about."

He watched as Colonel Hellin removed the map of Eastern Stronghold from the projector and replaced it with another he retrieved from his desk. The new map displayed contained the entirety of Peaceland, its five Strongholds spread across its three regions. It also included parts of Queens to the south, on the other side of a massive gorge appropriately named the Great Gorge.

Many believed the Great Gorge formed when the giant iifa-tree which had seized Rodina receded to its death. Its enormous roots were thought to have slithered into every corner of the continent, breaking the earth and splitting the Highlands before leaving behind forests and rivers after it withered.

Adherers of the New Book of Zaaj, a people known as Zaajars, worshipped a man depicted by the Ancients as the king responsible for the iifa-tree's extinction in this new found land. Although it was true there were enough gorges and rivers spread throughout Rodina to suggest it could've been left behind by the roots of a colossal iifa, it didn't take a researcher to see this was just another fable. The Great Gorge and its rivals were some of the more obvious natural phenomena lingering in the world.

There was, however, *some truth* to the tale.

In their journey to map the new world, which they had declared was revealed to them by the Daughter Rodina, the early Acadian voyagers were overwhelmed to find a leafless, fossilised iifa-tree near the centre of the continent. One as tall as the Salt Pillar of Queens.

Regardless, an iifa-tree would never leave behind life.

"There's too much red on the map," said the commander, watching as the colonel began circling points of interest throughout Peaceland.

Peaceland-

Each of her Strongholds, aside from the Fortress of the Citadel, was under the leadership of a brigadier who was responsible for their regional peace and stability. They also ensured the surrounding communities offered its count of soldiers and taxes in accordance to their arrangements with the Liberated Cause.

In the Eastern Lowlands, however, there was a red circle on nearly every village, while in the Northern Lowlands, the town of Summer Circle feuded with its neighbours over ownership of some recently unearthed natural gas.

They may have found a home within the Liberation, but the Lowlanders stood divided. Such was the case for every region now when he thought about it.

"Stormwater said she's handling it, but I'm worried we're not doing enough," said the commander.

I hope I didn't send my best Peaceguards to die.

"There's never enough to do in the Lowlands," said the colonel. "Leave it be."

The Lowlands were a place in Peaceland littered with unused farmland and desolate villages. Lands which were some of the richest in Middle Acadia and villages which were promised to migrants and refugees decades ago. When the Military Police first invaded Queens, a near destruction of southern Queens and its Ancient structures followed. Hundreds of thousands of Queenspeople were displaced from their homes as a result, and though Rockland was made to take in the bulk of asylum seekers, it was expected of Peaceland, with its vast open territories, to take in the majority of those dispossessed in future conflicts.

Something he was never opposed to, knowing what it could mean for the productive capacities of a society like his own.

"No," replied the commander, "We need the region."

"I suggest sending a small force there"

"We can't spread any thinner than we already have," retorted the colonel.

"We have nothing better to do," replied the commander, not wanting to argue but accepting he would if he had to.

A few weeks ago the Military Police initiated a campaign to conquer two communities near Newtown, Industria and Joran's Gates. Communities not protected by any force other than the rebels who opposed all foreign control. Brigadier Thornheart had suggested to intervene, but he and his high-officers reasoned this would only entangle them in another war they couldn't afford, or entirely collapse the markets they relied upon. So instead of joining the battle, they settled for peace.

More refugees and nowhere to place them.

Out of those who fled the conflict, most sought refuge in Peaceland, and there was no choice but to accept. The majority were sent around the Firstland Valley, a move which did not sit well with the Firstlanders, but the only alternative was to send them back to the arms of the enemy, or as Colonel Flowers put it, *"Watch them reorganise into another isolated, stateless community."*

He also considered himself to be an ambitious leader. Closer aligned with his sister and the last commander of Peaceland, Vaara Baltiar, than those who came before them. Including their father, Talan Baltiar. It was even a personal mission of his to carry on her legacy of undoing the decades of misery and stagnation accomplished by the established political and economic elites. Men and women who were all regarded as cruel by the have-nots and complacent and nearsighted by the intelligentsia.

"A village that spreads its stew too thin, is a village left without any children," said Colonel Hellin. "Or whatever the Rocklanders sing."

"This is for Peaceland's future," refuted the commander. "The only other option is falling further behind than we already have, and we just lost Windlehem"

"Just remember," said Colonel Hellin, "There's no space for bad decisions or mistakes."

"You're already well-invested in another project,"

"Don't overextend yourself Talius".

The ambition the colonel was referring to was his plan to secure enough labour for the mass production of new *Ancient automata*. The point the colonel always seemed to devalue was that such a step forward was necessary if they intended to compete with both the Military Police and the Frontier Army.

Though, it wasn't that he misunderstood as much as he failed to see there were no other reasonable alternatives. The system in place was inefficient at its worst, and feudal at its best. The researchers at the University had also warned of an upcoming population crisis which would undoubtedly leave Peaceland, and especially the Citadel, vulnerable to foreign expansion.

We've had record-breaking low birth rates almost every year for the last twenty years,

We can't end up like Old Acadia, there wouldn't be a world left to pick up,

This was the last one.

Labour was the base of any market, and his idea was to find proper stations for the most useful migrants and refugees, while sending the rest to the Lowland fields. He hoped to develop Peaceland through this method, forming new underclasses to occupy otherwise unused spaces with their labour. Every attempt at allocation and relocation, however, was met with resistance by competing Lowland rebels, now united under some common cause. This instability resulted in the once temporary camps located near the Firstland Peninsula to become permanent ones. Effectively transforming the land the Firstlanders regarded as sacred, into slums.

Finding new workers is going to be a problem in the future.... If there is a future.

The fight was on many fronts, and this was without counting Windlehem or the rest of the outer countryside.

"Waltz's on a lead at least," said the colonel, taking a pen to the map and placing a circle around Midland Stronghold.

That's right, the Landlords-

He had almost forgotten they were being investigated for using Old Royal coins and notes, a currency now recognized in Peaceland as illegitimate, to distribute loans and pay guild contracts.

"I hope he's onto something," said the commander, "We can't let this one slide, we gave them too much space."

"Don't forget about Workhammer," said Colonel Hellin, "He isn't happy about denying his search request, you know."

"I don't care if he's enraged," said the commander, "I'm not doing things with his interest in mind."

Sometimes, maybe... but not always.

"He said he's going to send Midland soldiers to the Gorge."

"Yeah, well, he's disobeying a direct command if he does." said the commander, "That's enough to arrest anyone, brigadier or not."

"Would you really arrest Workhammer?" asked Colonel Hellin, with some laughter in his voice. "That would be something."

"Why not? There's no law if anyone's above it," answered the commander.

"How are you going to explain that to the Lords? They still own half the courts."

I don't know.

"I'll figure it out," replied Commander Talius.

"What if they already found the bodies?" asked Colonel Hellin

"Who? Workhammer?" asked the commander, offended by the mere thought of it. "Then we arrest him along with his Landlords."

"No, the P-Police," clarified the colonel.

"Oh... then they know we're around, that's not new to them," said the commander.

Not too long ago, several Peaceguards were declared missing after a failed mission by the Great Gorge. The plan was to fabricate a landslide along its rocky walls, with the intention of demolishing a new Military Police outpost built within the Forest Gorge. Constructing outposts was a well-known Police strategy of inching closer to the land they hoped to occupy. It was no mystery they had their sights set on to seizing an Old Acadian hydro-electric power plant built near Newtown.

A power plant kept disabled by the Liberation Army as a means to retain control over the rebel communities in the region, and keep any potential sources of energy away from enemy hands.

We can let them have the rest of Uptown Queens,
But they're not getting the power plant.

According to those who survived the failed assignment, the soldiers responsible for setting the explosive charges miscalculated their setup and were sent down the Gorge by a mudslide near the rocks. There would be no searching for survivors as well judging from the discoveries. Some parachutes were recovered, but there were no bodies found. The Forest Gorge was home to big cats and even some species of terrorbirds as well, so it made no sense to search for some crushed bones.

It was a tragedy, but that would've been the end of it in most cases, had it not been that a few soldiers were recruited from Midland Stronghold, and belonged to some of the oldest and wealthiest families. Brigadier Workhammer of Midland, whose duty was to represent these families, pushed the Fortress to search the Forge or remove the order he made against his search request. One which declared the land was off limits unless a command came from his direct line.

An incoming transmission on the hand radio interrupted the two men.

"Commander Talius, the other Peaceguards are here," said the soldier on the other line.

"Let them in," replied the commander.

"I'll get the door," said the colonel walking to his desk and pressing a button underneath.

A group of seven quietly entered the room soon after with their hands by their hearts.

"Commander!" said a bright-red eyed soldier, in a black Specialist uniform. "The Peaceguards you requested."

She stepped aside to reveal four Peaceguards and two others, a woman, and a boy who looked no older than a pre-teen, standing behind him.

'Thank you, soldier." The commander saluted.

"Commander!" said the Peaceguards.

"Commander!" The civilians followed.

Another one of the Peaceguards, a young woman named Briaana Cryheart, stepped forward with her hand by her heart.

"Thank you for this assignment, Commander," she said, turning back to the two civilians.

"This is Professor Romina Lind and her student Willus Earthwind."

Wilona III

"What's this all about?" asked Colonel Flowers, wondering why she was sitting in a damp cold room with the major.

"He didn't tell me much," replied the major, "He just said it was urgent and required immediate mobilisation"

"Then let's get on with it-" a knock on the door interrupted her, and Major San walked over to answer it.

"I guess we're going to find out," he said, opening the door

She watched as Peace-sergeant Briggs entered the office with four others, a woman, a man, and two children by their sides. The small room quickly became crowded.

"Thank you for being here," said the peace-sergeant. "I know it's late and you all need to rest."

He was a red-eyed man of below-average stature, perhaps taller than her, but by no more than a pinky.

The group of four all appeared gaunt-faced, even the little girl who couldn't have been a day older than four, *maybe five.*

"It's okay," said the woman, with a tired but resilient voice.

She appeared to be around the same age as herself, but was much taller with a tired, but pretty face.

"What's this all about?" asked the major.

"You need to hear this," replied Peace-sergeant Briggs.

"Why? What do you mean?" asked the colonel.

"They're survivors from the incident,"

"They're all from Mineraltown."

"Mineraltown!?" said the colonel, turning to each of them.

"You're all from Mineraltown?!"

"Yes, I'm a teacher and this is my son," answered the woman.

She stood over a small boy with short golden hair and blood on his dirty middle school uniform.

"And this is our neighbour, Rupiya," she said, stepping aside to reveal an even smaller girl with a dark complexion similar to her own, hiding behind the others.

She watched her watch her, with rosy-brown eyes and eyelashes batting curiously whenever she blinked. She was *charmed* by her face and the two thick braids of curly black hair falling over her tiny shoulders, as well as the way she glimmered under the office light. It appeared as if someone had brushed a thin coat of molasses over her already dark skin.

"Hello Rupiya," said the colonel, smiling in hopes of having it returned.

She instead curled away behind the teacher.

I don't get it, kids never like me.

A cast was placed over her right hand while bandages covered the rest of her arms and legs, but it was hard to tell from the way she kept a straight face, whether or not she felt any pain.

Poor baby, at least she's still standing,

Still breathing.

"And who are you?" asked Colonel Flowers, turning her head to the man.

He was a brown-eyed Tautau like Major San, and much more muscle hardened. A sight to see considering the major was no first-year recruit himself.

"I work as a miner, my name is Wilbur," said the man. "I'm also a neighbour of theirs."

"I don't understand," said the colonel, "Why were you digging?"

"To escape," answered Wilbur. "We left right when they started arresting everyone, it was the only choice we had."

"Wait..." said the colonel, "Who is arresting everyone? What are you talking about?"

"Soldiers," said the teacher. "Wearing masks."

"Soldiers?" questioned the major.

"It's what the other survivors reported," said the peace-sergeant, taking his place among the high-officers.

"Well, the ones who could."

"What do you mean, soldiers?" asked the colonel, "What else were they wearing?"

"A uniform," said the teacher, closing her eyes.

"A black and red uniform, one I've never seen before. Though, some did have the patches the Temple guards wore on their shoulders."

"And how many were there?" asked Colonel Flowers.

"Nine t'ousand!" answered the little girl, raising three proud fingers to the air.

"What?!" said the major. "Nine thousand?!"

"No, no," laughed the teacher, "She just learned how to sort of count."

She sent a thumbs-up Rupiya's way, who returned the gesture.

The high-officers relaxed a little, even breaking into a chuckle amongst themselves at the absurdity of it.

"But it was enough to occupy the entire town, so several thousand at least," continued the teacher.

"What?!" said the colonel and major in near unison.

"So this is a force-," said Colonel Flowers, turning to the peace-sergeant.

"I think so," said Peace-sergeant Briggs.

"A-And they have weapons? " said the major, wide eyed.

"Yes," answered the teacher. "Rifles just like our soldiers, some even had flamethrowers."

"That's right." The miner nodded.

An outside force? Inside Mineraltown?

"Major," said Colonel Flowers, "Contact Colonel Hellin and tell him to order the land survey team to investigate this."

"I already did, Colonel." Answered the peace-sergeant. "Sorry, I should've told yo—"

"It's fine," said the colonel. "Good work."

This doesn't make any sense.

"Send a transmission to Mother Maaria, tell her if she doesn't respond within an hour we'll be taking action."

"Yes, Colonel," saluted the major.

"Don't bother with that," said Wilbur, "The Mother is dead."

"What?!" said the three high-officers.

"W-What do you mean she's dead?" asked Colonel Flowers, unsure if they had all just misheard.

"Mother Maaria... Dead?" continued the major, in disbelief.

"By dead, I mean she's dead," he continued, "They hung her from the radio tower right after they shut the gates. They started arresting everyone not too long after that."

No...

"She's not the only one they killed either," added the woman. "My son watched them execute his best friend and her family..."

It was all she managed to say before losing her voice to tears.

"I..." said the colonel.

"Why were they arresting everyone?" asked Major San, quite disturbed himself.

"None of us know," said the miner, "And we weren't trying to find out. They went to the mining communities first and gave everyone a choice before taking them."

Wilbur stepped away from the group and walked over the windows where he stood for some time, watching the night as if it had something to say.

"Would they rather work or be shot?"

"Some of them took the bullet and I would've done the same. Almost did it myself too when I saw them on my street, but I told myself they didn't catch me yet so I owed it to my brothers and sisters to keep running."

"I'm sorry," said the colonel. "And I'm sorry you saw what you did."

The room went quiet, and after some time she turned to the little boy standing by his mother.

"What's your name?"

He didn't respond, and it didn't seem like he would with the way he stared into their eyes.

I know that look, he's here, but nowhere near.

"Tell the colonel your name, sweetheart," said the mother, nudging him towards the high-officers.

"J-Jax," said the boy. "My name is Jax."

"You're a brave boy, Jax," replied the peace-sergeant. "You'll make a great soldier one day."

He waited for a response, but the boy went cold.

"How did you escape?" asked the colonel, moving the discussion forward. "Sorry, but this sounds absurd. Mineraltown is hours away."

"We left through the basement of our school," answered the teacher. "The miners in our community took their shovels and pickaxes before we left."

"A man named Rodin was going around gathering as many people as he could and he led us through the mines. When the mines ended, we took the sewers, when the sewers ended we all started digging with whatever we could."

She and other high-officers listened on silently, occasionally turning to one another in disbelief.

"We didn't know where we were going, we just knew we were heading east," she said, wiping her eyes. "There were hundreds of us and only enough food to feed everyone for a day. But we just kept on digging."

"And that's when the houses collapsed," said the peace-sergeant, tying up their story.

"I think that's enough for today," said Colonel Flowers, noticing all the survivors were struggling to hold back their yawns.

Don't need to keep them up any longer than we need to.

"Does anyone have anything useful to ask?"

The high-officers shook their heads.

"Well, actually I have one," continued the colonel. "Why are they still in rags?"

"Let them use our showers and give them a fresh set of clothes. The Army has uniforms in all their sizes."

"Yes, Colone—"

"I don't want to be a soldier," said Jax, breaking his silence as the high-officers finished their salutes.

"T-That's enough, sweetheart…" said his mother, drawing him closer and placing a hand on his mouth.

"I'm so sorry, he's jus—"

"No," said the colonel. "It's okay. I understand."

"Thank you, colonel," said Wilbur, already on his way out the door.

"'Tank' you," said Rupiya, smiling back for the first time.

It's far past her bedtime, but she's still on her own two feet.

She had fought many battles, first as a soldier no older than Jax himself, and then as a high-officer no older than the commander, but it did little to prepare her for the fight to resist the urge to take a bite out of Rupiya's face like she would a plum.

"No, thank you," smiled the colonel.

Wait-

"Wait-"

"You're her neighbour? Where are her parents—"

Before she could finish her sentence, both the peace-sergeant and the teacher quickly turned to her and shook their heads with vehement disapproval.

A signal to keep her mouth shut.

Raamina III

What if Isaarith's right? What if it's something serious? I mean, why wouldn't it be?

She quietly thought to herself as her guards led her through the Baltiar Palace, an Ancient neighbourhood made mostly of sea facing townhouses and apartments.

But why else would that excuse for a man want me at his desk? The only other explanation is if he somehow knew... But that can only happen if Vanfall... No-He wouldn't. Everything's fine. Don't think about it.

"Are you sure you don't want to take the low-roads, Mother?'' asked Lieutenant Virginia Calendar, a nobleman of forty-six and the head sentinel of her family guard.

He was a brown-eyed Tautau, a subgroup of Acadians who, along with the red-eyed Zacadins and the green-eyed Daaradins, made up the vast majority of all Acadian people.

"I'm sure," said Mother Raamina, ignoring the eyes watching her party as they shooed away the hordes of rabbits roaming the land.

"Shoo!" she said to one of them, a pitch-black bunny named Cardboard.

"I said shoo!"

She feigned a kick and was immediately upset by the sight of their frightened little faces as they flinched and cowered away. It was never her intention to harm them, *it was for their own good.*

The boots the guards were wearing were steel-reinforced and quite heavy.

Cute little bugs, just one step and the servants are having you for lunch.

The Baltiar Palace stood as one of the more well preserved neighbourhoods in Queen's Easton District and was thought to have once been the home of several Ancient noble families. A legacy fitting for the founders of the Liberation Army, the Baltiars, to inherit and succeed.

In the Courtyards, she found vines as ancient as the balconies they dangled from, in the Gardens she passed concrete flower-pots which reminded her of witch's cauldrons, and residing over the Palace walls was the Sea Tower. The greenstone spire which she fled to whenever she needed to escape.

She turned back to the balconies to see if the unwanted eyes were still gazing, and sure enough, they were.

Staring out the Ancient windows reinforced with Acadian glass, were members of lesser Baltiar and Honoured families, most of whom she despised.

They despise me too, the feeling was only fair.

She scoured the apartments, searching for the look of disapproval and resentment, as if she had been responsible for sending the soldiers of Inner Rockland to Windlehem. To her surprise, however, she was met with a display of genuine worry and horror for the times ahead. The sight of it rattled the bones in her back, but she still put on a smile for the ones she considered allies, and the ones no better than *parasites*. There were servants and slaves in the audience as well, but they carried on with their work for the most part. The ones who did watch, looked on with some sad indifference.

Her party continued through the Gardens' open fields, where they crossed paths with the statues of Ancient idols once employed as drinking fountains.

Though it was true the idols were once worshipped by the Ancients, a people who were now worshipped themselves, they no longer had a place in the world as gods. Something the Ancients seemed to understand in their later years as well with the emergence of the iifa tree.

What use is a god that can't save you?

Most were recovered from the streets of Easton and stored away by Old Acadian soldiers who regarded them as trophies. Since then, many lords and commanders sought out their destruction over the years, accusing them as brutal and unholy. She could never see anything beyond the art, however. Insisting instead they be decorated with repairs and distributed throughout the Palace, even if it angered or upset the other lords.

No. It can't be about Windlehem, they would've charged the gates by now

And a war would be fought for my arrest. It has to be about the Old-Royals.

"But how would they know we're using it?" asked the mother, under her breath.

"What are you blabbering to yourself now?" asked Isaarith, watching the sky with the painted stones she called eyes, walking the streets with her Solarite by her side.

"Braxas," hissed the mother. "I was thinking of other reasons he would want me at his desk"

"Maybe he knows we're using Old-coin?"

"Maybe he doesn't," said Isaarith, hissing back.

"Maybe he just wants to fuck you."

"And maybe you should let him, might solve all our problems."

She wanted to order Virginia to beat the swamp turtle's misshapen body senseless, but her only reaction was a shiver.

"The only thing I can think of is they caught Lord Hariya Baltiar using it inside Peaceland," said Virginia.

"But how could they?" asked the mother. "We have the only trade deal we need for decades."

Whatever promise the Liberated-piece, a currency introduced by Peaceland in the year 69 After New Acadia (A.N.A), held within the market, was gradually undone by its own limitations. It was partly responsible for the growth that Peaceland, and to a lesser extent the Liberation Army, experienced during its rise, but it's been largely irrelevant since then.

We had no choice but to keep using Old Royals, the Great Pilgrimage starts in a few months. If we didn't we'd have no income, but that's what they want.

"Maybe he changed his mind," said Isaarith. "Like all stupid men do when something new and convenient comes along."

"I hope you don't plan on going," said Virginia, speaking over her shoulder.

He was a very tall man, so it surprised her to find his head next to hers.

"No," laughed the mother. "I hope he's not expecting me."

"What if he makes it an order?"

"What do you mean?" demanded Mother Raamina. "What kind of order?"

Virginia was smart enough to understand he had crossed a sensitive line.

Jurisdiction over Rockland was a touchy subject, and full authority ultimately fell into the hands of the commander.

It wasn't always the case.

The Landlord branch of the Baltiars were once the ruling sovereigns during New Acadia, up until the moment the Old Acadian Military side of the family recaptured leadership in a relatively peaceful rebellion. In exchange for the entirety of Middle Acadia, the Landlord Baltiars were offered the lands now known as Inner Rockland, along with every holy site in Easton as a compromising gift from their faithless cousins.

One hundred and forty-three years after the end of New Acadia, the ruling Baltiars of Rockland continued to retain control over most of the remaining holy places.

He probably wants me at his fortress to cut a deal.

They've wanted the towers and shrines for years.

To strengthen the relevance of the Liberated-piece, however, the boy Commander Talius outlawed the exchange of Old-Royals within Peaceland, and like the drunk lap dog he was, Commander Braxas followed without question or protest.

In response to these policies, the Military Police exiled the trade of Liberated-piece in Newtown. An action which may have not mattered had it not been that the Military Police captured the entire southern region of Queens where most travellers, including pilgrims, entered from. This new expansion of Newtown forced every foreigner entering through their gates to exchange their currencies for Old-Royals, causing a massive problem for the Rockland Baltiars who derived much of their wealth and income from trades outside her walls, with the pilgrimages being the most lucrative.

We had to switch back to Old-coins, there was no other way-

"No," disagreed Mother Raamina. "It has to be something else."

"I can't see him doing something so stupid."

Or actually, I don't know-

It was hard to say how stupid someone truly was until one witnessed it themselves.

Her guards led the way through the hallways before taking a turn out of the main entrance to the Palace grounds. In one moment they were navigating a maze of paintings and portraits, in the next they were caught in the foot traffic of alley-like streets, wedged in-between crumbling towers and repurposed foundries. The scent of open sewers immediately replaced the flowers and gardens.

"Stay close, Mother!" yelled Untara, a guard at the front of the party. "It's getting crowded!"

She raised her kite-shield and short-glaive, the rest followed.

Jazzy – May ?

Murder Gang

He made his way through the murder of boys perched quietly inside a scorched apartment, knife in hand. The burnt tiles shattered under the weight of each step like the leaves in November, and it was difficult to say from the little light trickling in through the blackened windows, if the sun had risen or if the day had passed.

I want to go home.

At the end of a short walk in the dark, he encountered a burnt bathtub made of ash and soot, and the shadow of a boy curled inside. His arms, hands, legs and feet were strung together with thin metal wire, and tightened around his neck was an even thinner, sharper wire tied to the faucet. It reminded him of a hen tied to her merchant's stall, waiting to be butchered and sold in the market.

"You good, Cyrus?" asked Jazzy, taking a joint filled with jinx handed to him by his younger brother Wazo.

It was one of his favourite drugs.

"I said, you good, 'boy?" he repeated, taking a drag when he refused to respond.

He waited another moment, before losing his patience.

"You gon' talk b'woy," he said, taking a line of wire by the hand and twisting around his fist, tugging on it like a master would a Solarite.

The wires dug into his own hand, but he held the pull, waiting for the look of desperation in Cyrus's eyes.

When it surfaced, he let go.

"Don't kill him, Jazz," urged Quail, gathering around Cyrus with the others as he coughed bloody phlegm and snot all over his bare torso.

"Not yet" he continued, reaching into the bathtub and punching him in the jaw.

"I know, I know," said Jazzy.

There was something about the way he squirmed though, fighting to breathe while trying not to strangle himself, that reminded him of a worm out of water.

I forgot… I forgot to feed Joro today.

I know she' hungry.

"Yo," cried out a boy from the other side of a locked door. "Open the fuckin' door boy."

"Wazo," snapped Jazzy, "Go get it."

"Yeah," said Wazo, walking to the door and opening it without complaint.

It was Green and Red, two half-brothers from the same gang, and each of them entered with ice coolers on their backs like school bags.

"Y'all done?" asked Jazzy

"Yea—"

"Done?" said Cyrus, interrupting Red.

"Done what? What y'all do to her?"

"Why?" asked Green, a short brown-eyed brown haired boy with a sniffle in his nose.

"She' quiet, huh?"

"We gave her some witchleaf and did what we wanted—" said Red, approaching the bathtub before being cut off by Cyrus's shaking.

He fought with such rage the bathtub began to tremble and a few wires even came undone. It was enough to almost convince them for a moment he was going to escape and somehow find a way to strangle each of them with it. After their initial concern, however, the boys slowly erupted into laughter.

"We don't do that shit," said Green. "We ain't like y'all bitches."

"We let her go," said Red, "Bitch sang like a summerbird."

"Y'all are fuckin' stupid," coughed Cyrus. "She ain't tell y'all shit. Watch. She gon be back with the whole Summer—"

"Shut yo' bitch-ass up, boy," said Petrel, walking over and kicking his face in with a dirty brown boot.

"Watch it, birdy," said Ducky, holding Petrel back before he could strike again.

"I ain't tryin' to fish for some baby teeth."

"I am," replied Petrel.

"Your bitch ass friends ain't coming" said Red, cold and straight-faced. "I promise"

"Fuck you!" cried Cyrus. "Just wait 'til they hear about me."

"Y'all ain't the only boys who are tough. We' been 'round a couple summers," said Green. Wiping the mucus off his nose with the back of his hand. "Y'all bitches gon' see some dog years too."

"We gon' kill y'all Motherfuckers," cried Cyrus.

"Yeah," agreed Red, unstrapping the cooler from his shoulders and revealing a bloody bonesaw resting over crushed ice.

"Ain't shit savin' us, we all gon' die."

"We gon' be back when you all bones," said Jazzy.

"Nah' we need that too," said Ducky, "Those bitches go for good-coin."

"So do them' teeth, birdy" he said, shoving Petrel.

"Alright'," said Jazzy. "We just gon' be back then."

"Wait, wait!" begged Cyrus. "Timeout, Timeout, T.O! T.O!"

"We off the playground boy," said Green, removing a gizmo from his pocket and flicking on a switch.

"This ain't Queens"

A beam of light burst from the device, revealing the true condition of Cyrus's face.

He used to be a pretty boy, only a few years older than Wazo, whose voice had just deepened for the first time. A pretty boy with a smile almost as pretty as a pretty girl's. This was before they beat him bloody, however, before Petrel left his nose visibly bent.

"No timeouts here," continued Green, unstrapping the ice cooler on his back and retrieving his own bonesaw. "We gon' put all y'all in a box."

They left him up to Wazo to kill, and he did so without hesitation. Taking a knife to his neck while the others held the light.

Cyrus kicked uncontrollably as Wazo jiggled the sharpened blade as it pierced the flesh through to the other side. Petrel and Green eventually climbed in to help him take apart his head.

"Watch the organs—" said Green.

"I know" replied Wazo.+

He felt pity for him, but the feeling quickly vanished as he recalled why they had dragged him and *his bitch* to Roilmont in the first place.

They shot Blue and Paladin,

And fed Yellow to some rottweilers—

After that it seemed as if Petrel hadn't kicked him hard enough.

"You got him Wazo?" asked Jazzy.

"Yeah he' gone," said Wazo.

"Good work," said Red, "Now I can cut."

Up until this moment, Wazo had been the only one among them who hadn't killed before.

He's almost one of us,

He just has to lose a thumb.

He followed Red out the door, leaving the others to finish the job. A few doors down the lightless hall was another room, one with two other coolers resting over pools of crushed ice and blood. Red had said they let her go, and she was definitely *gone*.

They carried her down and out the apartment, like a school bag filled with some unfinished homework, and were careful not to drop her on the slippery stone tiled streets like a newborn.

The sun was absent in the ruined city oF Roilmont, much like the law, and the clouds were still and black, no different than the alley puddles and ponds. It was no easier to tell the time of the day from the outside.

"This way," said Red, guiding him to a motor-scooter stashed away in a nearby alley.

"I'll be back," said Red.

"Cool," said Jazzy, helping him place the box over the leg space.

"Gon' put this hoe in the sink like some dishes," said Red, setting a key into the lock mechanism and turning the ignition.

"Where' the leftovers at?" asked Jazzy.

"Huh?" replied Red.

He pointed to the box to clarify what he meant.

"Oh," said Red. "I left them in the room."

A plume of black smoke burst from the automobile, and he watched as it rose to join the rest of the darkened sky.

"Why?" laughed Red. "You hungry?"

"No," replied Jazzy, "My terrorbird is."

Valtus II

The Old Flag of Acadia dangled atop the cafeteria while her soldiers lined up for their morning meals. He stood alongside the other Generalists, waiting patiently for his fair share of Peaceland's famous and widely exported rice, as well as its renowned forever stew. Rice likely to have been grown in the Lowlands, and stew likely to have been boiling for centuries.

As the summer quickly approached, the soldiers of South Station would be returning to three meals a day, breaking their fast in the morning instead of the afternoon. Many had turned gaunt as a result of the loss in meals, but seeing the smiles on their faces whenever the servant-soldiers poured ladles of meat and undercooked potatoes over bowls of mushy brown rice almost convinced him it was worth the starve.

They're happy, I should be happy too.

He intended to smile at the girl responsible for serving him his plate, and maybe even ask her how her week went. Yet when it was his turn to be served, the moment came and went without as little as eye contact.

I should be grateful at least.

It was required of soldiers in South Station to gather in one of three cafeterias spread across the campus. In Cafeteria 2, several hundred plucked from every region in Peaceland, sat together in a hall large enough to reasonably fit only half that amount. Cafeteria 2 was also where the high-officers gathered in their corners, watching idly with full faces and proud bellies. The two-meal-a-day rule was only true for the soldiers under their supervision.

He carried his tray and utensils down the hall, marching past the uncountable rows of tables occupied with chattering soldiers. Some were comrades, many were peers, but most were still strangers watching on with the same scrutinising eyes they arrived with.

"Valtus!" waved a girl with a chipped tooth smile and hair cut to her chin.

It was *Taalia,* and she sat with their other friends from the Lowlands, some of whom were from their hometown Notwell as well. There were also a few strays joining them from other places, a rare sight in a space where most were loyal to only those they arrived with.

He sat with them, but had little to say in the discussion about how bad the food was and where the cutest girls from Peaceland came from.

"Firstlanders are the cutest, period," said Riya. "Just *look* at them!"

"Like, the red in their eyes?" she continued. "C'mon, shit's not even fair."

"But that's not just Firstlanders, that's all Zacadins," said Taalia

"Yeah, but still," said Riya. "There's just something *different* about the Zacadins from the Firstlands."

"Lowland girls are cute too," said Atlus, a small brown-eyed dark-skinned boy with piercings running down from the bridge of his nose to his lips.

He looked nearly identical to Riya, but with *metal*.

"They just smell like cows."

"Hey!" said Taalia, laughing.

"That's not nice!"

"Yeah!" agreed Riya, angered, but more so at herself for being unable to contain her laughter.

"Your mom is from there you know."

"Yeah, and?," said Atlus.

"You're so bad!" said Taalia, breaking into a hysterical laugh. "Don't say that!"

A few chairs to his left, Alric, Romin, Lamby, and Rodina listened as Wilaana went on about how unfair it was for the Army to confiscate every tool not made within their guild sites.

"I don't get it," she said, putting her fork to her plate.

"Last week I brought in a new sewing kit, and they took it away yesterday and put it on my permanent record."

"It's just for our safety," said Romin, "You're thinking too much about it."

"It's a sewing kit" pushed Wilaana.

"Yeah, also look at how they train us sometimes," interjected Alric. "I don't think they give a shit about our safety."

"I think they're just scared we're going to build our own skills," said Wilaana.

"And what," said Lamby. "Start our own guilds?"

"Maybe," said Wilaana. "Or just not need theirs."

"We could start our own little factories inside the dormitories." she smiled, wandering back into her own little fantastical world.

He wasn't sure if she was correct in her reasoning, but felt it was a *good point* regardless. There was a policy forbidding the crafting and importing of tools within the dormitories, and it was even forbidden to make modifications to clothing and equipment without an officer's permission. The Army claimed it was to ensure the safety and uniformity of every soldier and officer, but some of it *must've been a racket*, or so he figured.

Everything was pre-issued from the clothes to the utensils, and the names of guilds were found on every tagline and stamp. The contracts held between the two institutions were not a secret by any means.

Why would it matter if we build our skills? Would the Army really care about something like that? Would it really hurt them?

I guess if there's enough of us maybe, I don't know.

There were many other unanswered questions and unexplained tendencies as well. Like the tradition of treating lingering tools and materials from Old Acadia as irreplaceable objects, even if they were far past their days. Many were stamped with numbers too big for him to count, symbols too old to have any meaning, and the names of places known to no longer exist. The fork he was using to swirl his breakfast into an unappealing pile of mush read: Year Two-One-Seven-Three.

But it's only 143 years after New Acadia, and that only lasted two or three centuries.

How could it be Year 2-1-7-3?

"What's wrong, Valtus?" asked Riya, patting him on the back.

"Nothing," replied Valtus.

"Nah, it's on his plate," said Atlus. "He loves eating this shit and he's just…"

"Doing whatever he's doing with it," laughed Atlus. "I don't know."

He wanted to join in on their laughter, but he was too invested in padding the mush into a flat hilltop out of disinterest.

"I don't blame him," said Taalia, placing a forkful of mushy rice into her mouth. "It doesn't taste that famous to me."

"C'mon, what happened, Valtus?" pushed Riya. "Why are you so down?"

He sighed.

"Just got back from the major's office. Didn't make the cut."

"The reclassification test?" asked Wilaana

"Yeah," answered Valtus, cutting the hilltop into pieces.

"You tryna' be a specialist or some shit?" asked Lamby.

"No," replied Valtus. "Just make captain here."

"Good, that's a coward's fight"

Yeah, but it's living.

"Don't worry, Valtus," said Atlus, tugging his tray away from him. "Ain't shit savin' us, we all stuck in this bitch."

"At least we ain't stuck in Eastern Stronghold," said Taalia, "Making half of what we make now."

"Or in Notwell eating hard bread and dirty water for dinner," laughed Riya.

"Or working as servant-soldiers," added Romin.

They're not wrong. But still, it doesn't make me feel any better.

Notwell was a hell-hole, and mostly orphaned children ended up as servant-soldiers.

You're supposed to be better than that.

"Nah I'll take being a servant-soldier over this shit any day," said Atlus. "All they gotta do is cook and clean."

"Yeah? You're good with no honour?" asked Romin.

"Fuck honour gon' do for me when I'm gone?" said Atlus, taking a spoonful of stew to his lips. "I still gotta eat."

From a distance he noticed a Firstland soldier from a faraway table making his way towards theirs. He nodded a hello to a few of them before turning his full attention to Lamby.

What's this?

He watched as the two performed an awkward handshake, and though he couldn't catch it, he was sure hands were not the only things exchanged.

Maybe some jinx?

Along with the soldiers from the different regions, were soldiers who were once a part of the lineup, but since then turned inwards within the ranks to form their own *rings*.

Soldiers who were out to get it, selling whatever they could including fixes.

No.

Knowing Lamby, it's probably some sprey.

It was risky to turn a back against the Army, especially as an enlisted soldier. The punishment for disobedience and insubordination ranged from any combination of being jailed to losing a thumb to being cremated alive and sent to the frontlines as literal gunpowder.

Thank Mother these captains are so blind.

He turned to the officer's corner and watched as they sat around their round table, likely discussing the competition and contentions within their little world. The oldest among them were too old to notice their own bowels before they went, while the youngest were too busy climbing the ranks to complete their actual oversight duties. They were more concerned with adopting and appropriating the attitudes the older high-officers held over their peers.

And they wonder what's wrong with the army. Well, we ain't that much better either.

For years he spent trying to understand what brought his group of friends all together, and he had just figured it out at this moment. Aside from being completely *useless* to society, they were all broken in their own ways, and *stuck* like Atlus put it.

There was Rodina, who hadn't said much since her boyfriend got into an accident in Summer Circle three weeks ago and was left bedridden. Lamby, who came from one of the wealthiest Landlord families, and was now a drug addict. Taalia, Riya, and Atlus, who all still cried themselves to sleep after learning the Lowland recruits would be leading the vanguard.

And finally him, as much of a failure as the rest of them.

A failure who couldn't even make captain.

Though if he was being fair, the entire cafeteria was about the same or worse.

The Generalist was a force made up of mostly those who failed to be anywhere else. There were Firstlanders from wealthy guild families, Lowlanders who made it to the Citadel but never truly left the villages they crawled out of, and miserable children from Honoured and even Landlord families. Some were children who were cast away by their parents and still expected to not shame them. While others were the runts and extras, treated no better than street orphans their entire lives. Each one of them, however, were deselected from the workforce and streamed into the pool of soldiers who could not join a guild, university, or Army College.

"You gonna' finish that Valtus?" asked Lamby, pointing to the pile of gunk on his tray.

"No," said Valtus, pushing it toward him. "Take it."

"That actually looks really disgusting," said Atlus.

"Yeah, but it's all the same in your stomach," shrugged Lamby.

"F-Fair enough" answered Atlius, a little bewildered by his response.

In Peaceland, they were taught in school there was no time for complaints, that this was supposedly a society with limited resources and therefore little room for error. According to their teachers, only the most useful were sought out by the Citadel to do the most important things. There was no space for anyone in between.

Maybe I should've listened more in school... No.

I know I tried as hard as I could.

He sighed. *At least one of us made it out.*

The Army often declared they were all in the correct stations, each doing the work they were good enough for. Whether it meant designing new facilities, constructing new machinery, serving in the frontlines, or cleaning cafeterias.

But there has to be something better than this. I know there is. How couldn't there be?

It was easy to be useless in the world, and though the First Mother loved all her precious little children, she knew like any good mother, the ones who wouldn't make it.

Wilona VI

"What happened to her parents?" asked Colonel Flowers, watching Peace-sergeant Briggs close the door behind them as they left.

"They didn't make it," he sighed, waiting until he was sure they were gone.

"Times like this calls for peanuts"

He reached into the inside of his Army jacket and showcased an open fist full of crushed peanuts and pocket lint.

"You want some? I roasted them myself."

"N-No," said the colonel, "I'm okay."

"Hmph, well I do have something else" he continued, placing half a handful into his mouth and chewing aggressively.

Walking over to his desk he removed a small elixir bottle from one of the compartments, a jagged thing, and from another drawer he retrieved three small wooden cups.

"They say she had a baby brother too," he said, pouring a drink and taking a sip.

"He also didn't make it"

"Another one left without a family, what a tragedy," he continued, pouring the other two cups, "And such a beautiful child."

"I just hope I'm not around when they tell her,"

"I've killed men, cooked their skin and bones during war too, but I just can't stomach a little girl's cry."

"What is it?" asked the colonel, reaching for the glass.

"Witchleaf tea," answered the peace-sergeant.

Witchleaf?

"This is outlawed outside of hospitals peace-sergeant" replied the major.

"The commander doesn't mind if we have a drink or two"

"I'm not the commander," answered the colonel sternly.

"Just have one" he replied, "It helps with the shell-shock"

"Fine" she said, "Just this once,"

She took the drink to her lips and had a sip.

It was *sweetened*, like nectarines.

"Well," said the peace-sergeant, "We might s'well plan our next move since we're all here. Mother knows I'm not sleeping tonight."

He reached for his drawer once more, rummaging through it before settling on something. "I think I have it somewhere."

It was an untitled book, a pile of loose pages bound together by old string and glue.

They stood around him as he carefully flipped through the aged pages with the tips of his fingers.

"Wait!" she said, the moment something caught her eye. "Go back a page."

He did as he was instructed, and on the previous page was a map dated to the Year 2020 of Old Acadia and the title read: "*The Highlands of Middle Acadia Prefecture.*"

"Where did you get this?" said the colonel, with eyes frantically scanning every corner of the page.

The Highlands of Middle Acadia, but during a time when Queens was just a military excavation site, and it would be about another *thousand* years before the thought of Peaceland would ever be conceived.

The prefecture was also once home to the Old Capital, Roilmont. A city once widely recognized as the most prosperous in Rodina, and likely the entire Biosphere if any other lands had remained.

"A soldier found them in the blackmarket," said the sergeant. "I didn't believe it at first. Thought they were just good fakes, but here they are."

"A few of those are Old Acadian too," he said, pointing to the collection of books on the shelf behind his desk.

"Incredible," said Major San, with an agreeable sense of astonishment. "Near priceless relics."

"Yes," agreed the peace-sergeant, "I told the commander and the next day they were on my desk."

"How much did it cost?" she asked, lost in the pages.

"He didn't buy it," replied the peace-sergeant.

Something had caught her eye again, two Ancient clusters nestled to the east of Roilmont, in the once untapped segment of the Highland.

The Citadel before it was the Citadel. Mineraltown before it was even just a tree temple.

"We shot the traders."

She continued flipping through the pages until she found what she was searching for, a map closer to their time. It was the same Highland, but a very different place in *the year 110 After New Acadia.*

At some point the Westerians had come and gone, reducing Roilmont to a scorched ruin and forcing its people to scatter into Queens, and at some later point, the Landlords of Rockland took it upon themselves to reunify the torn country.

And failed.

It was never truly determined how many years had passed between the First Westerian Invasion and the rise of Rockland's Landlords. Historians, commanders, and others desperate to understand this post-war period marked the time as the 'Lost Years'. A time when new communities emerged and perished at the whim of each season, and any lingering societies were declared false-nations by the Landlords who campaigned against them through their centuries-long reign.

"We tried to contact the Peaceguard station inside, but there's been no response," said the sergeant.

"What do you think it could be?" asked Major San.

"Blacksheeps?" answered Peace-sergeant Briggs, with a question.

"Why would there be Blacksheeps in Mineraltown?" she refuted.

"Or how?"

"Who the hell knows?" said the peace-sergeant. "Why are we even here? I didn't expect any of this when I woke up today."

"That's fair," agreed the colonel, albeit reluctantly.

"But this sounds like a revolution"

"Could the Blacksheeps really stage a revolution?"

"Damn, it would've been useful to know what the captured knew," said the colonel, eyeing the outline of Mineraltown.

By the present day, 143 years After New Acadia, nearly all of the surviving post-war communities were no longer visible on the map. Many were completely erased, others had been gradually dispossessed and assimilated by the Liberation Army. First under the direction of the

Landlords, and later under the authority of their own conviction. Mineraltown was one of those communities.

Originally built around an Ancient mining site and a colossal ziggurat now used as a Zaaj Temple, it quickly developed into a small city before its eventual conquest by the Liberation Army centuries later. The city itself remained largely intact while the temple within its Ancient core was readjusted into a walled fortress rivalling the defences of the Citadel. It was now where a small government stood. Responsible for managing some of Peaceland's most important institutions like the Research & Excavation Facility, the Association of Mining and Metalworking Guilds, and the Orphanage where unclaimed Highland-children were sent to be raised.

"Well, that's the most reasonable explanation."

"There also couldn't be more than a hundred temple guards which could only mean they came from outside."

"Mercenaries?" said the colonel.

"Wouldn't be the first time mercenaries were snuck into a community."

"But where would all those mercenaries come from?" asked the peace-sergeant. "They would have had to sneak into Peaceland to go unnoticed like this."

"Maybe it's an uprising," suggested the major. "There are a few separatist groups running around."

"But the Mineraltown Separatists are just a gang of rejects," he replied, with his arms crossed. "I doubt they're inspiring a revolution."

The major let out a deep sigh.

"Well, this is not some squabble in the slums," he said, "We need an actual war plan. And if they really do control the entire town, we need to draw battle lines."

She knew something was wrong the moment the doors were closed. Denying access to space and resources was always a cause for concern, she knew this because it was what the Liberation Army specialised in. It was also a cause for concern when people were escaping a place with children.

"Well it doesn't matter what the reason is."

"I agree," said the peace-sergeant, "But we can't just storm in, especially if there's an army on the other side."

"We can't attack them with artillery either, we have to think about the remaining residents," said Major San.

"And the Ancient sites," added the peace-sergeant.

"And the nearby Firstland farmlands," continued the colonel. "We can't do anything without Brigadier August."

"We need her or her officers at the table."

They turned their attention to the Firstland Region on the map, a place on the Highland to the south of the Citadel and next to the Iron Valleys. The Firstlanders were one of the few people lingering from the Lost Years. Believed to have originated from a community of mainly displaced Zacadins who managed to survive in the fringes of Middle Acadia. They eventually went on to develop their own society and customs. Most notably rejecting the Old Faith, and centuries later, revolutionising the New one.

They were regarded as the first followers of the Book of Zaaj, and their practice resembled something closer aligned to the Ostarian and Astormi faiths. Among all those who feared the Ancients, they were the first to develop the practice of pilgrimage to the Ancient sites. A revolution which has had an undeniable impact upon the world.

"No we don't," said the peace-sergeant. "If we bring them to the table that'll just legitimise the Firstland separatist argument. They are not a stakeholder to the land and we can't let them think otherwise."

"We can legitimise one of their claims or we can ruin our relationship with them entirely," said Colonel Flowers. "The villages are close enough to matter and we're going to need to surround Mineraltown anyways, it has to be a joint mission."

"Without them we'd suffer major losses surely"

"With them Mineraltown would be ours in a few weeks, even with an army hiding behind its walls."

The peace-sergeant grumbled in disdain, and his concern was not unfounded.

For many years the Firstlanders had contested their territory extended beyond the current borders, both to include parts of the Iron Valley as well as most of Mineraltown. Acknowledging their presence now would set a strong precedent for any future arrangements on where to draw the line.

It would've been unwise, however, to not invite Brigadier August to the war room, and it would've been inhumane and unreasonable to send soldiers off to die when there was space to avoid it.

"Besides, the pilgrims in Mineraltown are trapped as well, and most of them are Firstlanders," said the colonel. "I think they would care about that."

Last thing we need is more tension.

"We also don't know if it is a defection or not," said Major San. "There could be moles in our ranks."

"T-That's a good point," she said.

A wave of existential dread silently swept over the faces of the three high-officers, and for a moment, she felt their eyes judging her and one another.

She was doing the same.

"Quietly assemble the regiments," said Colonel Flowers, regaining some composure.

"Tomorrow we're cutting the lights."

Emmi II

"I-I can't believe that just happened" said Ashley-Ann catching her breath against an Ancient umbrella-pillar inside one of the plazas.

"I don't think that guy was any merchant" replied Nia, "He was probably a Liberation spy or a soldier somewhere"

"What makes you say that?"

"I remember seeing a Liberated flag in his stall" she replied, "That and he had a gun-"

"We should hurry, they might just start their own war and we could be late for it" said Emmi, gazing above and finding a public clocktower.

The hands read *12:16.*

"We can go now while it's still hot" said Nia

"Are you serious?" asked Ashley-Ann, plain faced and with genuine curiosity.

"Shouldn't we just call it a day?"

"The Police are going to be all over this place, we could get caught"

"No, we can do it" said Nia "Now's a good time, while they're still distracted"

They agreed to press on, following a steady stream of foot traffic leading into the bustling heart of Newtown District. The road was lined with colourful shops, lively cafes, and vibrant street performers, creating a medley of sights, sounds, and experiences for pilgrims and travellers, and just three blocks west they found their destination, *Trevino Plaza*. The plaza itself was home to a pearly white limestone palace overlooking an enormous marble fountain which depicted a great Ancient battle, though as historic and grand as it were, she knew it was neither *their* history, *or even Acadian* history.

Just mostly men going off to rape and kill, and steal
And only Mother knows what else.

Not too far away to the south of them stood a mega-structure, one as tall as the clouds were high and made of earthstones green and blue and grey. It was the *Salt Pillar*, one of the most revered Ancient sites in the City, commanding the attention of all those who merely gazed in its general direction.

"Remember not to make any mistakes" she said, taking in a deep breath of the scent of Highland water pouring from the marble fountain.

Mist from the fountain filled Trevino Plaza with a mossy aroma which gently caressed and cleared her nostrils and the sound of it also furiously beat away at their eardrums like the nearby band of young teens who were playing homemade instruments on the side of the road for a pence. They belonged to a race called the Solarites, a resilient people that had long suffered the burden of centuries long conquest and enslavement under Westeria, only to be brought into the cities of Acadia as captives.

Amidst the grandeur and history, the bustling streets also offered a delightful treat, an *ice cream store*, known far and wide to locals and tourists alike. It was where they had settled in Trevino Plaza, waiting and watching for a congregation of cult followers to end their weekly gathering and leave their prayer hall, another marvel itself. The building was once known as the Flower Temple and its exterior resembled an elegant rose bush with pillars of brick acting as its stems with protruding earthstone serving as leaves and thorns. From afar it appeared to be a real-life enormous budding flower. It was the inside, however, which interested them today, as it was where the Cult of Asherah gathered to perform rituals and celebrate their exploits in the Acadian sex trade.

"Do you remember your spot?" asked Hania to Ashley-Ann.

"Yeah" she replied, gathering herself and tightening the straps of her school bag around her shoulders.

"Emmi, can you watch my back?"

"I sure can Ashley-Ann"

She watched from atop a set of steps leading into the fountain as Hania and Ashley-Ann scurried around the crowds and took their place as was planned and practised. Ashley would go into the backstreet while Nia would take a side entrance, each of them removing a small slab of the Ancient foundation which they had prepared beforehand, and inserting a sticky clay-like substance, glued to an electronic device.

It didn't take long for the girls to complete their assignment as the road leading to and from was surprisingly *empty*? She thought to herself.

The shooting must've moved everyone away,

Great for us.

Nia was the first to finish, and she made her way back to the lookout as if nothing had happened.

She did it!

Now just Ashley!

Though they had entered a new era of peace in Rodina, it wasn't quite theirs to enjoy. Places like Newtown were paradises where occupiers like the Westerians, and even Acadians in the Military Police had their way inside brothels and lived out their years exploiting the local population in ways that were even disallowed in Westeria herself. It was an artificial space between foreigners and locals, but it was constructed well. Well enough to almost not notice that members of the local community were slipping through cracks and falling into some Newtown trap. Well enough to almost forget some of the things being traded were alive and sometimes still human.

For one reason or another, the price for little Tautau girls had soared over the years, and it wasn't uncommon for young brown-eyed women to be taken away in broad daylight and chained to some bedpost somewhere. Young Tautau boys were known to be stolen, bought, and sold too, and she couldn't trust the Military Police or Liberation Army to do anything about it either. Sometimes they would turn the other way, sometimes they were the patrons.

It was for these reasons, and others, that walking on the roads made her feel uneasy. Being surrounded by a world she wasn't a part of already made her feel small, smaller than she already might have been. Now here she was, nearly eighteen with supposedly something special between her legs, special enough for many to forsake their humanity for. It put her on edge all the time, knowing she was as vulnerable as she was, and it was also what forced many like her to turn their backs on both the Liberation Cause and the Military Police, and join the Blacksheeps instead.

"We might hurt some innocent people today" said Nia, breaking the silence between them.

It was about the worst thing she could have said at the moment as she wasn't prepared for the existential crisis awaiting her ahead.

Along with the Pilgrims who took the City as something sacred, both Armies were responsible for the destruction of Queens. They were both guilty of carving out and colonising the City, while turning it into a contradiction with its supposed holysites sitting across from its Red Light District. Both sides were responsible for dispossessing them and their people within, but still they *had to be careful*.

The original plan was to detonate an explosive in a busy Zaaj Temple situated deep in Military Police territory. Some of the top Blacksheeps believed it would be enough for the Military Police to blame it on the Liberation Army and start another war. She was no follower of the New Faith, but still could not bring herself to target its temples and civilian population. As a result there were major disagreements within upper Blacksheep circles. In one particularly heated argument, they came to an agreement to disagree with the three of them suggesting their problem wasn't with the pilgrims necessarily, but rather the exploiters in the market, and their fight wasn't necessarily with the Ancients or their constructs, but rather how they were revered and misworshipped.

"The Frontier Army is on our side"

"What does that have to do with any of it?" asked Nia, quietly and unexpectedly.

"We *save* innocent people, we don't target them" she told both herself and Nia.

Although it upset some of the other Blacksheep members, the three had volunteered themselves to take on the mission, believing they were the best ones up for the task of sparking a war between two of the largest armies of a fractured Acadia.

Some of the others wanted to target the plazas and some New Faith settlements,

We couldn't let them,

Not when there's sex traders right down the market.

Their new goal was to cause some chaos on the streets, hoping it would disrupt the Westerian migration while frightening enough pilgrims to put an end to the Great Pilgrimage before summer. Before they were dislocated from another community for its Ancient sites, before Queens could be flooded with Westerian sex tourism.

Still it made her question if what they were doing was justifiable. They were being displaced all around Queens and left hungry, and homeless or dead.

This was just retaliation, right?

They're the ones who started the war and we're just punching back?

Right?

"Okay we need to leave right now" said Ashley-Ann, returning to their circle.

"Before we get caught"

"Don't panic Ashley-" said Nia, "But I see some Police heading our way"

"What?!" blurted Ashley-Ann.

"Quiet!" hissed Nia, "I said don't panic!"

"Shit, I see them too" said Emmi.

"Here, this way, follow me" said Nia, leading them forward down a *wet* back road until it *finally* led back into the main parts of the district.

They clasped hands as she led them through the crowded plaza, avoiding as much of the rest of the population as possible, before taking a turn into a pathway made of some of the most *miserable looking gardens* she had ever seen. The walkway was filled with idols and their worshipers, and the air buzzed with prayers, the scent of burning exotic herbs, and the hum of conversations in various foreign and strange sounding languages.

She glanced down and observed the streets slowly transitioning from a new piece of work, to a curiously glittering greenish-brown shade of well-aged stone.

She searched for the Trevino Plaza fountain and when she couldn't find it, she sought out the *Salt Pillar.* One could always figure out where they were in the City if they found the menacing tower, which was nearly impossible to miss.

And there it was, the *west side* of it at least.

"Hania-"

"We're heading west,"

She heard, but just continued on.

Though all things appeared ordinary, with each step they took, the bustling crowd seemed to fade away like a Highland mirage, and the once packed market grew eerily silent, as if everyone there had been taken by an *unseen* force. Soon the sounds of chatter and activity dissolved into hushed whispers, until only the faint echo of their footsteps remained. Nia and Ashley-Ann exchanged bewildered glances, as they realised the three of them were now alone in the pathway. The vibrant tapestry of sounds and sights had dissipated, leaving behind an unsettling void. The market stalls, once brimming with life, now stood empty and abandoned. Strands of colourful, but faded fabric swayed gently in the breeze, and there was no one, except for her to admire their beauty. The aroma of *something* lingered in the air, but there was no one around to claim or explain it.

"We should start heading back," said Ashley-Ann.

"I think so too" she added, more creeped out by the atmosphere than she cared to admit to herself.

"We can't," said Nia, "What if they followed us here?"

"What if they didn't?" she asked, almost arguing.

Hania didn't respond.

"Nia?" she asked once more, only to bump into Ashley-Ann, who then bumped into Nia in turn.

"W-What is it?" asked Ashley-Ann

"I-I don't know" answered Nia.

Their journey had unwittingly led them into a street littered with *idols*, and one peculiar shrine dedicated to an unfamiliar deity stood out more than all the others, leaving each of them apprehensive in their own little way by its presence.

It was an imposing thing, *a genie* she recognized immediately, and underneath it was another imposing construct, a black metal gate adorned with dog headed bats, and other *winged demons*.

"Welcome to Witchtown" read Ashley-Ann, murmuring whilst she read its signage.

Talius V

In Peaceland, the children of Citizens were placed into classrooms to be arranged and stratified according to their merits, talents, and *usefulness*. It was also determined within these classrooms, who amongst them would support the Cause with a life of full-time work and who would be dedicating their lives to active duty. Standing before him now were a few of the surviving Peaceguards from the failed explosives mission, and two of the most promising researchers available to them.

"Commander! Colonel!" said Briaana Cryheart, one of the more outstanding soldiers in the Peaceguard.

She was a young woman, still in her early twenties and distinguished as a special intelligence operative. Along with Daaria Earthwind and Omaara Strong, she was unknowingly in contention for a top position as a high-official within the Force.

She's as useful with a gun as she is without one,
A soldier with a future as bright as her eyes.

The other three Peaceguards, Jovaana Wells, Toshi Hara, and Olisa August followed her lead. "Commander! Colonel!" they said with heartfelt salutes.

The professor and her student stood in silence with their hands by their hearts, as was the custom for civilians in the presence of high-ranking officers.

Wait...

He turned his attention to the professor, a woman who had dedicated a life to the study of Ancient physics, both as a science and history. Currently she was working adjacent to researchers tasked to lead a highly classified Army initiative titled 'Project Orphan'.

She's beautiful-

"I don't think we've ever met, professor," said the commander, approaching her with his best foot forward, and the most masculine frame he could think of. A cold expression which conveyed no emotion, but still suggested some underlying mystery. One incapable of being solved by any one woman.

"Very few have," replied the professor, glancing up and locking eyes with him. "I spend most of my nights alone."

She was a small woman with frail shoulders turned slightly inwards, a light brown complexion, and what would've been an otherwise average appearance if it had not been for her unusually charming smile. She wore a white lab coat and a pair of black leggings, as if anyone had doubts as to who she was, and nothing in particular stood out about her other than how young she was for a professor, and of course, *her smile.*

There's no ring on her finger.

"Thank you for funding our research," she continued, placing her obstructive strands of silky black hair behind her pointy uneven ears to reveal a pair of wide green eyes.

"We're very close to seeing the first Acadian computer built within the last two centuries," she said, smiling. "If the researchers from the previous generation had a commander who was half as supportive, we'd be there by now."

She also spoke with a subtle inflection in her voice, a soft melodic tone which concealed her K's and C's relative to her H's and F's. It was something characteristic of most women from the Lowlands, and though it was faint, it was still there. Resisting the harsh Highland dialect, in the same way many had resisted the New Faith and all other pieces of culture considered alien to them.

"Well, we now have people like you to invest in," said the commander. "Thank you for being here."

She seemed to enjoy the compliment.

Standing idly next to her, with his hands still by his heart, was her lab assistant, Wiluss Earthwind, a *dweeby* looking kid who was also cut out right out of what one would expect from a lab assistant.

He was a small boy and wore a white lab coat several sizes larger than his body.

That's right-

He's the neurobody-

Wait... Should I be worried about sending him out to the field? That's a good question. I guess they do need to get out sometimes, but it is a risk whenever they do.

Hmm... He needs to be there.

He'll be useful to make sense of whatever they find, and besides, there's a whole team of Peaceguards watching his every step.

He couldn't trip if he tried.

Neurobodies were highly sought-after beings, recognized for their ability to generate breakthroughs in research fields thought to be already entirely discovered, and well-established crafts thought to be already developed and mastered. They were fragile creatures, however. Often born with abnormalities which left them prone to chronic suffering, and an inescapable early death. An extremely rare and poorly understood birth defect was the cause of their beyond average intelligence and physical incapability. As a part of an internal Army policy, those inflicted were no longer informed of their disease, yet the Classification Test was still used to identify them wherever they were. Wiluss, along with his older sister, who though not a neurobody, was distinguished in her own right, served as strong evidence of good things coming from backward places.

There's definitely more of them out there, we just need to fish them out wherever we can.

It was a race against the clock to make use of neurobodies as the defect was known to reduce the brain to pulp by the time they turned twenty-one, rendering them entirely obsolete and needing to be replaced.

Wherever they are I just hope they're old enough to get to work, we can't wait on any newborns.

"Are you from Summer Circle?" asked the commander, walking over to meet Colonel Hellin under the projection, though not without first crossing her path.

"Why do you ask? Is there something in my demeanour?" she asked.

"There is," said the commander, "I had a feeling you were a Lowlander when you walked in."

"Oh?" she said, intrigued. "And how did you infer that?"

"The women from Summer Circle are always the prettiest," he said, smiling for the second time all year.

"Oh... thank you," she said, covering her smile with a hand.

The others in the room watched on, some more unsure of what was happening than others, but all a little concerned for the passing time.

"But I'm not from Summer Circle," she continued, smiling balefully at his direction, almost as if she could read his intentions.

"Oh…" said the commander. "W-Where are you from?

"I'm from a small village outside Peaceland. One which no longer exists in Northern Acadia," said Professor Lind, expressing her words with some pain.

"My family moved before the Frontier Army put it to the torch, I was ten when I joined the Liberation."

"Though, I suppose you're right about the Lowland part," she said.

"And the pretty part too-." he said before the colonel cut him off.

"Okay," said Colonel Hellin, giving him *the look* while setting down a new slide on the projector.

It was a photo of the Great Gorge and its forests in the foreground.

"We have a lot to cover."

"Really?" pronounced Wiluss, unable to contain his excitement. "Did we really find it?"

It was almost inappropriate of him to burst out the way he did in the presence of the two high-officers, but there were smiles across their faces as well.

Though the quality of photos were below ideal, it was clear a large segment of the cliff rock had once been submerged with the way the sediments were stained with the ocean's purple waters. There were also odd protrusions and misalignments in the rock wall which did not match the surrounding formation of the Gorge. Almost as if a piece of the Highland had fallen off and a new patch of stone grew over it like a scar. Almost as if the Highland was alive and always trying to heal.

Such was the fable spread during the Lost Years to quell any curiosity about the clearly unnatural formation at least.

"We think so," answered Colonel Hellin. "The miners found something that's worth checking at least."

A wide-ranging continent inhabited long before the first Acadian was ever born, Rodina had awed the early Gran Acadian voyagers the moment they took sight of her shores, and perplexed them the moment they began exploring and inquiring about its history.

In the Lowlands, they encountered wild fields of undiscovered grains growing freely on some of the richest earth, dense forests home to the toughest trees known to humankind, countless rivers which appeared like the roots of a tree itself, and the scattered ruins of a people thought to have been conquered entirely.

In the Highlands, they encountered vast cities made of a *fascinating* and resilient substance later determined to be an advanced form of concrete, and a strange source of energy later named *electricity*.

I couldn't imagine what they first thought of it. He looked up to the lights radiating above. I still don't know what to make of it.

For hundreds, if not thousands of years, it was undetermined what the lights in the abandoned Highland cities exactly were, as up until this moment, electricity was something foreign and misunderstood by the newly arrived Gran Acadians who ventured into the lost continent. The Astormi, a people nestled between Rodina's southernmost islands, had no interest in trying to understand or even exploit the energy for their own use, declaring it along with their neighbour, the Ostorians, to be sacred, forbidden, and cursed.

Though it was ever present, there existed no true knowledge of light outside what was found in nature. What was simply understood of the phenomenon was that it came from the star called the sun, was found in fire, and according to Gran Acadian folktales, "*Whenever the Whitestar reared its ugly face.*"

Whatever that meant.

There were many competing theories regarding the nature of electricity and its source, the most dated of which included the widespread belief that Rodina's Highlands were some kind of living organism. One capable of repairing itself, as well as producing an electromagnetic field which could be harnessed and used. Such a belief was passively accepted for much of Acadian history, Old and New. Partly because it conveniently answered the question of how electricity worked and where it was coming from, and partly because of the Landlord's centuries long efforts to conceal their true suspicions.

It wasn't until the year 116 A.N.A that an Old Acadian theory was proven to be correct. That a network of deep underground generators were responsible for providing the energy, not some creature. What they didn't expect to discover, however, was an entire subterranean city and an entire *people* still persisting on.

Daaria VI

"Will!" she shouted into the crowd of soldiers, as loud as she could.

"Will!"

C'mon, look this way you blind kid, don't tell me you're deaf now too.

It took several attempts for him to catch the sight of her waving like a deranged woman, and even then he wasn't exactly sure who she was.

Yes, it's me!

When he did eventually realise it was his big sister, he sprinted to her as fast as he could with his little legs.

She couldn't count how many times she kissed him on the face.

In Peaceland, some of the best performing student-soldiers were delisted from conscription and permitted to work for the cause as professionals. Though there was a useful trade for every civilian to dedicate their lives to, the most lucrative and rewarding, and therefore the most desirable and competitive disciplines were found inside the closed doors of the guilds or at the University's lecture halls.

These were institutions tasked with identifying the correct stations, as well as designating the appropriate field for students upon graduation. To be even considered for admission, however, one was expected to arrive complete as a person. Both with the willingness to compete with others, and the readiness to do so.

In the Northern and Eastern Lowlands, however, the schools did little to prepare the children for the world ahead, and their communities had little to raise them as well. Especially relative to the rest of Peaceland. Paired with the political and social instabilities of day-to-day life, the occasional outbursts of violence, as well as the pressures to conform to the cultural attitudes of their peers, it left many without a true path to be included into the wider society they supposedly belonged to.

Even with these barriers in place, however, her baby brother still found a way. At only seventeen, he was already a postgraduate student at the University teaching maths and Ancient art.

I'm so happy he made it as a civilian,

He would've never made a good soldier,

Or a servant-

"Stop!" pleaded Wiluss, "You're hugging me too tight! I can't breathe, it hurts!"

"I missed you so much," said Daaria. "And I was so scared."

"Huh?" Why were you scared?" asked Wiluss, with a voice still higher than usual for a boy his age.

"I thought you were stuck in Mineraltown," said Daaria. "How'd you get out?"

In a handwritten letter addressed to her, he had stated the University would be transferring him to the excavation site's research facility in Mineraltown to work as a lab assistant. That was six months ago, however, and she hadn't heard anything from or of him since.

She knew she would be losing sleep the moment she learned of the rumours surrounding Mineraltown, and was practically convinced he was dead when Jotan broke the news of the escapees earlier.

Yet here he was, fully intact and as *adorable* as ever.

"Stuck in Mineraltown?" said Wiluss.

He looked visibly confused for a moment, but then his face lit up with excitement.

"Oh!" he said, "I never got to tell you! I haven't been there in months!"

"Huh?" said Daaria.

"Yeah! I've been taking field assignments from the commander."

What!? Field assignments? From the commander?

"Why are you taking assignments from the commander?" she asked, feigning composure so as not to frighten him.

What does the commander want with him? He'll never survive out in the field. He can't even survive without his night light.

"Um..." said Willus, before going quiet and positioning his feet slightly inwards.

It was something he did whenever he was about to withhold information *or lie*.

"I-I..." he stuttered. "I can't tell you, even if you're my big sister..."

"What's going on here?" asked a voice, one belonging to a young woman.

She looked up to find August approaching with Briaana and two other Peaceguards, Toshi and Jovaana.

They all exchanged a salute, but it felt a little half-hearted, especially from the Firstlanders.

"Good morning," said Toshi.

"Good morning," replied Omaara, "Where are you guys all heading? Wait... don't tell me. You're headed to search the Gorge for the others."

Omaara... You're sneaky.

"No," said Jovaana, with a hint of sorrow she made no effort to hide.

There was a brief and slightly awkward silence before she continued on. "They're not missing, they're dead."

"What?" said Omaara. "Dead? No."

"It's true," said Toshi, "We shouldn't have gone there in the first place. The cliffside was too muddy, the plan was never going to work, b-but they're always sending us out," continued Toshi, with enough contempt in his voice to be written up for insubordination. "They don't give a fuck about us."

Toshi! Not so loud.

She turned to find Briaana and August standing quietly, observing the conversation more than they were willing to engage in it.

I shouldn't be surprised. These things happen, and I should've known when they were declared missing in action. There's no such thing as missing.

Not in the Army.

"On your way to Eastern Stronghold?" asked Briaana, making her way into the circle, and with eyes occasionally glancing towards Wiluss.

"Huh? How'd you know?" asked Omaara.

She just smiled.

There was always something cold and distant in Briaana's voice. It was faint, *but it was there.*

It's the same exact pitch every single time. I don't even remember what her laugh sounds like.

Wait... Has she ever laughed?

In the years she had known her, she couldn't think of a single moment.

"We were assigned to the Lowlands before they found something more important for us to do," said August, following Briaana into the circle. "Your team is probably better suited for that work though."

"I'm sure Daaria knows her way around," she said, with a malicious smile which casted away any doubts as to whether she was intentionally insulting her or not.

Though that's not new. She's been like this since we met. What's wrong with you, August?

Though the name August was originally an orphan-name, it now belonged to one of the most well-established Firstlander families. A renowned family in Peaceland with inseparable ties to both their regional Army and elite guild society. She was also apparently a close relative of Brigadier Wildred August, the leader of the Firstland people. A coincidence which she must have confused for justification to act like *a total bitch.*

"I hear some of the others are on missions to Mineraltown?" asked Briaana. "You' hear anything about that?"

"No," replied Omaara. "They don't tell us those things."

She pulled her brother to the side as the others continued their conversation. The thought of him being placed in any harm's way made her heart flutter.

At least he's alive., thank Mother.

"What are you doing tonight? I have some free time. Let's go to the night market," said Daaria. "I'll buy you whatever you want."

"He can't," said Briaana, quickly disengaging from the others and taking him by the arm. "We have to go," she said. "Now."

"Go where?" asked Daaria, trailing her before she was cut off by August.

"None of your business," she replied.

Raamina IV

"Lower your hand," ordered Untara, speaking to a man who refused to allow her party to continue out of protest. "And step aside before I take it."

"Not until she answers for her crimes!" shouted a young woman who, at first glance, appeared different from the others with her well to do clothes and little round face.

An upper class girl.

Maybe even a lordling's daughter.

Or a rich whore's-

Someone ought to make an example out of her

"False priestess!" added four others. "False Mothers! False teachers in our temple!"

"False priestess! False Mothers! False teachers in our temple!"

"False priestess! False Mother—"

"Shut the fuck up," shouted Dolarin Weight, a Zacadin man of sixty-two, who along with a few others, was responsible for safeguarding her family.

Even at his age he was still a frighteningly large man. Though not quite as tall as Virginia who stood just under two metres, he must have weighed twice as much.

He still hasn't lost an ounce of muscle after all these years. How?

"And get the fuck out of the way before I send you back home in pieces," said Dolarin, with arms shaking under the weight of temptation.

His grievance, however, did little to quell the protesters, and if anything, only awakened their resolve.

"False priestess! False Mothers! False teachers in our temple!"

"False priestess! False Mothers! False teachers in our temple!"

A crowd of some fifty or so Rocklanders had gathered around her party, and they watched on, with silent cowardice, as the group of some thirty delinquents continued to publicly berate their sovereign-Mother.

So not a single one of them are going to strike on my behalf?

Well, maybe that's a good thing, for now at least. It would have to change, however.

An army can only do so much without starting a revolution

"We're not leaving until *she* answers for her family's crimes!" shouted the first man with a curled up newspaper pointed toward her.

It was then Untara took her short-glaive and swung it with such grace that she was awestruck by her ability as a soldier, not even concerning herself with where the blade went.

"Oh my God!" cried the man, "My hand!"

"You cut off my fucking hand!" he screamed as blood fell, "Why?!" he pleaded.

"She told she would" said Dolarin Weight, "And I told you you'd be going home in pieces-"

"Enough!" finally said Virgina Calendar, removing an auto-pistol from the side of his hip, and firing two shots into the air.

A further panic broke out amongst the bystanders, while a nearby guard of her family's sentinel took the opportunity to chase and capture the protesters.

She didn't see much as they carried the man and as many dissenters as they could off into a dark alley, but she did hear more screaming and pleading.

I wonder which crimes they were talking about.

"Untara," called Virginia from the back of the party as they pressed forward.

"Sorry, Lieutenant!" said Untara, wonderfully sheathing her glaive and turning to him with a hand placed on her metal breastplate.

She was a beautiful thing, with hair as pink and pleating as the roses in the Palace Gardens, and with eyes as green and resilient as the stones used to build her favourite mansion.

"I should've waited for an order."

"It's fine, you had cause" replied Virginia, dropping his concern for the situation.

It was only a short walk between the Baltiar Palace and the Zaaj Temple, perhaps no more than ten minutes, but it didn't take long for their path to be obstructed once more. This time by an even larger crowd spilling into the streets from the neighbouring apartments and townhouses.

Her heart leapt at the sight of them, but it quickly settled in its place when the cheers erupted.

"What are they cheering for?" asked Quill, another beautiful emerald-eyed creature.

He was a boy of sixteen, who also happened to be one of the youngest soldiers entrusted to protect her life.

An honour which rightfully belonged to him as well.

By the age of ten he had already established himself as an expert crossbowman, beating out some of the most veteran archers in the Interior Army in several competitions, and by fourteen he was proclaimed the greatest rifleman to have never fought a war. A title handed to him without a drop of irony.

"The protesters," replied Isaarith. "They're cheering for what happened to the protesters."

"I hope they get torn to shreds in the streets," she continued, under her breath.

Several hundred, *or maybe a thousand,* had gathered in the streets leading to the temple and many others were proceeding to the gates where the bodies were likely still trickling in, but still there were those who stood for her. Watching her as she passed, with cheers, tears, and whimpers..

Braxas can't arrest me. I did what I had to, for the future of my family. For the future of Rockland-

Hold on… No. What am I saying? I did nothing. I had no part to play in this, I'll just say it was all Vanfall's idea-.

Wait, no. If I knew he was planning this, then I'm at fault for not saying or doing anything about it. I have to be careful. I can't know anything I shouldn't. Or accuse anyone who only I would know is guilty.

Earlier she had dismissed Lieutenant Virginia when he mentioned the idea of Braxas violating their sovereignty for her arrest, and like the hair lice which nearly ruined her childhood, the thought continued to itch her head.

What if he does make the order? No. He wouldn't dare.

She instinctively placed a hand over her heart to soothe the fluttering, only to realise a moment later that it was inadvertently the correct thing to do in the presence of countless grieving Innerlanders who took it for a salute.

Would he?

"Both my sons are dead!" cried a woman, bursting from the audience and approaching the party.

She had gotten too close, however, and it forced Untara to act with her shield.

"Stand back!" shouted Untara, shoving the woman.

"They'll be in my thoughts and prayers," replied Mother Raamina, extending a hand out from a small gap between her guards and petting the frail Tautau woman on her head.

"And cry not, mother," said Mother Raamina. "You will meet your children again. First at the temple, and then someday back at Home in bed."

She continued to cry, however, as the party carried on without her.

"Stay close, Mother," said Virginia, "This is going to take longer than usual."

"Yes," replied Mother Raamina.

As they neared their destination, the Highland air had noticeably thickened, and a community distinguished for its industrious working folk, was found idling the streets.

Field workers who ensured the Landlords earned their share of the harvest, had carried with them their shovels and ploughs as they joined the masses.

Butchers and smiths who laboured every day to deliver useful commodities to the markets, were now unconcerned with the passing of time and its losses.

Even the slave-families imported to hand-pollinate the orchards and gardens with the extinction of the Highland bee, had now forgotten their stations like some civil defectors and artists.

I should've taken the lower roads, this is going to take all day.

It was clear from the way the Ancients had planned the community now known as Rockland, that only those responsible for building the structures were permitted to imagine its design. The roads were standardised and had once been separated from the sidewalks with impermeable steel grates. The parks were void of trees and assembled together with flowerless fields of coloured concrete, while the living quarters were kept far apart from the factories and foundries, and appeared to be segregated with some kind of class structure in mind. What that structure may have been, however, was long lost to time.

It was as if each space had been built to serve its designated purpose, and nothing more. Or at least that was how it was before the Old Acadians were forced to retreat into the City and settle.

Like a scattered colony of ants in search of shelter, their ancestors had crawled into every Ancient corner and crevice in an effort to evade the Westerian Army, and much like a restless house cat, they made it their home without much thought or care for those sharing or inheriting the space.

Grand libraries were made into granaries, great factories were replaced with ranches, open streams became open sewers, and apartments became indistinguishable from slaughterhouses and unsanitary hospitals. Even whole stadiums and arenas were infilled with unplanned houses and high rises until they transformed into well-fortified strongholds as the centuries marched on. There was also once enough space in the streets for trucks and other large vehicles, but now the roads unreliably narrowed and widened as a result of shifts in the reutilised land. Such near-sightedness not only permanently deformed and scarred the built-space, but also resulted in the eventual stagnation of their development.

Their early ancestors, the Gran Acadians, upon their arrival to Rodina, had discovered a lost civilization more advanced than their own. In the pursuit of survival, however, their successors the Old Acadians had torn it to the ground to make it their own. Technologies, constructs, and facilities which may have not been useful during the Lost Years, were now regarded as priceless instruments and artefacts, with wars still being fought over what little remained.

But I suppose it's likely they wouldn't have survived had they not melted down the Ancient world to construct walls.

The Old Acadians were nearsighted, but it necessary, and I suppose without them there wouldn't be us-

"It won't be much longer, Mother," said Untara. "I can see the temple."

"Walk faster, boy!" screeched Lady Isaarith, slapping her slave across the back of his head. "Before I hand you over to some madame"

She needed some discipline herself.

"Isaarith, stop screaming please," said Mother Raamina. "I'll have Virginia poke your eardrums in if it means you'll shut up."

I think my ears are bleeding.

"Sorry, Mother," she apologised.

"You also know it's not *his* fault there's a crowd ahead"

It was uncertain for several centuries just how much time had actually passed since the fall of Old Acadia and when her descendants emerged from their walled sanctuaries, after the Lost Years. Yet it was here, behind the confines of a makeshift wall made of melted engines, vehicles, and instruments, where the largest Old Acadian refugee and military settlement persisted. Encircled by an outer walled crescent of repurposed steel and concrete, and a rocky cliffside which marked the end of the Highland to the east, was now the Interior of Rockland, a bustling community within a community, which together in its own right, was a well-established empire within the City of Queens.

The birthplace of New Acadia, and even the time after-

"Step back, boy!" shouted Dolarin Weight.

"No! I have to talk to Mother!" shouted back a boy from not too far away.

She turned to find one of her plainclothes guards pressing him back against the crowd, and when he refused, he too was struck against the head.

That voice sounds familiar…Wait! I think I know it!

She turned to find her suspicion correct.

"Stand down!" ordered Mother Raamina, from a short distance. "He's my servant."

The guard placed the boy down.

"Callum, what is it?" she asked, signalling him to walk over.

But he stood his ground.

"Mother! This way!" he called out, his voice cutting through the chaotic crowd behind him. "Hurry!" he urged, leading the way into a narrow alley. "There's no time!"

"It's about your uncle, L-Lord Hariya!"

M-My uncle?!

Without giving it much thought, she removed herself from the party and followed him recklessly into the backstreets.

Wilona V

The moonlights fell through the passing sea of clouds, brightening the world an ominous glow, before settling over the dreary streets of the Citadel. She wasn't sure exactly when, but at some point a storm had come and gone. By the time she thought to place the hood of her raincoat over her hair, however, she was already drenched

I forgot how good this felt-

Almost like a dream, but I'm wide awake.

She took the elixir bottle to her lips once more, hoping to add more witchleaf into her veins, but this time she found it empty.

She sighed frustrated, "How long have I been up here? "I should be in bed soon"

It was unwise to stay up this late or be as inebriated as she was, especially considering the events of the day. A good night's rest was important if one hoped to complete their chores, or compete in the day-to-day antagonisms of human interactions. Being half asleep while others were awake, more often than not, led to falling behind one's duties and others in the world, and as the Colonel of the Peaceland Generalist Force, she was directly responsible for managing the entire southern half of the Citadel. This included no less than twelve thousand active duty soldiers, and some three hundred thousand residents spread across an area of sixty kilometres. A deeply political affair as much as it was a martial and bureaucratic one.

Though, it wasn't as if she's going to actually get any sleep, not tonight at least. The thought of a possible betrayal from within their ranks, and what it could mean for the Liberation Army as a whole was enough to drive any soldier to the sanatorium with anxiety.

Armed soldiers in Mineraltown and it could be a rebellion.

If we're right, we need to re-evaluate every officer before they could be trusted with orders, every soldier before they could be trusted with arms.

But where do we even start? And who does the work?

As the witchleaf took its grip, her sense of balance and focus became increasingly elusive and the worries which had plagued her now seemed distant and insignificant. The colours emanating from the starry night-sky also began to sharpen with each passing minute, granting her the ability to gaze into space without a concern for her place in the vast universe.

Derived from the precious sap and oils of a rare species of thornbush, witchleaf was often regarded as a botanical treasure. Found only in the most remote and inaccessible regions of the Forest Gorge, it was a widely shared tradition to share a drink during the making of peace and forging of harmony. High-officers also secretly consumed the drug to reduce anxiety in the war room, and in higher doses, it was also considered a powerful pain reliever and aphrodisiac. A side-effect which she figured would, unfortunately, only be going to waste.

If we're right, and it is a rebellion, what reason could they have?

Is there even a reason one can have?

Well, I mean... to be honest, maybe.

When the Liberation Army crossed the Great Gorge into this land in the Year 12 After New Acadia, they had arrived with the intention of conquering it from the various communities refusing to join their Cause. Well-experienced from their ventures under the Landlords of New Acadia, they had made it a duty of theirs to reunite every patch of dirt across the war-torn land to those who saw themselves as its true stewards.

Before the start of what would be their most prized campaign, the legendary Liberation General Hadrial Baltiar had made a sincere promise to all the feral states occupying the Lowlands of the north-easternmost corners of Middle Acadia. The Liberation Army will include all those who surrendered to the inevitable new country, and oppress those who resisted it for countless generations. This proposal, however, did more to unify the warring communities of Peaceland than it did to incite fear. The Lowland ruler Daaramon the Drunk, most known for his feats in alcohol consumption and tribal warfare, had even famously sent back a portrait of his genitals after reading the terms set forth by the great general. A mistake which successive generations of Lowlanders continued to pay for.

One by one, and unnamed massacre after unnamed massacre, each of the regions were consolidated. Communities which had survived the Westerians, now fell to the Liberation Army who sought out the reunification of the country, as well as living space for themselves. Communities which had formed out of desperation and isolation after the

Lost Years were now vanquished before their roots could settle into the land like an iifa tree.

The few who managed to successfully resist were reluctantly awarded with independence, but where conquest failed, coercion and control would not. Long after the wars were fought and the storms were settled, the Army continued their relentless pursuit of dispossession. The destabilisation of markets, the seizure of natural resource rights, and the overthrowing of dissenting leaders for agreeable ones, were just a few of the ways the remaining independent states were weakened, overtaken, and assimilated, until eventually only the Firstlanders were left. The Landlord Campaigns were over, but its imperial legacy continued on.

Even if Mineraltown had a reason, it wasn't any more than any other community.

But maybe that's the problem. Maybe we failed to share what little remained of Middle Acadia.

She drew her eyes from the land below to the space above, where they remained for some time a captive to the stars. Dwelling beyond any imaginable distance was a dense ocean of clustered stardust - gold and green, purple and orange and blue, spread across the undefined void of space itself. Yearning to be explored, or at the very least, understood.

There might be more stars than there was ever time to count.

Closer to home, she found the servants of the goddess Wilona quietly observing the world - the claymoon Amestris suspended with her rings of captured rock and rubble, and the seamoon Maaria with her perpetual storms. She also searched for the mythical lux belonging to the small moon they called the *Whitestar*, but it was absent tonight as it often is.

That poor little girl...

What was her name again? Rupi? Rupa? I can't remember.

She had initially reminded her of the kind of daughter she always wanted, but now she could only think of herself when her little face came to mind.

Another orphan, another Tautau.

In Peaceland, each region was responsible for housing its own orphans, and each orphanage was responsible for bestowing an orphan-name for its generation of lost children. In Mineraltown's orphanage, she along with the other children of her time, were given the last name *Flowers* to wear.

There were many with orphan-names running around, names which were still a hot iron stamp on the skins of those who wore them without any class or privilege. They were rarely told much about their origins as well, including what caused them to be displaced and left without parents in the first place. From the little information she managed to gather of the years, however, she was able to infer she was born to a family likely living Downtown or Midtown Queens, just around the First Military Police Invasion. This suspicion, however, did more to raise her curiosity and fuel her imagination than it did to quell her frustrations.

She often wondered about the relationship which led to her birth. Who were her parents and how did they meet? Were they in love? And did they have any other children? For as long as she could remember she had searched the world for boys and girls, women and men, who shared the same or similar features. A skin tone as dark as rockwood, paired with ears and eyes which could have belonged to a cat.

Though, like most true-born and war-torn orphans spread throughout Acadia, she was born a brown-eyed Tautau, and such facial features were not uncommon among such Acadians. There were many orphaned Daaradins as well, and it was never quite certain where any of them came from. Countless battles were being fought in every corner of the country and continent, and many were too young to remember if they even had a family.

If anyone of them could've been a lost brother or sister, then they were all her siblings as far as she was concerned.

My brothers and sisters, I haven't forgotten you. I just can't remember where they buried you.

She had grown up in an orphanage in Mineraltown, huddled with the other forgotten children under itchy bed sheets rarely washed and sheet-metal roofs which rang like steel pan drums whenever the rain knocked. She wasn't the brightest, but stood out enough to make it to where she was, wasn't the prettiest, but found a boy who loved her enough to make her believe she was. He ended up a medic and they ended up *married*.

When she closed her eyes, she could still see some of the faces of the other children who she had regarded as siblings.

There was Vallan, who never took a bath, the twins, Tayl and Vivi, who fought over the same boy.

Apollo, who was that boy,

Daaron, who took everything too seriously, and Atlus, the class clown.

Even on her deathbed, succumbing to the illness which would have claimed her memories before stealing her life, she still wouldn't forget the time Atlus in kindergarten had asked their priest-teacher if Mother Maaria had been the First Mother mentioned within the holy books. It was funny because it was a serious question, and unforgettable because of their teacher's response.

"Atlus, I wouldn't be surprised if your parents aren't actually dead and just left you here instead."

What a terrible thing to say to a child, she giggled, just like the little school girl she was back then.

I think that was the first day I ever smiled. The first day I ever laughed. "But gone are the days," she sighed aloud to herself

And with it Mother Maaria. The only mother I ever knew. A beautiful woman. A woman who put duty above her health. A woman who never cared for the differences between others. Something I can't say for many people.

She had spent the majority of her life supporting the poverty stricken and defending the orphaned. Arguing that such children were not any one person's sole duty to house or feed, but rather everyone's shared responsibility as members of a civil society.

"And now she's dangling somewhere with a snapped neck."

Well, If the petrels didn't already tear her head off.

"Colonel!" called out a soldier from somewhere atop the rooftop.

"Yes?" she answered, turning around.

But no one was there.

A G-Ghost?

"Colonel?" cried the demonic spectre once more, "Are you there?"

It took her longer than it should have to realise the voice was communicating to her through the hand radio attached to her hip.

"Um… yes," she said, taking it and answering with a press of a button." What is it, Anna?"

"I-It's Amilia," corrected the soldier, "And your husband is here to see you."

"What?" said the colonel. "My husband? Are you sure?"

"Y-Yes, Colonel," she answered. "From what I understand, at least."

Did he just get off work? What time is it?

She checked the mechanical watch on her wrist. It was working just fine, but for some reason she had forgotten how to read again.

Oh no. I think the sickness is taking me-

"Colonel? Are you there?"

"Oh... huh, what?" she asked, again losing her train of thought.

"I asked if I should send him away?" asked Anna.

"Who?"

"Your husband," she replied, confused and slightly annoyed.

"Oh, right, yes," said the colonel. "No, I mean no, let him in."

I have a husband...What a nice surprise.

A brief moment later, a tall, dark, and handsome man entered through the door leading into the rooftop. He had a head full of short curly black hair, a hand-chiselled jaw still well defined in the night, and a thick beard which appeared *rugged* under the moonlight.

Alright, play it cool, Wilona. And don't be so easy.

With him he carried what appeared to be food and *flowers?*

She melted.

"Hey," he said, making his way towards her.

"Apollo," she said, finding his embrace.

They didn't talk much these days, just hugged, but that was enough.

"What's wrong, dove?" he asked, taking her hand and placing his fingers in between her hers.

It stopped the pain in her heart, but the trembling travelled to her knees.

"Everything," she said, looking up at him, still feeling like the luckiest girl in Rodina.

He was always doing sweet things for her, even when she didn't deserve it. Today he had even brought her flowers and hadn't forgotten irises were her favourite.

"I love you," he replied, hugging her tighter.

She placed her head on his chest and he took his lips to hers. His kiss was as gentle as the breeze in spring on a warm spell, and his breath smelled like the clouds when the mist fell.

It's too late to go to sleep, might as well stay up the night.

Valtus III

He was on his final lap before he realised the others in the race were not catching up to him anytime soon.

"H-How the f-fuck…" said Jupitar, meeting him at the finish line, after maybe two or three seconds later.

Tarcus and Varna followed shortly, and behind them came the rest.

"Damn, you ran like a Motherfucker, boy," said Barya, a Citadel boy of average height and near average build, had it not been for his large hands and longer than usual limbs.

"H-How d-did you beat me at long sprint?" continued Tarcus, fighting to catch his breath with a light jog. "You on some shit?"

"Of course he is," replied Casimir, another young Citadeler.

He was also of average height, but possessed a well-defined muscular frame well-beyond his years.

"Last week he fell off and now he's up on everyone," said Jupitar.

"Yeah that's a pretty good point," said Varna, "He's always with Lamby too."

He dismissed their claims with a laugh. "Shut up Varna, you don't know what you're talking about."

In the Playgrounds were where the soldiers of South Station gathered in their track shorts and cut off shirts. Testing and pushing their limits in activities they may never get a chance to use, even within the sweltering heat of battle.

"Nah his eyes' been clear," said Laith, a green-eyed Midlander.

"You can still drink sprey," suggested Jupitar.

"Bro', who the fuck drinks sprey?" laughed Laith, "You trippin… Hold on, why are you so mad about this?"

"Because it's cheating," answered Jupitar. "And that's unfair to the rest of us."

"Jupitar, don't act like you're not on some shit," he answered. "None of us talk about it, but everybody knows."

Jupitar didn't reply.

"Thanks Laith" said Valtus, "It feels great to have somebody stick up for you around here for once"

"It's always a rat race with you guys"

It was always a bit of a mystery as to why or how Laith ended up a Generalist. Though not from a particularly wealthy family by their own standards, as a natural born Midlander it was reasonable to assume they were well-educated and doing relatively well compared to the vast majority of Peacelanders. He was also a smart kid, and had the self-awareness to challenge the world's perceptions and misconceptions.

As Generalists, most of the energy afforded to them in the way of food and rest went towards their training, and if they were lucky, part-time work contracts with the Army. In addition to their rifle training, they practised swimming, hand to hand combat, weight-lifting, Acadian-wrestling, and navigating spaces made to resemble Ancient City alleys. Each day they were not preparing for war, however, the boys and girls of South Station contended for high-standing amongst their peers, within competitions they had constructed for themselves. A top twenty finish was considered the threshold for bragging rights while top forty was respectable.

Two weeks ago he had placed third overall in the long sprint before dropping out of the ladder entirely. Today, however, he finished first, and by a considerable margin as well.

Still not good enough to make captain though.

No matter how hard I try, it's never enough.

He had something to prove, if not to the officers, then at least to himself. The attention didn't feel too bad either, even the serious attempts to diminish his achievements. It only meant they were recognized and *real*.

In Eastern Stronghold, he was top of his class in the physical, but here things were different. Though they certainly possessed their share of runts, addicts, and out of shapes, the difference amongst those striving for a lead was much narrower. Some were made for the competition, excelling in nearly all of the physically demanding courses and exercises, while others, like Laith, Barya, and Varna, were never the best in any one area, but were good enough to challenge those who were. It was how they earned their respect amongst the boys.

"I guess if he was on some shit he wouldn't be sixtieth for bench press," said Varna, jumping into the pile of Army-issued training bags they had left in the field.

As the youngest boy in an Honoured family of three daughters and four sons, Varna too wasn't raised to meet the expectations his society held quietly over him. Not quite treated as a potential heir by a business-minded father, and too adored by an overbearing mother to learn anything useful, he gradually slipped through the cracks as the years passed.

Him, I feel sorry for.

"Or ninetieth at squat," added Barya, taking off his running shoes and socks before tossing them into the pile.

They all shared a laugh at his expense.

"It's those Lowlander legs," said Varna. "Can't keep up with them, can't win a war with them,"

"For real," agreed Barya.

"Y'all stupid as hell," said Tarcus, a Summer Circler himself. "Lowlanders have won plenty of wars."

"Yeah?" said Barya, "Name one."

"The War of Crying Men," said Tarcus, proudly. "In the Year 6 After New Acadia."

"The war of what?!" said Varna, nearly bursting into tears, but of laughter.

"You just made some shit up, boy'," said Barya, bringing him in for a playful headlock.

"No I didn't," said Tarcus, shoving him away. "And fuck off!"

"That was a great war"

Every Lowland student had at some point dreamt of one day reaching the Citadel to represent their village as a soldier in the national Specialist Force. The only opportunity presented to the vast majority of them, however, was the Generalist, a place for failures, but a rat race in its own right. Due to the shortage of teachers and school supplies, only those who showed promise early were invested in, while the rest were left to work and compete with their bodies. All under the hopes of one day being selected over their peers by Army scouts who scrutinised their every effort. Among the most well-trained soldiers in Eastern and Northern Stronghold, only the best were permitted into the Citadel, and even then it was hard to believe this was their best.

They laugh at us, and we can't even prove them wrong.

Though I did put them in their place today at least.

Though the Lowlanders were known to perform well in many games, it was true strength in particular was not their specialty. A common trait which puzzled him for many years as they were genetically *just as Acadian* and most of the food produced in Peaceland were grown and raised in the Lowlands.

The Lowlanders grew most of the food, but still there was somehow never enough to eat at home.

The Highlanders just claim everything they can with their few victories over us.

Being underfed did well to prepare them for a life of being overtrained, but it led to their further exclusion from certain traditions, particularly the toughest competition on the Playground, tug of war. A sport now reserved for the Citadelers, Midlanders, and Firstlanders to struggle over.

"Varna, you laugh a lot for a kid who never made top ten in any lift or sport," said Tarcus.

"Tarcus, you talk a lot for a little ass boy," said Varna, "You only ever finished top twenty in anything 'cause those Firstlander boys stick to their own."

He took a moment to wonder if there was any truth to Varna's words, but didn't dwell on it for too long.

"Yeah," agreed Tarcus, albeit reluctantly. "That's true."

"But what does that say about you?"

Varna went quiet while the rest of them tried to contain their laughter.

"That's true Varna" laughed Laith, "He got you there"

Varna was on to something though,

If the Firstlanders weren't so weird about not being friends with us, most of us wouldn't have a name on any list.

He joined the others as they turned their attention towards the corner the Firstlanders had carved up for themselves. There were *odd*, and often unspoken, customs established within the different spaces spread throughout the entire station, and those who realised this early on were amongst the most well off.

In the cafeterias, they were made to keep to their own kind, only crossing tables and aisles to trade lunches and make deals. In the dormitories, disputes were handled with open fists to avoid unwarranted trips to the Army's emergency room, and when it came to the Playgrounds, soldiers continued to antagonise one another through competition. Yet they also found some sense of comradery within it. Leading many from different groups and identities to come together when they otherwise would have never considered it.

Well, all except the Firstlanders.

They still kept to themselves.

They watched on as two Firstlander boys attempted to obstruct a third from completing his set on the bench press. There were a hundred kilograms worth of plates attached to the barbell, and likely over three hundred kilograms in total after including the weight of the two pressing down on it.

This didn't stop him from completing an entire set of eight repetitions, however. He even laughed it off.

"Goddamn," said Tarcus and Varna, in disbelief.

"What the fuck?," added Laith and Barya.

"Yeah, they sprey," said Valtus.

If these guys are the dropouts, I can't imagine the real Firstland Army.

Sprey was a drug originally manufactured by the Military Police to be administered to Police-soldiers who were arriving to, or returning from battle. It was primarily used as a medicine to help cope with anxiety and recurring nightmares, but strength, mental clarity, sight, and stamina all improved as a side effect. These useful traits, however, came at a cost. It was a highly addictive drug which made its use a massive risk, and there were many otherwise star students and athletes who, only after a few sprays, mistook the high as their true life's purpose.

Most of the sprey the dealers bought and sold in the Generalist Force were smuggled in through the Firstlanders. They were some of the biggest users of it as well, and the way it redden the whites of their Zacadin eyes left many looking like *demons.*

"Good thing they only want to play tug of war," said Laith. "We'd get no girls if they tried us in our dorms."

"We don't get girls anyways," said Tarcus.

"Yeah, but at least *they* don't have anything to do with that," said Laith.

Other than maybe Laith on a good day, no one seemed to enjoy being stuck in the Generalists as it was clear what it meant. Being held back from the rest of society while still being expected to die in the frontlines for it.

Yet, even when the others found something to gather and socialise around, the Firstlanders still preferred to be isolated in their corner.

They don't mess with us, we don't mess with them. Fair, I guess.

"Valtus," called Barya, "'Sarge said we got some free time cause the lights went out again. We gonna' go shoot some crossbows, you in?

"Fucking South Station" said Valtus.

"Nah I'm good,"

"Go without me."

He retrieved his belongings from the pile of smelly bags, and carried them to the top of a nearby set of cascading raised steps believed to have been the ruins of an Ancient outdoor auditorium. It was there he took a seat, nursing his bruised ego and resting his sore feet.

There wasn't much to spectate from the top row when the Army wasn't hosting tournaments between the regiments, or when the soldiers weren't running their own games, but the view was still pleasant.

Especially on such a warm windy day.

From atop the steps, he could see the women's side of the field, separated by Ancient-steel grates which more or less split the Playground in half. Their training regiments were about the same, but the number of repetitions needed to complete their courses were cut down by a third. They were, however, held to an unspoken and unofficial standard. One which expected them to match the boys at every turn.

Back on their side, he found the flag of Old Acadia fluttering at half-mast, as it often were, and a few of the boy captains peeking through the grates, as they so often did. Though to be fair, some of the girls were peeking back.

What's so special about them anyways? How come they made it and not me? They can't be that much better.

Can they?

Though there were only two positions available and something over two hundred soldiers taking the Reclassification Test, he felt he did well and was quite confident in his chances. He had even managed to outperform most of the star athletes in the physical. It was just the writing section he had trouble with.

I just can't get it right, even though I practised every day. What's wrong with me?

Why am I not okay?

He still wanted to climb the ranks, but he had already failed twice prior and now he only had one last chance to prove himself before being blacklisted from re-examination entirely.

I'm not that outmatched... Am I?

"Good work, soldier," said a man approaching from the steps below.

He looked up to find Sergeant-Captain Granite.

"T-Thank you, Sergeant-Captain!" said Valtus, standing and raising a hand to his heart.

"But um... For what?"

"I heard you did well on the test," replied the sergeant, padding him on the back with a bear claw for a hand.

It nearly knocked the wind out of him and hurt tremendously.

"Just a little more, keep pushing."

Sergeant-Captain Granite was as honest and kind as sergeants in the Army were permitted to be. He had always believed in him even when he had given up on himself.

"Thank you, Sergeant," said Valtus. "I'll try my b—"

A sudden explosion rocked their eardrums, and it would've knocked the sergeant off the bleachers if he hadn't caught him.

"What the fuck was that!" said the sergeant, eventually finding his balance.

"I-I don't know," replied Valtus.

The sirens soon followed.

Hiran V

"Your fathers' big, like me," said Arther Guildmen, sliding a glass of starmilk over the counter. "But you ain't grown in years."

"Huh?" said Hiran, with a mouthful of buttered bread and slices of some cured meat. "How'd you know?"

"I saw him once," answered the old man, "General Harlan Baltiar, the living legend" he said with some added poise.

"He was leading a force through the overworld at the time and I was tagging along with my caravan, in the back with the other merchants,"

"You never told me that," he said, quickly washing down the light meal with the milk, but still finding a way to savour it.

"This was way before you were born, back when Newtown was still Ancient," said Arther Guildmen. "And I was still a travelling man, trying to survive anyway I can."

"Did you ever talk to him?" asked Hiran.

"No," he replied, quietly.

The Guildmens were an old Westerian family belonging to a merchant class in Acadian territory. Like Zacadins, the Westerians also possessed red eyes which they found more acceptable and appealing relative to other Acadian groups. Unlike most Westerians, however, the Guildmens found a lucrative trade in dealing with Acadians rather than seizing their land and treating them like subhuman others.

"They wouldn't let a man like me near the general," chuckled the old merchant.

Though he managed to retain his broadness and the strength of an ox which came with it, it was clear that time was quickly catching up to Arther Guildmen. His voice grew coarser by the week, he was tired more often, and his once silky black hair had greyed significantly over the passing winter.

He wondered if something similar was happening to his father, who was around the same age. They used to write to one another often, but it's been several months since his last letter or transmission, and many years since his last visit.

Dad.

His father was partly responsible for him working as a courier for the Liberation, tugging him closer towards the Army while his Mother pushed him towards ruling for the family. He didn't want either, however, and joining a guild or the Zaaj Temple was out of the question for his father, a war hero.

"Those are not the duties of a soldier!" he so often proclaimed in his letters. *"He has a cause to inherit!"*

It was this disagreement between his parents which led him here, under the suggestion of his uncle Braxas who argued it was best to find a middle ground. He was not offered a say in the matter himself, but was pleasantly surprised when he learned he would be making deliveries between the many trading posts the Army owned or at least had a stake in.

In Rodina, there were several races to gather whatever useful remained of the world, with Ancient gizmos and artefacts being the most sought after. His uncle had argued the Army needed stronger links between their markets and the Newtown underground, which was enough for his parents to accept. It wasn't soldiership, but the role required a loyal actor. It wasn't at home in the Inner Ring, but at least he was in Queens and still in reach. It was a compromise to keep both parties content, but it left neither truly satisfied.

Maybe it's better that way. I was going to do this anyway.

He carried his plate off to the side the moment he noticed a line of customers forming behind him, and continued to make space as others entered the General Store. Many wandered in search of their gods before even considering searching for their desired goods, while others simply left the moment they finished worshipping their shrines.

It was good practice for travellers and foreigners to only enter cities and spaces where they could find their gods at rest. For a business like the General Store, this meant housing as many idols together as possible.

A foreign-looking woman stood chanting a prayer before a thunderbird made of maglith, while another woman searched the entire store for her god before giving up, yet still settling on some starmilk. In the southeastern most corner, a group of Astormi stood silently before a painting of a young Ancient king surrounded by a scorched forest, and to the opposite end, several Daaradins had gathered before a shrine similar to his own faith, but without a child cradled in the Mother's arms and a tree with a crown full of leaves instead.

He approached the painting after the group of Astormi left. The Acadians called him Zaaj, the Ancient King, and his eyes always followed, judging both beast and men, and cursing all those who idled under his breath. He was the principal reason for the shift from the Old to the New Faith, and sometimes he appeared as an old disarranged man, with a beard as grey as cement and a face as hollow and brittle as the trees native to the Highland. Here he was portrayed as a young man, with golden hair like a stallion's mane.

"Hiran!" said Guildmen, handing change to an Ostorian woman who wore an elaborate turban, something resembling a bee's nest, over her head.

"Why' you still here?"

"I-I don't know how to get there," said Hiran, a little distracted by the sound of patrons entering through the backdoor, and the sound of footsteps heading down into the saloon below.

"Oh," replied Arther Guildmen, scratching the ridges on his forehead. "Go through Newtown and cross the Queensbridge," said the old merchant, "After you do that, keep walking north until you reach…" continued Arther Guildmen, jotting down the remaining directions on a piece of paper and handing it to him.

"Cool," said Hiran, taking the note and carrying his bicycle out the front door.

Talius VI

When the Military Police first invaded Queens through the southern city of Astor, little was spared of the Liberated communities occupying its Downtown District.

Though the Police-soldiers were few in comparison and largely not accustomed to the Highland altitude, their forces still managed to overtake the southern gates using the gift of Westerian technology. City block after city block was lost to armoured land vehicles and wall piercing auto-rifles, and as valiant as their efforts may have been, the Liberated frontlines fell without a major victory.

Thousands lost their lives as a result of the conflict, and tens of thousands more were captured and enslaved in labour camps. Instead of mass graves, the dead were incinerated and left for the vultures, and instead of cherishing the land as the blessing it was, its Holysites and complexes were pillaged and put to dynamite.

It was a relatively short but brutal war, and like nearly all wars, the resulting damage to the world could never truly be repaired.

"We're not quite sure what we found," said Colonel Hellin, distributing the contents of an orange envelope he had removed from his desk. "But we do know it's a lead."

The room tightened as a collection of photos made their rounds, with confusion and speculation following closely behind.

"Huh?" said Toshi Hara.

"What is that?" asked Jovaana.

"It's a wall" said Wiluss, "Or actually- No! It's a door!"

"Okay" said Jovaana, "But what's on it?"

"We think it's a bird," said the colonel, "Or at least, I think it's a bird."

"It's not a bird—" replied the commander, before being cut off.

"A flightless bird" continued the colonel, "Maybe a chicken"

"I don't know," said Wiluss. "It looks like one of those great giant dodos to me,"

"It's a terrorbird" said Professor Lind, taking a hold of several pictures and placing them under her eye as she would a microscope. "One called the elephant bird"

"Or it *was*"

"Wait..." she said, turning toward him with such fury that he had almost forgotten he was in charge. "Don't tell me you tried to force it open."

"N-No," said the commander. "The excavators found it that way."

"Couldn't it have just been the elements?" asked Olisa August. "I mean, it's been buried for, like, thousands of years."

"It could have," answered the professor, skimming through the different photos of the wall.

"I'd have to get closer to it to say for sure, but that looks like someone tried breaking their way in".

"The Ancients have tried to break into these cities before," said Wiluss. "Maybe they did it?"

"No, it looks like there was an explosion" retorted the professor.

"That's a real shame" added Colonel Hellin, "We were hoping to study it later"

"There's still so much left to learn"

The Commander stepped forward into the room,

"So a part of your mission is to go examine the door and find a way in without further damaging it"

"I expect to be paid for this" said Professor Lind, with some noticeable disdain in her voice.

As costly as the First Military Police Invasion was in terms of lives and buildings lost, it was the resulting political instability that truly threatened the Liberation Army.

Countless Acadians were displaced throughout the war with many, flooding the streets in search of communities willing to take them in. Most were turned away by societies who sought to remain isolated, under the assumption it was necessary for their own preservation, but a few did open their doors.

Rockland was the first to accept the waves of refugees crashing at their gates, with much of Liberated Easton and Westown following closely behind. These communities were quickly overwhelmed, however, and as the days passed, internal disputes between Landlords and Army officials, common-folk and asylum-seekers, arose and escalated. Soon their doors would be closed as well, and with nowhere else to go other than off the Highland cliff and into the Ruined Sea, the left-outs were driven underground to escape the violence.

Much of the story from there on remains unclear even to this day, but the most reputed sources claimed the survivors gathered in the Ancient subway tunnels, before being forced to dig when the Hellraisers came.

For days, men, women, children, and elders too, clawed away at the soil, rock and concrete. Some with their bare hands, others with simple tools, and all compelled by the echoes of approaching flamethrowers and the stench of scorched flesh and earth.

"So if the seal is unbroken, does that mean we're the first ones down there?" asked Briaana Cryheart, collecting all the photos and handing them back to the colonel with an unimpressed look on her face.

I smile more than she does, is she always like this?

"I hope so…" said Wiluss.

"Hold on," said Professor Lind. "If we are, then doesn't that mean there's a good chance of…"

"Yes," said Colonel Hellin. "And we've prepared for that"

"Translated recordings to help with communication, photos of the outside world to calm any suspicion, and full body suits to avoid physical contact."

Th-that's right-

His people-

"There's also gift bags in the supply truck," continued the colonel.

"Sorry to interrupt," said Toshi, raising a hand and placing the other by his heart. "But make contact with who?"

The room fell silent.

As convincing as their campaign seemed early on, the Military Police were eventually driven off the Highland by a coalition of Liberation forces led by the then Colonel Harlan Baltiar. This failure came as a surprise to the Police-generals who later unconvincingly blamed it on the disparity between the number of soldiers.

But that's not why they lost the war, they know it too.

Though the Military Police took on several victories early on in the campaign, they had spent an unreasonable amount of resources pursuing

Queenspeople as they fled into and beneath underground bazaars, pathways, and train lines to avoid the barrage. They trailed them at every twist and turn through Queens' subterranean network of sewage systems and canals, though, as the war continued upstairs, the survivors were never found.

Not found. Not anywhere.

Without any conclusive evidence, they were eventually, and rather reluctantly, declared already incinerated by the Hellraisers or devoured by giant carnivorous earthworms. The only other explanations were that a horde of refugees, without any sustainable provisions, somehow dug themselves out of a web of tunnels. Of which there was no evidence for, not even in Liberated territory.

This mystery was said to have driven several hundred Police-soldiers mad with obsession, with some officers going as far as to refuse senior commands to discontinue the search. The war itself was lost before it could be truly determined, however, and its failures were noted in Military Police history as learned lessons never to be repeated.

There's a half-decent chance they're still in the dark about Lowtown after all these years.

Though I wouldn't bet on it, not any more at least

According to those who witnessed and still remember the times, the survivors dug deeper and deeper into the Biosphere, until it was unsure how far they had travelled or how many days had passed. Some had even forgotten why they were fleeing, but the digging never stopped.

Hundreds if not thousands perished from illness and fatigue, and in the final hours of their resistance, it was said that a broken-vault-like door, one with an enormous boulder wedged in-between its frame, was discovered at the end of a particularly cold and windy wormhole. Believing it was an exit to the outside world, the survivors scattered the dead and collapsed every nearby pathway, before rushing down a promising light-filled tunnel.

It was there they stumbled upon what was later described as the edge of an ancient underground city. A city made of glass towers, running water, its own skies underneath the earth, and electricity.

Lowtown-

It's hard to imagine you're real, I need to see you for myself.

Like field mice discovering a human settlement for the first time, the survivors scurried into every corner of the unexplained settlement, unaware of its dangers, but still trying to understand what it had to offer. In the days following, they would gradually relearn the value of a good night's sleep, as well as what it meant to be a human being. Finding sustenance and a sense of community within self-contained farms mistaken for some distant part of Queens, while resting their sick and injured in the company of shadows dismissed as shell-shocked visions and fever dreams.

"The people who live there," answered Cryheart. "Who else?

"B-But that's not true is it?" asked Toshi Hara, visibly bothered by the idea. "That's just a story, right? And this is all *just in case?*"

"Who do you think all this stuff is for?" asked Professor Lind. "And who do you think built the cities inside the Highlands?"

"I-I don't know," said Toshi. "I thought it was the Ancients—"

"No," said the Professor, glancing toward Colonel Hellin who stood quietly by the corner.

For a moment it appeared as if she was about to speak, but nothing came out when her lips parted.

Yeah. I wouldn't know where to start either.

It wasn't clear how or when *they* had introduced themselves, but the survivors stood in awe before the small underworld as they began their worship, celebrating their miraculous escape from the Military Police. They rejoiced for hours, dancing and singing and hymning their hearts away, all under the belief they had uncovered a lost Ancient colony. Their saviour Zaaj had saved them once again. The story beyond this point was shaky, as the truth of the tale was slipping from those who were there to witness the events. Many had or were fading to illness, and there were conflicting reports amongst those still with enough memory to speak of the incident.

Even Flowers had her version of the story.

According to her account, it was believed there had been something trailing and stalking the survivors as they ventured about the facility. It was only after the prayers were sung and the dances were danced, however, that it occurred to them they were not the only ones dwelling within the glistening underground town. The tales described them as an elusive people, silver haired like the colonel, but primal and feral like wild cats. Others describe something more unsettling, suggesting they had caught glimpses of one-eyed creatures trying to pass as human beings. Whatever it was, it had fled upon the first sight, retreating into the caverns etched into the rocky undercliffs. How had they gone unnoticed? How long were they watching? These questions remained unanswered, shrouded in the haze of fading memories, and for years the events went misunderstood. Many clung to the belief they had indeed stumbled upon an Ancient colony, he and others however, had their doubts.

These people could not be the descendants of the fabled saviour of Rodina, he thought to himself, their features were entirely different from the depictions and descriptions the Ancients had left of themselves, and something closer to that they left of others. As time would eventually reveal, these were a people even more ancient and at one point, even more advanced than those widely treated as gods. They were the true indigenous people of the continent, *the Gihon*.

Jazzy II

They quietly drove their motor-scooters to the end of a narrow alleyway before carrying their backpacks to the top of a metal stairwell which served as their usual spot.

"Who got the zap?" asked Quail, falling onto a bed of blankets laid over the metal grates, his favourite place to roost.

"Here," answered Jazzy, handing Red his black and blue school bag.

It still had the name of the boy he had robbed it from written in white marker, as well as the hole he caused when they stabbed him for it.

"Cool," said Red.

He rummaged through the bag until he found a small glass pipe and a pink tablecloth folded onto itself. Wrapped inside were half a dozen small grey tablets.

"These pills are Paladin's," said Jazzy.

"Damn, for real?" said Green, peering over Red's shoulders.

"Yeah," replied Jazzy. "He tossed 'em to me before the blackhouse got stormed. Last I saw him."

If I stayed with 'em then maybe we'd be here now.

"We gon' cut up all those bitches," said Quail.

"For real," said Red, "And sell them off"

There was little time wasted, and even fewer words exchanged as Red placed enough pills into the pipe to heal a heartbreak, and lit the glass underneath with a lighter.

"Y'all don't got hands or nothin'?" said Red, annoyed with the wind.

"No," answered Green, being funny.

"Shut up," replied Red.

The three of them huddled around the fire with their hands cupped, until eventually the pills heated to a bright red and began to smoke.

"We good," said Red, drawing a few short pulls before taking several deep breaths. "This shit kick, boy, damn!"

The pipe slowly made its way around the nest, and each of the boys had a turn to get as high as their last.

By the time it came to him, the others were already laying with their backs turned to one another. Quail was the first to go with Green following shortly behind, and Red might've still been awake with the way he was twitching, but it was hard to tell.

My turn.

He had tried many drugs in his short life, but none of them interested him more than zap. Jinx was a great start and something he would always enjoy, hex was a daydream and something worth staying alive for, but zap was *different*.

Zap was disassociating, zap was personal.

He placed his mouth to the pipe and inhaled as deep as he could without bursting his lungs. The smoke burned as it travelled down his chest where he held it for some time, drawing as much as he could from the drug before being forced to cough it out. The ashy blue smoke escaping him was the same colour as the sky, and it wasn't long before a shimmering glaze blanketed his eyes.

This shit feel good.

He continued to smoke while the others drifted away, racing to finish the zap before it bewitched him like the rest.

Things quieted by the second hit, until all he could hear was the shining sun, and by the third and fourth hits, he had forgotten where he was and what he had done.

On the sixth and final pull, the tether which tied him to reality quickly loosened like a worn-out shoe lace.

Not too long 'til I'm gone.

When there was no zap left to smoke, he turned to his brothers and found them shaking and shivering.

These were some of the boys he thought of when he thought of himself. Boys who he had huddled up with every winter and roamed the City with every summer. Boys who were his brothers and his sisters.

I love these boyz.

None of their mothers had chewed their food for them when they were still chicklings, and none of the other children in the playground wanted to play with them when they were still friendly. Some fell from their nest at a young age and lived along the edge of Queens ever since, while others were born on the streets and knew nothing of a home beyond the company they kept.

There was Green, whose shoes were always on the wrong feet, Red, who was one of the smart kids but always skipped school, and Quail who had put them all under his wing when he still had some growing left to do.

They might have once been good boys with proper names, he and Wazo were at least, but now the only names they had were the ones they had made for themselves, and the only lessons they learned were the ones they taught others along the way.

I love these boyz for real.

Resisting the high as much as he could, he crawled over to make sure each of them were tucked to bed before collapsing without a blanket himself.

In his pipe-dreams he dreamt of better days, and of all the people he once knew before he went his own way. Parents who were too lost to parent, fellow gang members who were too busy following to lead, and even what was left of *Cyrus and his girl.*

He once had a girl in his life too, though whenever he tried to remember her name or what she looked like, the only thing that ever came to mind were the sounds of summerbirds taking flight.

Birds-

What he knew of people he learned from watching the birds, and over the years he learned that some birds were vultures, some birds were doves, some birds were eagles, and some birds were *bugs.*

Mama was also like a mama bird. She loved all her children, but only fed the chicks with the loudest chirps.

His eyes shot open sometime later, unsure how much time had passed, but noticing the day had advanced without them.

I'm... I'm up. I think.

The others were still asleep, but they would gradually awake as well. Breaking out of their high like hatchlings emerging from their shells.

W-We can't be doing this shit.

They'll pluck us off in our sleep.

He wanted to tell them maybe smoking outside in the open like this wasn't one of their best ideas, even if they were deep in friendly underguild territory. Queens was a big city and it wasn't as if anyone was going to watch their backs for them.

When he opened his mouth to speak, however, nothing came out. Almost as if he had forgotten how to, and he wasn't alone.

There wasn't much talking after they came down from their highs and climbed down from their nest, and if there was something on their minds, none of them shared it.

One by one they returned to their motor-scooters, but he left his behind to walk instead.

"Where you goin' birdy?" asked Quail, noticing he was straying away from the flock.

"To my cage," answered Jazzy.

Daaria V

She laid with her still wet hair spread over her pillows like a tree with invasive roots, watching the ceiling fan jitter uncontrollably as it spiralled above. Hoping today wasn't the day it decided to collapse and take her neck off.

Did they really have to nail the beds to the floors too? Whose idea was this?

Acadians at their best, she figured.

After arranging their trip, the three of them were sent to lead patrols through the Citadel's working class neighbourhoods. They were in search of suspected union leaders, but didn't find anyone important enough to arrest, nor did they expect to.

The Army knew the top union leaders were hiding in the slums, their presence as Peaceguards was a demonstration for the working class folk more than anything else.

I hope they're in line. I don't want to see any more closed-door executions.

For the first time all day, she was able to relieve herself without worrying about falling behind, and for the first time in days she had taken a proper shower without a cap on. Very few things had beaten the sensation of kicking off her hard leather boots and changing into a fresh pair of pyjamas after a long hot shower. Except maybe taking off her Army-issued bra, which truly felt *liberating*.

I can't wait to go home, I've missed it so much. It's been years... Wait. I almost forgot.

Something wasn't right about earlier, what was the commander talking about?

She lifted herself up and reached under her bed, patting the floor until she felt the cold metal of the container which housed her most precious memories and invaluables.

They haven't confiscated you yet.

With legs crossed and the covers over her head, she sifted through the letters and postcards sent to her from her mother. Her parents couldn't read or write so the contents of the letters were often dictated to a man named Higar, a local clerk who usually transcribed her family's letters.

She scrutinised each sentence and page with her most careful eyes, searching for inconsistencies or abnormalities in the wording, phrasing, information, parchment and ink, but nothing strange stood out to her.

The more recent ones are written with a typewriter, but it's still his signature at the bottom.

Higar was one of the oldest scribes in the Eastern Cratertowns, of which Notwell was a part of. He was well known and well regarded, and it felt almost inappropriate and disrespectful to suspect him of something. Especially when the Army could easily have been responsible for anything concerning or out of the ordinary.

She wanted to not worry about it, but it wasn't in her nature.

Organised attacks and rebellions, burning down guild sites and villages.

What's going on down there? It's impossible to say when nothing was said.

She placed the letters back into the box and peeked out of the covers to see if she was still alone in the dormitory.

She was.

I gotta be quick.

The Army rewarded soldiers for dispossessing themselves of their personal attachments, and many who aspired to be soldiers by trade and spirit did so without resistance. She always had a hard time releasing herself from her upbringing, however, even when she faced pressures from her peers to do so.

It was easy to feel homesick in what felt like a foreign land, and in the presence of those who were no more than strangers.

Even after all these years.

She neatly organised the contents of the box, and was just about to close it before a photograph caught her eye.

"What's this?" she whispered to herself.

It was a photo of her and Omaara, dated a few weeks after they first met and taken from an Ancient gizmo they called a camera. She was wearing her old clothes, blue denims torn at the knees and a pink shirt likely sewn for a boy, while Omaara wore her favourite garb. A yellow summer dress with blue freckles.

They were standing at the edge of the Highland with their eyes closed and the wind in their hair. The purple waters of Primordia appeared calm in the still image, but she remembered how fiercely the waves were crashing against the rocks that day. As well as why she was crying.

She reached over and carefully placed the photo into the pocket of her jacket which hung over her night desk.

In its place she found another photo, one which contained the two of them and as well as Jaxas. It was taken a few weeks after they met him and they were all in their Specialist uniforms, holding peace signs.

Jaxas and Omaara.

Like many others in the Army, the two of them kept their relationship away from the officers as well as their peers. They had also trusted her to keep their secret, which she would take to her grave. She had been the one who introduced them afterall, and was happy to see them together, but as much as she tried, she couldn't brush the image of Jaxas leaning in and locking lips with Omaara.

They were made for each other,
I knew right away, and so did they.

In the Army, there were too many duties and worries, too many hours of training, hunger, and fear to think of anything other than oneself.

She had learned over the years that most soldiers in the Citadel had little interest in being loved or pursuing any form of intimacy. Many tried, some made it happen, but most were too tired or afraid of being caught. The punishments in place for soldiers for even just holding hands were also unusually harsh, even by the Army's standards.

The ones who felt something, however, always took the risk and found a way to make it work.

Good for them too.

As content as she was with her ways, there were still some days where she wanted something only a cute boy could provide. Out of those who reached for her heart, however, she wasn't interested.

They can't have me,
I don't really know them well, and they don't really know themselves.

But even then there was *this one boy*, however. A boy who kept her secrets and even lied for her, a boy who lived like her and sometimes smiled like her. He was the only boy she ever bothered twisting her hair for, and she still held onto his letters along with the drawings he drew for her.

I wrote to him, but he hasn't written back.

And it's been months since he sent me anything.

Who does he think he is?

At first she thought he died, until she went through the records and found him still alive in South Station.

She still couldn't get over how relieved and angry she was that day.

Whatever. it doesn't matter, anyway. I have to give up on him. Generalists don't age well, or often.

Where one's position was in the Army during peacetime determined where and when one fought during wartime. She was in the Peaceguard, while he was a Generalist. Not only were they not in the same unit, but their ranks were too far apart to ever reasonably expect to see one another, during war and peace.

He probably found someone better anyways.

The thought of him holding hands and kissing another girl like how Jaxas kissed Omaara hurt her, but she would be happy for him.

Wait. No I wouldn't.

He better be thinking of me-

What if he isn't?

No he wouldn't do that.

But what If?

The abrupt sound of footsteps approaching from the hallway startled her, and she quickly tucked away her things as the other girls made their way to the dormitory.

Well, I guess I'm just going to have to find out.

Jaana entered with Orina and Gadolin, who smiled half-heartedly at her. The two took notice, but pretended they didn't. Gwendolyn and Wilona followed soon after, with the rest of the Firstlanders trailing behind. It wasn't long before the room was filled with the sound of chattering girls.

And just like that, my peace is over.

Though they were all in the same unit, it was hard getting to know the other girls sometimes, and it wasn't exactly a secret some of them didn't like her very much. They were never truly nice to her and were not afraid to show it either, and for many years she questioned why. First out of desperation, then out of curiosity.

She reasoned they were mean to her for the same reason anyone was mean without a real justification.

To feel better about themselves, but why?

This question led her to many inferences, some she suspected were more probable than others.

Initially she considered their differences in religion to be responsible for the tensions between them as Lowlanders were generally uncompromising in their Old Faith, while Highlanders were often Zaajars.

But faith hardly played a role in most of their lives, especially as Peaceguards. So she abandoned the explanation for a more likely one.

Maybe it's competition?

The idea of perpetual competition was something hammered into every child born into Peaceland like a stubborn nail. They were even told in the first week of training that though there was space for all of them in the Peaceguard, their classification test was not over.

That must have something to do with it, surely. I know it does.

It was useful to remember most of them, including herself, were working towards some kind of leadership role in the Force. It was a steep climb to the top amongst equals, however, and most rarely had a second chance at completing a high-profile assignment. This environment of limited opportunities required competitors to hold back what they knew and felt. They listened closely when others were speaking, but had the self-awareness to never truly reveal much about themselves or what they were up to. Every question asked was a probe into something deeper, every question answered withheld their true intentions. Gossip was a means, exclusion was the objective.

I can't trust them. They're not my friends, they don't give a fuck about me actually.

She was nervous to be around them in her first few years as a Peaceguard, partly because it was a given they were some of the smartest soldiers in Peaceland, and partly because she always doubted she belonged in their presence. She did eventually accept there was a good reason she was here, even if they tried to make her feel otherwise.

But it took years.

Years!

I wasted years worrying about why these other kids don't like me. These random kids from random families from random places.

The pressures of competition seemed to explain much of what was going on below the surface of everyday interactions, or so she hoped.

Though it was just one explanation, *there were others*.

Raamina V

Her funeral gown grazed the murky alley waters as she chased Callum through the skyless backstreets of Inner Rockland. She turned back to find her guards trailing behind, unable to keep pace with her in their heavy armour, while she had trouble keeping pace with Callum. Though, he did wait for her like a good servant.

What does this boy eat? He's so quick

"This way, Mother!" said Callum, taking another turn through the labyrinth-like passages.

She was always struck by how silent his movements were. Even Isaarith, with her exceptionally sensitive hearing, often missed his presence in the room when she wouldn't miss a mouse.

It reminded her of the stray big cat that used to sneak into the chicken coup her father had built for her, before he became too preoccupied with lordship to care about being a father.

She would enter through the back gate in broad daylight, snatch up a chick or two, and be out before the hens could do anything about it. They never caught her, but they did find her corpse rotting in an alley like this one day. How she ended up that way was a mystery, but she never gave it much thought. She was just happy she was gone.

"Where are we going, Callum?" asked Mother Raamina, placing a hand against an alley wall in an effort to cross around a murky puddle.

"It's only a little further, Mother," he answered, "They told me it couldn't wait."

It better be important. I'm not ruining my shoes and dress for anything less.

After a few more turns in the dark, they found a fat man in black trousers leaning with his hands against the wall, fighting to catch his breath.

It was *Lord Valtus Oldfield?*

What is he doing here? This can't be good.

"B-Bad n-news, Mother," said Lord Oldfield, after finding some wind.

He was quite overweight so they were patient with him.

"What is it?" trailed Isaarith, with an air of indifference in her voice. "Did your wife finally leave?"

"N-No," said Lord Oldfield, wanting to bite back, but not having the energy.

Callum-

"Callum," said Mother Raamina, realising she needed to get rid of the boy before he learned of anything he wasn't supposed to.

"Go to the Temple and tell them I'll be a little late. Take him too," she said, taking Isaarith's walker by the hand and directing him toward the servant-boy.

His hand was slimier than she expected.

"Yes, Mother!" said Callum, strolling away into the dark with the boy without a proper name.

"Who's going to hold my hand now?" asked Isaarith, trying to be funny. "Mr. Oldfield?"

"I-It's Lord Oldfield to you," said the Honoured man of fifty-two, visibly and understandably agitated with the swamp woman.

He came from an Old Acadian line of Landlords who, though disposed of their rule many centuries ago, were still bestowed with Baltiar property to manage and preside over.

"No it isn't," said Isaarith, rejecting his refute.

"Isaarith, be honest," said the Mother, "Do you really *need* a walker?"

The priest-woman didn't respond, but that was enough.

Yeah, that's what I thought, She just wants a pet to abuse.

"What is it, Lord Oldfield?" asked Mother Raamina, "You don't look all that well."

He wore a gold and purple doublet which fell over his belly like a blanket, and his shoes were likely among the most expensive in Acadia, if not Rodina. It appeared as if he was dressed to attend a wedding instead of a funeral, and there was a look of uncertainty and dismay on his face which led her to worry.

I've never seen him look so miserable before, and this is Lord Oldfield.

She recalled seeing him somewhere within the audience as she left the Baltiar Palace earlier in the day, and she was certain he didn't have any dark circles around his eyes then.

Now he looks like a fat raccoon.

"The Baltiars of Peaceland are being accused of treason," said the lord, trying to hide the panic in his voice.

"What!? What are you talking about?" said Mother Raamina. "What do you mean, treason? Accused by who?"

"Treason as in high treason, and accused by Commander Talius," he answered.

"W-Where is this coming from?" she asked, demanding a good answer. "Are you sure it's not falsehood?"

"It came straight from Lord Hariya Baltiar himself, he sent me a transmission I received just after you left the palace," said Lord Oldfield. "Unless he's been day drinking, it can't be falsehood."

Uncle Hariya... Accused of treason by that little urchin of a boy. It can't be!

"Does Talius know we're trading in Old-Royals?" she asked.

"He's not sure," replied the lord, turning both ways to ensure no one but her and her party were around.

He reached into his doublet and retrieved a letter. It was a transmission address to her, but someone had opened it.

"But Lord Hariya thinks there's an informer in the Midlands," he said, whispering as quietly as he could without going unheard.

"An informer?" said Mother Raamina, taking the letter by the hand.

I guess we're not the only traitors in town.

"We need to cut ties as soon as we can," she continued, "Old-Royals could be coming in from the overworld. That's our only good defence and we have to stick to it."

Several months ago, the Baltiars of Rockland and their Peaceland cousins had struck an under the table agreement after what might've been their last day as instruments of the Liberation Army.

With Midland Stronghold acting as the bridge and broker, it was decided the Peaceland Baltiars would be sent Old-Royals in exchange for enough provisions to keep the Inner Ring reliably independent from the Outer. A mutually beneficial decision with a greater shared vision in mind for the future. This was done after the *boy commander Talius* announced an end to the Liberation Army's involvement in the Great Pilgrimage, suggesting it's been the source of so much conflict and has only been something that had emerged out of the Lost Years.

Something which sounded blasphemous and reminded her of Blacksheep.

"Thank you for relaying the message, Lord Oldfield."

We could be screwed, but at least we have friends.

She had accepted there was a chance the families of the Baltiar Palace could not be unified in a single lifetime, and that sometimes being a great leader meant understanding where the boundaries were laid. Yet it was nice to be assured every now and then that she had loyal allies inside and in arms reach. Especially when the battle for supremacy was perpetual and war inevitable.

"Don't thank me now Mother" said the lord, "We haven't escaped yet, I'm in this as much as you are"

"Our commander follows the lead of a boy commander half his age," said Dolarin Weight, standing with Untara and the rest.

"We'll know his next move if we know his."

"That's a good point," said Lord Oldfield, "I'll send Brigadier Workhammer a transmission right after this. They might have their spies, but we have ours."

Workhammer, that's another fool, but allies are allies, I suppose.

Take them where you can, and leave when they were past their use.

"We already know what his next move is," said Mother Raamina. "He's not making accusations without some evidence, and sooner or later he'll make an arrest."

Talius is predictable, it doesn't matter if it's family or if it's going to cost him politically. He's principled, not spineless.

"And what of my husband? Is there any news regarding his release from the Military Police?".

"We haven't received any word from them yet, but I know the Police well" replied Oldfield "I'm sure they'll be back before the summer ends"

"They *must* be back before the summer ends" she clarified, "Or else we've sold ourselves to faithlessness"

The deal was to compromise the location of the invading Liberation Forces entering Windlehem in exchange for the prisoners of war captured in the Lowlands some months ago. Her husband *Harlan* was a top General in the Liberation Army and would have condemned this trade, but she wasn't going to allow him to rot in some dungeon cell being tortured for decades.

"Hey! You!" shouted Isaarith. "Dolarin! Untara! Over there!" she said, pointing to a dark spot in the alley.

They turned their heads to the direction of her pointing finger, and Dolarin rushed into the corner with his short-glaive drawn. After some yelling and screaming, he returned with a boy clutched under the crushing weight of his headlock.

His championship wrestling headlock.

"He's been watching us," cried Isaarith, "He heard everything."

"He's just an alley kid," said Lieutenant Virginia.

"Who knows too much," replied Lady Isaarith.

"Is it true? You've been watching? Listening?" asked the Mother.

He didn't respond, but his shaking legs did all the talking after Dolarin had set him down.

"I'll take care of it," said Untara, unsheathing her short-glaive, still bloody at the blade.

It screeched as it slid against its metal scabbard as she retrieved it.

"Stop!" ordered the lieutenant. "There's too many people on the streets, and there's no way we can explain this to the public."

"I wasn't going to take his head off," said Untara. "Just his tongue."

"It doesn't matter, stand down," he replied with a stern face.

She reluctantly placed her blade away.

"What if he heard everything?" said Isaarith. "What if he tells everyone?"

"He's still a child and we still have the rule of law," answered Virginia Calendar. "And even if he did hear it all, how much did he understand? "Who would even believe him?"

Yeah, he's right. What do we do with him? What can we do with him?

He was a little Tautau boy with some Zacadin in his eyes, and for clothes he wore a stitch ridden cowl over his frail torso with pyjamas torn off at the knee.

"I'll take him," said Lord Oldfield.

"I'll go with you," said Rodin Tallwater, another young Daaradin man of average stature.

He was one of her youngest serving private family guards, and was considered by many including her, to be the heir to the legacies left behind by the likes of Dolarin and Virginia.

Though as great of a soldier as he was, he was a better fly on the wall.

"Where are you taking him?" asked Dolarin, holding onto the boy by his neck.

"The watchtower," answered Rodin, stepping into the foreground.

"You intend to jail a child?" asked Virginia Calendar, visibly perplexed and a little out of place.

"Why not?" asked Rodin.

"Because his mother is going to be looking for him," answered the lieutenant. "And she'll come to us at some point."

"So?" replied Rodin, "If we can't kill him, we have no choice but to take him."

"Mother Raamina?" said Virginia, turning to her for an answer, or at least some guidance.

The others turned towards her as well.

My day keeps getting worse. Why can't I just catch a break?

"J-Just question him," ordered the Mother. "See what he learned, but don't hurt him."

"And if his mother starts looking for him?" asked Dolarin.

"Hand him back and pay her to keep both their mouths shut," said Mother Raamina. "I doubt he understood whatever he heard, but I know he understands what's happening now."

"Mother, are you sure?" asked Untara.

"Yes."

As tempting as it may have been to silence the child, they still had an obligation to uphold *some* rule of law, as the lieutenant had put it.

This isn't some feral land, this is still Rockland.

We can bend the law, but not break it.

Well-

Unless we must.

Dolarin released the boy and handed him over to Rodin who promptly placed him under his shield.

"We'll talk later," said Lord Oldfield, placing a hand by his heart and walking off into the darkness with the two. "Goodbye, Mother."

I wanted to be a school teacher, how did I end up here?

"This way," said Untara, pointing to a winding path. "We can keep talking if we have to."

They eventually proceeded out of the alleyway and turned into an empty side street where no one was expecting her.

"We need to be more careful," said Dolarin, with eyes scanning the townhouses and low rise apartments. "We can't arrest the whole town."

It took longer than usual for her eyes to adjust to the sunlight, but when it did, she found the seamoon quietly receding behind the distant blue sky and the Salt Pillar standing proudly atop its corner on the Highland.

As it has for countless millennia.

It was a colossal thing, a spire as tall, and blue, and grey as some storms.

It was believed by many that the Ancient King they had named Zaaj had built it to reach the heavens, and that his tomb could still be found at the top floor behind a sealed door.

The control and access her family possessed over the Pillar was vital to not only the survival of Inner Rockland, but also to the successive generations of Baltiars poised to inherit their rightful place. For as long as Middle Acadia remained divided, it would serve as a useful strategic outpost, with its line of sight having thwarted many past attacks and deterring current attempts to advance into Liberated Easton. Arguably even more importantly, however, it was useful as a cultural device. Made entirely of concrete coloured with bluestones mixed with grey and some serpentine, it was the most attractive Holysite in Queens, and served as the foundation of the New Faith and for various other pilgrim seekers who ventured into town in hopes to worship such structures of Ancient magnitude.

Arrest the Landlords-

Yeah, right. It's the Landlords who established order when there was none. Peace when there was chaos. Civilization when it was lost.

They found a way to feed a society when its people resorted to feeding on the old and young.

But that was well over a hundred and forty-three years ago. That's true.

Hmm… What to do?

It took several generations to reorganise their society after the Westerian Invasion, but those who persisted through the Lost Years eventually went on to rebuild Acadia in their image.

A new empire had emerged from behind the walls of this once Ancient settlement, and under the direction of those descending from its Old Acadian Military leaders, it sought to re-seize and liberate its territories lost and left feral. This march forward led to the era known as New Acadia, and it was within those short two hundred some years that the Liberation Army experienced its greatest success. It was also when the Baltiars had established themselves as competent rulers.

During New Acadia, the top Army officials took political office while the most decorated and honoured soldiers were granted lands as feudal rent collectors. After their deaths, their descendants took over as the Landlords and Honoured men of Liberated Acadia. The Oldfields, the Workhammers, the Lancias, and the Winches were amongst the most noble, but it was the Baltiars who came to rule the Highlands of Middle Acadia. They reforged men and women into working people, and re-built the world with the labour they captured with each conquest. Out of the working class citizens, the most skilled in the most useful trades found their rightful stations as the heads of guilds, and were regarded as Honoured themselves.

Together with the Landlords and other remnant forces spread through the country, they had established a functioning market economy and built upon their well-deserved wealth through a system of exclusion made possible by a clever repurposing of their Old Country's currency.

A very clever repurposing, manufactured by very clever men and women.

There were two parts to the Old-Royal coin, the pushed out silver centre-piece now known as the 'good-coin' and the remaining copper shell named the 'bad-coin'. The good-coin was reserved for the purchase of skilled labour, scarce materials, and valuable commodities, while the bad-coin was used to pay peasant wages and purchase common goods. A useful system which laid the foundation for rebuilding Acadia.

And they're trying to take it away from us.

Peaceland had sought to weaken this system when it first introduced the Liberated-piece, a substitution currency without the market exclusion, in the year 69 A.N.A., but it was clear now that Talius had some intention to replace the Old-Royal entirely before the end of her lifetime.

Yeah, maybe over my dead body.

In their journey to the Zaaj Temple, they took a complete detour around a circular apartment complex built twelve stories tall and stretching three whole city blocks. It was one of the many properties owned by the Baltiars and rented to working class families, but it also housed a secret as well. Deep below the network of tunnels and low roads, and even further below the Ancient catacombs, the Mining Guild had been conducting a digging operation outside the knowledge of Commander Braxas and the Outer Rockland Army.

"Mother," said Quill

"Hm?" she replied.

"Are you okay?" he asked, handing her his canteen.

"Do you need a drink?"

What a sweet little thing.

"I'm okay, Quill, thank you."

"I was thinking about our defence should we need one," said the lieutenant.

"Probably not," answered Dolarin. "They would be crossing the line having us explain ourselves."

"We can pin the use of Old-coins on the Military Police," replied the Mother. "Or traders from the Outer Country. It's not like the rest of Acadia abandoned using it."

And why would they? There was never a good enough reason to.

Its markets were well-established and its value better understood and regulated. It also possessed greater purchasing power, especially in foreign affairs. A space the Liberated-piece lacked sufficient influence in. Traders were also losing favour with the Liberated-piece even before the recent Military Police policy to obstruct its trade, and their confidence only dropped with each battle lost by the Liberation Army.

"I don't get why they have such a big problem with it," said Untara. "It's not like any of the commanders ever stopped using it."

She stopped walking.

"What's wrong, Mother?" asked Untara.

Wait-

That's true-

Even before the new Military Police policy, they taxed our Old-coins and spent it in Newtown.

I-I can't believe a word any of them say-

"What the Landlords do between themselves is their own private business," she spoke, almost out of the blue. "Maybe they should switch coins too if some metal was enough to collapse their market."

"Well be ready to tell him that," said Isaarith.

"No, I don't have to tell him anything," said Mother Raamina.

Men were loved as much as they provided and whatever little Commander Braxas did for Rockland was packaged in misery for his people and his own family.

She never took him seriously as a man, and she was not going to start today.

"I'm not going," said Mother Raamina.

"What?" said Virginia Calendar in a loud whisper, "He's still the commander! You have to!"

"No she doesn't," said Dolarin.

"No I don't," repeated Mother Raamina, practising the dismissive voice she would write her response with.

"I'm the sovereign Mother of our temple and a Baltiar princess, and besides, this is just a ploy to seize my family's property. Like every other policy they've ever made."

"We just have to wait until the Military Police is ready to—"

"Shut up," hissed Lady Isaarith. "I can hear it."

Silence took over their party.

"There are others around," whispered the priest-woman, "And they're listening."

Each of them searched for what she was referring to, but ended up just taking her word for it. They journeyed the rest of the way in silence and as they neared their destination the temple bells loudened. It wasn't much longer before she could see black smoke billowing from its spires like a dirty candle.

"Looks like they started without us," said Quill, placing a hand on his forehead like a visor.

"I hope so," said Mother Raamina, "I don't have all day."

Emmi III

They stood beneath the shade of a Highland-tree, watching as a percussion of beating drums and metal pans led a march down an open road. It was a festival, and the gatherers and parade goers were venerating their own cults, carrying their God-forsaken idols like trophies over their heads and championing them like pit fighters. In the foreground, a small replica statue of a genie was passing through an audience of occult seekers, while tribes of magic men who commanded *strange* and antique animals were walking on their knees as a display of servitude to *some other god*. Though there had been a shooting not too long ago, the world seemed to stand still for Witchtown, which was business as usual.

"I'm so *tired*," groaned Ashley-Ann.

"We can take a break here," said Hania, stepping deeper into the shade and taking a seat on the grass.

She watched as she swung her backpack from her shoulder, bringing it to the front in one smooth motion along with some of her hair.

"Want some?" she asked, brushing away strands of long pitch black braids from her eyes and face and rummaging through the front pocket of her school bag.

There were pencils, erasers, pens, gel pens, eye-liner, a small mirror, hair ties, hair bands, hair clips, nail polish, nail polish remover, and *lip gloss*.

"I got this from the new make-up store" said Nia, removing the lip gloss brush from its container and applying a thin coat of sparkling pink gloss on her already pouty lips.

"In the Fashion District"

Her tone had a hint of youthful innocence, like a *baby-girl*.

"Yeah, can I try some?" asked Ashley-Ann with excitement.

"Me too" said Emmi.

"I also bought it so don't ask" she continued, with an attitude that was betrayed by a wide smile she tried to contain.

"We weren't going to," laughed Ashley-Ann.

While stealing could've been in her blood, Hania was the type of friend that wouldn't hand her girlfriends stolen lip gloss.

"Are the Police still on us?" asked Emmi.

"I haven't seen them" replied Nia, glancing over her shoulder just to make sure.

"We should still keep an eye out-" said Ashley-Ann.

She reached to pluck a berry from the Highland-tree, but stumbled and almost fell on her backside after something caught her eye.

"W-What the fuck is that!?" she screeched, pointing back to what appeared to be a bundle of raw bones tied around some feathers and attached to a low hanging tree branch.

"That's black magic!" said Emmi, immediately recognizing it, "Don't touch it!"

"Did you touch it?" asked Nia, more so demanded.

"No!"

"Are you sure? I don't want any fucking spirits around me"

"Yes I'm sure" replied Ashley-Ann, "If I touched it I'd still be screaming"

If she touched it we would have to go to a proper exorcist and spend at least a good-coin getting her cleansed.

"Okay good, you better not have" she replied,

"Hey! You're the one who brought us here" refuted Ashley-Ann, *a fair point.*

It seemed as if each turn they took down the narrow market they were met with walls draped with animal hide and pungent jars containing supposed cures for diseases from foreign continents.

"I wasn't trying to" she replied, "The Police were on us"

"We have school too Nia" said Ashley-Ann, "We're going to be late"

"Don't worry, just trust me" she replied, "I know way out of here and we'll all be back on time"

"We should get going then" said Emmi, "I have to get back to work soon too"

"And Ashley is right" she continued with eyes scanning the peculiar foreground.

"This place is seriously giving me the creeps"

Witchtown was a small town, about the size of any neighbourhood found within Newtown District, and it was here inside the witches market where all things spiritual could be bought and sold, even souls. Magical candles flickered on stands selling gemstones, fetish idols, and ape skulls from tropical islands, garments and jewellery were traded in from lost and conquered civilizations, and palm reading and love spells were sold by seasoned oracles. There were tents displaying hallucinogenic cacti from Roseland Prefecture, toad venom from the Forest Gorge, and thousands of trinkets and elixirs, potions, and cursed oils, and even *hexing powder* she read to herself as they crossed paths with rows of sorcerers sitting by the side of the road.

They watched on as a few peddled their goods to other cult and occult members, one was selling genies supposedly entrapped inside spell-forged amulets, the other was selling *some sort of shiny yellow stone* crushed into a powder. She noticed a few sitting under the shade of umbrella-pillars taking lines of it by the nose before entering *some sort of* mystic trance.

"This way" said Nia, taking the lead again.

They followed her out of the road they found in Witchtown, the sun scorching their backs as they weaved in and out of the crowds spilling onto the streets and joining the parade. At some point they had crossed into another animal bazaar, but one that slaughtered under the name of something other than any god, false or not, and at another section they came across an alley home to scryers praying to dolls and casting curses for a pence.

"It looks like the magicians took the City," said Nia.

"We should've saved some of the plaster-bomb for this place" replied Ashley-Ann.

"No kidding" agreed Nia.

Unlike most Highlanders, the three of them did not worship towers or conform to some sort of faithless practice like demon worship. Instead they clung to the Old Story of Acadia, the true account of Acadia. This story spoke of the First Mother who had tamed the iifa-trees with her three daughters—Rodina, Romina, and Wilona—and taught the rest of Acadia to coexist with the invading alien species. They did also pray to an idol, but in contrast to the tower worshipping Zaajars they solely revered the First Mother and acknowledged only Her as divine, rejecting the notion of venerating the Ancients, their structures, or any sovereign among them. Although it was true there were no living iifa-trees left on this new continent, with many attributing their demise to some Ancient king they dug up from the ground, this absence was still no warrant for worship. Within the pages of the Old Mother's Book, it was repeatedly mentioned that the iifa-trees had periodically returned to the Biosphere and would continue to do so at the turn of every *myriad*.

Whatever that meant.

In any case, Zaaj was *just* a person, just like every Ancient before and after him. He didn't descend from space on a winged ship like the Goddess Mother did, he was *born* on the Biosphere *like everyone else.*

It'll be time at some point and then they'll be back,

The iifa-trees we were warned about,

And then the end of days because we didn't listen,

But the Mother will be back too, with her ship, and she'll take us believers back Home.

All these thoughts reminded her of *some boy* from the New Faith who she worked with. A boy she was more and less in love with, but was never sure it could work out between them due to such differences and more.

Hiran Baltiar-

He believes in the Mother, but also the Ancients-

I wish he would just listen.

It was clear to many amongst the tree temples that the New Faith had just been some sort of merger between what was taught in Gran Acadia and what was found in the new continent of Rodina. It was a fabricated religion and such was their contradiction, and it was in this regard the New Faith was truly pagan, along with *all this sorcery* they found in Witchtown.

If they had armies that pillaged and raped she wouldn't hesitate to raze it all to the ground, but these people were just the occult. For now they had other forces in the City, more seeable ones, in their sights.

The Westerians,

The Military Police,

The Liberation Army,

And the Pilgrimage,

"We're here" said Nia, leading them to a flight of stairs by the street which descended past a gate below.

"Y'all ready?" she asked, taking out a small gizmo from her pocket, a remote detonator.

"'Cause I'm really about to press this and we really gotta start movin'"

"Wait! Let me tie my hair first" urged Ashley-Ann, quickly gathering her long silky black hair into a ponytail.

"Okay, here it goes," said Nia, pressing down on one of the buttons.

A moment later they could hear it in the distance, a roaring boom followed by a loud thud which shook the market. Not too long after, the sound of crowds erupting from various pilgrim sites took over the streets like Military Police sirens.

"C'mon" said Hania, pacing herself down the flight of stairs.

"Let's get lost"

Talius VII

"The second part of your mission," continued the commander, "Is to locate the generator and retrieve as much sunstone as you can without disrupting Peaceland's energy output. We just need enough to study and complete Project Orphan."

"Also, if you do make contact with the Gihon," said the colonel, "Try to convince one of their leaders to follow you back"

"I want to meet them"

"B-But what about the stories?" interrupted Wiluss Earthwind, visibly worried. "About the *creatures*?"

"Those are just fables" replied the Commander,

"Told to children like you to stay away from the Forest Gorge"

For a long time, it was understood that Peaceland and Queens shared the same power source responsible for lighting their cities from beneath the Highland. When new evidence arose from Mineraltown's Excavation & Research Facility suggesting otherwise, however, the top academics from the University scrambled to prove and disprove the findings.

It was now widely accepted there was another subterranean city below Peaceland, one possibly as large as Lowtown.

"Well, we can try to bring back the sunstone," said Professor Lind, "But I'm not quite sure how likely we'll succeed in either of those two assignments, if I'm being honest."

"What do you mean?" asked the commander. "Why couldn't you bring back the sunstone?"

"There's a chance it's unstable by now," she answered, adjusting her hair once more.

"Why would it matter? Isn't it still usable?" asked the colonel.

"Only when it's left in its generator," answered Wiluss, beating his professor to the answer. "We can't get near it if it's past its second half-life. It'll kill us all."

"Which, intuitively, makes no sense either," continued Professor Lind. "Most properties turn stable as they decay, but this *thing* just lives on."

No-

That can't be-

"Don't be sad," said Professor Lind, likely taking notice of the change in his expression. "It takes approximately ten thousand years for sunstone to begin decaying. There *is* a chance it's still stable."

"How good?" asked the colonel.

"Fifteen percent."

He tried very hard not to react, but he couldn't help but slam a hand on the desk before searching for a window to look out of. It took longer than it should have to realise they were some six stories deep below the earth inside an office bunker.

Is it really going to end like this?

While most commanders before him had built a legacy based on some combination of conquest and defence, ending the technological freeze may have been the most important policy decision he had ever made.

No, not like this.

Years of work out the window.

It was always believed, within myth and story at least, that there was a world long before the ocean Primordia came into existence. Pre-Primordia, or so the theory went. Beyond speculation and amateur archaeology, however, there were no real leads or interest in unearthing what this world may have held and who could have built it.

With the discovery of Lowtown, however, scientific inquiry into this time was now made possible, and after another researcher, a woman named *Helissia*, made a breakthrough in deconstructing a golden-stone material simply referred to in Gran Acadian legend as the 'sunstone', Project Orphan was established.

The stone was said to be an otherworldly property with incalculable potential energy. It was also theorised to be the core component to the generators which continued to power the Highlands even after all these millennia. He believed the answer to liberating all of Acadia rested within it as well.

Trapped within the sunstone, waiting to be tapped into.

The target was to build something the researchers called a dark energy generator, with the understanding it was the first step to harnessing the true extent of the sunstone's power. An energy source if utilised properly, had the capacity to raze entire empires, let alone cities.

After some initial optimism and minor success, however, the project was shelved due to reasons he could not quite understand, other than it was much more of a distant technology than previously thought.

He would never forget the day Helissia and her research team entered his office to break the news of their failure. His heart had sunk, but they were more or less celebrating, arguing there were heavy costs to exploiting the material, both in war and in nature.

But we still have a war to fuel.

We can worry about the cost when we have a country to worry about. The generators can go out tomorrow, and we have no way of knowing today.

Acadians were always a people learning as they went, the only difference now was that there were no space for errors. They could no longer rely on or even trust the Guilds to innovate and push Acadian society and technology forward either. The entire guild system itself was a relic of New Acadia, a time when the Landlords assumed control over the land and worked to rebuild the world with the help of skilled labour and self-serving campaigns. A system which seemed promising at first, even leading to the successful conquest of Peaceland, as well as the production of the first flying instrument in over two hundred years. It became apparent after generations of stagnation, however, there was little interest among the Guilds and Landlords to support the Army in researching and developing beyond the trades and crafts they had established for themselves.

It's been centuries since the guildmasters developed anything new,
And whenever they did, they kept it to themselves.

The guildmasters were a powerful political and business group who were largely content with the current state of affairs regarding Acadian scientific knowledge and machinery. They primarily benefited from this stagnation as rather than striving to create new technologies and opportunities, they made it their life's ambition to accrue wealth, as well as advance their own expertise and private interests. War and conquest were often at the forefront of their agenda, but rarely were the interests of the Liberation Army and its Citizens in mind when they advocated for it.

These circumstances were what led to the formation of the University and the National Program designed to select the brightest students to fulfil the research and development needs of the state. It was a necessary measure if they had any desire to compete with foreign powers, let alone deter their expansion.

But still we needed something more.

Our communication lines aren't as good as they could be.

The energy grid is ageing and we don't know what to do about it, and now Windlehem is lost.

We can't fall behind them any further than we already have.

Not if we want to stay relevant on Rodina.

Currently, there was an irreconcilable difference between how Ancient and Acadian technologies were conceptualised, designed, and ultimately engineered. The lack of remaining Ancient gizmos and artefacts only widened this gap and this was initially a major concern, until it was later discovered the great Ancient legacy was in reality, a dead end.

The Ancients had made progress with working with coal, steam, and even gas, but tracing their development revealed little technological progress after it was believed they had discovered the generators below the Highland Cities. It was unsure whether or not, however, if they had abandoned such pursuits or if the Old Acadians had melted down too much of their world to piece back together. What it did mean, however, was that their remaining artefacts were still useful for the rare metals and components found in their make-up, which, interestingly enough, made them priceless.

"Commander," said Jovaana Wells. "What about the Military Police?"

"What about them?" answered Olisa August, turning to her peer.

"Well, aren't they right around the corner?" asked Wells,

"How do we know we won't be spied on?"

"I wouldn't worry too much," said the commander, "We have the entire Gorge under surveillance. If they're around, we'll know."

"That's all I have to say for today, make sure you get a good night's rest. The supply truck will be waiting for you at sunrise."

"Yes, Commander!" answered the team of soldiers and researchers.

"And thank you, professor, for taking this assignment on."

"Did I have a choice?" she asked as she headed for the door. "I have to eat and pay bills. Though, I don't know if I can say no to the commander either," she continued, smiling with her eyes.

"Uhm…" he said, clearing his throat, unsure of what to say.

By the time he figured it out, she was already *gone*.

Wilona VII – May 6th

After taking an elevator down twenty stories from the University's main research centre, and walking down an additional ten flights of stairs, she arrived at the Machine Hall, the underground power station responsible for managing nearly all the electricity in Peaceland.

"Over here, colonel," said Professor Datum, a distinguished mathematician who led the way.

He guided her down a soothing light filled path, until they reached a tall green door retrofitted between the ruins of a crumbling arch. The walls and columns around the structure were deteriorating, but the damage done to it appeared artificial rather than the result of time, or from braving any nearby elements.

Looks like someone wasn't happy to find this place.

There were also images and inscriptions of strange beasts and even stranger alphabets, the likes of which she hadn't seen before.

Horses who might've been part human, humans who might've been part terrorbird, and enormous tusked beasts with snakes for noses and giant leaves for ears.

Those letters, what are they?

They're definitely not Acadian, Westerian, Astormi, or Ostorian, and I know what Ancient looks like, it's not that either.

"Just through here," said Datum, approaching the door and placing a hand on it.

"Sure," replied the colonel, unsure of what was awaiting ahead.

The door creaked open with a gentle push, and on the other side of the narrow passage she discovered a sea of metallic silos, ventilation channels, and electrical cabinets.

All of which were constructed entirely from maglith?

What? I've never seen this much maglith at once-

I-I didn't even know this much existed.

The way the structures were designed and assembled made her feel as if she had stepped into a small city. Complete with its own tiny apartments, winding streets, and even the occasional cool breeze.

Something doesn't feel right though. What's going on?

Her hands began to tremble as she searched the room for an explanation for the wind, but it remained a mystery.

W-Why am I so nervous? I-I want to turn back but I can't.

"I've never seen this much maglith at once," said the colonel, sparking a conversation in hopes it quelled her worries, or at least kept her distracted until it slipped her mind.

"Yeah," chuckled Datum, "The entire circuit is made of it. Wouldn't be surprised if half the world's total supply was down here."

He was trying to be funny, but she didn't think he was joking.

Maglith was a natural resource the Liberation Army had declared worth fighting and dying for. It was an extraordinary light and malleable metal, weighing a tenth of titanium per gram, and with a durability rating which had yet to be determined outside of mathematical assumptions.

There's enough of it here to make a thousand fortunes.

"Colonel!" said another man, revealing himself from the corner of an eye and approaching with a salute.

He wore a pair of sunglasses which blended well with the curly black hair that fell over his face, a white lab coat which was spotless but in desperate need of a tailor, and *pink slippers*.

Those are some nice slippers, man.

"Hello," replied the colonel. "And you are?"

"My name is Ocil," he said. "I'm an electrician, I work here."

"I couldn't imagine taking that many stairs every morning just to get to work," said the colonel, with a smile. "That's impressive."

"Oh, I also live here," said Ocil, pointing to a dainty looking tent in the corner. "My apprentices bring me food and there's a cat somewhere that keeps me company."

"Oh," said the colonel, quite sadly.

"Yeah," replied Ocil, placing his head down with a bit of shame, likely mistaking her surprise for judgement.

"So are these the generators I hear so much about?" she said, changing the subject to spare him of any embarrassment he may have perceived. "The Ancients always surprise me."

"These aren't the generators," said a woman, from somewhere inside the room.

Huh? The voice startled her, but she recognized it almost immediately.

Is that... Yeah, it is... But where is she?

"Where are you?" asked the colonel.

"Your Ancients also didn't build this place either," she replied, ignoring the question. "Or the generators for that matter."

Several steps ahead and in-between two electrical towers, they found a dark-skinned woman sitting on the floor with her legs crossed. She had a head full of fiery bone white hair which flared like the sun whenever the wind blew, and on her lap laid a black cat which was well past its best years, but *still cute.*

"H-Helissia!" said Colonel Flowers.

"Hello, Wilona," she replied, unfolding a small rectangular gizmo like a briefcase, and placing it before the cat. "What brings you here?"

"I was curious about how this all works," she answered, before realising that was no longer her most pressing concern. "I-I haven't seen you in years! Where the hell have you been?"

"I've been around," she shrugged, "And it doesn't feel that way to me. I see you all the time whenever I pass by South Station."

"What?" replied the colonel. "How come you don't say hi? I Thought we were friends?"

"Oh..." said Helissia. "Is that what friends do? Sorry, I'm still learning."

If specialisation meant keeping an eye on one thing more than others, here was a woman whose eyes could not help but wander.

Most researchers at the University were regarded for their dedication to a field or two, but her name was found behind the books of several disciplines. She had a head full of rabbit holes, some of which spiralled into wormholes, and if reality had a pulse, *she had a finger on it.*

A true genius she was.

"Ocil?" said Helissia, turning to the electrician.

"Hm?" said Ocil, approaching the open cabinet.

"I don't understand why this isn't working?" she said, pointing to the glass screen of an electronic device commonly known as a computer. "I've been trying to boot the system, but it won't work."

"That's not good," said Ocil.

He took a moment to inspect the switches and circuits inside the electrical cabinet, before turning back to her.

"Oh, I see the problem."

"What?" asked Helissia, with a worried look.

"It's not plugged in," he said, taking the end of the computer cable and inserting it into an empty socket somewhere inside the cabinet.

The screen lit up with a flash of red.

"Oh, right," replied Helissia, scratching her head.

She was also once an advisor to the commander, before convincing him to let her pursue her own research full-time at the University.

But that was years ago.

The last I heard she accidentally burned her apartment down doing some experiment the University wouldn't allow her to do.

"Wait…" said the colonel, realising something important had slipped through the cracks of the conversation. "If these aren't the generators, then what are they?"

"It's an electrical facility," answered Datum, "A sort of substation which houses the capacitor banks and system controls we use to power Peaceland. Without it we wouldn't have any lights, or be able to communicate through those hand radios the Army seems to love," he said, pointing to her hip.

"The actual generators are far below here," added Helissia, before locking her attention into the computer screen.

"And here I was thinking you were just going to pull a plug, or turn off a switch or something," she said, quietly feeling out of place.

"It's not that easy," said Ocil, "I mean we could, but Mineraltown and its nearby villages likely won't ever see power again."

"Why not?" she asked

"Because we can't turn the system on and off by demand," he replied.

"W-Why?" she asked, fully recognizing she was being annoying.

"Well, even though we learned how to build upon this pre-Ancient infrastructure, we still didn't build the subcircuit beneath it all, and no one can say for sure what'll happen to the entire system if the connection was severed, for even for a second. So it's best we don't try."

"It's a miracle it's still up and running," added Datum, "Not only do we *not* know how old the subcircuit truly is, we haven't actually seen it either."

"So how are we removing the power from Mineraltown if we're not unplugging anything?" she asked.

Every answer they provided seemed to only lead to more questions.

"Through codes and algorithms," said Helissia.

Algorithms? Codes?

She took a look at the screen and immediately wished she hadn't. Rows and columns of pure nonsense, placed into an array of sequences and matrices which only made less sense.

The numbers she recognized, but the letters belonged to a language she had only ever seen on her way to this room.

"You already know what I'm going to ask," said the colonel.

"Algorithms are like sets of steps, instructions, and commands," said Datum unfolding another mobile computer and taking a seat nearby Helissia. "From what we understand, they operate within these electrical channels made up of these gate-like structures, and by manipulating the numeric values which exist at their roots, we can do things like monitor and manage energy use.

"Though, to access and instruct a part of the electrical grid we have to sift through and decrypt hundreds, and sometimes thousands, of codes.

"Each block on the grid is protected by a firewall too, and the security algorithms are always changing which only makes it harder for us to exploit."

"Such a counterintuitive piece of technology," said Ocil. "With nothing really more than numbers and language systems, we've been able to manipulate subatomic particles and connect into the literal physical space around us. Well, that and sets of strict logical and conditional parameters."

A smirk flashed across Helissia's reflection on the computer screen.

"Almost as if it's a bridge between abstract logic and physical space," she said. "Almost as if it's an incision into reality itself."

The cat meowed, seemingly in agreement.

"Maybe logic has a physical, empirical structure after all, and just like its abstract form, it's *useful.*"

She had no idea what they were trying to explain, but continued to nod her head in agreement, nonetheless.

"Don't worry, I don't really understand it myself," said Datum. "Only five people across Peaceland actually know how to access the security system, we're three of them"

"Can't you just teach it?" she asked.

"It's not something you want too many people to know," said Helissia. "Trust me."

"I forgot to mention," chimed in Ocil, "We can't actually *cut off* the power as you might understand it, we can only reroute it."

"Well, we could," interjected Datum, "But just like we didn't built the subcircuit, we also didn't build the program, and just like we don't know how the entire system would react if we unplug it, we won't know how it'll respond if we shut down a part of the grid completely."

"There's a strong possibility we won't be able to access the system again," said Datum. "If I'm being honest, we really don't know what we're doing. We still have so much to uncover behind these algorithms."

"Though we did learn a lot thanks to the Giho—" said Ocil, before Helissia's glare cut him off.

"Uh, yeah, basically we have a lot to learn. Both in the maths and in the original language it was written in."

"Does that have anything to do with why Project Orphan was shelved?" asked the colonel, trying her best to connect all the pieces.

The three others turned to one another and a long silence followed before one of them answered.

"No," said Helissia.

Hiran VI

He rode his bicycle through the reconstructed streets of Newtown District, with eyes and ears out for any special deals and interesting news. The marketplace was about as crowded as one would expect for the season, which made for a frenzied, but orderly environment, and aside from the few wispy clouds in the sky, it was an otherwise clear day.

The first warm spell of summer, and the summerbirds are singing too. It's going to get real hot, real soon.

The wind pulled his wavy black hair to the side as he passed by the hordes of tourists and foreign traders, early pilgrims and migrant workers, all entering the City with their newly exchanged money and need for consumption. Though each district had a past and reputation of its own, Newtown was a place most unlike any other in Queens. The day bazaars were assembled over brick laid streets and under colonies of white tents shaped like umbrellas, while housed inside the Ancient apartments overlooking the marketplace were more well established merchant stalls and businesses. Often trading the same goods and services found outside, but for a higher price, and at times, better quality.

"Though, just because it's well-known doesn't mean it's well-made," his mother always used to say.

His path through the busy street was littered with store signs and regulatory notices, some of which were indistinguishable from the medley of language and information, while others were difficult to ignore. One such notice read: *"OLD-COINS ONLY!"* While another simply contained a red circle around a fish with three wide circles for eyes, and the words *"NO OCEAN FISH! Indefinite Imprisonment!"* written beneath.

In this part of the City, nothing entered or left the gates without the oversight and approval of the Military Police who tried to observe the markets like an eagle would field mice. It was a district home to trades both free and forbidden, and it split Queens between its two allied Liberated fractions, Westown and Easton District.

I forgot to kiss mom before I left home today.

He continued to elude the swarms of buyers and sellers as they spilled into the main streets and town squares, until at some point, the entire path was overrun with an outburst of patrons and peddlers.

The crowd forced him to get off his bicycle and carry it into the mob.

It's fine, I'll be back before sunset.

In his walk through the bazaar, he passed sugar and salt stands, spice-traders and flower vendors, and artists hustling paintings of well known gods and other idols. He met Ostorian coffee makers who wore loose fitting garments and elaborate turbans on their heads, and crossed paths with a woman who made a show out of butchering jungle fowl for their meat and feathers, as well as a man in a wheelchair selling wild boar tusks and giant snail shells.

There were flea markets where Queenspeople pawned off their hand-me-downs and second hand goods, wet markets where wild animals were butchered for their raw meat and hide, and the Red Light District which was only truly ever opened to the night. The specialty market further down the street was also bustling. Made up of the most skilled craftspeople and accomplished merchants, it was where one could find the finest textiles and leatherwear, gemstones and jewellery, as well as overvalued goods like imported Westerian craft beer and artisan bread.

He considered taking a short detour through its stone tiled streets, and perhaps spending a good-coin along the way, but what was there to buy? The silk in his shirt, as torn as it was, had been spun from the most expensive wormsilk in Rodina, and his sandals, as beat up as they were, were crafted from the rarest known woodcow hide and stitched together by the best shoemakers in Rockland.

I'm good, I got all I need.

Still bored as Hell though.

Hey-

What's that?

His attention was drawn toward an audience of mainly foreigners and drunken labourers, gathered around a company of performing actors and actresses.

That looks like it's something...

He stood there for some time, first out of curiosity for the show, and then later trying to understand why the crowd was so entertained by a theatre of street dwellers who were probably a band of thieves themselves.

The group was publicly rehearsing lines from a famous Old Acadian play, '*The Fourth Knight of the Dungeon*'. It was one of his favourite plays and he wanted to watch them as well, but left the moment he remembered they usually had pickpocketers working the audience.

"Hey, kid," said a man to his left, "You need a ride?"

He turned to find a Tautau man dressed in ragged clothes sitting atop a rickshaw, behind him were a dozen or so others lined up with their own, all waiting anxiously for employment.

"I'll take you anywhere, and it'll only cost you a couple bad-coins."

I could take a rickshaw, but I don't know if I could trust them either.

Throughout the marketplace, he had noticed a rise in the number of wanted posters and sketches of Blacksheep Gang members, and with the way the public ignored their pleas for work as they passed, it was clear he wasn't the only one who had a guard up.

"No, I'm okay," he answered, feeling a little sorry for him.

Blacksheeps... If they knew who I was, they'd cut me up and sell me back in pieces.

Turning his eyes away from the market, he searched the busy skyline for the source of the faint birdsong chirping quietly behind his ears, and it only took a glimpse of the Ancient world around him to forget what he was looking for. The way the towers and apartments, both distant and near, lined up against the backdrop of the City, made it difficult to distinguish between their individual pieces and one enormous wall of gradient concrete. His mother once told him no matter how dull, small, unfinished or damaged, or even how many Acadians hung their clothes out to dry from their balconies, each and every Ancient structure was something to admire and marvel at.

"Something holy and worthy of worship," she had said, while running her fingers through his hair and kissing his forehead goodnight.

All Ancient structures were composed of some combination of Ancient concrete and coloured earthstone, and no two Ancient buildings were alike. Some protruded into the foreground with elaborate and often invasive exteriors, while others were made to fall far behind, seemingly to create some illusion of depth. Even those uniform in design, such as the row of townhouses inside Inner Rockland, were still distinguished by slight variations in size and the amount of detail invested in their construction. Maroon, dark blue, and serpentine, were the most common colours, but there were many others, and each varied in shade and tone. Even if only slightly.

The Ancients. I wonder if any of them are left.

Probably not...

An aching feeling near his belly caused him to suddenly stop, and a faint ringing in his head interrupted his thoughts.

All that milk and tea is catching up to me.

With nowhere else to go, he turned into a nearby alley to relieve himself.

What's in this anyways? He thought to himself, staring at the parcel while having a go in the cleanest corner he could find.

Eon said he couldn't tell me.

Why?

He once carried a package all the way across town, only to be informed later that it was a fresh human hand. In another time, he delivered a fossilised Ancient fetus to a woman he was convinced was a *witch*.

It could be anything.

Oh well. I shouldn't lose sleep over it, it's none of my business anyways.

Whatever was inside likely came from the blackmarket, and belonged there as well.

He stepped out of the corner and continued down the alley, bicycle in hand and courier bag still strapped tightly around his shoulder. Just as he was about to step back onto the main road, however, he felt a cold hard metal object press against his temple.

"Don't move," said a girl.

He dropped his bicycle.

Th-That feels like a gun-

Valtus IV– May 5th

"Wrong!" said Riya, high-fiving Rodina. "That's not our signal!"

"Okay, I'm done," said Atlus, walking over to the arms of a boy who laid on a bed nearby.

His name was also Valtus, and he welcomed him with a warm embrace.

"What? No come back!" laughed Riya. "We'll change the game, you like poker, right?"

"Nah, I'm done," replied Atlus. "I'm gon' play with him instead."

At the end of their duties and daily routines, the soldiers of South Station were ordered back to their dormitories where they were expected to rest and wait for war to break. More often than not, however, they spent the evening playing cards and sharing scary stories, or in the case of Atlus, kissing boys.

"How about our Valtu—?" said Wilaana.

"No," he said, dismissing the idea before it could be entertained.

"C'mon you can be on my team," said Rodina.

"I'm good." He smiled. "I'll just slow you down."

Rodina's doing better now, that's good to see.

Yesterday they learned her boyfriend was placed under stable condition for the first time since his accident, and that he was eventually expected to make a decent recovery. The good news lightened her mood, and everyone else around her seemed to have felt her improvement.

She's been gone for so long. I'm happy she's back.

He was still feeling sorry for himself for failing the Reclassification Test and not making the cut for captainship, but after a few days of rest and self-reflection, he learned not to project his deficiencies onto the others around him. As close and interconnected as they all might have been, they were still on their own separate journeys to survive and make the best of the days.

However many might've been left.

Earlier today, they were also informed the Generalists were to receive a two-day holiday. The news meant they could finally relax and take a break, but in the back of everyone's minds they knew what it truly meant.

It was another opportunity to enjoy the last few moments of a fleeting life and communicate any remaining farewells to loved ones.

Even if it meant they were destined to die in the frontlines, he was happy he was still with Taalia, Riya and Atlus, and had gotten to meet boys and girls like Alric, Romin, Wilaana and Rodina in the Highland.

In the Generalist Force, they were taught to set aside their differences and expel from their minds any ideas they held of what made a man or woman. They were all soldiers and until they proved otherwise, all equally *useless* in the eyes of the Cause.

Though, there was some value in placing them together in the same environment, he figured, even if saving space and other resources were the main concern. It taught him there wasn't much separating the girls from the boys, and that removing such pre-constructions from the mind was a useful endeavour in itself.

He couldn't remember when, but at some point it occurred to him that all boys and girls, regardless of their outward appearances, superficial differences, and sexual preferences, were members of the same species. It was a mundane thought, but its implications did well to raise his understanding and self-awareness of the world, or so he believed.

It was by mere coincidence he was born a boy, pure chance Riya and Taalia grew up to be women, and if the dice had set in any other way, in another space and time, he may have been in their shoes or even kissing boys like Atlus.

This understanding wasn't just helpful in making sense of the reality surrounding him, it also equipped him with an interesting set of tools to navigate his society, as well as those fighting to stand in his way. He didn't consider it a coincidence that the day he began accepting others for how they identified themselves, both willingly and unknowingly, was also the same day he gained a clearer picture of who they truly were. Both behind the masks worn for faces, as well as their true intentions concealed behind their choice of words and actions.

"If you're looking for someone, why don't you ask Taalia?" said Valtus, noticing the sombre look on Riya and Rodina's faces.

"Oh she's with some boy somewhere," said Riya, packing the deck of cards away. "I wish I was with some boy somewhere," she said, sighing under her breath.

He returned to what he was doing before they could call out to him again, lying on his bed whilst flipping through the pages of his Old Book. Though he was unable to read the hymns and prayers, and mostly knew of their sound from the memories of his mother singing him to sleep, he enjoyed the pictures, nonetheless.

Mom, I couldn't repay you with the rent, or the medicine you needed so badly.

I'm so sorry.

Just as he was about to immerse himself into the pages, he was driven back to the room with the sounds of laughter and *snorting?*

Even before he turned to see what the noise was about, he knew he would find Lamby, and not to anyone's surprise, there he was. Spraying sprey into his nose with Misty and Ashton, two drug dealers and addicts from neighbouring dormitories.

Lamby, you really got no one else to kick it with?

And y'all really got nothing else to do?

Ashton had lost half a thumb last winter for stealing food and supplies from the pantry, while Misty would've seen years in Army prison for drug-trafficking, had she not been related to one of the high-officers overseeing her case.

He understood it was hard to be a soldier when you were always worried about your next meal, or licking some stubborn wound that wouldn't heal, and he also understood why they sold drugs to get by. A single Generalist's income was hardly enough to support oneself and many of them had families and entire villages to feed. There were those who were in it for themselves and that was fair as well. Everyone was trying to jump the line over one another in their own little ways, or at the very least, just get by.

There were those like Rodina who cut hair, Wilaana and Riya who sewed and designed clothes, and even Atlus had his own business offering his advice and judgement on life and relationships.

He had his own hustle on the side too, drawing sketches and portraits for other soldiers, often of their parents, lovers and friends, and sometimes just of things they took an interest in.

It was for these reasons he had a hard time respecting the dealers, however. It was undeniable many of them worked hard and took care of their families, but more often than not, they ruined lives and pulled others back in line just to get ahead.

What type of shit is that?

Though, if I'm being honest, it is still useful having them around.

As much as he hated to admit it, there was some value to having friends who were willing to take the risk and do the dirty work others could not or refused to do. Drugs may have made up the majority of all trafficked goods in South Station, but many smuggled in or manufactured items like *good* soap and shampoo, dorm-made rations and snacks, and even offered services like fixing hand-radios, portable computers, and other gizmos. In most cases, all they ever asked for in return, aside from a couple coins, was help to squeeze back in line with the other soldiers who stood with their thumbs still intact.

And that wasn't all, either.

From a young age they were taught the importance of brotherhood and sisterhood, citizenship and civil duty, but even before such ideas were instilled into them, they were told they belonged to the Cause before they belonged even to their families.

The Army had convinced or coerced most student-soldiers into surrendering their labour and sense of self, and as much as he disliked them and what they did, boys and girls like Ashton and Misty were a reminder they had a purpose and identity outside of what the Army had declared.

Some had something to teach, others were the lessons.

He returned to his Old Book once more, but found himself on a page he didn't remember turning to. There were rows and columns of poetic hymns and sonnets, as well as a detailed description of the world through the eyes of their ancient ancestors, the Gran Acadians.

To the right of the compositions, stood an image of three moons dangling above the Biosphere, and in the page next over, he found the three daughters, *Rodina, Romina, and Wilona,* sitting beneath the shade of an iifa-tree. Plucking its fruits in the presence of their Mother, who judged the world as it passed.

I missing going to the tree temples,
It's a shame they only worship Zaaj here,
They could at least give us a storage room to pray in.

It was believed by the Gran Acadians, as well as his grandmother, that a woman named Utia created the universe over the course of tens of billions of years, birthing and destroying all life and matter until it suited her aesthetic appetite.

She was said to have existed since existence itself, but only revealed herself to humanity when they needed her the most.

When the iifas arrived.

It was written she descended down from the heavens on a winged ship and taught the Gran Acadians how to tame the iifa after they had failed to wage a winning war against the tree.

Along with her three daughters, there was another child, a child who was said to have gone missing shortly after birth. The worshippers of the New Book took the young boy for Zaaj the Ancient King and placed him alongside the Mother as her sovereign successor. Which made little sense to him considering it was stated explicitly throughout the Old Book that only the First Mother was worthy of worship. It was also never mentioned whether or not the child was a boy or a girl, let alone a *king.*

They were only ever referred to as *Orphan,* and only ever depicted as a faceless figure with an over looming spectre for a mentor. It was quite obvious to *anyone with half a brain*, that such a story was made up by Highlanders who sought to encourage pilgrimage into the Ancient cities.

The sound of laughter in the room interrupted his thoughts once more, but this time he decided he would just join in.

Can't beat 'em.

He closed his book, put it back into its place inside the box underneath his bed, and walked over to the group gathered around Atlus' bed.

"What' you guys doing?" asked Valtus.

"We're reading palms," answered Riya.

"This line means you're going to die young," she said, gliding a finger across Alric's hand.

"What about this one?" he asked, out of genuine concern.

"It means you're gay," said Atlus. "Come over here,"

Laughter erupted.

"Shut up, Atlus," replied Alric, "You can't read palms."

"Yeah, but I can read boys," countered Atlus. They all shared another laugh, and even Alric was unable to contain his smile.

"All right I'm bored," said Riya. Y'all ain't got nothin' else?"

"What about scary stories?" suggested Wilaana, whilst etching something into her bed frame. "You hear the one about those four Old Acadian kids who broke into Queens and went *missing*?"

"Yes," they all answered.

"What about the forest women with backward feet?" she asked.

"Yes," they said once more.

"What about the things that crawl into your bed at night and take you down to Hell to breed?"

"Yes," said Atlus, cradled in Valtus' lap. "We heard it all."

"I wish someone crawled into my bed at night," quietly slipped in Riya.

"Okay then I'm all out," said Wilaana.

Hey... I think I got one.

"I got one," said Valtus.

"Is it about the Mother?" asked Atlus.

"Yes," he replied.

They all groaned.

"What? What's wrong?" asked Valtus.

"You gon' tell us some sorry-ass story from the Old Book again," said Atlus.

"No I'm not! It's a good one!" he responded. "And hey! What's wrong with the Old Book?"

Atlus shrugged. "It's lame as hell."

"But that's all the books, Old or New," said Riya.

"Yeah that's true," agreed Atlus.

"Okay, but' any of you ever hear' the other story? The one they never tell in the tree temples?" said Valtus.

"The other story?" said Wilaana, intrigued.

She moved closer and the others reluctantly followed.

"They say the woman who taught the Gran Acadians about the iifa-tree wasn't actually the First Mother, but a feral woman."

"A *witch*, actually."

"They say she made her husband hang their daughters one by one, and when there were no children left, they misled the nearby village kids right into the iifa-tree's mouth-belly"."

"What the hell!" said Alric, who had sat quietly in the corner the entire time. "That's what you believe?"

"Damn dude, I changed my mind," said Atlus. "The Old Faith is pretty cool, how do I join?"

"No," laughed Valtus. "It's just a story. My dad used to tell me whenever my mom wasn't around."

Dad... I miss him too-

"Hey, guys!" interrupted Taalia, storming into the dormitory with a pretty Zacadin boy, likely a Firstlander, who looked out of place.

"Daaria is here!"

Daaria VI

"Your hair," said Orina, running a finger through her ends. "It's so pretty."

She smiled. "I don't use the new shampoo they gave us."

"What?" said Orina, almost outraged by her lack of knowledge on the subject. "What do you use?"

"A recipe my mom showed me," said Daaria, "I have some if you want to try..."

"That's the first time I've seen you smile all day, Daaria," said Gadolin. "Is everything okay?"

"Y-Yeah," replied Daaria.

She thinks she got to me earlier.

Don't worry, Daaria. You'll be fine.

"I'm fine."

"Oh, okay," said Gadolin. "I was worried you were upset about earlier."

"Oh," said Daaria. "No, it's fine. I didn't think much of it."

"Wow," said Gadolin, feigning an interest in her. "You really know how to handle the truth, that's really mature of you."

Why are you like this, Gadolin? I don't even know you. I don't know any of you, and none of you know me.

Unlike the regional strongholds, the soldiers stationed inside the Citadel were collected from all throughout Peaceland, and she had learned the hard way that this meant something to many of them. Some were here to further themselves while others were here to push forward the Cause, but each one of them regardless were tethered to their upbringing and experiences. Carrying with them the burdens placed upon them by their communities, as well as the ones they picked up along the way.

That's something I can't forget.

The most memorable moment of her first year as a Peaceguard was when she tried, for the first and last time, to sit with the Midlanders at the cafeteria. In the middle of their discussion about those expected to rise through the ranks next, Airica, a friend of Gadolin who was no longer alive, had looked her right in the eye and said, "*Just 'cause you got here don't make you smart.*"

August had once told her something similar as well when she tried to sit with the Firstlanders a few days later.

"*Just 'cause you got here doesn't make you one of us.*"

It was hard to say how similar those things were, and at times, difficult to deny its merits.

The classification exams handed to student-soldiers in the Firstlands and Midlands were much more difficult and competitive than the official Peaceland Classification Exam administered in the other regions. In both regions, the top one third of students-soldiers were delisted from the Army out of merit, the middle third were honourably enlisted into their respective regional strongholds, while the bottom third were offered to the Citadel to meet their quota to the Cause. The Lowlanders had their contracts with the Citadel too, but unlike the Highlanders, they didn't have to be forced to send their children to war.

For the Northern and Eastern regions, joining their strongholds was a rat race and a privilege in its own right. Most had *no choice but to be a soldier* as it was the only opportunity presented to them with a secure enough income to survive meaningfully. From there on only the best were selected to represent their communities within the Commander's Forces.

They didn't call the Lowland Armies bottom-dwellers for no reason.

The best student-soldiers from the North and East were sent to the Citadel while the top performing Midlanders and Firstlanders either enrolled into University, a guild academy, or inherited the responsibilities of their family's property and assets.

And even after making it to the Citadel, it wasn't like most of them made it past the Generalist.

The Specialist Force was primarily made up of the citizenry living within the Citadel, with any remaining space quickly being taken up by Firstlanders and Midlanders who were not competitive enough for positions inside their own communities, but used the opportunity as a backup.

I guess I'd be at least a little upset if I was in their shoes. I mean... They deserved better.

Like many of the other Firstlanders and Midlanders in the Peaceguards, Gadolin worked her entire life to make the top of their classes in an effort to avoid being sent to the Citadel.

But here she was. All that hard work, only to be selected by the Commander anyway.

In their eyes it was where the failures from their communities ended up, and though it didn't justify how they treated her, she still empathised with their frustration. If Commander Talius hadn't plucked them from their stations, it was likely she would have never met them.

Not even on the battlefield.

There were many other moments over the years, and she could never quite remember what they did or said, or even the context and whether or not she deserved it. All she could ever remember was just how she felt.

Very,

Very,

Sad.

She knew what it meant to feel and be cheated, she was a Lowlander after all, but that was never enough for them, and if anything only singled her out.

She had learned the hard way her upbringing wasn't going to help her here, and that it was better to just leave it by the door whenever she stepped out of her dorm.

It was just baggage she couldn't unpack, so she kept it tucked under her bed.

I'm a Lowlander before I'm a Peacelander. That's my birth class, my birthright, and the way they treat me.

Gadolin is about as Daaradin as I am, and yet she's always hating, and thinks I don't notice. But I noticed that too. Damn, I can't believe I thought we were going to be friends.

Whatever, forget that bitch-

She turned her attention to the Firstland girls, and watched as they gathered in their little corner. They were never the type to willingly interact with others, and with each passing year their circle only seemed to tighten up.

She had some suspicion as to why, as many Lowlanders were guilty of something similar as well. They only kept to themselves under the belief they had to in order to survive and retain their identity from the Liberation Army.

The Liberation Army screwed us both, we got that in common. But why don't they like us? Most of them came from families as rich as the Honoured Citadel and Midlander kids. But they don't get along with them either. So, it can't just be just class or status.

It was that very inference which led her to suspect *something* else from the Firstlanders.

Most were Zacadins and they were quite proud of it, which was an odd thing to celebrate as throughout Peaceland they were reminded the colour of one's eye was not a measure or indicator of Acadianness.

Regardless, many Firstlanders felt the Daaradins, Tautaus, and other minor Acadian groups fell behind as a result of their own doing, and therefore, should be left behind. Others simply believed Zacadins belonged to a higher order. Not all Firstlanders believed this, but it was the popular attitude of the times, and like all rhetoric, it had manifested itself within the politics of the region.

Where was this even coming from? What did we ever do to you? What did I ever do to you?

Such virtues and beliefs reminded her of the Military Police propaganda quickly spreading throughout the country, as well as a dark part of Peaceland's history which many have tried for centuries to sweep under the rug and deny.

Before the Liberation Army conquered Peaceland, the people now known as the Firstlanders ruled over the Tautau and Daaradin communities spread throughout the Lowlands. When the Liberation Army conquered the land, they made a promise to end their oppression, but instead of true systemic reform, the only thing that changed was the oppressor.

This history was hard to forget or accept, especially when the way they treated her was a constant reminder of it. A constant reminder that her ordeal and plight was a symptom of a wider illness spreading across Peaceland and now what remained of Acadia.

This morning when I caught them with Will, did they know he was my brother?

She thought about it and yes, she remembered telling them earlier in the month, after the rumours about Mineraltown first broke out, that her brother was working at the excavation site beneath the Zaaj Temple there.

They must've known, and never told me. No, there's a chance they didn't know they'd be working with him until today. Either way, it doesn't change much.

The Army had kept her baby brother away from her and it made her a little bitter. She had every right to know if he was dead and every right to see him if he was alive.

What's so important anyways? He's not even a soldier. I guess I could just ask them straight up... No, I'll only embarrass myself again.

I could try to dig it out of them, but August would never spill.

And Briaana... Well, Briaana is Briaana, she'll know what I'm really poking for. She's too smart to slip, and I'm too smart to try.

Damn... Why does life have to be so competitive all the time?

They treated her as if she was something different and she was starting to believe it. If being in the position she was in as a Lowlander and a Daaradin was somehow a reminder of their own failure, then maybe they were the actual failures.

My path here is an accomplishment, and it's not like I chose to be a Lowlander.

Or have green eyes.

Or have black hair.

Or be as tall as I am.

Or be born at all.

Who are they to judge me the way they do?

For many years she used to think she was just overthinking, until one day she started trusting her reasoning, and now she was certain of many things.

That you can only see people's true colours when they look down on you, and for some people, every engagement was a political one for one reason or another.

Whatever reasons they had for not liking her, *it was personal*, but it was *theirs*. As a result, she wasn't going to do anything about it. Trying to win someone over implies you lost something to them.

"What' you thinkin' 'bout?" asked Omaara.

"Huh? said Daaria, startled. "Oh, it's nothing important, just something on my mind."

Omaara, I'd be so alone without you.

Omaara was one of the few girls, if not the only girl she could be cool around. She always accepted her for who she was and never made her feel out of place, even when she was.

"You ready to head out tomorrow?" asked Omaara. "We gotta'' be up early."

"I can't go with you guys," said Daaria.

"Huh?" asked Omaara, "Why not?"

"I have something to do first," she replied, "'I'll meet you there."

"How? Isn't Eastern Stronghold like days away?"

"Yeah but I'll figure it out."

"But what if we get lost?" cried Omaara with a hint of laughter in her voice which she tried to hold back.

"You mean like how you and Jaxas forgot to bring your radios and ended up getting lost in the slums today?"

"Yeah." laughed Omaara. "Exactly," she said, hugging her head.

Wilona VIII

"Well, not exactly," said Helissia, typing away.

"Professor," hissed Datum, "This is classified information!"

"It's fine," she replied. "She's on the project committee."

Helissia turned to her with a scornful look. "She just doesn't go to any of the meetings and *clearly* doesn't read the notes left on her desk."

The colonel laughed, albeit with some embarrassment

"Sorry."

"Project Orphan wasn't shelved just because of our lack of knowledge in computing," said Helissia, continuing from where she left off. "Well, I mean that certainly had a part to play in it, but there's a lot more to it than that. We can only classify things when we know what it is and isn't relative to other things, and this is true for all things.

"Or it *was*"

"What do you mean?"

"Well, we only know what a chair is from what it isn't, we can only define what mammals are from what separates them from other classes of animals, and we can only organise the chemicals inside the table of elements as their properties relate to one another."

"Are you with me?" she asked, removing her attention from the computer and turning to her.

She was *gorgeous,* and felt her eyes scanning for any hint of uncertainty and self-doubt.

"Y-Yeah," replied the colonel. "I think."

"When it comes to the material you know as the sunstone, there appears to be nothing unusual about it at first glance," said Helissia, turning back to the screen.

"It seems to possess no intrinsic value, like any other useless decorative stone, like an emerald or a sapphire, until it interacts with *maglith*."

"Maglith?" asked Colonel Flowers.

"The generators built into the city below are made entirely of maglith," answered Datum. "When the sunstone interacts with the metal, it produces an interesting reaction. One that spills into our reality as electromagnetic energy."

"*Spills into?*"

"Yes," answered Ocil, ominously.

"The strange part is that we can't see or detect its particles," he added. "Not even as waves."

Waves?

"Waves?" asked the colonel.

"Please don't ask," said Helissia, "That's a completely different rabbit hole."

"The important part here is that though we can see, touch, and feel maglith and sunstone, we cannot measure or detect their combined reaction. Not yet, at least."

"Why not?" she asked, but only to feign the appearance of comprehension.

The two researchers shrugged without noticing the other doing so.

Helissia turned to Datum begrudgingly. "To this day we don't have an answer."

"What?" said Datum. "Why are you looking at me?"

"Didn't you write your Ph.D thesis on this?" asked Ocil.

"Yes," said Datum, "But I'm failing to see your point."

"Anyways," said Helissia, "It forced us to re-evaluate where to place both the sunstone and maglith on the table of elements."

"Maglith and sunstone," said Ocil, caressing a nearby electrical cabinet. "Two things that don't seem related at all, but together they power every Highland city in Rodina. Isn't it *incredible?*"

"Yeah," said Colonel Flowers, in genuine awe. "It truly is."

This was a part of the world she had relied so heavily on but had no real knowledge or understanding of. It felt as if she had been standing on a rug her entire life, only to just have it be swept from under her feet.

"It's even more incredible when we consider neither maglith or sunstone is conductive of electricity *or* magnetism," said Datum.

"Huh?" said the colonel, "That doesn't make much sense."

"You're catching on," said Helissia. "That's good."

"It's a little counterintuitive, isn't it?" said Datum.

"A little?" Ocil laughed. "The great researcher Haritah Lancia died thinking her equations solved electromagnetism. What a peaceful death that must've been."

"So what does all of this mean?" asked Colonel Flowers, scratching the top of her head.

"There's only one explanation to this," said Helissia, "And I don't care what the other researchers at the University say," she asserted, with a glare aimed at Datum and Ocil.

They didn't attempt to challenge her idea, but they did turn to one another and chuckle nervously.

"We can infer there *must* be another property to electromagnetism," said Helissia, "A third field that's existed alongside us within the same time and space, but in another place hidden deep within reality. One we can interact with as electromagnetic energy, but can't observe it for one reason or another. A field which unifies the electric field and magnetic field into a wider natural force."

"The *Missing-Electromagnetic Field,*" finished Ocil, "Or the MEF"

"Something revealed to us only after two seemingly unrelated things were utilised."

"And it's been evading us for hundreds of years." Helissia nodded in agreement. "There haven't been any exciting breakthroughs, but we do have a lead."

"W-What's the lead?" said the colonel, with a newfound investment in the subject.

"The electromagnetic energy derived from the generators isn't much different from the electricity we can derive from let's say, hydroelectric magnetic turbines," explained Helissia. "Except for that one feeling." She gestured vaguely to the space around her. "You know, that warm, *soothing* feeling? The one you get when you walk into a room with the lights still on? The one that calms your nerves? The one that reminds you of home?"

Soothing?

Y-Yeah...I know that feeling, I felt it at the Hospital. I felt it when I walked in here. I felt it all my life-

She looked up toward the lights beaming down from the glass tubes attached to the ceiling.

I feel it right now.

"Yeah," she said, lost in the light like a fly. "I know that feeling."

"Well if you ask me," said Helissia, "I think it's bringing something back from the Missing-field."

"What?" asked Colonel Flowers, excited by the idea.

"Toxic radiation," answered Helissia, as flat out as she possibly could have.

"We're hoping she's wrong," said Datum quickly, following her response.

"Yeah well I'm not," Helissia bit back. "So get back to work," she said, returning to her computer.

I-I didn't even know you could do this with maglith, she thought to herself whilst toying with the maglith eagle pinned to her breast pocket.

"Maybe our science is wrong, maybe there's something obvious we missed," said Helissia. "But I'm not that surprised to be honest. I always had a feeling there was some kind of *Mother-force*, which all the other forces of nature derived from."

"But then where would the Mother-force come from?" asked Datum.

"Stop asking questions, get back to work," barked Helissia.

The cat meowed, seemingly in support.

"So that's why Project Orphan was shelved, and if we don't figure this out, we might have to abandon it entirely."

"Interesting," she replied quietly.

Glad I didn't read the report.

"Ocil," said Helissia.

"Yes?"

"Can you give me a reading?"

"Sure thing," said Ocil.

She watched as Ocil ran to his tent and retrieved a tablet-like instrument which she initially mistook for a radio. He turned the tool on and connected it into the cabinet Helissia had been working out of.

"If she is right about the Missing-field," said Ocil, "Then we still have a long way to go before we can reach it. At the moment our understanding of the physical world is held together by splints and duct tape, and for the last few centuries, we've been trying our best to work backwards. Reverse engineering things we barely understand while taking steps entirely in the dark.

"And now we have to reject everything about our intuition," said Datum. "It's true our engineering hasn't caught up to our physics, but it's just as likely that our physics just isn't good enough. Or *worse...*"

"Worse?" she asked.

"There's something fundamentally incorrect about our mathematical assumptions of the universe," answered Datum. "Or *even* worse..."

"Can it really get worse?" laughed Colonel Flowers, both at the absurdity of the situation, as well as her naivety.

If I only knew what I was getting myself into this morning, maybe I would've just stayed home.

"There's a good chance we don't have the right metals or materials to test the relationship between the two objects," said Ocil. "So much of the Biosphere is lost to us. The right material may no longer be on the visible planet."

"Or *ever* at all"

"If that's the case then we're really better off giving up," finished Datum.

I guess it can always get worse.

"In any case," continued Ocil, "We don't know how the main generators work and we won't really know until we see it for ourselves."

"It seems like no matter how much we learn, there always seems to be a gap between our understanding of the universe and what reality dictates. This gap seems to only widen the further we dig."

"And the better we get at conceptualising the physical world as states of pure mathematical principles," added Datum.

He set his mobile computer aside to stretch his fingers.

"Which makes sense when you think about it, reality as it appears to us is likely the intersection between physical matter and human consciousness.

"If that is the case, then it's only a given that our natural perception of the cosmos is a distorted one. Maybe some things are just not meant to be observed or understood, maybe that *is* the human experience."

"One thing I learned over the years." Helissia smiled. "Is that the only contradictions which exist in the universe are found in our understanding of it."

"If the Missing-field truly exists outside of our perception of reality, then my work is finished and I'm retiring. No point in draining public funds like some of these other *academics,*" she said.

"Makes me wonder what else reality is hiding in plain sight," sighed Datum, "Sometimes I think I don't even exist."

"I think we might understand the Missing-field better if we find a way to make use of it," said Helissia, turning to him. "Utility seems to be a substrate of reality as much as reasoning itself, but I suppose until then this is the only use we have for this energy, powering homes and hospitals."

She turned back to her. "Which, you would think, is all a society needs, but it's never enough for you Acadians," she said, making no effort to mask the disdain in her voice.

"The early Peaceland researchers discovered a way to work off Ancient and Old Acadian designs and even managed to develop a functioning grid system, but according to Talius, we need a country, not a *fucking* habitat."

"With all these issues, I don't understand how Project Orphan was even considered a viable option?" asked the colonel. "I'm sure we could be doing something else with the resources we have."

"Because we managed to build a maglith microcircuit which successfully harnessed the sunstone's energy. Though it only lasted a split second, it was a promising experiment and that's where the optimism comes from," replied Datum. "Scaling it up to a fully fictional generator is a few generations away, however."

"I don't know if we have a few generations to spare," said the colonel.

"That's a part of the problem, isn't it?" reflected Ocil, with his head down.

"I lost all my brothers to the frontlines, there might not be much of us left by the time we figure any of this out. I know I won't be."

I'm sorry," said the colonel, placing her hand by her heart.

A cold wind pressed through the facility, and with it came a silence which took over the room. She took the opportunity to wander the space, trying to make sense of all that was discussed, but trying to forget it as well.

This was all too much, and something tells me it's just the surface.

After maybe fifteen minutes or so, she returned to find the three of them still hard at work, and the cat clawing at Helissia's arm as if it was typing itself.

She looks so zoned out, but there's something's on her mind as well, something she can't hide. What could it be?

"Doesn't that hurt?" asked the colonel, pointing to the scratches on her skin.

"Yeah," said Helissia, "But there's nothing that can be done."

She took a hand to the cat's chin and returned the gesture.

"Come here, Pigeon," called out Datum, with a hand.

It was ignored.

Pigeon? That's a cute name for a cat.

"Hey," said Ocil, with a worried look. "Something's wrong with the storage capacitors. We can't transfer the energy to the Citadel for some reason."

"Huh?" said Helissia, "What are you talking about?"

"Come see for yourself."

Helissia stood up with Pigeon safely clutched in her arms and walked over to his station.

She and Datum followed.

"Hm," said Helissia. "You're right."

"Does that mean we can't cut off Mineraltown?" asked the colonel.

"No, we can," said Helissia. "Though we have to reroute it to another power station."

"Oh, okay," said the colonel. "So there's no problem right? Everything's fine?"

"Well, the only other power stations in Peaceland are in the Firstlands and Midlands, and if we reroute to either of those places, we'd likely either permanently short circuit their systems, or explode their facilities."

A look of panic was her only response.

"We can override the Midland power station and send it to the entire Lowland," said Ocil. "It's about enough energy to light the whole region for the entire summer."

"Great," said the colonel, "Let's do that then."

"The guilds aren't going to like that," said Helissia.

"The guilds?" she replied. "What do the guilds have to do with any of this?"

"Well, not all the guilds," said Ocil. "Just the electric companies, mostly."

"The electric companies?"

"Oh right!"

"The contracts"

Dammit.

At some point during the consolidation of Peaceland, the Landlords were awarded contracts to develop and manage the newly conquered territories. Within a few decades, they monopolised control over the extraction of various minerals and metals, as well as the management and distribution of electricity, water, and other utilities like road construction and natural gas.

It took the introduction of the Liberated-piece to weaken their empires, and successive policies designed to dismantle their oligopolies for the Army to regain ownership over such industries. In the absence of their oligarchical control over the politics of Peaceland, several guilds were established as mediums between the Landlords and the needs of the general public, and they competed amongst themselves in the free market to provide and manage utilities to the Midlands and Lowlands.

"We're literally the Citadel," said the colonel. "Don't they answer to us?"

"Yes," replied Helissia, "But it's going to cut into their profits, and I don't know if that's a conversation you want to have with them."

"It's fine," said the colonel, "It'll take more than a summer to stave them, and besides, this is a national security concern."

"You sure?" asked Helissia, hovering her finger over the keyboard. "Because I *will* press this key."

"Yes," replied Colonel Flowers, "I'll explain to the commander."

"All right," said Helissia, a brief moment later. "We're done here."

Talius VII– May 6th

He swept his telescope over the waters of Primordia, watching the seabirds as they circled off the cliffside of Queens.

Standing some three thousand five hundred metres above the water's surface, and separated by a layer of clouds between its Lowland valleys and Midland Plateau, the Highlands of Middle Acadia was the second highest summit in Rodina. With an approximate total area of four thousand three hundred kilometres, it was also by far the widest.

Even with its impressive height and enormous landmass, however, it was still not enough to see any meaningful land, beyond except a few rocky islets and the remnants of a glass complex protruding from out the waters far off into the distance.

Even with a good telescope on a clear day. Nothing.

Primordia was a vast and unforgiving ocean, a detail said to have been miscalculated in the legends the Gran Acadians had relied upon in their retreat to this land.

A journey thought to have taken only a few weeks to complete, took several months, or even years, the history wasn't clear, and nor was it made clear by competing scholars who drafted contradicting accounts of the past.

According to the diaries of the Great Voyager Aaj Firewind, however, she had led the escape from Gran Acadia with a fleet of a hundred iron long ships by her side, and an emerald vessel at her steer.

She possessed no clear maps to direct her or competent advisors to counsel her, but still managed to sail to the shores of Rodina by locating and following the *Whitestar*. A celestial object too bright to be a planet, and far too small to be a star or even a true moon, but still heavy enough to claim its own belt of shattered asteroids just outside the Biosphere.

In her own words, she had described the once fabled, and now newly discovered land, as a *"Haunted body"*.

"Cold upon arrival and void of people, but not their constructions."

Along with the understanding that such a journey was never taken before *or since,* such were some of the details agreed upon even by the most disagreeable scholars.

Moving along, he swayed his telescope westward where he found an Ancient tower reaching for the heavens, and a flock of enormous seabirds terrorising the streets of Queens.

"Huh?" he said, removing his eyes from the telescope. "Hey! Get out of here!" he said, shooing away the summerbirds hanging around his balcony.

"Stupid birds."

When they were gone, a clearer picture of Queens was left, and he stood there for some time. Peering over the rails and admiring the sight of the Ancient world and all its marvels. Wondering if he would ever get to see more of it before they left him for the worms to eat, or if he would be confined to this single tower for the remainder of his life.

I haven't been to Queens in years. How long have I been stuck here? There's still so much I haven't seen.

Though much of Rodina was yet to be discovered, it was clear there were no other structures on the continent like the great bridges separating Queens from Peaceland, as well as the *Salt Pillar*.

Several centuries before the three competing armies of today ever existed, during the height of Old Acadia when Roilmont was a bustling capital and the Acadian Republic was a free and prosperous empire, the Military had recorded several decades worth of unsuccessful expeditions to Gran Acadia, before abandoning it entirely as an un-costworthy project. The most widely known expedition was the one of an Old Acadian researcher named Elysiaa Ann. She was the first to fly a hot air balloon over Primordia, flying for an entire week and transmitting as much information as she could before losing all contact in what was thought to be a sea storm.

The expedition which fascinated him the most, however, was a project to develop a machine the Old Military called a submarine. The effort was a partial failure in that it only managed to dive half as deep into the ocean as was predicted, but it did lead them to something more interesting.

The clear, still waters of the Ruined Sea.

A place thought to be a myth by the masses, turned out to be a well-documented place in Old Acadian Military records.

If I could only get to the Salt Pillar, maybe I can see all I need.

But the Great Pilgrimage is in the way.

A tale fabricated by the Firstlanders to draw people and traders into their markets.

Accepted by the Lords of New Acadia as a way of enriching themselves.

All at the cost of research and development and true state-building.

Putting an end to the Great Pilgrimage was a radical step away from the Liberation Army, but a necessary one for the continued survival of Peaceland. Countless had been displaced as a result of the last few wars and the ongoing conflicts for the Ancient City.

The pilgrimages have always denied us access into the Ancient world.

It was hard to say what really happened as Old Acadia fell about half a millenia ago and Gran Acadia several thousands of years before that. What little was known from remaining Gran Acadian scriptures was that they had traversed over a clear sea in the middle of purple-blue ocean, and glimpsed into it like a window into the seabed. There they found the remains of a long lost civilization with structures behemoth in size and suspended in time and almost entirely made of glass and steel. He wanted to see this for himself, it was something he was not taught even as a son of a Baltiar, and he only learned later why it was left a secret and made into a fable after prying into the coffins of New Acadia's rulers.

The Lords of New Acadia had hid the existence of the Gihon to hide the Ancients within a shroud of divinity. To conceal them as deities was something crucial for the pilgrimage to be functional and successful. It was a shame because researching the sea might've been helpful in piecing together Acadian history and spreading the truth about their shared past could at least be useful in unifying them.

The answers were there, but as one historian wrote, *"Atop the tallest tower in the Middle Highland of Rodina was a clear view of the clear sea, of all the Lowlands and the stars. But Gran Acadia was a world long lost, a bridge too far"*

He turned his attention away from the ancient world which often preoccupied his mind, and returned to his apartment where he was greeted by a life he had all but entirely neglected.

There's so much to do. Where have I been?

Though he hadn't actually left the premises in what may have been months, he still felt like a stranger in his own apartment.

Like a soldier returning to the homeland after decades on the battlefront.

Spread throughout the concrete floor were boxes filled with gizmo parts he tried to repair, but never could, laid over the kitchen counter were stacks of official Army reports he was told to read but never did, and on the round table positioned near the centre of the room was an unfinished game of Hegemon he had been losing for weeks. A part of him worried the pieces currently set in place had already determined the outcome of the game, but he was too afraid to check. So he left it unobserved with hopes his opponent, Helissia would eventually forget about it.

Next to the reports on the counter were letters arriving to his office from nearly every corner of Acadia. They were sent to him by the Generals who were leading war campaigns in the distant overworld and Acadia's remaining prefectures of Northland, Southernland, and Roseland.

Though it was their duty to produce for their plates, he couldn't help but feel they wrote their letters with little understanding of the affairs within. They begged for supplies when supplies were scarce, sent them old unsalvageable equipment while expecting new and serviceable ones in return, and demanded well-trained soldiers to replenish the frontlines in exchange for the uniforms they mailed back.

We can't turn our backs on them, but what more can we do? We haven't won a war in years, and now Hariya Baltiar's been captured-

Damn, I need a drink... No. I said I was going to quit, and I really meant it.

But what else is there to do?

Maybe just one.

Inside the cupboards of the walk-in kitchen, he found bottles of witchleaf and cactus-water, but reached for the red wine instead.

For a moment he considered just settling on the tap water, knowing it was what he should be doing, but by the time he finished the thought, the glass was practically empty.

Maybe another one, just for good luck.

He placed the bottle of wine on the counter and poured himself another glass, which he finished in one go, and then another which lasted just as long. He repeated this until he could no longer feel the glass pressing against his lips.

Wh-what am I d-doing? I c-can'-t even s-sttop m-myself from drinking. I'm just a failure.

"Aren't I?" he asked aloud, as if expecting an answer from someone or somewhere.

He was only a boy, no older than eight when he was taught the craft of running Army supplies through the sewers and storm drains of Queens and Roilmont, and about eleven when his father sent him out to fight his first war.

He should've died then but here he was, alive and *alone*.

Out of the original twelve Liberation Armies, only seven remained. Most had fallen within his lifetime and though he wasn't directly responsible, it was a grim reminder of not only the pressures he faced to succeed, but also of his failures to accomplish anything he set his heart to.

I can't end up like father, I can't end up like those generals.

I can't end up like the men I look up to.

There was a broken typewriter on the counter which he couldn't help but always caress after a couple drinks. It was an Old Acadian gizmo, outdated even for its time, but charming, nonetheless.

The last of her things... Katherine.

There was a fleeting pain in his chest whenever the name came to mind, but he fanned those feelings away.

Those were feelings that should've died along with her.

I wish I could call her.

He loved many over the years, but it was *her* he could not forget.

Professor Lind was the first woman to catch his eye since, and only because she reminded him of *her*.

I'm losing the Lowlands, like I lost Windlehem. I'm going to lose this war. Like I lost Kat—

He couldn't remember when he had passed out, but he did eventually awaken sometime later with his face pressed hard against the kitchen floor. There was a ringing in the back of his ear which *wouldn't go away*, no matter how hard he tried to ignore it.

What is that sound? Why is it familiar? It sounds like... It sounds like my name? Wait... It is my name!

"Talius!" called out a soldier from the radio on the counter.

"Open the door, Talius!" she begged. "It's Flowers. We're in trouble."

Valtus V

She was the most *beautiful thing* he'd ever seen, and everyone seemed to notice. Even the boys who showed little concern in anything other than their own survival.

So now they like girls?

"Daaria!" yelled Riya, finding the quickest path to her through the other Generalists lounging around the courtyard.

"Girl!" said Taalia, trailing her.

He watched from a short distance as the three of them took turns lifting one another up with a tight embrace.

"Daaria!" said Atlus, running to her with some disbelief and hugging her like the rest. "I missed you so much!"

"I missed you too!" she said, slightly winded. "How is everything?"

"Terrible," said Riya, "I'm still single."

"Great," said Taalia, "I found a man."

"Really?" said Daaria, "Where is he?"

"Yeah!" replied Taalia with elation, "He's right ther—*Huh*? Where'd he go?"

"He left your sorry ass already?" laughed Atlus. "Damn."

"Hey!" said Taalia, "No he didn't! He wouldn't—.I'm sure he's around, *somewhere*."

"Don't worry," said Daaria, covering her giggles with a hand, "I believe you."

"Some apartment crashed the other day," said Atlus, taking a step back and pointing back to the Playgrounds, the general direction of the incident.

"They sent a bunch of us to go clean it up, but other than that, and Taalia's imaginary boyfriend, it's just the same ol' boring-ass South Station."

"I know," said Daaria, looking down at her black leather flats. "I heard a lot of people got hurt, but I'm happy you're all safe."

"How about you?" asked Atlus. "You're still so small and sorta cute."

"Hey, what do you mean *sorta cute*?" said Daaria, flicking her hair to the side with a little attitude. "I've been cute."

"Girl, true," agreed Taalia.

"Daaria, have you met Wilaana?" asked Riya, taking Wilaana by the hand and bringing her into their circle.

"No, I haven't," said Daaria. "Nice to meet you."

"My pleasure," replied Wilaana.

The two exchanged smiles and salutes.

"And that's Romin and Alric," she said, pointing to the two who stood far off in the distance.

Too afraid of approaching, but not too shy to *stare*.

There were a dozen other boys watching from the sideline as well, and they all gazed at her with *hungry*, lust-filled eyes. It boiled his blood, and he wanted to do something about it like maybe telling them to find something else to look at, or maybe just take turns punching them all in the face.

Ugh... Can't they just look at something else? Well... I guess not really.

As much as it upset him, he also understood.

It was rare for most of them to meet girls outside their regiments, as Generalists were rarely permitted to leave their stations unless their hard labour was needed, or if they were being sent out to war. So the moment one showed up, something seemed to awaken in them.

He understood the feeling, he just never thought he'd be this jealous.

"I'm so happy I caught you all at the right time," said Daaria.

"Please stay," said Atlus, "I can't stand these people, especially these two," he said, pointing to Riya and Taalia.

"Hey!" said Riya.

"Atlus, it's annoying how annoying you are," said Taalia, shaking her head. "Unbelievable."

Daaria laughed. "I don't want to go, but I can't stay for too long."

"Did you run here or something?" asked Valtus, breaking his silence out of sight.

Her head quickly turned to the sound of his voice.

"Y-Yeah," she said, glossy-eyed. "Why?"

"You just look tired and a little sweaty—"

He stopped talking when she gave him a look.

"Smooth," whispered Taalia.

"Wait..." said Atlus. "They just gave us a holiday and you're telling us you can't stay?"

"My team got assigned to a faraway assignment," answered Daaria. "I'm leaving tomorrow."

"Where are they?" asked Riya, "I remember that Omaara girl, she's *gorg*."

"Right?" agreed Daaria. "They left without me. Well... we had a ride to catch today, but I told them to go ahead. I wanted to come here first."

"You came here just for me?" said Taalia, with glitter in her eyes.

Daaria smiled. "Of course, I didn't get a chance to say goodbye when they were assembling the Generalists for Windlehem, so when I heard the campaign was cancelled, I just had to come."

The others were too focused on her eyes and smile to notice the worry leaking from her voice.

Her shoulders are also raised, and her knees are a little caved in too. Her guard must be up. Why?

She was never the type to openly reveal her emotions, but it was clear *something was wrong*.

"What if you get in trouble?" asked Taalia.

"It's fine, I'll take a horse," she answered, turning her head to him, but glancing away the moment their eyes met.

"Um... guys?" said Daaria. "Can I talk to Valtus? Alone?"

"He's in trouble," said Riya, whispering to Wilaana who quickly caught on.

They did as they were asked, and the crowded courtyard no longer seemed as busy or noisy with just two of them standing there face to face.

"What's wrong?" asked Valtus.

"What do you mean?" asked Daaria, keeping her distance. "Nothing's wrong."

"Don't lie," said Valtus, "You're leaking."

"What!?" said Daaria, looking down and back at her pants. "Where?"

"Huh?" said Valtus.

"What are you talking about?" she said, trying not to shout and draw attention, but failing to do both.

"Y-Your voice, you sound worried," replied Valus.

"Oh..." she said, visibly agitated.

"What did you think I'm talking about?"

"N-Nothing," replied Daaria. "And I'm fine."

"Okay, well… that's good," said Valus.

"Yeah," said Daaria.

"I guess everything is good then," said Valtus.

"Yeah," said Daaria. "Everything's great."

"Great," said Valtus.

"Good," replied Daaria.

"All right then."

"I guess so,"

Silence.

"Okay, so where is she?" asked Daaria, with eyes piercing into him like a terrorbird.

"Who?"

"Your little girlfriend," answered Daaria. "Where is she?"

"Huh? What are you talkin' about?" said Valtus. "I don't have one."

"So why didn't you shave your beard?"

"Why would I shave my beard?" said Valtus. "I like it."

"Okay, but I don't," said Daaria.

"What?" he said, quite perplexed by the situation.

Damn, I forgot how crazy she was.

"The last time I saw you was months ago."

"So you don't want to see me?"

"What!? That's not even what I said!"

"Well that's what it sounds like to me," said Daaria, "And you didn't send me back a letter so I guess that means it's true."

"You know I'm not a good writer."

He always knew reading and writing was important, but the words always seemed to dance, and his eyes couldn't help but follow.

"I don't care," said Daaria

Her voice softened, and the anger in her face fell just a little.

"You could've sent me a drawing."

"I'm not good at that either," he replied.

"Then send me a potato," said Daaria, "I don't *care*."

Daaria, you really are still the same girl.

He thought about her often over the past few months, but figured she had found better or moved on. They had grown up together in the same dirty playgrounds, eating bugs for breakfast and watching the sun set over the crater ridden lands with the other children who were heading nowhere fast. As much as he wanted her, he always knew she deserved better than a life in the Lowlands, a life better than anything he could've provided for her.

I can't give you what you need. Why would you want a boy like me?

She was the prettiest girl in Peaceland and likely the smartest person he'd ever met. Always performing better than him and the other children in class, and now she had something to show for it.

She deserved better, and yet here she was.

Smiling with the same eyes she owned when she was just a little girl, wearing the same simple clothes she wore when she left Eastern Stronghold.

A green t-shirt, blue jeans torn at the knees, and a pair of little black flats.

I really thought I lost her that day.

"You know what happens when you think like that," she said, taking a step towards him. "Did you forget what I told you?"

"N-No," said Valtus. "Well, maybe a little."

She had once told him while they were digging for crickets that *"How you see yourself is how you see the world."*

It took him several years to understand what she meant, and a few more to accept she wasn't wrong when she told him, *"You also have it in you to make it out,"* in the days leading up to her transfer to the Citadel.

It was what he needed to hear when he was broke and stuck in Eastern Stronghold, and it was what he needed to hear today.

"Are you mad at me?" he asked, too embarrassed to meet her eyes.

"Yes," she put it bluntly.

"I'm sorry."

"Don't do that again," she scorned.

"Okay," he said with his head still down.

A silence descended upon them once more, but it was quickly broken with the sound of her approaching footsteps.

"What now?" he asked, looking up to find her standing right in front of him.

With eyes gleaming like the seamoon on a rainy day, with lashes tangled and flickering like the lights in the classroom where they first met.

"Take me out to eat," she answered.

Emmi IV

Like several marketplaces atop the Highland, the district continued through an underground passage made of long-winding maze-like corridors. It was where the largest market of all sprawled beneath the rest of Newtown, held up by blackstone pillars sprouting from somewhere beneath the red earth. A place the locals called the 'Undermarket' and the foreigners called *lawless*. A place as crowded and busy as above, and it was only getting busier with people trickling in from all its corners, likely fleeing the eruption outside.

It was here she learned if something had a use then it had a place, and if it had a place then it had a price. Here were slave houses where one could purchase an orphan for a small cost, and indulge in animal baiting rings where different species were betted against one another and against man. One could even find human organs, limbs, teeth, other body parts, along with a surgeon to stitch them in somewhere.

"There was an explosion upstairs!" said a man by a mining enlistment desk.

He was breaking the news to several others who stood awaiting employment, so the three took another moment to eavesdrop.

"Is that what all that shaking was about?" asked another as he finished signing his forms.

"I thought it was a tremor"

"Yeah, no" replied the man, "Someone set off a bomb by one of the pilgrim sites"

"What?!"

"Don't tell me it's another war"

"I don't think so", "The Military Police are looking for three suspects".

"I bet it was those Blacksheeps"

"What—?" she blurted, almost loud enough for them to hear.

"Three suspects—? That's us!" added Ashley-Ann.

"That was quick" said Nia, pondering to herself, "They must've already closed down the streets".

A crowd had gathered around the man telling the story by the desk, but the three continued on before they caught anyone's attention. Word travelled quickly in Newtown, but she didn't expect it to be so soon.

"Hania, what time is it?" asked Ashley-Ann

"12:46" she replied.

"What!? We only have fourteen minutes to get back to school?!"

"You two should start heading back then, I think I'll be okay" said Emmi.

She was concerned about entering the Undermarket until it struck her that she could take the underground entrance back to the General Store, the discreet entrance where mostly elite patrons snuck in from.

I should be able to make it back before Morten or Garett catches me,

Though I should stay away from that red door,

Just in case the old man's there,

Smuggling in orphans and Solarites

In addition to the well populated tunnels leading into the marketplace, there were paths leading out of the corridors into open air bazaars and villages made of concrete huts. It was where many Tautaus now lived and where the Blacksheeps did much of their smuggling into the city. Bringing in supplies from the Frontier Army, the third major force in Acadia's history.

While the Military Police were a remnant Acadian branch of the Westerian Army, originating from territories conquered by Westeria, the Liberation Army was said to be a force which had emerged from the Lost Years in Queens, made up of families which had survived Westerian occupation and later, Military Police invasion. Alongside the Landlords who claimed the City for themselves, they brought forth an era lasting several hundred years known as New Acadia. This rise was promising at first, and to their credit they did liberate many communities early on, however the Landlords gradually made it clear where they stood with their army. They wanted Queens for themselves and it mattered little who or what dwelled within its buildings. Together they were responsible for oppressing hundreds of thousands as they claimed communities under the banner of Zaaj the Ancient King. Imposing rent and taxation as a way of enriching themselves and spreading the idea of pilgrimage as a way of gathering people into their markets. While the Landlords have been more or less removed from power within the Liberation Army, the underlying system they helped consolidate largely remained the same.

Surviving such schisms in Acadian history was another force—the Free Acadian Frontier Army, a now mainly rural coalition found in the outer lowlands, they were the truest to Old Acadia, and the Blacksheeps relied on them for survival. It was where they received their plaster bombs, as well as the willingness to resist the forced occupation. It was now said the Frontier was in control of Windlehem, a victory which they quietly celebrated in Queens.

"Nia, Emmi" hissed Ashley-Ann, from their rear, her voice filled with urgency.

"What is it?" asked Emmi

"I see some police-soldiers. I think they're from the shooting.

"They're definitely following us"

The words sent a jolt of fear through her spine, and they quickly turned their heads to steal a glimpse. Amongst the sea of people flooding the gates from above, they spotted a small Military Police unit of three scanning the crowd, accompanied by a vigilant rottweiler.

"You see them?" Nia asked, her voice tinged with concern.

"Yeah, they're from the shooting," said Emmi, immediately recognizing the *tall blonde* who threatened her with a gaze and *sunglasses* who she came to hate.

"I recognize them"

"Are you sure?" asked Nia

"Yeah I remember the blonde one watching me"

Mother,

Please don't let me get caught today.

I promise to pray-

"What do we do now?" asked Ashley-Ann

"We can lose them in the sewers" she replied

"No" said Nia, "I just did my hair"

"What about the catacombs?"

"No" replied Ashley-Ann

"We could get lost in there"

"Just keep moving through the market" said Nia, "Before we get stuck in this crowd"

They crossed the underground streets, weaving in-between the canopy of stalls, trying to shake the police-soldiers by cutting through crowds of betting men and women who were eagerly waiting to watch two endangered species fight, a black lion against a giant terrorbird.

"Are they still following us?" asked Emmi

"Yes," said Nia, turning back.

"They're getting closer"

"Just keep moving" she replied, "Don't be afraid to push your way through"

They continued until the crowd had thickened and there was no space to press forward.

The Police were *somewhere*.

"Okay, what now?" asked Emmi, her voice quivering with desperation, her mind racing for a solution.

"We have to lose them but we can't make a scene" whispered Nia.

Then, a spark lit up somewhere in Ashley-Ann's often blank and ditzy eyes.

"I think I have an idea," she said, readjusting her ponytail.

"What is it? asked Nia "

"I forgot to set my charge off"

"What?! Do it now!" urged Emmi

Ashley-Ann swiftly pressed down on the button, and a split second later a loud thud reverberated through the market, shaking the stalls and the surrounding area. Panic swept through the confused market-goers as they scrambled to find shelter and she felt her heart race as the chaos ensued, providing the perfect opportunity to disappear into the commotion.

"See you guys after work!" Emmi yelled, "I'm running back!"

"Okay, I love you," Hania called out, her voice filled with a mix of worry and care.

"I love you too!"

Raamina VII

She stood inside the kitchen chamber in her mud-soaked gown, watching the servants as they nourished the fire beneath a foundry ladle the size of a small house. What was once used by the Ancients to likely pour molten casts of maglith and coloured earthstone, was now used as a cooking cauldron to feed thousands of temple goers and Rocklanders.

Even the ungrateful ones, they had their share too.

When she closed her eyes, she could feel the faint chants of the temple choir resonating throughout the halls, and when she placed her ears to the wind, she could hear her own daughter within the medley of voices. Hymning her heart away with the other righteous and self-righteous souls.

Don't sing too loud, baby, you might hurt yourself.

According to her Aunt Wila, when the Old Acadians lost track of the years, they started counting the summers, and when they lost track of the summers, they began counting the stars. Not much was recorded during that time, but much of what emerged still lingered, and in the case of Rockland, a legacy continued to boil.

Entrapped behind the walls of their own constructions, and under the pressures of a Westerian blockade which may have lasted centuries, the Old Acadians were forced to turn to the unexplained world for sustenance. Without any means of preserving what they managed to grow, butcher, and forage under the Highland sun, they placed whatever they could raise and scavenge into a perpetual boil. Survival here was a communal effort and there was no space for pickiness. If it could be consumed, it was tossed inside the cauldron, and if it could burn, it was considered wood fuel.

They named their newfound creation the *forever stew*, a concoction now simmering for over half a millennia, and likely until the end of all Acadia. Along with the splitting of the Old-coin, and the fables which founded the New Faith, it was one of the many persisting customs conceived after the Westerian Invasion.

I wonder if those stories of cannibalism were true.

"What the hell are you doing here?" said Lady Isaarith, startling all the servants with her crackling.

"Thinking," she replied, unbothered.

"Can't you think somewhere else? You know, maybe on your bed after the funeral? You know, the one we're all waiting on you to finish?"

She didn't respond, preferring to stare at the pyre instead.

Do I really have to go out there? In front of all those people? Couldn't I just stay home? Hmm… Maybe if I stand closer to the flames I can fake a fever

"Mother Raamina!" called out a girl from the back entrance to the chamber.

What now?

Through fire she found Luna, the eldest daughter of her head servant Maggy, approaching with a little Solarite boy who knew his way around the City like a street rat, and Larcia Winch, a choir-girl who was madly in love with her son.

"Where's Hiran? She asked, eager to expect some good news for the first time all day.

She had sent the three of them out to Queens earlier in the day, after learning he had been summoned by his uncle somewhere. Their job was to fetch him and tie him down to one of the bronze statues in the main hall until she returned. An assignment which excited Larcia more than it should have, *but as long as she was motivated*, who was she to judge?

"We saw him in Newtown, but we lost him in the crowd," said Luna.

Her head was down and her hands by her side.

"Sorry, Mother."

Unlike Maggy who looked like a toad, she was a beautiful creature who never mis-stepped and rarely misspoke.

Why must that boy go out on Braxas' orders?

He always puts him in danger with these assignments.

He already has a bad habit of keeping others around longer than he should, too. When is he going to learn?

She always told him that while friends can show you new things and lead you to new places, few will ever take you back home, and even fewer in one piece.

"It's fine," said Mother Raamina, "Thank you for trying. You can all return to your post."

"Yes, Mother," they said, leaving with their hands by their hearts.

"You're not okay, are you?" said Isaarith, dismissing the rest of the servants in the kitchen with a hand.

They all turned to her for direction before complying with the lady.

She simply sighed and nodded.

"I just don't feel right about this," replied Mother Raamina, waiting until the chamber door had shut behind the last of them, and only after she was certain no one else was around.

"It- It wouldn't be right, I'm responsible for all this."

"Responsible for what?" asked Isaarith, placing a hand on her shoulder.

Her fingers were long and spindly, like a spider's legs. It was unnerving, but she welcomed it, nonetheless.

"I killed them," said Mother Raamina, "And now I have to bury them."

"Oh," said Isaarith, delighted to hear that was the extent of her worry. "No, you didn't."

"Huh?" said the mother, "What do you mean?"

"Did you forget what you once told me to do? Lie to yourself until it's true?" said Lady Isaarith, almost smiling as if she could.

T-That's right. Who am I crying for? I'm here to build a country, not to make friends.

"I-I'll be there in a few," said the Mother, returning a smile before realising Isaarith couldn't see it if she wanted to.

"While I'm still cute, please," said the lady, limping away.

I do feel better, but I still hate funerals.

Why is this my life?

She disliked many things about Motherhood, but at the top of the list were ceremonies which required her to take part as an officiate. Which practically meant every important funeral and high-class wedding ever.

Faith was never her first choice and she never asked for this, but after her dear mother, the former matriarch of Rockland, passed away from a sudden illness, she was left with the burden of picking up after the temple. Or suffer watching it be handed to some undeserving lord-woman.

Aside from the few oil lamps scattered around the room, and the fire raging beneath the cauldron, there were no other sources of light within the darkened chamber. It was intentionally kept this way, both to conceal the images of the ancient world etched into the walls, as well as to draw attention to a shrine of the First Mother and her three daughters placed to the side of the main entrance.

In ancient history, it was never truly certain if some things happened or not, and at times it was difficult to untangle the tangible experiences of a people from the dominant cultural values of a particular period. According to Westerian traders, the Westerian Invasion ended a little under five hundred years ago, but many others like Wila Baltiar, believed it lasted closer to a thousand years, so such was the belief made history.

Many communities during this period developed their own understanding of the world as well, finding their own answers and explanations to what may have happened, who may have been responsible for it, and why. This caused a major problem for the Landlords who learned the hard way that denying the liberties and sovereignties of feral communities was only half the battle. To truly defeat or reclaim a people, it was necessary to replace their history and culture with stories, values, and customs of their own.

And that was exactly what was done.

First with the burning of tree temples, and then later with spreading the new lie to erase their legacies.

History did not always require a traumatic catalyst to be recorded or remembered, but such seemed to be the case for the Acadians and anyone *stupid* enough to live amongst them. In some instances, the time before the catalyst were lost to the ages, as was the case in histories found even in the Old Book. While in other cases, it was well placed and accepted as truth, like the *fabrications* in the New Book. In all incidents, freethinking vanished in favour of group-think, and a state of repetition ensued so long as the same stories were told with unyielding regard.

The First Mother may have never existed and her three daughters may have never been born. It was likely some village discovered the dangers of the iifa-tree, and then made up some useful story around surviving its spread.

But it still didn't answer the question.

Why was it this particular story and not some other?

It seemed like a silly question at first, but the more she thought about it the more it bothered her.

Why the Mother? Why the daughters? Why all these stories and hymns? There must've surely been some reasonable explanation.

Her eyes turned to the ceiling above where they met Utia's supposed son. Though here he was not depicted as a child, but rather as a long bearded decrepit old man who wore a serpentine crown made of every beast found in his kingdom. An ear here, a mouth there, and a few eyes and horns to match elsewhere.

How can idols be divine if their faces and figures were carved by man? How can events occurring in the Biosphere be holy, let alone other wordly? How foolish can we be?

But does it mean there's no God? I-I don't know. I-I'm too afraid to say.

She could hear the sound of hymns fading away until the halls went silent.

As much as she wanted to run back to the Sea Tower, she understood it would've been inappropriate and unwise to hide her face during this time. This was when the public needed her direction the most, when they were vulnerable and susceptible.

I-I guess I should go. Yeah... I'll be back.

She turned away from the fire and headed out the main entrance to the chamber. The hymning returned, almost with a vengeance the moment she entered the ceremonial hall, and with it followed the melodic sound of cradles, a musical instrument played by gently rocking its bellows like a newborn and plucking its strings like the feathers of a jungle fowl.

Leading the choir was her daughter, Romina Baltiar. A young woman of twenty-years who had beautiful brown hair like her father, and was next in line to inherit the endless burdens of her society like her mother.

She looks nothing like me but must play my part,

I don't think she can do it, not until she loses her heart.

After climbing an unreasonably long flight of Ancient concrete steps, she made her way towards a makeshift stage and a podium placed at the centre. It was there she hid her body, both from the crowd of people who gathered beneath her, as well as from the bodies piled in the foreground below.

The music stopped.

I should've faked that fever.

She wanted to throw up a little, but managed to swallow her fear and step forward.

Even Isaarith, a woman who cared for little beyond herself, was visibly upset. If she could have she might have shed a tear, if not for the dead, then at least for the stench of decaying flesh.

"Daughter Rodina tries her best to guide misled souls back home," said Mother Raamina, breaking the silence. "But it's up to her Mother, Utia, to let them enter."

She had never heard the sound of her own heartbeat before, but there it was. More pronounced than ever and in the presence of over two thousand Rocklanders no less.

"Mother Utia does not give without asking," she said, "And out of all her children, she feeds only those who have begged."

She paused to check their faces, scanning for signs of dissent and whether or not her body language had failed her. She found working men and women, Honoured-folk and Lordlings, most of whom clung to her every word, while others clung to their chests.

It was an opportune time to pivot her stance.

"Every generation has its turn to learn the true nature of humanity, but some things cannot be taught. The world had ended many times before, but it was our faith and the Honoured descendants of Old Acadia who ensured it would not end again.

"The Temples of Zaaj," continued the Mother, "Where no Acadian was left behind or without prayer, shelter, and warmth.

"The Honoured folk, who always sought to protect their people and ensure they were perpetually fed."

"Even the peasantry had their hand in rebuilding this great land," she said, understanding well enough a great leader was also like a good tailor.

Both understood where the seams lie.

She searched once more and was delighted to find she had captured their full attention.

"We also rightfully pay our debts to the Army with work and life, but how many more Rockland children? How many more Interior children? Where is the promised country? Who among us received a pittance for our labour? The wars we fight, we fight without consent, every tear we've shed, we've done with anguish and contempt!"

She had never asked for Motherhood, but it was a part of what remained of her inheritance, and she was going to make the *most* of it.

Daaria VII

She couldn't recall the last time she had spent an evening out in the Citadel, let alone off duty and in her plainclothes, let alone with *Valtus.*

He shaved, good boy.

His face was covered in fresh bumps and cuts, as if he had taken a razor to it in a hurry, and the scars hiding beneath his beard reminded her of an apple grown in the wild. Damaged by the world and left to heal on its own.

He looks more hollow than I remember. The others looked a little half-starved too.

They don't feed Generalists often, do they?

"This is nice isn't it?" said Valtus, placing both hands behind his head. "Being out like this?"

"Yeah," agreed Daaria "It is."

He had changed into his plainclothes as well, a black t-shirt with black shorts and sandals to match.

She didn't recognize the outfit.

Everything looks new.

"Why did you buy new clothes?"

"Hm?"

"Are you trying to impress those girls at South Station or something?"

He opened his mouth to respond, but let out a defeated sigh instead.

"I'm just kidding," she said, smiling and pulling him closer by the arm.

He may not have been the most handsome boy, but he did have his charm like the scorching dry Highland wind on a humid summer day.

You should kiss him. Wait... No. He has to work for it.

Or does he?

Hmm... That is the question.

"Hey!" said Valtus, taking his arm away. "What if someone sees us?"

"It's nice and crowded here," said Daaria. "We blend right in."

"Yeah," said Valtus, "But what *if?*"

She pouted and crossed her arms like a child.

What's the point if we can't even hold hands? Ugh... This is just like the time he wouldn't let me eat that weird-looking bug. Or the time he wouldn't let me swim in the ocean with the other kids.

I-I shouldn't be upset at him, he's right.

He's always been right.

"I guess you're right," grumbled Daaria, disappointed by the special moment they were denied.

Along with breaking up gangs and drug-rings, the Army fought hard to dull the interest soldiers may have had in one another, fearing such ties threatened the bond soldiers held with one another and the Cause. They were made to care for the Army before they cared for themselves, and forced to care for themselves before they could care for another, and the Army had achieved this for the most part with strict rules and punishments against dating.

There was even a policy to prevent soldiers from having children before their first deployment.

She wasn't alone in suspecting it was their way of motivating them to go to war with the intention of winning, or at least incentivizing them to compete for a safer position in the force. Though, there was some sense to such rules she figured, especially with the persistent threat of hemovaria underlying every sexual interaction between man and woman. The worry was enough for the Commander to routinely issue every soldier to keep their desires distant from one another in fear of another outbreak within the Force. Though it often sounded like a plea more than anything.

"Are you hungry?" asked Valtus, tapping her by the hips to let her know he still loved her.

"I am," she replied, leaning in a little closer.

They walked along the stone tiled streets of the night-market, scraping shoulders with a few hundred others who seemed just as lost in the world. Their path resembled a labyrinth or an unkept garden with the way the market-stalls sprouted without any clear direction or meaningful plan. The night was also illuminated with strands of brightly lit light bulbs weaving through and under each merchant tent and army post.

She had patrolled the same streets earlier in the day with her team, and she wondered now if anyone would or could recognize her with her hair down and lipstick on.

Soldiers, especially Specialists and Peaceguards, were generally well regarded and respected, or at the very least feared, by civilians and migrants. It was common for many to take advantage of this valour and privilege, often pushing for free lunches with some even resorting to extortion and bribery. Even she was guilty of accepting a payment *or two* in her early days as a Peaceguard, but only because she faced pressures from her peers. It was something she regretted everyday as her hands were dirty, so they never quite left her pockets whenever she was out.

In the nearby unwalled and impoverished slums, however, it was often the case that neither was true. That soldiers, regardless of their rank, were respected or feared, rather they were resented, and at best, tolerated. It didn't affect their ability to order and command, however, as it was understood by the masses that acts of civil disobedience could mean the difference between their conditional freedom and imprisonment.

The slums...

We should still be careful, there are rebels everywhere.

R-Relax, there's hundreds of others outside.

But what about Mineraltown?

What if-

Okay, you need to stop, there's nothing going on.

It was already hard enough to let her guard down, even when there was no real threat around, but without her uniform she felt *naked* and *see-through.*

"Daaria?" asked Valtus.

"Huh?" she responded, as if she had just awakened.

"I asked if you knew what you wanted to eat," said Valtus.

"Oh..." said Daaria. "Hmm..."

What do I want to eat?

She took a moment to ponder the answer to such a deep and perplexing question.

Hmm...

"I don't know," was her best response.

"All right," sighed Valtus. "Let's just walk around 'til we find something."

"Sure," she smiled.

If I could eat you I would, stupid boy.

Another half hour of wandering the night market passed like a few seconds, and at some point they crossed into the wealthier, better kept side of the market district. It calmed her anxieties a little, but she could tell he grew a little more nervous.

Things were a little pricier here.

"Damn," said Valtus, gesturing to every lineup and public spectacle they skipped out on. "Look at all the stuff."

There were street vendors and trading posts, crafts shops and tea coffee emporiums, and among the sheep herders and cattle ranchers, they found

"A woodcow!" shouted Daaria, pointing through a gathering of on-lookers.

"What?" said Valtus. "A wood-cow? All the way up here?"

They walked over to the crowd with some disbelief, but sure enough, there it was. Kneeling on all fours while its owners collected the fares they charged to touch and climb it.

It was a longer line-up than she expected or hoped.

How long has this been going on?

Woodcows were *gorgeous* ancient creatures which many Lowlanders regarded as sacred for the moss and microbodies of greenery which they carried on their bodies. Here, however, it was made to carry a shoal on its back. A shoal made of cowhide and decorated with the flowers plucked from its back, as well as cheap gemstones likely pulled from some Highland stream.

Someone has to report this. Woodcows can't survive up here, these ranchers know that better than anyone. I'll take it to the commander before I leave.

They continued on through the market in silence, still unsure of what they were doing, where they were going, or how to make the most out of this time together.

"How's the Peaceguard?" he asked, at some point.

"I don't know," she replied.

"Is there something wrong?"

"No," she answered, understanding that he was carrying her weight in the conversation.

"It's just… Some days I feel stuck, some days I feel better."

"Yeah," said Valtus. "I know what you mean."

"How about you?" she asked, grazing his fingers with hers, craving more.

"Every day feels like a past life," he replied, "And the last few years feel like a blur."

"I'm sorry," said Daaria.

"For what?"

"For going through what you've gone through."

"It's okay," he replied, with eyes set on a group of migrant women taking a break and sharing a laugh around a wooden crate they used as a tea-table.

"As bad as the Generalist is, it's crazy what some people go through just to make it to the next day. It's hard to make it a world that's already made."

"Yeah," she agreed.

Peaceland was a place founded upon an extraordinary difference in wealth and privilege, and nowhere else on the land was this more apparent than inside its capital, the Citadel.

Over one million people were accounted for in Peaceland, over half of whom were spread throughout the Highland with a majority of those residing within the Citadel. To the northern end of the city were communities made up of Honoured families, stripped of their Landlord status but just as wealthy, and in every other direction leading away from the markets were where the working people, slum dwellers, and every Citizen-born class in between, fought to earn a living.

There were also foreign labourers who, though not expected to fight for any cause, were kept out of the social contract which would have granted them rights in the citizenry if they had been. As a result of their migrant status, they could not own land, take public office, or send their children to school, but still continued to pay rent and taxes, and supply the Army's needs with their labour.

"Hey! What about that place?" he said, pointing into the backdrop.

She followed his finger to a quaint little place with a painting of a skewer running through two love hearts for a name.

"There is no lineup and it looks good."

"Yes!" said Daaria, quickly approaching the stall.

"Two, no, four curry skewers please," he said, following her to the young woman at the counter before reaching for his pockets.

Aww...

He wants to pay.

"It's fine," she interjected. "I'll pay."

"No it's okay," said Valtus. "I have to make it up to you."

Aww.

"No, I told you to take me out," she smiled.

He's still after my heart like it's not already his.

"Sorry but we only take Old-Royals," replied the woman, looking down at her open palm full of Liberated-pieces.

"Huh?" said Daaria. "What do you mean, Old-Royals? This isn't Newtown."

"Yeah but it's a new practice," answered the woman, "To be honest I don't know why, either. I just follow what the owners tell me."

"Oh," said Daaria. "Well, I don't know how to get any Old-Royals."

"And I don't know if I'll be back." Valtus laughed, scratching the back of his head.

No! Don't say that.

"Okay," said the stall keeper, "On the house, don't worry about it."

"Really?" asked Daaria.

"Yeah." She smiled. "I see you're both soldiers."

"Huh? How did you know?" asked Daaria.

"I can tell by your posture, only the good soldiers stand upright."

"Wow, that's a good eye," replied Valtus.

"Yeah, and also her *gun* is showing."

"What!" she shrieked, turning to check the side of her jeans.

Sure enough, there it was, still attached to its holster.

Uh oh… I forgot to leave it at the Armoury.

That's not good.

They thanked the stall keeper for her service and hospitality, and continued on with their skewers on hand.

He's so cute. Okay, kiss him now. No don't, your mouth is full stupid.

There were a few other soldiers who were strolling the streets, some pretending to be on patrol, while others pretended to not know another, but were obviously on dates like them.

She knew because she had an eye for risk takers who chose love like them.

It's hard to find moments like this, it's so easy to forget we're people sometimes, and so rare to see soldiers happy.

There was always some underlying understanding that it was inevitable for soldiers to take a liking towards one another, for one reason or another. As a result, they were encouraged to report those within their ranks who were suspected of being in unapproved relationships, with the promise of one day being rewarded for their disclosure and betrayal. To be reported for such a crime more often than not resulted in disciplinary action, as well as a file on their permanent record which was a stain nearly impossible to scrub away.

War and disease may have meant the end of intimacy, but it was nice to see love still persisting.

She would never forget how happy she was on the day she learned he was going to be transferred to the Citadel, even if he was stationed across town and inside the Generalist. It meant he had worked incredibly hard, and at least she could see him like this.

But still, don't forget rank matters, they're not on holiday to celebrate.

Generalists were often also called deathmarchers and they earned the name, not only because they marched to their graves, but also because they often were better off that way. A significant portion of those on the street and those living in poverty were once Generalists who had served their purpose to the Army, and were no longer considered serviceable.

With no skills other than fighting, there was no place left for them in their own society upon returning, and even if they did have a trade or two tucked under their belt, they were likely too maimed to work. If not in body, then in mind and spirit.

The thought of him not returning whole was something she had spent many years preparing herself for. She never did come to terms with it, believing it was another one of the many injustices perpetrated by the Army against their own people, but she did learn how to sweep her feelings under the rug over the years and enjoy the moment regardless.

If only she could sweep *this bra under some rug* too, she thought whilst trying to adjust it without him noticing. *It's killing me.*

"Is something wrong?" asked Valtus.

"Huh? Oh no it's nothing."

How do I tell him it's not my bra?

"It's my bra," said Daaria. "It never fits right and it kills."

"You don't have tailors?"

"Tailors?"

"Yeah, you know, people who make clothes and sew things together?"

"The girls in South Station always get theirs fixed or just do it themselves."

"Oh," said Daaria. "No, no one does that here."

They used to, but not any more.

"Why don't you learn?"

"What's that supposed to mean?"

"Hm?" he said, turning to her with a sincere look on his face.

He didn't mean it that way, don't make a scene.

"You're saying I'm not as good as those girls?"

"What?" said Valtus, visibly confused.

"Maybe you should go look for one then," said Daaria. "I'm better than that anyways."

A wave of embarrassment washed over both their faces, while the awkward silence *killed* her.

I can't believe how stupid I am.

"Yeah," agreed Valtus, "You are…"

"Look… I… That's not what I…" said Daaria. "I'm sorry."

What's wrong with me?

"Y-You know I just don't want to lose you," she said.

"I-I know," said Valtus, "And you know I don't want to waste your time."

"Don't say that," she said, taking him by the hand. "I just missed you so much."

"I missed you too, Daaria."

My name sounds so pretty when he says it.

He pulled her closer and she let him, maybe a little too easily.

She felt him searching her body *and eyes* for any sign of opposition, but before he could kiss her, she kissed him. It was a long kiss, followed by a longer hug.

His eyes were reddish green and his hair smelled like the earth.

This boy, where did he come from?

This can't be a coincidence, can it?

I don't know.

I just know I have to let him go, and that I'll tear my hair off if anything bad ever happens to him.

Talius VIII– May 7th

Far below the Commander's apartment, and even further below Colonel Hellin's bunker, was an Ancient temple built deep within the rock and earth. It was here the War Council of Peaceland convened and deliberated.

"They're late," said Colonel Hellin, with knees tapping against the underside of a round table.

"It's a long trip," replied Colonel Flowers, a Tautau woman who was likely among the last of her time.

It amazes me how far she's come. It's a miracle she's still alive.

"Yeah," said Colonel Hellin, "But *three* hours late?"

"The elders aren't here either," said Colonel Flowers, "We just have to be patient."

"Okay," replied Colonel Hellin, standing up and reaching over to the centre of the table without needing to adjust his position. "I'll be patient, but I'm done waiting on the food."

It was always difficult to ignore how tall and long limbed Colonel Hellin was, but nowhere was this more apparent than inside the temple. Here he was made to watch his every move so as not to knock anything over by accident, here he was forced to bend his neck whenever he stood.

"Eat while it's still warm," said the colonel, claiming one of the cafeteria trays for himself.

Each of them contained a generous portion of rice and meat stew from the Command Tower's kitchen.

"Nevermind," he said, taking a spoon to the rice like a shovel to the snow. "It's already cold."

They followed his suggestion, nonetheless.

Waiting with him in the presence of naked idols and reliefs depicting Ancient cult ceremonies, were the two high-officers responsible for maintaining the forces fighting under the banner of the Citadel. Colonel Wilona Flowers whose thoughts on things were always worth considering, and Colonel Hellin who never left his side.

In addition to lecturing him on his poor decisions on *practically everything*, Colonel Hellin managed the Specialist Force, a regiment tasked with educating and employing soldiers within highly technical departments.

Sitting next to him was Colonel Flowers, whose patience was always tested within the Generalist Force. An Army division composed primarily of soldiers expected to be the first in line to brunt every conflict. Together they were the main reason he could be left within an arm's reach of the entire Peaceguard, as well as be left alone with his telescope.

"Careful Wilona, don't work yourself beyond repair," said the commander, noticing the hand on her tray was shaking more than it should have.

"I'm fine," said Wilona Flowers, walking back to her place.

I hope so.

It was another twenty minutes of waiting before the first knock on the chamber door occurred.

Before any one of them could answer the call, however, a black-haired woman in sunglasses had already found her way inside with her walking stick.

It was the leader of the Firstland People, Brigadier Wildred August, the *Little Dead Girl.*

She had earned the name after surviving a Hellraiser's inferno unscathed when she was just eight.

"Brigadier," said the three high-officers, handing her a salute.

"Commander, Colonels," saluted the brigadier, limping into the room with the same melancholic expression he learned to expect from her.

"It's so good to see you, Wildred," said Colonel Flowers, drawing a chair out for her.

"Likewise, Wilona," she said, ignoring it.

Though she was the highest ranking officer within the Firstland, she still insisted on wearing the uniform she wore on the day she acquired her most career-defining achievement. A plain field-grey infantry suit without a single medal pinned by the breast pocket, and a bright-red beret to draw attention away from the metal prosthetics replacing both legs.

To survive a fire in one war, only to lose your legs in another.

I can see what they call her, the Little Dead Girl.

"Couldn't we have used the telecom?" she asked, examining the trays and turning away without the slightest bit of interest.

"It's not safe—" suggested Colonel Flowers, before being cut off.

"It takes my party half a day to reach the Citadel and it's not exactly the safest trip," said the brigadier, taking her own place across the table. "Not with the way the roads are, at least. Though, I suppose that's not something you would care about."

She turned away from the colonel before she could respond, choosing to observe a statue of a woman with demons suckling at her nipples and breasts instead.

"What's wrong with the roads?" he asked, taking note of the subtle infliction in her voice.

"Didn't you hear?" she said, with deep condescension. "They're all destroyed. From the Firstlands to Mineraltown, from Mineraltown to the nearest Army posts in-between."

"What!?" said Colonel Hellin. "What are you talking about?"

"We rode our trucks here off-track," continued the brigadier, "Through old mining shafts and rifts on the Highland."

"No... there's no way," said Colonel Flowers. "We just sent out our surveyors, they didn't find anything wrong with the roads."

"You don't have to believe me," said Brigadier August, glancing at the hand-radio he had placed atop the table in arm's reach "The news'll get here, sooner or later."

She can't be serious can she? Yes... of course she is. Why would she lie about something like this?

He fought the urge to pick his radio up and call the Command Center, but did so anyway the moment he recognized it was a losing battle.

"Commander!" answered a Peaceguard from the other line.

"Have you received any transmissions or reports about Mineraltown? Or *anything* about the roads and posts nearby?"

"Um... no, Commander, not since yesterday," answered the soldier. "Should we have?"

Though she may have appeared uninterested, it was clear the brigadier had her ears to the conversation.

What she had in mind, however, was beyond him.

"N-No," said the commander. "But please have someone check it anyway."

He ended the call and set the radio aside. Promising not to touch it unless there was an incoming call, or if there was an urgent order to make.

If there's news, it'll come.

"What could it be?" whispered Colonel Hellin, turning to his peer.

"Maybe they retaliated," replied Colonel Flowers. "But I don't understand, when could this have happened?"

"Retaliation?" asked the brigadier. "Who? For what?"

"We'll get to it when the time comes," said Commander Talius. "As far as the telecom, I'm sorry, but we just can't risk it. We will consider meeting closer to the Firstlands, however. Once the dust settles."

She was as unimpressed with his answer as she was with the food, likely in belief he had no intention of fulfilling his obligation. Instead of challenging his answer, however, she simply turned away.

Guess it's no secret.

Insecure communication lines, though still an issue for them across vast distances, was only one reason as to why the War Council meetings were always held in person. In order to consolidate a country, it was crucial to recognize and disentangle the mannerisms of political rivals and allies, especially in the midst of contentious discussions. Of which the council often devolved into.

Forcing them to gather in one place provided him with a better read on each one of their characters and intentions. Things he could only infer by paying attention to the ways their bodies betrayed them. Political strife were more often than not, matters of honesty and dishonesty, not differences in ideology. Truth was not subjective, the relationship one had to it, however, was relative. Even if they weren't giving it away with words, there was information in everything, and intentions were difficult to hide if one knew what to look for. Actions were not simply louder than words, but oftentimes unspoken words left to interpret.

"Life is a charade and there are dishonest actors," his sister once told him after seeking out her advice on how to deal with some unruly Lords. *"But things are easy to read if you know what to look out for. And people are always leaking, you don't have to poke holes."*

The next knock on the door occurred some ten minutes later, and in came a *large* Zacadin man with a rock-cut face tucked away somewhere underneath a layer of fat. He wore a black uniform adorned with yellow stripes along the shoulder blades and cuffs, as well as more medals pinned to his chest than most Queenspeople could count.

It was Brigadier Quintin Workhammer of Midland Stronghold.

"Welcome, Brigadier," said the Commander, sliding one of the trays in his direction.

"Thank you," said the brigadier, saluting with one hand and reaching out with the other. "I could use a meal."

He was once a decorated wrestler and tug of war champion in the Army, and though he entered the meeting with a limp similar to Brigadier August, his glory days were still etched all across his body like a tattoo.

That's battle hardened muscle he's hiding under his coat. Some fat, but muscle mostly. Incredible. At fifty-five, he could still break most soldiers with a single arm.

As famous as he was for his tug of war medals, he was more widely celebrated for leading his share of the Coalition Army through the Second Military Police Invasion without suffering more than a single major loss. A staggering accomplishment which proved vital to the war effort.

"Hellin?!" he asked upon noticing the abnormally tall figure in the room, "I thought you were on your way to Windlehem!"

"I was," sighed the colonel. "But something came up."

"The Frontier Army is going to be at our gates if we don't—"

"Windlehem is lost," said Brigadier August. "Let it go."

"Let it go?" said Brigadier Workhammer. "Are you out of your mind?" He turned to him. "Please tell us she's out of her mind."

What am I supposed to say? Neither of them are completely wrong.

He sighed, not wanting to talk about it, but understanding he could avoid discussing the matter for only so long.

"I don't know. None of us do. Rockland lost too much trying to take it back, we'd be marching our soldiers down the same path."

"So then what's the solution? An armistice? Peace?" asked Brigadier Workhammer.

"Perhaps," replied the commander. "We'll know only when the time comes."

"And when's that? When we lose our colonies in the overworld?" replied the brigadier.

"When the retreat is over," answered Brigadier August, with an empty glare.

Workhammer grumbled and returned to his plate.

The conversation was put to rest.

Two retired soldiers entered about twenty or so minutes later. Wallace Lancia, a former war general, and a man who simply went by the name Lint, a former rifleman. They were both brought in on wheelchairs by their servant-soldiers who also made sure to sprey each of their eyes before they left.

Like many Acadians who reached an old enough age, they suffered from milky-eye, a disorder which reduced their vision to that of a mole. It occurred mainly in Zacadins, but Tautaus, Daaradins, and other minor Acadians were susceptible to the affliction as well.

After a single dose of sprey, he could see the whites in the old general's eyes fading to reveal a sea of red.

"Ah, I finally see now," said General Lancia, searching the room with clear eyes. "Our Commander and the Colonels, and the Brigadiers as well, it seems."

"General," they all responded with their hands to their hearts.

Lint had fallen asleep and it was likely he wouldn't awake for some time.

There was a long silence after the initial greetings while all, except for Brigadier August and the sleeping soldier, had their fill of the stew. It was tradition to not argue on an empty stomach and he hoped this was at least a decent start, but even after all the trays were taken away and the tea was served, it was *just more silence.*

Not even small talk. Why does this always happen? Is it that hard for us to get along?

Each member of the War Council served their regiments and constituents with grace and distinction, and together they made up the highest council in Peaceland. Though some forces, such as the Lowlanders, were usually missing at the table, it was argued the officials and citizens currently represented were more than enough quorum and diversity to decide upon public and foreign matters for all of Peaceland.

The two Brigadiers, August and Workhammer had inherited their forces and were tasked with the responsibility to represent a class and community of Peacelanders who were consolidated under the Citadel's rule. There was a significant age gap between them which was difficult to ignore, and along with their regional differences, made it difficult to rule.

He was the youngest in the room along with Wildred August at twenty-eight, while the old general was somewhere in his eighties, and Lint was thought to be nearing a hundred and twenty. He looked the part as well, and at times it was hard to say if he was alive or not. Though it was usually safe to assume he was closely following along.

Few things were ever truly decided upon, however, especially not without some insufferable dispute.

"I know it's a long trip," said the Commander, taking a stand with his hand by his heart. "And apparently some of the roads need work—"

"Yes," interrupted the old general. "The roads do need work, but in my day we rode on terrorbirds the size of cows."

No... Not another story.

"You see in those days, the terrorbirds were huge, big birds we used to call them, *big birds* that could run faster than a cow."

"Do you mean a horse, General?" asked Colonel Flowers.

Flowers, no! Shut up! Don't encourage him.

Even if her intention was to help him get through his thoughts quicker, it was never quite certain where a conversation with him would lead.

Especially when he starts telling one of his stories.

"Horse?" asked the old general. "Oh no, I think the stew was chicken," he said, brushing his cold grey beard, chuckling.

I think he needs more sprey.

Though the retired soldiers were far past their prime, and it made little sense for them to be at the table in many respects, it was still required for them to be present.

In addition to being regarded as national heroes and irreplaceable political figures by those who lingered from their time and in the generations following, they were also partially responsible for his reign as Commander. A title which had historically been an intergenerational contest among the Baltiars.

To determine commandership, sometimes it took a knife to the back of an over ambitious uncle, other times it was a national election held between the different Strongholds. In his case it was a bullet, *several bullets,* in the heads of many cousins and their families.

I should be more grateful, they're the ones who told me where to point the gun. I'd be dead without them.

The high-officers turned to one another in relief to find he had finished or forgotten his story, only to break out into silent frustration the moment he began speaking again.

"I think I was seven when I rode my first bird, seventeen one when I rode my last. Though this was before the Military Police left their cities, when a cup of coffee still cost about a Liberated-piece."

He sighed with unease. "T-Thank you for the story, General—"

"Though we didn't pay for things with Liberated-piece at the time, that was a burden we pushed down to the colonies. The colonies... How are they doing these days? Do we still have them?"

"Uh... General?" said Colonel Flowers.

Thank you, Wilona.

"Yes, Colonel?" answered the general.

"You were talking about your first terrorbird," she replied.

No... Why?!

"My first what?" said the old general, "I don't remember owning a leather shirt."

"Okay, enough of this!" said Brigadier Workhammer, turning to his Commander. "Even without Windlehem, we have serious issues to talk about. Why did you stop the search for the Peaceguards?"

"Stop? We never started," he answered.

"What!?" he said, failing to adjust his discomposure. "I'm sending my soldiers to the Gorge tonight. Their families demand a proper burial, and their children deserve it!"

"No you're not," said the Commander, "And there are plenty of soldiers in mass graves who deserved a proper burial. Half the continent is a bonebed."

"But—" tried the brigadier.

"That's an order," he asserted.

He knows the Gorge is off-limits. Midlanders must still think they can push around the commander and hijack the national interest.

"We pay more than our fair share in taxes, we deserve free rights," said Brigadier Workhammer. "Commanding our own forces with our own interests are a part of those rights. And speaking of taxes," he continued, "Why are our property taxes going to the Lowlands?"

"Because they need it to build roads and schools," he answered, plainly.

We already cut their taxes. What are they complaining about?

"Roads? Schools?" said the brigadier, clearly distraught. "The Lowlands are their own domain! Let them fund their own development. That's their problem, not ours!"

"There's only one domain," replied Commander Talius, with his sternest face. "Don't forget, Brigadier."

"Either way you took our best and put them in your Peaceguard," retorted Brigadier Workhammer. "These were student-soldiers who always belonged in the Midlands. Not in the Citadel, and especially not rotting in the f-fucking Forest Gorge," he said, stammering through his words.

"Those are the terms all regions are subjected to," said the Commander.

"Maybe our third and second class soldiers," replied Brigadier Workhammer. "But not our best!"

"What are we left with? You don't think that's a problem, Brigadier?" he said, turning to Brigadier August who was slow to take notice and even slower to respond.

"The Firstlanders are with the Cause, and my allegiance rests with the Citadel," she said, without much resistance in her voice. "I accepted a long time ago they weren't my soldiers anymore."

She turned her head to her Commander and smiled, but it faded the moment he returned it.

"I also learned it doesn't matter what the Firstlanders think, and that they'll always be left behind unless they take matters into their hands."

What? What is she talking about?

"So, if you think you deserve free rights for paying taxes, then we deserve absolute freedom for enduring what we do," scoffed Brigadier August.

"What are you speaking of?" asked Colonel Flowers.

"I'm talking about the *city rats* our Commander unleashed into our lands, Wilona. They've desecrated our farms and fields, our towns and villages for long enough. Our public council has decided it will demolish every new homeless camp that dares to sprout, and jail any newborn that dares to spawn," she said, letting it all out like a bad cough. "Until all of them are relocated and removed."

"New homeless camps?" said the Commander. "What are you talking about? We haven't let in any new migrants yet."

Though the name August itself was an orphan one, she represented a long line of Firstland leaders who fought to prevent new arrivals from entering Peaceland. Especially when they believed it would affect their lands.

"They're all outside Peaceland's walls."

"They're close enough," said the brigadier. "They spill in through the cracks and where do they go? The closest villages they can, and that's the Firstlands."

"You say it like they're cannibals coming out of Roilmont," added Colonel Flowers. "They're not any different from any other Peacelander, They're just like you and me—."

"More like you maybe," said Wildred August, adjusting her sunglasses as if there was shine to block. "Not like me."

The Colonel was visibly staggered and left speechless by the comment, but instead of finding the right words to respond with, she just placed her head down and kept her trembling hands to herself.

"August. Be careful with the lines you cross."

"It doesn't matter," said Brigadier August. "The Firstlanders have made their decision. "You should be grateful we even told you."

"So, should we leave them for the actual cannibals then?" said Brigadier Workhammer, attempting to chime in with some wit.

"If you want them so bad why don't you tell your precious Landlords to take them in? I'm sure they have the land to spare and wouldn't mind —"

"I was still speaking," said the old general, with a voice as deep as the sea, and a look *as cold as steel*.

It more or less frightened each of them to their cores, and it served as a reminder who he *truly* was.

He's still a general, was this just another front?

"S-Sorry, General," said Colonel Hellin. "Please continue."

"T-That's okay, Colonel," he replied, gradually returning to his sickly self. "You did nothing wrong. Now where was I?" he mumbled, "Oh right, as fast as a horse, no, even faster. We used to race them down into the Lowlands and even the lands beyond Summer Circle."

"The overworld, the outer-country." said General Lancia, "Where the air was thicker, like the ladies."

Wilona IX

It was still early in the afternoon when they entered the rooftop of the University. Just her, Helissia, and the cat named Pigeon. The sun was gone, however, and it likely wouldn't be returning with the way the greying clouds had assembled over the Highland sky.

"It worked," said Helissia, with eyes peering into an Old Acadian remake of an Ancient device they called a binocular.

"Mineraltown is like two hours away," said Colonel Flowers, uninspired by the professor's conclusion. "I doubt you can actually tell from this far."

"See for yourself," said Helissia, stepping aside and handing the gizmo off to her.

She accepted it with as much excitement as a schoolgirl finding her crush in homeroom, placed it over her eyes as she tried to her sleeping mask every night, and set her sights to the distant cluster of concrete, steel, and stone. The view made possible by the University was just enough to peer over the walls of Mineraltown, which were tall, but no more than the fences found separating the boys from the girls in South Station.

"Huh?" she said, lifting the device from her eyes and placing it back on.

"What?" asked Helissia, "You see something?"

She scanned as much as she could of the holy town. From the roads leading into its mismatched towers to the tall rockwood in the foreground. She also searched for any signs of a forced entry, as well as the massacre reported late last night, but the day seemed to pass like any other,

"Wilona?"

"No," she replied. "How can you be so sure? Everything seems so normal…"

She turned toward Helissia and screamed when she found her face through the binoculars.

"I'm sure," replied Helissia, unamused and annoyed.

"Have another look, there" she said, pointing back to the land.

The darkest spaces on the Highland were usually found in-between the villages sprawling out and away from the Citadel, but Mineraltown on *second glance* appeared nearly indistinguishable from the dusk ridden land.

Wait-

She's right—

It... It does look cold and bleak.

Like a fly caught under the spell of an unfixed fire, her gaze was captured by the dreary skyline of the small city, and though she stood empty and seemingly void of all activity, Mineraltown like all Ancient constructs, appeared threatening and alive *without her light.*

Wait- No- Hold on- I think I see something.

With a press of a button, she zoomed in as much as she could into the cave-infested mining town, and in its northernmost corner, she located a colossal whitestone monument resembling a *pyramid* sliced in half. It was the First Temple of Zaaj, a great Ancient ziggurat with walls still glistening without the sun, and stairs cascading down into the town like the brackets of a tree fungus. It was where Mother Maaria once ruled from with open arms, and it was there she found what appeared to be a group of workers hauling some kind of machine into its entrance.

What's going on here?

It was too dark and too far to tell if they were soldiers, miners, or nuns, but she was sure the machine in question was an *engine*, or at least belonged to one.

"Hmm..."

"There's definitely something going on. I'm curious to hear what the surveyors find"

"What is it?" asked Helissia

"I see four people, they're carrying something into the Temple-"

"It looks like a machine"

She continued to step forward, searching for an explanation to what she was witnessing, or at least a better angle to the scene, but then she felt something warm and *alive* coil around her feet.

"Huh?!" she said, lifting the binoculars and looking down.

There she found Pigeon nibbling on her laces, as well as the University's student lounge resting directly below the gap between her legs.

Another step forward and she would've retired her career with an even earlier funeral, and maybe a shorter school year for the students.

"Pigeon! You saved me! Thank you so much, girl. Wait- you're a girl, right?"

Pigeon meowed.

"I don't know what that means, or why I even asked, but I owe you my life," said the colonel, saluting the cat and turning back to the town.

She was determined to follow the group as they carried out their operation, but by the time she readjusted her vision, they were *gone*.

Damn.

She scanned the stairs for any other suspicious activities, but it was empty.

I hope I didn't miss anything.

"Seems like wherever there's a wall, there's tension," said Helissia, approaching her from the side.

"Yeah," agreed Wilona Flowers "I've always felt the same."

"You might as well get a look at the rest of it while you're up here" said Helissia, gesturing to the general direction of Peaceland, "At least here the view is nice"

She was silent, but nodded and did as she was suggested.

"*Wow!*" she immediately thought to herself upon turning toward the Midland Plateau and the Lowlands, "You can see almost everything from up here".

It was *menacing* and *colossal* the way the Highland descended down into the mist of the Midlands, but the view made her too nauseous to continue beyond that one observation.

"I can see why Talius is so crazy about that telescope"

Speaking of which, I wonder if I can find him.

She turned toward the Citadel, adjusted the scope, and strolled the rooftop for a better view of the capital.

Though many of the major institutions and establishments possessed some kind of allure, her eyes were quick to locate the six-story apartment block welded to a concrete long hall. It was the building which housed the Hospital, where this *ordeal* more or less began.

Yesterday I was thinking of retiring. Today I'm preparing for war and questioning reality. I didn't expect any of this.

266

Her attention gradually drifted from the medical facility and toward a stalagmite-like structure protruding from the Fortress, *the Commander's Tower*. She was expected there for a War Council meeting tomorrow, one that would likely *disfigure* the current social configuration of Peaceland, or at the very least, *change* who stood to benefit in her future affairs.

Well, I guess none of us expected this.

She searched the windows of the uneven tower, as well as the balconies strewed throughout its varying floors and spires, hoping to find him working, and *there he was*. On the rooftop with eyes dead set searching the Ruined Sea, *almost like a little boy actually*.

She continued her stroll atop the University, adjusting the binoculars and widening her view to include South Station and her sisters to the north, east, and west, as well as every community in between. There were Peacelanders scavenging the streets next to children returning home from school, a lovely couple dancing their hearts away with their curtains flared, two stray cats fighting over the wings of a summerbird, and a son feeding his bed-stricken mother with his only hand.

Nothing unusual here.

Well maybe other than the two soldiers making out by the park.

"I'm sorry we couldn't find a cure for you," said Helissia, out of the blue, "Our people always warned us about getting too close to that place you call Lowtown. They must've lost their minds when they found all those Acadians making a home out of it."

"Yeah," said Colonel Flowers after collecting herself a little. "It makes me laugh whenever I think about it."

"Do you remember anything?" asked Helissia.

"Only that I was really tired and thirsty and…" said the colonel, trailing off. "Someone handed me a cup of water," she continued, after a painful head ringing moment of failing to recollect anything else. "I can't say for sure who, but it could've been my mother."

Helissia sighed. "There is some good news, well, sort of."

"What do you mean?"

"Even if your reproductive system was damaged, you'd still be able to bear children."

"It would just be to a stillborn or a…" said Helissia, pausing to find the right word. "… Creature." She cleared her throat before continuing, "So the problem could be your husband, not you."

"Thank you," said the colonel. "But I love my man, so it doesn't make me feel better."

"It shouldn't," said Helissia. "It likely means something else is going wrong, and if I'm being honest, it's strange you've kept on for this long without a proper diagnosis. You might only have a year or two left at best."

"You'll find out when they cut me open," said Wilona Flowers.

"I'm sorry," said Helissia, taking her hand and holding it.

Her touch, though coarse and bristly like a new paintbrush, was still warm and affectionate, so she welcomed it.

She must work hard.

"I always warned we needed more investments in research." continued Helissia, "It's possible for societies to heal and persist after viruses and wars, but the end of a people is almost always reproductive. The biologists and anthropologists seem to understand that. Same goes for the generals who order down rape during war."

Damn… She really doesn't care anymore, does she?

"The information we currently have about the world and its substrates are disjointed at best. Too many centuries on the warpath will do that."

"At least the technology freeze ended," said Colonel Flowers, "Maybe the next generation has a better chance."

"A better chance at what?" said Helissia, with contempt.

"When the early Peaceland researchers discovered a way to build on my people's circuits and grids, they managed to power every region with hardly any cost. When the guilds learned of this technology, they tried hard to tear it down before attempting to seize it themselves."

"The Citadel didn't fight for those founding researchers either."

"Well, they did when it was being developed," she corrected herself, "But the moment key breakthroughs were made, the ownership was transferred to the Landlords. It wasn't much longer before the industry was subcontracted to the guild society and a price was placed on access. It's not like much has changed since then either."

"Project Orphan itself was only born after we could prove our research was useful to your cause. And don't forget, we're standing here as we are, as professionals in our own rights, because we're able to more or less contribute to this system."

"At least the Liberation Force has the regulation and control it does," said Colonel Flowers, "Over the market and state."

"Yeah, but does it really matter?" replied Helissia.

"Markets and states, like all arrangements and institutions, are human constructs, and in many respects, are expressions of our ingenuity. But like nearly all systems in place, they required dispossession to emerge and disaffection to persist. It doesn't take long for entire meritocracies to be passed down like possessions."

Helissia shrugged. "There is the result," she said, pointing down into the Citadel. "A people stripped of their humanness and boiled down to their most useful components at best. A people stratified in pursuit of some long-forgotten empire, almost like the vessel on the flag."

"Sounds *feudal*, if you ask me." she shrugged.

She turned to her with a stiff face. "And besides, you and I both know the Army could've taken back Acadia centuries ago if they truly wanted to, peacefully even."

"They could have even rebuilt the scattered country while they were at it. But it wasn't the Old Republic they were seeking, it was the New Empire."

She's... not wrong. It took decades for Westeria to establish the Military Police, and the emergence of the Frontier Army was our own doing. If the Lords and Generals of New Arcadia cared for reunification as much as they did for playing class and politics. They could've had a country in that time, but they settled for the first system which served them instead.

"Inequity isn't always some side effect or symptom," said Helissia. "Sometimes it's an intended outcome,"

"So is that why you left the Army?" asked Colonel Flowers.

"More or less," she answered, nonchalantly and without much hesitation. "But I lost myself before I left... lost myself," she repeated, but with a whisper. "Lost myself trying to understand why things are the way they are and not some other way. Lost myself wondering why I'm alone and not okay."

"Helissia..." said Colonel Flowers, taking her by the hand.

"For years I couldn't stop thinking about the nature of reality, and for years I failed to find some kind of meaning or explanation. *Years*...I lost years. And all I learned was that reality is a rabbit hole of information no matter which way you go," she said, pausing for a brief moment. "And that I also forgot to count the turns I took."

"But look at you now," replied Wilona Flowers. "You're here and you don't look a day older than thirty-five."

"I'm thirty," said Helissia, "But I take your point. I don't know when, but one day it occurred to me that all things, no matter how much we fail to understand them or their relationship to the universe, are grounded in reasoning and therefore have a cause and effect."

"Realising this wasn't a lead out the rabbit hole, but it did provide me with a flashlight, and it did show me most strive to understand their environment and make useful observations about it."

She felt Helissia's fingers unravel from hers one by one before slipping away completely.

"I suppose competing to survive and be useful is everyone's cause, but I want to be useful to people and communities, not armies and private interests. I believe any society hoping to advance must organise around justice as a rigid principle," she said, with eyes fixed to the space above the sky, like a cat to a mouse in the dark. "The ancient Gihon seemed to understand that."

She looked down to find Pigeon staring too, but if there was anything other than inconspicuous starlight, *and the Whitestar,* her eyes couldn't catch it.

"So... I, uh," said the colonel, trying to change the subject. "I heard you lost all your research trying that experiment."

"M-My research? Who told you I lost my research? How do you know?"

"T-Talius did," said the colonel.

"What!?" Helissia burst out. "What else did he tell you? Tell me!" she said, approaching with eyes as wide as an ocean fish.

It frightened her enough to impulsively take a step back, and it was there in that brief instance she noticed the professor re-adjusting her strategy.

"I promise I won't be mad," said Helissia, softening her voice and facial expression to appear more agreeable, though rather unconvincingly.

She also forced a smile which was more *self-defeating* than it was reassuring.

"All he said was you accidentally burned your apartment down," said Colonel Flowers, "I assumed it was trying one of your experiments the state rejected."

"Y-Yes," said Helissia, with shifting eyes. "That is exactly what happened, and don't let anyone tell you otherwise."

She cleared her throat before continuing, "And yes, I did lose most of my research, but it's fine. I know where to look should I need to reassemble my findings."

"Wait… so where are you living now?"

"Under Talius in the Command Tower," she said with a thumb pointing back in its general direction. "I miss my old room, but the new one will do."

"My ideas are still homeless, however," she said, placing her hands inside her jacket. "They were never accepted at the University, but I think they deserve a school, though I wouldn't mind if they ended up in the fringes if that's where they belong."

"That's quite poetic of you, Helissia," said Wilona Flowers, charmed by her choice of words.

"Yeah." She shrugged. "I also know where to look for a cute guy if you still want those kids."

"Helissia!" shouted the colonel, scaring the cat. "I'm married!"

"What? You wouldn't?" said Helissia, closing her eyes and smirking. "I would."

"No I—"

She was interrupted by a call from her radio.

"Yes?" she said, answering and placing the device to her ears, with eyes still scorning the professor. "Huh? What do you mean? What!? A-Are you sure?" she said, quickly placing the binoculars down and turning back to Mineraltown. "W-What the hell? It can't be."

"What is it?" asked Helissia.

"I-It's Mineraltown," said Colonel Flowers. "The lights are back on."

Hiran VII

"Emmi! What the hell!"

"Sorry," she said, laughing with a hand covering her mouth.

"Don't do that!"

"Relax," said Emmi, failing to contain her laughter, though not really trying at all.

She took a step back to search the corners of the backstreet, and tossed out the metal pipe she used to scare him nine-tenths to death.

"It was funny," she said, turning to him with a closed, but malicious smile.

"Does it look like I'm laughing?" said Hiran, "'Cause I'm not. So say sorry... Hey! Stop laughing!"

The angrier he got, the more amused she seemed.

"Whatever," he said, turning his back and walking away. "See ya!"

"Wait!" she said, still giggling but tagging along. "Where' ya' goin'?"

"Just some delivery."

"Where?"

"I don't really know," said Hiran, after thinking about it. "A place in Roilmont, I guess."

"Roilmont?" said Emmi, with a raised eyebrow. "Don't they eat people there?"

"Right?" he chuckled.

"What's the address?"

"Oh,," he said, removing the note Arther Guildmen had slipped to him. "I forgot to check."

Together they read the words: *12 Old Queens Avenue.*

"How do you get there?" said Emmi, scratching the top of her head.

"Guildmen said to go through Newtown and cross the Queensbridge," said Hiran.

"The Queensbridge?" said Emmi. "Are you trying to die or something?"

"What' you mean?"

"You have to cross Industria before you cross the Queensbridge."

"So?"

"There's a war?" she said, with her hand up and out like a server carrying a tray.

Oh, right... The war.

"You'd need a Military Police passport if you're heading through that side of Roilmont anyway," said Emmi, "Take the Kingsbridge instead. It's safer." She shrugged. "You'll pass right by Rockland too."

"Yeah, I think I'll do that actually," said Hiran. "Thank you, Emmi."

She smiled *her smile.*

They left the alley and continued along the way together. Silently walking the streets with their small shoulders fighting for space inside the crowded market.

In Newtown, it was easy to miss something if your eyes glossed over the world as it passed by. There was a lot to see and even more to hide, and some things were tucked right in plain sight. The seemingly narrow dead end alleys actually led into underground markets littered with hex dens and bone collectors. The long line of nervous day labourers waiting outside the Military Police construction offices, were not just trembling for the possibility of being turned away, but also being hired. The Salt Pillar stood not too far east as well, watching over the entire Biosphere and therefore all of life. Many, including his Mother, claimed the tomb of the Great King Zaaj was resting in its highest floor, while others believed it was where a coven of witches congregated. In either case, whatever lurked within was more or less a matter of faith as every path leading to the top floor had been demolished centuries ago.

There has to be something up there though, he thought to himself while observing the vultures still circling the windows.

He turned his sights to the concrete floor.

And something down here too,

Though I guess if there was a lead, the gizmo hunters would have found it first.

"Do you really think there's something down there?" asked Emmi, breaking the silence between them.

"Like, below the Undermarkets and catacombs?"

Huh? Did she just finish my thoughts?

"I don't know," said Hiran, "I think about every day."

"I wouldn't be surprised if there was, or even if Lowtown was a true place" said Emmi, placing her hands behind her head like a pillow. "There's a whole world out there. I know, 'cause I had nothing to do with building it."

He was always caught off guard by how well she spoke, especially for a saloon girl. Like many others throughout Queens, she once went to school before the Military Police, took over her community and locked their gates. Though it's been a few years since then, he figured some of it must've still stuck.

"What if there is?" she asked, suddenly cheerful of the idea, "Would you take me there?"

"Of course," said Hiran, turning to her with a smile. "I'd take you anywhere, even to the moons and keep you there."

She turned away before he could see her wide-open smile, but he was sure it was there.

Smooth Hiran.

They returned to their silent ways not too long after. Speaking was something they did a lot less of whenever they were outside together, and it was likely one of the main reasons why they got along so well.

"Wait!" said Hiran, stopping abruptly. "Where are you going?" he asked, pointing to her bike.

"Huh? Oh… I was just riding around."

"Don't you have to get back to work?"

"Right," agreed Emmi.

"O-Okay well, shouldn't you go then?" he laughed.

"How come you never came to see me?" she asked, with her head down.

"I waited all winter"

Aw… Emmi.

"Is it 'cause you found a new girl?" She gasped. "It's that choir-girl isn't it? What's her face? The Winch girl"

She paused to think for a brief moment.

"You're lucky I forgot her name."

He laughed. "Mom doesn't let me out of the Interior in the winter. You know that."

"So you're not even going to try?" asked Emmi.

"Of course I tried," said Hiran. "You really think I wouldn't want to see you?"

She giggled.

Aside from her cheerful demeanour and well-spoken ways, he was always caught off by how *pretty* she was.

Her clothes were just a cut above rags, but her shoulders were dainty like his, and her hands, though overworked and festered with scars, still appeared soft and delicate like a ball of yarn. There was some colour in her cat-like eyes as well, colours which resembled an ore of brownstone unearthed for the first time.

She's so pretty, just like the City.

"I missed you," said Hiran, stopping to enjoy the view.

"Really?" asked Emmi, with a wide uneven smile and a chipped tooth she couldn't hide.

"You can kiss me if you want to," she said, staring down at her torn up sandals. "Just don't touch me with your hands."

"Hey!" said Hiran "Were you watching me?"

"Um…" She smiled, with eyes pointing away from him. "Maybe."

She dropped her bike, wrapped both arms around his neck, and placed her lips to his.

They shared a long kiss, just like how they always did, and he stood there like she told him to, with his hands by his hips.

Her skinny arms made her feel safe..

"Bye, Hiran."

"Bye. Emmi."

He watched her for as long as he could before she disappeared into the crowd with her bicycle.

I should keep it moving. I don't have all day.

He continued through the back alleys of Newtown, peddling and pushing and coasting on his bicycle, and always looking both ways before crossing, even when the streets seemed empty.

This is still a war zone.

After a certain point he had reached the mainroad, and after another point he had passed by Guildmen's directions. There were half a dozen police-soldiers armed with auto-rifles and spraying their eyes and noses with sprey. They were lined up against the side of the road awaiting their command from their direct officer and when that order came they each took turns climbing into the back of a supply truck. One likely heading into the rebel communities neighbouring Newtown.

Emmi was right.

At some point he took a turn east and continued along the street. Following the rows of newly assembled wooden pillars and the electric lines strung between them. The sky had blackened a little and the summerbirds began flying westward, while the seabirds flew eastward to the Ruined Sea and the vultures patiently circled the City above. There were signs leading to different holy ruins and shrines, as well as signs hanging over stores along the District's main avenue, and after a certain point, clothing lines came to replace the electrical lines and a rocky dirt path came to cover the road. The further east he travelled the further the crowd seemed to thin, until there were only a handful of stragglers left on the streets.

Easton was only a few minutes away.

Valtus VI– May 7

The last time the soldiers of South Station stood for the National Anthem of Peaceland during lunch break was for the Fall of Windlehem two years ago. Today they stood with their hands to their hearts, hymning together a New Acadian anthem for all those who failed to retake the city from the Free Acadian Frontier Army.

I don't know what it is, but something doesn't feel right. The officers weren't at their table, and someone turned off all the lights.

It was a strange atmosphere in the station to say the least, especially considering the security alarms were raised around Mineraltown, but their schedules were still not tightened around wartime. There were also more bodies than usual in the already crowded cafeteria, many of whom belonged to former peers and familiar faces.

Among those who were forced to abandon the campaign to retake Windlehem, were those who were removed from active duty and placed on the reserve list. The non-essentials, or so they were collectively referred to as, and along with the retired veterans and part-timers, they were now just returning from their ordinary lives as line cooks and assembly workers, farm hands and restaurant bussers.

Everyone's looking as miserable as ever. That's great to see.

When the anthem ended, the unified sounds of screeching chairs and scraping forks took over the cafeteria.

"Looks like the part-timers are back," said Wilaana, with her elbow to the table and a hand on her face. "Now I gotta wake up even earlier to use the washroom."

"I hear the surveyors they sent to Mineraltown never made it back," said Riya.

"What?" said Rodina, putting her fork down. "What do you mean? They're dead?"

"No," answered Riya. "I don't know."

"The Colonel's probably gonna' announce something at the ceremony," said Taalia, placing a spoonful of stew into her mouth and regretting it immediately.

"Doubt it," replied Wilaana, cutting into an apple with a butter knife. "They've never shared that kind of information with us before. Why start now?"

"Fair," said Alric. "But the commander is coming,"," "Maybe we'll learn something?"

"He's only ever here to announce war, too." said Atlus. "So I guess the rumours are true."

"Who knew the Temple had an army" he chuckled

"I was headed for Windlehem now I gotta fight some nuns. What a life."

Something still isn't adding up though.

Colonel Wilona Flowers and her high-officers were expected to make an announcement later in the day, in a formal ceremony in which all Generalists in South Station were expected to attend in their assembled regiments. There wasn't much said about the affair, other than that it was in response to the collapse in the marketplace a few days ago, and that Commander Talius would be sitting somewhere in the bleachers with his Peaceguard.

"Something doesn't make sense," said Valtus, "Why would the Commander be sitting with us? And why does everyone know?"

Wilaana shrugged.

"Moles in the force?"

"I think you're right," said Atlus, with a sudden drop in his voice.

As much as he tried to resist, his eyes darted around the cafeteria like a honeybee before returning to the table where he noticed each one of them eyeing one another with the same concerned look.

"I also don't see any Firstlanders around"

"Relax, guys," laughed Riya. "We're overthinking again."

"I just wish we knew what happened to those surveyors," said Alric.

"I feel so sorry for them-," added Wilaana,

"Who cares," interjected Lamby, dismissively from across the table.

"Lamby!" burst Taalia. "Don't say that! They're soldiers and comrades."

"Sorry, but I don't feel sorry for Specialists," replied Lamby, digging into his tray. "And I'm sure they don't feel sorry for me."

"You're high again aren't you?" asked Rodina.

"No," said Lamby, dropping eye contact.

It was quite clear he was *lying*.

"You're going to get caught one day," continued Rodina. "What then?"

"Fuck they gon' do?" said Lamby. "Write me up? They ain't even here."

"Probably went to sprey with the Firstlanders somewhere"

"That doesn't even matter," said Riya. "It's still not good for you. Don't you care about that?"

"Can y'all drop it!?" shouted Lamby. "We not liberating anybody and no one gives a fuck about us. We all gon' die, so stop killing my high."

They all turned back to their trays, not wanting to cause a scene.

Like many others who carried with them the privilege and honour of being born to the Midlands, Lamby was expected to compete to remain a part of his community. Due to a contract with the Cause, however, he was one of the many lagging Midland students sent to the Citadel to live out the rest of their days in the Generalist.

It was true reality was intolerant of failures, but Lamby was a different kind of failure, a greater kind of failure, *an absolute failure*. He was the son of a Landlord and ended up a *Generalist*. Even the Honoured kids had rejected him from how far he had fallen from grace.

Well... He can be annoying too. Though, it's not like any of us are or better off.

As much as he was tired of his whining and self-destructive spiral down into misery and illness, he understood how he felt.

Not too long ago he was feeling a similar way.

The feeling of being abandoned by a system you fought every day to be included within. The feeling of living out your days without any sense of freewill or agency. The feeling you were stuck, the feeling you won't survive, the feeling you never had a fair shot at life.

He knew that feeling well, that feeling was an old friend.

"At least you're on active duty," said Valtus. "Those boys over there *just* got paid."

"And look at all these other kids," added Atlus, nodding over to a group of soldiers who were just a few years older. "Half of them probably sittin' on a guild certificate or some degree."

"All that work and debt and they ain't learn shit," shrugged Atlus.

"Atlus," said Riya. "You're not helping."

"What?" said Atlus. "I'm just being honest. I don't got a problem being here. Better a trade soldier than a lost cause."

Though there were plenty of fields to scour and trades to master, it was hard to deny there were few opportunities presented to them to become professionals.

The knowledge and level of literacy required to achieve a top score on the Peaceland Classification Exam, the main metric used to funnel and allocate students into their proper stations, was often beyond the learning curve of most residing within underprivileged communities. The intention of the standardised test may have been to identify and select students into competitive programs on the basis of their merits, but it achieved this by punishing them for their errors and disqualifying them from accessing future opportunities.

Maybe that was the opportunity.

That was not the end of it either, as while academia appeared to be a space primarily reserved for those who could prepare for and afford it, striving to join a guild had its own challenges as well. Established during or near the founding of Peaceland, the guilds were a society of professional trade networks now under the control of Peaceland's most well-off Citizens. Many of their academies formed long before the Lowlands were even a part of the state as well, and the knowledge and craft behind their trades were strictly kept secret and regulated with their best interests in mind. This was done not only to keep the value of their labour high and to protect their positions, but also to maintain the position they held within the market and in the pockets of Peaceland's officials.

It feels like there's nothing really for us sometimes. Even someone like Wilaana, as smart as she was, still couldn't find a place in pharmacy school. The same went for Alric and Rodina too. They both studied merchant technology, but still couldn't find a place in the Highland guilds or its markets.

Though he never achieved an education past middle school, such barriers in hindsight seemed to have saved him effort and time, as neither a degree or certificate was a true guarantee *out of war*. It was a competition to stay as far away from the frontlines while working for the cause to earn a living. This was the balancing act for their generation and many went far into debt to pay for their schooling and training.

Those that could no longer contribute to their field, however, often ended up on the Generalist after years of falling behind on their training. Some tried to bandwagon a trade or research subject, but they were usually the first to get kicked off. Then there were those who took a turn down a narrow street and found there was no space for them in their field at the end of the road. Not to mention those who were made obsolete with each passing improvement in automata.

No matter their background or expertise, here they were now. Skilled and unskilled workers, class clowns and star students, all wasted potential found ageing together in the same cafeteria, disowned and in debt. All that work, time, and money just to end up funnelled down and forgotten.

With these things in mind, failing the Reclassification Test wasn't bothering him as much any more. Even though he had no skills other than being a soldier, he was a good soldier, and that was enough to provide for his family. Seeing *Daaria* also motivated him to meet her at her rank one day, or at least try to close the gap between them. As strange as it sounded, he was grateful to be here. He could have easily been stuck in Notwell with all the other boys who were in love with her, but would never see her again.

I'm going to read more and write her a letter every week until she's back.

Sergeant-Captain Granite was right too. I just gotta keep working for it—

The sudden sound of sirens, when they were expecting the ringing of bells, had rattled half the room to its feet.

"Take cover, this is not a drill!" ordered a woman's voice through the speakers.

Take cover?

"What's going on, guys?" asked Lamby.

"Just do what the speaker says!" shouted Riya.

It was only a few seconds later when they heard it. The screeching sound of rockets soaring through the skies like an eagle, and it was approaching quickly.

Is this it? Am I really going to die? No! I can't! I have to get to Daaria—

Jazzy III

The Highland sun blistered the back of his neck as he wandered her streets aimlessly in search of somewhere to be. It must've been several hours since he left the others behind at their usual spot, but he still wasn't too far away from the alley. Or far enough to feel alone.

At some point during his walk, he had spent a considerable amount of time throwing his lunch up against the side of some drug den, though it easily could have been a whore-house or a Military Police station. He was too high to tell the difference, or who was yelling at him as he wandered off. At another, much later point, he had inadvertently crossed out of Newtown's southern territories and into the wasteland nested between South Easton and Downtown Queens.

It was a part of the city that was as missing as the sketches of lost children whisking in the wind. A part of the city as missing as the nails once used to hang their portraits to the posts.

I know some kids who goners,
I know some kids who ghosts.

Newborn Highland-trees, known for their soft maroon brown wood and delicious tree berries, poked and protruded out from the rubble as if someone had nurtured their growth, while enormous slabs of ruined concrete blossomed into flowerful hills of red, blue, yellow and orange, and even some purple too. In this side of town, anything of value was scavenged long ago by hordes of metal scrappers and bands of gizmo hunters who were at times, as much of an annoyance as rival underguilds. What remained of the landscape was either left to erode under the elements, or quickly seized by nature.

There was also a corpse of *something* rotting away along the street. It appeared to have been dead for many months when he had first discovered it years ago, and since then he had watched it grow more unrecognisable with each passing season until it became indistinguishable from the corner it died on.

Just like everything else.

He spent some time sitting atop the flowery hill, watching the clouds as they quietly passed alongside the Salt Pillar, wondering if this was all there was to the world, and if the seabirds knew of an end to the Purple Sea.

What' mom use' to say?

"The Purple Seas' only for the birds to see."

No. That wasn't mom. I... I don't remember what mom used to say. I don't remember mom, I don't remember the day.

A nearby colony of wild rabbits grazing against a patch of shallow grass caught his attention, and he considered for some time the idea of bringing one down with his pocket knife and maybe taking it home. Except rabbits were never worth the trouble, and he didn't think he had it in him.

Wait- Home.

I remember-

I was going home.

After climbing down the hill and leaving it behind, he ventured further into the desolate plains of South Easton, all the while maintaining as much of a distance as he possibly could between those who crossed his path. Though it was not a particularly windy day, he still felt the breeze combing through the twists in his hair like some girl named Hania once did, and though he could no longer put a face to her, he still wished she was around to braid it again.

Maybe someday she'll see me again.

It took perhaps another hour, or at most, the rest of the mid-day before any semblance of a civilization returned. What had appeared to be homes from a distance, however, were in actuality ruins, and what appeared to be trash at first glance, turned out to be *people*. Some slept the day away under army tents as tattered as their uniforms, while others tossed headless bunnies into boiling steel drums with spirits as broken as their faces. There were men, women, and children too, and every one of them were strangers. Even those who had watched him grow over the years with his demons.

At some point, the City reemerged with its marvellous high-rises, and it devoured him the moment he stepped foot into its barren outskirts. Wherever he looked, he found a world neither he nor anyone he knew of had a part to play in designing or constructing. Towers so tall and invasive that it took an unsafe bend in one's neck to catch a glimpse of the Highland sky, traffic signals and street lamps still radiating with their colours, as if someone had forgotten to turn off the lights.

He took several turns down the weathered streets, until he found a quiet little park tucked away behind the shadow of the Salt Pillar. There was a playground resting at the centre of a sandy field, and a pile of rubble tangled within a frenzy of overgrowth at its southwestern most corner. He walked over to the ruin while removing and unloading the auto pistol concealed within his jacket, and when he was sure no one was looking, he placed the bullets inside his pockets, and the pistol under a rock. Though they didn't have a part in the city's foundation, it didn't mean her streets didn't belong to them.

He left the park as cautiously as he entered it, and after walking about another half block south, stopped to search his surroundings before lifting up a broken slab of the sidewalk. Slipping into the rift below, he found the passage quite dark and narrow, and though he had no flashlight to lead the way, he was worried little. It was *home* where he was headed, not some stranger's place.

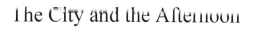

The City and the Afternoon

1

"I think it's that way" said Atin, pointing to the unbeaten path leading only further into the thicket.

"You think?" asked Vaara, with some protest in her voice, "Let's just keep to the tracks. We only just got here"

"No, that'll just lead us to a dead-end" said Atin, "Trust me"

She didn't have to trust him, she knew he was right. She just hoped Wilona and Altus didn't know that.

They had spent the last half-hour hiking through the Forest Gorge and she was tired of it. The woods clawed at her body, leaving cuts from her shoulders to her ankles, while the mud from the stormy night before soaked into her brown leather sandals, coating her toes with a *slimy* texture. She was uncomfortable and hated herself for agreeing to join them. Turning back to Roilmont was on her mind the moment they crossed Queensbridge, but it was *too late to turn back now.*

"Trust me Vaara" urged Atin, continuing on up the trail ahead.

A long walk to nowhere might've been enough to convince them this was all a stupid idea, but his words were enough for the other two to follow.

"Me and Romina smoke jinx here all the time" he said in a half-hearted effort to reassure her.

That helps,

Thanks.

Earlier he had told her it wasn't his fault she wore shorts and a crop-top after complaining about the bush-thorns and tree branches. She was prepared for a walk to the Queensbridge and no further, but he kept pushing them to continue before bringing up the idea to sneak into the Ancient City they called *Queens.*

Also, it was summer, what was she *supposed* to wear?

She knew things weren't going to go her way when they all showed up in their hoodies, sweatpants, and boots. She also knew to turn back when Atlus started showing off his flashlight.

That could only mean he's looking for some adventure.

Yet here she was. All because she *couldn't say no.*

Well, at least I got my sandwich and water.

"You got any jinx?" asked Wilona to Atin.

"I wish" he replied, "I'm dry like a nun"

She did also have some jinx in her school bag, but she wasn't sharing with these *losers.* If anything, they taught her she had made the wrong friends.

They're not really my friends,

If they were then they rarely acted like it.

"We could also find a witchleaf bush and boil the leaves" laughed Atlus,

"That'll get us high".

"No!" shouted Atin, "That'll get us lost!"

Atin's reason for sneaking into Queens was a *stupid* one, to search for an Ancient artefact to bring home. Not only was it against Military Law to enter Queens, but it was a crime to bring back even the dirt on your shoes. Wilona's reason wasn't any better either. She had some problems at home and had to do something *fun* to get away from it. Yet somehow Altus's reason was worse than both of theirs.

It would be fun because Wilona thought so.

It was a bad idea to think sneaking into Queens was a good idea. Whatever the reason, for every hundred or so folk stories and urban legends about children going missing, at least a dozen had actually disappeared in and around the Ancient City.

But those were *just mostly stories,* she told herself.

Stories told by the tree temple and the Military to keep children out.

Besides, kids run away all the time.

She trailed behind as the others climbed the wooded hills, the thorns and leaves brushing against her tender brown skin, cutting her and sealing the wounds with their oily saps. It was painful, though oddly, she found it *soothing.*

"Vaara's right," said Wilona, struggling to catch her breath.

"What if something catches us?"

Not too long ago she had told her to *"Quit bitching"* and *"Go home then"* when she pointed out the Forest belonged to big-cats and terror-birds, and *now* she was *right*?

Bitch-

She would have gone home by herself, except in class they were taught big-cats and terror-birds preferred to stalk lone prey, and she was alone in wanting to turn back.

"It's okay," said Atlus, reaching into his backpack.

"I found a this rock"

He carefully removed a thin shard of blackstone wrapped around a dirty blue table cloth.

"Yo, careful" said Atin, "Don't play with blackstone!"

"Don't worry," said Altus, taking the cloth and folding it around a dull part of the stone.

"Nothing can fuck with us now" he said, proudly holding it up to the moons.

"I feel so much safer," said Wilona, turning back and rolling her eyes.

"Don't worry," replied Atin, revealing a small crossbow inside his own bag.

"We'll be fine"

At some point then it occurred to her, if there had been anything lurking within the Forest, they may have accidentally covered its tracks.

"Just a little further up ahead" shouted Atin, every five or so minutes until another half-hour passed.

Eventually they stumbled upon a construction site with a case of concrete stairs crawling up and along the rocky red walls of the Great Gorge.

"I told you," said Atin, pointing to the stairs.

"W-We can get in through there"

The faint rattle in his voice made her worry enough to think of hymning a prayer, but she was never a holy person and she wasn't going to start pretending now.

After a near hour-long climb they entered a mine carved into the Gorge itself and after passing a maze of tunnels, they reached a tall iron gate with the words 'MILITARY EXCAVATION' and 'KEEP OUT" guarding the road ahead. Whoever decided the City was not to be tampered with, however, was doing a bad job at stopping them as a gentle press against the gate swung it wide open.

The *Ancients* were waiting ahead.

2

There was a peculiar smell to the City which made it difficult to enjoy the afternoon. Like so many other Acadians, he often watched the clouds pass over Queens from his apartment in Roilmont. Though he couldn't have guessed just how colossal and quiet it was on the inside. From roads twice as wide and apartments thrice as tall as the ones in Roilmont, to drinking fountains dedicated to Ancient idols, grey and coloured concrete encircled their reality, and it was getting *unpleasant*.

The clouds and moons also seemed to take on a new appearance when observed from the empty streets and even the summerly winds blew through the City *a little differently*. It was interesting, but the novelty of the experience was over the moment he learned Wilona would rather stare into nothing before she would acknowledge his presence.

Wilona, thought Atlus, watching her as she watched the sky.

She stood quietly next to a whitestone idol of a woman who stood naked over a bed of torn human heads. The idol was beautiful, but not nearly as *pretty as Wilona* whose brown eyes and dark-brown skin glimmered under the sun, almost like the blackstone knife he crafted to protect her.

She hates me-

Why?

"Can we sit somewhere?" asked Vaara, "My head is hurting"

"We shouldn't," said Wilona, cupping her hand beneath the idol's fountain, where water flowed out from the mouths of each of the nine heads.

"Not when there's so much to see and do," she said, raising her hands to her lips.

"Stop!" shouted Atin, "We don't know if it's good!"

"I'm thirsty!" said Wilona, shouting back.

"Let's head back then" said Vaara, "There's water in Roilmont"

It wasn't a bad idea, he was getting hungry too, but as long as Wilona wasn't turning back, neither was he.

They had spent the better half of the day silently wandering Queens, without a sense for the passing afternoon. Even Atin who was obsessed over finding some artefact to take home seemed to forget why he was here. That was a great thing. It was no secret why the Military was so protective of the City.

Though the wild inherited much of their lands, it was the Acadians who made great use of what the Ancients had left behind. Within the first century of excavation and research alone, they learned how to construct sewers and engines, proper roads and bridges, and even grand cities like Roilmont and Lindblum. All without an understanding of their language or an idea of who they were.

He should know better.

At some point down the road, a cluster of Highland-trees protruded from the road, shrouding the streets and littering their fruits for the doves and boars to eat. It was clear this was a place retaken long ago by beasts, and yet every animal they encountered scurried in fear at the first sight of them. Around one corner they even crossed paths with a family of a dozen big-cats chewing on the carcasses of what appeared to be a drove of hares. Though the four of them were too frightened to move, it was the cats who fled first, even leaving their kittens to catch up.

Guess we're the big cats in town.

"You can go home now Vaara, we scared off all the cats" said Atin

The three of them shared a laugh, but she didn't think it was funny.

They turned to find her leaning quietly against a crumbling idol, falling with eyes shuttering frantically.

"V-Vaara!?" shouted Atin, rushing to her before she fell.

The moment he caught her, she caught her balance and looked around. Almost as if she had forgotten where she was.

"I-It's f-fine" she said under her breath, "I j-just need some-"

She reached into her school bag, removed a canteen, and poured water over her half-parted lips.

"You okay?" asked Atin.

"C-Can we go now?" she sighed.

"Y-Yeah let's turn back" agreed Atin.

She handed the canteen around and there was enough for each of them to get a good swig. He was handed it last and he downed what was left, with eyes wandering in search of whatever else could have sent the cats running.

3

"C'mon" said Wilona pointing down towards a set of stairs hidden behind a slab of wood and sheet metal.

"It won't take long".

"Let's just go home," urged Atin.

But she wasn't ready to go home.

There was still so much to see and a lot on her mind she wasn't ready to deal with yet. Besides, this might've been their only chance at Queens for a long time. The Military was off fighting the war against Westeria and most if not all of the soldiers were re-stationed into Summer Circle.

"Okay, whatever, let's get this over with," said Vaara, angrily approaching the metal sheet and squeezing herself into a narrow gap in the wood.

She's mad, thought Wilona, dismissively.

Whatever.

One by one they each followed and soon found themselves descending a long flight of stairs into the darkness.

"Altus" snapped Wilona with her hand out in the dark.

"Flashlight".

"Right," said Altus, rummaging through his belongings.

"Where are yo-"

She snatched the flashlight from his hand before he could finish his sentence, flicked it on, and led the way forward.

They snaked through the tunnels, taking a turn down every stairwell emerging from the dark, and wherever else the flashlight showed some promise, until eventually, they stumbled upon *train tracks?*

"I think I know where we are!" proclaimed Wilona, excited "This must be the subway tunnels they warned us about!"

"We should turn back soon then" said Atin

"What? Why?" asked Wilona, "There's gotta be something good down here!"

"We could be wandering too far away from Roilmont or we could just get lost" he said, taking her by the arm and drawing her back toward the group.

"C'mon Wilona"

Yeah,

I guess he's right.

Smart , assertive, and cute,

Just my type.

Vaara was her type as well, though she was more annoying at times than she was cute or smart.

"So? We can keep going, it'll be fun like Wilona said" said Altus

Though she wasn't as annoying as Altus, who couldn't take a hint.

"Alright, we'll turn back soon" agreed Wilona, stepping deeper into the dark.

It wasn't much longer before Atin cried out again, "W-Wilona, w-we have to turn back!" he said with a short breath.

"Something's wrong with Vaara!"

She turned to find Atin carrying Vaara on his back, and Altus standing next to them, smiling stupidly at her.

Vaara had fallen apart. Her entire body was swollen and limp and though her arms were around Atin's neck, it was clear they were placed there from how they hung.

Damn,

Poor girl.

I'm so sorry Vaara.

I should be nicer to you.

"Yeah, let's go," sighed Wilona.

"Y-yeah" agreed Altus.

"B-but wait" said Atin, "I didn't track the turns".

"Shit",

"I didn't either".

"I did," said Altus, turning to Wilona. "I'm pretty sure we went right-left-left-right, so that means we go back the same way, right?"

She wasn't sure if he was telling her or asking her but she replied with an unsure "R-right".

"That doesn't sound right to me," said Atin.

"You got a better idea?" replied Altus, snapping back, "You're the one who brought us here to begin with Atin, you should lead us out".

"It's fine," said Wilona, not wanting to deal with any arguing.

That's the last thing we need.

The four retreated, agreeing to take the first right turn they could. After a short walk along the path, however, there was something on the floor which didn't *seem right.*

"Wait!" shouted Wilona, stopping the moment she noticed it.

"What?" asked Altus bumping into her from behind, "Huh?" added Atin following forward with Vaara on his back.

They screamed as they plunged down into the dark rift below.

4

Wh-

Where am I-? She asked herself, awaking to meet the dark for the first time in a long time.

Mom? She asked again, after her eyes had adjusted.

Her whole body felt *so sore*, but she wasn't sure if it actually hurt or if it was just another feeling in her head. The same went for the sounds of a nearby rustling.

"Mom?!"

"Dad?!

She sought out her legs to use, but couldn't feel them.

"I-I can't get up" she said, "Someone help me!"

No one answered.

Clawing at the earth, she pulled herself into the darkness like a slug, until something found itself inside her clutch.

I remember this-

I know this, she said to herself picking up the object.

She flicked the thing off and on several times, but it was only after rattling it out of frustration did it burst with light, illuminating the pit around her. In the space right next to her she found Atlus and Atin, quietly asleep. She wanted to call out to them, but didn't want to wake them either. It was a long afternoon and *they could use the rest*.

She waved the light around the darkness. In one corner, it revealed a large crack in the wall with a tall sheet of metal placed off to the side and in another corner she found a bed of rocks

"Mom?"

"Dad?" she said, whispering to the dark.

There was no reply, only more rustling.

She continued to wave the light until she neared the source of the sound in a nearby corner. There she found a family of women and men, boys and girls, gnawing away at *Wilona*.